# Meant to be Together

Eva Manning

**ISBN:** 9781793460950
**Imprint:** Independently published

To Garth who gave me the time to write and Carl who inspired the story.

May you never have to deal with all the crap Wren deals with.

# Author's note

Although the characters in this book are fictitious, spousal violence is a serious problem that occurs in families of every race, class, and sexual orientation. Sometimes the signs of abuse are not obvious. Abuse can occur in the form of financial abuse, verbal abuse (including bullying or threatening), emotional abuse (including isolating), physical abuse, or sexual abuse. Usually, physically abuse does not occur first.

Instances of abuse, particularly physical abuse, usually occurs within the cycle of violence. The cycle of violence starts with a period of increased tension which leads to an acute explosion (abusive event). Usually this is followed by a honey moon period where the abuser is apologetic. The relationship may seem 'fixed' during the honey moon phase which can make it particularly difficult for victims to leave the relationship.

Unfortunately, members of the LGBTQ2+ community can face unique challenges when they are victimized. There can be fear of being outed to friends or family, there can also be concerns around being believed or treated respectfully by police and the justice system.

If you think you or someone you know is the victim of domestic violence please seek help.

Call 911 if you or someone you know is in immediate danger.

Other resources:

- Alberta provincial abuse helpline: 1-855-4HELPAB (1-855-443-5722) for assistance in more than 100 languages from 7:30 am to 8 pm, Monday to Friday
- The Family Violence Information Line: 310-1818 to get help anonymously in more than 170 languages
- For those living in the United States: National Domestic Violence Hotline at 1-800-799-SAFE (1-800-799-7233)

# Part One

# Things get fun

# Chapter 1
## Aiden

*He slid his hand up the naked spine on display before him. He felt each of the muscles quivering below his light fingers and could hear his partner's breath quickening at his touch. His hand continued as he reaches the tips of the soft brown hair and he ran his hand up into the hair letting the feeling of the soft strands play through his fingers until he suddenly fisted his hand in that hair and pulled it back, causing his partner to gasp in both excitement and surprise.*

*Holding his partner in place with his hand in that hair, he leaned forward and kissed behind the man's ear. He then used his lips, teeth and tongue to slowly retrace the path his hand had just followed, reversing his way back down the now arched back. He spent an extra few seconds to kiss the small dimples at the base of the man's spine before he took a gentle bite out of the left buttocks.*

*His partner was now panting loudly and visibly shaking in his desire to be touched more and in his effort to remain still. He keened with desire, wordlessly begging Aiden to move his hand up and because he wanted nothing more than to please his partner, he followed the instructions and moved his hand to firmly gripped his partner's leaking cock.*

*Fluidly he raised himself back up as he stroked the cock which sat heavily in his hand. Once he was standing with his front pressed against his partner's spine, he leaned forward and whispered, "Now I get to fuck you."*

*He slid his cock into the man, relishing how tight he was. He felt himself become more and more desperate to fuck harder and harder while his partner pushed his body back onto him, forcing his cock deeper inside. He let go of the man's hair and used that hand to hold on and guide him so their thrusts were in perfect harmony. He used his other hand to continue stroking his partner faster and faster.*

*He felt his balls rise with his desire to come. The amazing sheath of heat making it harder and harder not to fill his partner.*

*He could feel his partner was right there with him. His cock somehow becoming even harder as he leaked more and more precum.*

*He moved his free hand back up to grab at the back of his partner's head, using it to steer his head so they could see each other's faces. He needed to look into those eyes. He needed to see him while they both came together.*

*The head turned...*

Doo da dodo do. The first few notes of loud his ring tone jerked Aiden awake.

"FUCK!" he swore into his empty apartment. His balls ached, his cock pulsed with excitement. He could feel his breath coming in pants as the sex dream faded, unable to do anything but retreat in response to the happy song coming out of his phone—his mother's ring tone.

Aiden flailed his arm over to the coffee table beside the couch where he'd fallen asleep, desperately trying to grab the phone, either to answer it or make it shut up. In that second, he wasn't sure which he'd prefer.

Glancing at the boner tenting his shorts obscenely he knew the last was a lie. He definitely just wanted the phone to shut up.

Finally getting hold of the phone he raised it to look at the screen.

Yep. His mom was calling.

Aiden had thought he finished having her interrupt him mid-orgasm when he moved out of the house and she stopped being at risk of barging in while he masturbated. Apparently not.

He moved to ignore the call. He wanted to finish what his dream had started. Then he noticed the time.

Shit! He had less than an hour to get to his mom's house for their weekly dinner. Obviously, he'd slept for longer than he'd thought.

"Hello," Aiden answered gruffly. Sleep and sex coating his voice and making it sound gruffer and more gravely than normal.

"Aiden, dear, were you sleeping?" his mother asked, hardly pausing to breathe before continuing. "Well, wake up! Your sister just called and said she forgot to tell me earlier but she finally invited Wren to join us for dinner and so I need you to stop and get another steak on the way to our house so we have enough for him. There should be enough of everything else.

"Of course, I am happy he is coming and hope he knows he is always welcome, but I wish your sister had told me earlier since I only bought enough steak for us when I went shopping earlier and was already worried there wouldn't be enough for everyone tonight."

"Wait," Aiden said as soon as his mother took a breath. "Wren is in town?"

"Yes. Apparently, he moved back in with his mother last summer. Now that he is back in Edmonton, I'm hoping he will come to our dinners again. It's important to me that things go well tonight so he comes back.

"So, shake off the sleep or whatever you were doing and go get me another steak." She paused briefly before saying, "Love you. See you soon, honey." And with the marching order's given she hung up the phone.

Aiden stared at the phone for a second, letting his still tired brain catch up with what had just happened. He saw the time again and realized he really would need to hurry if he wanted to make it to his mom's on time, especially since he would apparently be stopping at the store on the way. He guessed he wouldn't have time to revisit his dream. He glanced down.

Luckily the thought of hanging out with his parents and sister had helped deal with the problem.

Though the thought of seeing Wren again after all this time was enticing.

# Chapter 2
## Wren

The second the door opened, Wren was engulfed in a tight hug. At first, he felt his body tense at the unexpected contact but felt himself relax into the familiar embrace. Lillian wasn't his mother, but she had sure been a big part of his adolescence. Standing there in the tight hug he realized he'd missed her and Steven almost as much as he'd missed his own mother and Lucy.

Wren remembered the first of many meals he'd shared with this family. He'd come over to Lucy's house to practice lines for a group project in their drama class and ended up staying for dinner. He'd met Lucy's tall and quiet father. "Just call me Steven or Lucy's dad." Wren also watched the interaction between Lucy and her brother and how the siblings interacted with their parents.

To say it was more relaxed and openly affectionate than it was at home was an understatement of epic proportions. Wren never questioned whether his mother loved him. She constantly makes sure he knew. She just liked things done properly and cared a lot about appearances.

Steven differed totally from his dad, though. During their first meal together, he'd seen Steven pay more attention to his kids than he had ever seen from his own father. Every moment since had reinforced Wren's opinion that Steven genuinely cared about his children's life, paying attention even if what they were saying was trivial or just a stupid joke.

Wren had seen Lillian and Steven a few times during the years he was living in away. He'd come back to visit his parents and Lucy a few times and more than once he and Lucy had ended up over here, eating food and sharing laugher with her parents.

Wren had even seen Lillian and Steven a few times when they had travelled to Ontario to visit Lucy while she was studying at the University of Waterloo. Although Toronto was almost three hours away by train, he'd made the effort to visit Lucy when her parents were visiting so he could visit with them too.

Plus, he'd known if he hadn't, then it would have hurt Lillian, likely Steven too.

"It is so good to see you again, Wren," Lillian said as she finally pulled back, her hands gripping his arms to hold him in place while she looked at him.

"You've lost weight," she accused before pulling him back into a tight, but this time, at least, brief, hug. "Aiden is picking up a steak for you. You will eat the whole thing. Get some meat on your bones."

Wren just laughed. What else could he do in the face of such overbearing love? Plus, she was right; he had lost weight, including some he didn't have to lose. Stress could do that to a person.

He followed Lillian into the kitchen. Luckily, he heard the squeal and managed to brace himself in time to catch Lucy when she threw herself at him. Despite bracing himself, he stumbled back from the weight of Lucy's taller and likely heavier body.

"I love you, Luce, but you are not a kitten anymore," he grunted as he caught the door frame to steady them.

Lucy just laughed. Her happiness at seeing him and having him finally agree to come for dinner shining out of her face.

Standing there in the familiar kitchen, Wren wasn't sure why he had been so reluctant to come back. It was nice being here. Almost like coming home. He'd spent just about every weeknight in this house from grade nine to grade twelve enjoying the welcoming embrace of Lucy's family as he tried his hardest to avoid going to his father's house where he was forced to live every Monday to Thursday.

Barry had fought dirty in court to ensure his mother hadn't been able to get full custody of Wren, Barry's only son. It had sounded like an act of love, except Barry then made it clear Wren didn't fit into his new bachelor lifestyle. Coming out had only made their relationship worse.

No, if Wren had had a father growing up, it hadn't been the one on his birth certificate.

Shaking off the melancholy, Wren smiled at Steven who also pulled Wren into an embrace. Here was a father that was worth smiling about.

They sat down to a drink each and a plate of cut raw vegetables and dip while Lillian grilled Wren about his life and explained the food was all made except for the steaks.

"Steven cannot start the steaks until Aiden arrives since he is getting the last one. He sounded as though he had been sleeping when I called him earlier so I can only hope he remembers I asked him to pick one up on the way."

Luckily, Aiden quickly arrived bearing gifts, a nice large cut of steak.

Looking up at Aiden from his seat at the kitchen table, Wren felt he could argue there were many more impressive things about Aiden than the steak he held out to his mother.

"Hey, Wren," Aiden said, holding out his hand for Wren to shake. "Long time no see."

Long time indeed. Wren hadn't consciously realized it before, but when he'd visited with Lucy's parents over the last decade, Aiden must not have been around. Wren's last memory of Aiden was of a little kid.

*The door to Lucy's house flew open before Wren had even rung the doorbell. Before he even realized what had happened, he was on his ass looking up at a kid, who appeared to be about seven or eight years old. He was short and skinny, wearing an assortment of clothing that was both too large and too small. His hair was messy, like he had been running his hands through it, or maybe like he had recently stuck his finger in an electrical outlet. He also had one of those adorable oddly proportioned faces that kids sometimes had where his ears and eyes were just a little over sized for his small face. Or maybe it wasn't actually that his eyes were that large, but instead that he was wearing a pair of glasses which made his eyes appear larger than they were.*

*"Oh gosh, I'm so sorry. Man, wow, I didn't even see you there." The kid stammered. "Umm, do you want a help up or something?" He extended his hand up to Wren.*

*Wren was by no means a giant but he had a few years on this kid and probably weighed close to twice as much as him. He shook his head and stood up, awkwardly trying to move out of the way of the kid's hand which remained extended for a few seconds beyond necessary.*

*"Ah, hi," Wren said once he was standing. Now he was looking down on the kid he could see there were red highlights in his hair and it had a slight curl which probably contributed to its general disorderliness. Wren could also see the tag of the kid's shirt, showing that his t-shirt was inside out. Wren suppressed a laugh. This kid was adorable. "I'm Wren. I'm here to see Lucy."*

*"Oh, oh ya," the kid said, pushing his glasses up his nose and stepping back to open the front door again. "You are the guy from her drama class. The one that's in the play with her. She talks about you all the time. That's cool you could come over. Umm, I'll just get her. I mean I guess could just ring the bell since I'm supposed to be heading over to see my friend, Rachel, but—I mean, since I'm right here—I can just let you in."*

*The kid was rambling. Wren wondered if he was making him nervous or if he was always like this. Wren tried to appear less intimidating, but since he was pretty short and not especially athletic, he rarely had to worry about that sort of thing. "Thanks. I'm glad I'm at the right house."*

*The kid nodded his head and lead the way into the house, shouting Lucy's name as soon as he entered the house. Wren winced, impressed at the volume coming from such a small kid.*

*"Aiden, stop shouting and just go get your sister," a woman instructed, poking her head into the hallway from what Wren could only assume was the kitchen.*

*Aiden grumbled something under his breath which Wren didn't entirely hear but turned to go upstairs. Wren wasn't sure whether he should follow but decided not to when he saw Lucy's mother looked at him expectantly. "Hello dear, you must be Wren. Lucy told me she was expecting you to come over to practice your lines."*

*"Umm, yes Mrs. Walker," Wren answered. He tried to be casual as he looked around the entryway and looked over at Lucy's mother. She differed completely from his mom. Even Lucy's house was totally different from his. His mother always wanted their house to be clean and tidy. Sometimes his mom and dad argued because his mom said his dad acted like a child. Wren didn't really feel that was fair to him since he was pretty good at cleaning up after himself.*

*He wouldn't have described Lucy's house as dirty. He wasn't worried about there being mice or bugs or anything like he'd seen on TV but there was a lot of stuff just lying around. On the stairs there were several piles of things which appeared to be on their way up or down the stairs. One pile appeared to be clean clothes, another a pile of papers which Wren suspected might be Lucy's homework since he saw a handout from their drama class. There was also a box which seemed to have a large magnifying glass sticking out the top.*

*At first glance Lucy's mother wasn't anything like his mother either. She was wearing a loose sweatshirt and a pair of jeans which had a tear in them. His mother would never wear anything with a tear and he wasn't sure if she even owned jeans. She had some casual clothes but rarely wore them.*

*"Aren't you sweet," Lucy's mother answered. "Such nice manners but call me Lillian. Only telemarketers call me Mrs. Walker." She rubbed her hand on her legs and Wren realized she was leaving a streak of flour on her pants. She was baking.*

*He turned his head as he heard two sets of feet running down the stairs.*

*"'Kay bye, I'm off to Rachel's. I should be home before dinner," the kid, who Wren realized must be Lucy's little brother, yelled as he passed Wren and ran out the door.*

*"Wren!" Lucy said, giving Wren a tight hug. "I'm so happy you came."*

*"I said I would," Wren responded.*

*"I know but I'm still happy you're here." Lucy released Wren and took his hand, pulling him up the stairs.*

*"You kids have fun," Mrs. Walker, Lillian, shouted after them. "I'm making cinnamon buns for dessert tonight and we will have butternut squash soup with chicken Parmesan for dinner. Wren, you are welcome to join us. Just be sure to let your mother know if you plan to stay." Then she turned around and left.*

*"She making all that from scratch?" Wren asked Lucy as they walked into her room. The walls were plastered with pictures, magazine cut-outs, handwritten words, and drawings. He hardly knew where to look.*

*"Ya, my mom's food is great. You should stay. Plus, Aiden might stay at Rachel's which would mean I might be able to steal extra cinnamon buns for us."*

*"Aiden's your brother? He's super adorable. Barrelled me over when I came to the door though."*

*Lucy burst into laughter. "What a dweeb!" She laughed more.*

*"He was pretty apologetic after but he's what, seven, it's not like I'm gonna to get mad at a kid." Wren's comments seemed to make Lucy laugh harder.*

*"He's nine not seven. Man, I'm going to bug him about being mistaken for a little kid again."*

*"No, don't make fun of him. I feel bad." Wren begged. Wren did feel bad. He knew what it was light to be short and mistaken for younger than he was. He was usually better at not making that mistake. Plus, the kid seemed sweet. Wren didn't want to embarrass him.*

*"You're no fun!" Lucy said, throwing a pillow from her bed at Wren. "But, fine, only because Aiden really isn't a bad little brother and I know he's pretty sensitive about how tiny he is. My dad says he was small until he hit puberty."*

Steven's prediction that Aiden would grow turned out to be true. He had grown over a foot and was now much taller than Wren. His face had matured into a handsome, well-proportioned one. His muscles had also grown until his lean strength was obvious through his clothes. The only thing remaining from Wren's memory was Aiden's goofy grin.

Then he smiled and there it was.

# Chapter 3
## Aiden

Aiden froze in the doorway to his parent's kitchen. He could hear his mother thanking him for getting the steak and nattering something about how she'd worried he would forget but he couldn't focus on her words. He had eyes only for the smaller man sitting at the table across the room from him.

Wren was sitting in one of the kitchen chairs with his back to the wall. His hair was shorter than the last time Aiden had seen it and even sitting down Aiden could see Wren had put on some muscle through his shoulders and arms. The muscles suited him and increased how attractive Wren was although his general appearance and fit of his clothes suggested he had lost weight recently. He was also no longer wearing glasses and Aiden briefly wondered if he was wearing contact lenses or if he'd had his eyes corrected.

Despite the differences, it was like someone had suddenly thrown him back to the last time he'd seen Wren.

*Aiden pushed up his glasses up his nose and sighed in frustration. He'd only gotten his new glasses three weeks ago, and he already regretted his decision to buy them. They had a thicker rim and the sales person convinced him that this look was in style. He'd thought they'd been kind of fun, like a hat tip to a 1950s engineer or something and agreed to get them. A week later he wished he could still wear his old busted up glasses. At least his old ones stayed on his face properly or at least they had before Aiden had accidentally stepped on them.*

*Maybe the problem was the glasses looked a little too much like Aiden had stolen them from a real 1950s engineer. They made him look like a dweeb. Or more of a dweeb than he was anyway since his geeky nerd status was pretty entrenched.*

*The thick rims somehow made him look even younger and skinnier than he was, which was difficult given he was already basically the shortest boy—person—in his grade nine class.*

*The worst part, though, was that he'd made an effort today. He wanted to look good. He had brushed his hair and bugged his dad into taking him to get a haircut last week. He'd gone out with Rachel to buy a new t-shirt and a new pair of jeans. He'd embraced his small stature and had picked out a really tight pair of skinny jeans. Lucy had joked he wouldn't be able to have kids, but he didn't care. For once it actually looked like his pants fit. Plus, he knew his ass looked good in his new clothes, which, honestly, was the whole point.*

*After looking in the mirror on his way out of his room he'd worried that the jig was up and everyone would immediately guess his secret but either everyone already knew or his outfit wasn't as obvious as he'd feared because no one had blinked.*

*Not even Wren, which was a monumental disappointment since the entire outfit was for him.*

*Yes, he'd dressed up for Wren, who of course hadn't even noticed because why would he? Even if he was the light of Aiden's life.*

*Unrequited love was the worst.*

*Wren was the first gay person he'd ever met. He was also the first person he'd ever had a crush on and the boy who made Aiden realize he was gay, or at least bi.*

*Wren was the man who Aiden spent way too much time thinking about especially since he was Lucy's friend and probably couldn't care less about Aiden. He was always nice whenever they talked but that just meant he wasn't an asshole since Wren had practically been living at their house for the past four years since his parents got divorced.*

*Unfortunately, he was leaving town and might never come back before Aiden admitted to anyone that he was in fact a complete homo and would really, really, REALLY like to make out with Wren.*

*Aiden wanted to cry.*

*He also wanted to take this moment and just announce to everyone in the room that he was gay and hope that maybe Wren would kiss him goodbye. Except... one kiss would never be enough and Wren was leaving. He was going away to university, moving to the big city to attend the University of Toronto. There was a real gay village there, and a thriving pride parade, and support for LGBTQ students on campus and why would he ever want to come back to boring, redneck Edmonton?*

*No, Wren wasn't coming back and Aiden was just going to have to get over his crush. But... maybe not today.*

Aiden mentally shook himself and took a step forward, putting his hand out for Wren to shake. "Long time no see," he said as a joke and watched as Wren nodded and smiled while he held out his hand.

The moment their fingers touched Aiden felt a rush travel from his hand to his cock.

Damn. Maybe he hadn't grown out of that adolescent crush after all.

Or maybe he just needed to get laid. Aiden suspected that might be a strong contributing factor since he had seen no action since he'd broken up with his asshole cheating ex- almost a year earlier. It had been hard to get his head back in the game after the sudden and dramatic end of their two-year relationship. The fear of something similar happening again had mostly killed Aiden's interest in having sex with other people.

Except between the semi he was getting just from looking at Wren in his parents' kitchen and the sex dream from his nap earlier Aiden was wondering if maybe he was finally ready to rejoin the dating game again.

Although he could get his dick under control—being an adult rather than a teenager had a few advantages—Aiden found himself increasingly fascinated by the man that Wren had become. The outward changes he had noticed when he'd first laid eyes on Wren may have been the most obvious but they were not the only ones.

Aiden was so focused on his own reaction to seeing Wren again that it took until part-way through dinner before he noticed Wren was talking far less than he ever had when they were younger. Wren had easily held his own against Lucy's high energy and talkative nature.

Tonight, he barely spoke more than three words at a time. It wasn't immediately obvious since, like always, Lucy and his mom were chatting with a constant stream of conversation which filled even the possibility of silence.

What finally clued Aiden in was when his mom asked Wren a question about his job at the hospital and Wren used the simple two-word answer, "It's good." Lucy picked up where he left off and spent twenty minutes telling everyone about how Wren had done really well on his MCAT and had just finished applying to a bunch of medical schools but how she was really hoping he would be accepted into the University of Alberta because she didn't want him leaving again.

It had initially annoyed Aiden. Why wasn't Lucy letting Wren talk? Then he realized she was doing the same thing their parents did. His dad had always been quiet but his mom didn't want him left out so when she didn't think his answer said enough, she'd expand on his answer to the point of practically answering the question for him.

It worked for them.

Aiden wondered if Wren appreciated Lucy's verbal assistance or wished she would just shut up. Lucy and Wren had been friends for so long Aiden tended to trust her ability to be a good friend to Wren. Except Wren seemed so embarrassed when Lucy talked about him that Aiden wasn't so sure. It was almost like he didn't like her pointing out his accomplishments.

The entire situation confused him. It was so different from when Lucy and Wren were teenagers Aiden couldn't help wondering what had caused treechange.

Maybe it wasn't anything bad. Aiden knew he knew barely anything about Wren's life these days.

Something that unfortunately hadn't changed were the flashes of melancholy which Aiden could see occasionally between the smiles and laughter. That was something Aiden had seen in Wren's face off and on throughout the divorce and the years after until he'd moved out of town. Aiden had never heard the full story, but he'd known Wren's relationship with his father hadn't been great and that was why Lucy and their parents had practically adopted Wren when he was fifteen.

Aiden wondered if it was still his father or if it was something else that put those flashes of sadness into Wren's adult eyes.

Wren rushed off to work the night shift at the hospital shortly after they finished dinner. While they stood side by side doing dishes, Aiden couldn't help asking Lucy what was going on with Wren.

"It was weird seeing Wren again after so long. I realized I haven't seen him since high school. He's changed a lot," Aiden commented.

Lucy splashed Aiden with some water. "Like you're one to talk. I'm pretty sure you've doubled in size since we graduated."

"Ya, but it isn't just that he is an adult now. He's so quiet and sometimes he looked so sad. His dad still giving him a hard time?"

Lucy looked at him seriously and then bit her lip, like she was trying to decide how to answer. "Barry is still an asshole but I think Wren has mostly come to terms with his dad. No... this is something else. Sure, we are all older, not kids anymore, but Wren's changed a bunch just in the last three and a half years since I moved back from Ontario. I think something happened but he won't talk about it. I can't even get a straight answer about why he left Toronto.

"I know he was seeing someone for a while after I left but he hasn't even mentioned the guy since he moved back. I wonder if things went south before he left Toronto because he's oddly isolated, and as far as I've seen, he hasn't even looked at a guy since he moved back in with his mom."

Aiden thought back to his last bad breakup and could sympathize.

"It's hard to pick up guys when you live with your parents," Aiden pointed out. Lucy shrugged her agreement but Aiden couldn't help wondering if it was more than that. He wondered if Wren needed another friend, maybe someone in the Edmonton LGBTQ2+ community. Lucy was great, but she was straight and a girl. Possibly he was looking for someone who could introduce him to other gay men; although that idea didn't sit well with Aiden.

If nothing else, hanging out with Aiden's friend, Zane, made everyone else feel normal by comparison.

As they finished up the dishes and the conversation wound down, Aiden suggested Lucy give Wren his number and invite Wren to call him if he was ever looking to hang out or do something with another gay man.

"Sure, sounds good," Lucy agreed. "He doesn't do much besides work and hang out with me. Hanging out with your weird group of gay friends might be good for him."

A cheeky grin spread across her face as she continued, "Plus, maybe you will both end your weird dry spell together."

Aiden didn't know how to respond to that so he remained silent but he worried his blush spoke for him as he felt his face and ears heat up.

"Oh, my god! I was joking but you actually like him, don't you?"

# Chapter 4
## Wren

The entire time he was at work and for the next few days Wren couldn't get his dinner with Lucy's family out of his head.

No, that was a lie.

He couldn't get Lucy's brother out of his head. Somehow during the past ten years Aiden had gone from an awkward little teenager to—to a hot man. A tall, smoking hot man.

There had been a moment when Aiden had first walked through the kitchen door when Wren had barely recognized the boy he'd spent so much time around when they were younger. His face had matured and grown from his old weird adolescent face. His hair was also a darker brown now but the most dramatic change was Aiden's height.

Aiden must have grown close to a foot because when Wren had left town, he had still been several inches shorter than Wren. Now, he was several inches taller and well muscled. He wasn't bulky like a gym rat would be. Instead, despite his wide shoulders, he had a lean strength suggesting he spent most of his exercise time doing cardio, Wren's favourite kind of muscles.

It was weird having to look up at Aiden. It was even weirder when he looked up at Aiden and noticed how pretty his brown eyes were—or how long his lashes were, or how full and kissable his lips were.

There had even been a moment when Aiden and Wren were touching, shaking hands, that Wren had felt a zing of... something. They had been looking each other in the eyes, just saying hello but Wren had almost wanted to taste those lips. He'd ended the handshake and sat back down but the feeling, that zing, had stayed like a ghost for several minutes after.

It wasn't all changes. Aiden was clearly still a geek—a leopard couldn't change its spots after all—but he carried himself with a level of confidence and sophistication he could never have pulled off when they were kids. Even his interactions with his sister held a level of self-assurance which showed their friendship was genuine instead of a forced product of living together and a heavy dose of younger sibling hero worship.

That new confidence only added to Aiden's appeal. Wren had caught himself a few times during dinner and even after thinking about what it would be like to have Aiden focus his attention on him. How would he kiss? How would he hold someone he cared for?

The thoughts had made him nervous and embarrassed. It was hardly cool for him to be interested in Lucy's little brother. He didn't want to do anything to mess things up with her, especially since these days she was his only real friend. He had lost touch with almost all his old friends from before he moved to Toronto. Even in his new job working as a clerk at the University Hospital, he had only made a few casual acquaintances; no one he would want to spend time with outside work.

Plus, Wren thought to himself wryly, his experience was that confident men were mostly assholes. Even if Aiden was someone else's brother, Wren wouldn't go down that road again.

Over the following week, Wren had decided he needed to just put Aiden out of his head, no matter how hot he had become. Following his own advice was not as straightforward as he would like but Wren knew he was heading in the right direction when Lucy called him and Wren realized he hadn't thought about Aiden all day.

Lucy had been calling to invite Wren out for coffee after work the next day. Since Wren had it off, he happily agreed to go—anything to stop his mind from continuing on the same path, stressing over the same things including continuing to wonder what Aiden tasted like.

Unfortunately, meeting Lucy didn't help at all.

"I'm pretty sure my brother has a crush on you," Lucy announced the second they sat down at their favourite south-side coffee shop.

Wren sputtered and almost choked on his coffee and had to grab a napkin to wipe his mouth and a few drops off the table. "Your brother is gay?"

"Oh ya. Didn't I tell you that before?" Lucy looked so confused and surprised Wren didn't seem to know. "No, I'm sure I told you. I mean he's been out for like... forever. Plus, I know you and my mom have talked about her involvement with PFLAG and why would she ever join, let alone become such an active member if she didn't have a kid that was LGBTQ2+. I mean really?"

Wren felt a bit dumb because, of course, he did know Aiden was gay. It was just that Aiden's sexuality had always been sort of an abstract thing until now. Even over the past two weeks while Wren had been thinking about how attractive he was, deep down Wren had still thought of Aiden as a kid—well, maybe not a kid—but at least nothing more than Lucy's brother.

"Anyway," Lucy continued, ignoring Wren's silence. "He was asking about you after you left the other day and when I suggested you guys could hook up, he totally blushed like a tomato."

They ended up talking about other things before making arrangements to get together for lunch the following Saturday but the echo of Lucy's words kept repeating in Wren's head, *"I'm pretty sure my brother has a crush on you. I'm pretty sure my brother has a crush on you. I'm pretty sure my brother has a crush on you."*

Now, how was Wren supposed to get over his crush on Aiden?

# Chapter 5
## Aiden

"Lucy, I doubt he wants me there," Aiden had tried to argue with his sister. He was almost positive she was playing match maker since she had invited Aiden along for the lunch she was having with Wren the following day.

"Nonsense," Lucy argued, completely ignoring everything Aiden had been saying for the past ten minutes. "You and Wren have always gotten along well before."

"But..." Aiden started, then just sighed in exasperation. He wasn't sure why he was arguing against going. He wanted to be there. Lucy knew it, he knew it. Hell, he was sure basically everyone in his life knew it. His two best friends, Zane and Rachel, had gone out for drinks with him last week and his inability to stop talking about Wren had clued them in that Aiden had fallen back into lust city.

It was just that, well, Aiden didn't want Wren to be annoyed with him. He didn't want to seem like some sort of stalker. Sure, he wanted to hang out with Wren, but he wanted Wren to want to hang out with him too. He didn't want to be a third wheel; the kid clutching to his big sister's skirts, trying to play with her friends.

Even if it was what he wanted to do.

Once he had agreed to go, the idea of seeing Wren again soon got him excited. He practically floated through the rest of work on Friday. He was so giddy that after going for a run he agreed to go dancing at Flitter with

Zane and his boyfriend as a way to get rid of some of his excess excited energy.

The next morning, he woke up in a good mood and a boner. Then he enjoyed a delicious breakfast and coffee on his way to the farmers' market where he wasted time until lunch. All morning everyone kept smiling at him and he realized just before leaving the market that the reason everyone was smiling at him was because he couldn't keep the giant grin off his face and they probably thought he was smiling at them. Whatever, he didn't mind spreading the joy.

Fuck! This wasn't a date. This wasn't an anything. He needed to get himself in check or he would come across as a complete freak over lunch. He tried to take deep breaths on his way toward the restaurant where they were meeting for lunch, but had to admit to himself he was only partially successful in reining himself back to reality.

Luckily, or maybe really unluckily, reality pulled him back down to earth the moment he walked into the restaurant and saw Wren sitting at a two-person table alone.

Shit, Lucy didn't tell him Aiden was coming.

Fucking Lucy!

Then she pulled the second trick of the afternoon. This one worse than the last, she sent Aiden a text, "Not able to make it. Enjoy lunch with Wren."

With a fucking winking emoji.

This was entirely planned.

Aiden felt himself blush and had to force himself not to turn around and walk back out of the restaurant. Wren wasn't only not expecting him but he wasn't even going to get to have lunch with the person he wanted to.

What if Wren thought this was all Aiden's idea?

Aiden saw Wren pull a phone out of his pocket, read the message and look up in confusion.

Shit, Aiden thought. Not only isn't it planned, but he isn't happy. Aiden took two more steps toward Wren's table, once again forcing himself not to turn around and walk out before Wren spotted him. The only thing keeping him going was he didn't want Wren to think Aiden had stood him up. He was sure Lucy had said something about Aiden coming instead of her in her message to Wren.

When he was about two tables away from Wren their eyes met. Aiden felt a connection form between them but blinked and tried desperately to tell himself it was all in his imagination. There was no way Wren was into him. This must all be Aiden's adolescent self taking him on a journey into fantasy land.

"I swear I didn't know Lucy was going to do this," Aiden pleaded the moment he got to the table. "She invited me yesterday and promised she had asked you about me coming with her, not replacing her. I'm not trying to force you to eat with me. If you want to, you know, just not do this and go home or do something else on your own I totally get it." Aiden knew he was rambling. He knew it but it was like his mouth had separated itself from his brain and he couldn't stop.

Eventually Wren interrupted him, "No, no. Lunch with you is fine." The words finally acted as the trigger allowing Aiden to stop talking for long enough to regain control of his mouth. He hoped.

"Actually," Wren continued. "I know Lucy well enough I should have seen this coming. She suggested this lunch right after she told me you have a crush on me."

"She told you what?" Aiden asked in mortified surprise. He put his head on the table, trying to hide his face since he could feel himself blushing so hard his face could probably be used as a frying pan. He might literally murder his sister after this. No jury would convict him. Not a single one.

Jesus Christ!

"You know she is trying to set us up?" Aiden asked, raising his head and looking Wren in his gorgeous hazel eyes. "I swear I didn't ask her to do this!"

Luckily Wren really knew Aiden's idiotic sister and instead of being angry with Aiden he laughed. "Ya, I know but whatever is going through Lucy's head, it doesn't mean we can't enjoy a meal together."

Aiden felt himself smile. It was true. As long as they both were okay with this and knew what Lucy was doing, they could make their own choices.

"Thanks for that," Aiden smiled. "On the plus side, Lucy's machinations mean she isn't here. Maybe today we will get a chance to talk to each other."

Wren laughed at Aiden's joke. This time he looked bashful before changing the subject to ask what Aiden thought he might like to order. Of course, since Aiden hadn't even glanced at the menu, that forced Aiden to look away from Wren. Aiden suspected that had been the point.

They decided what they wanted to eat in silence and just as the silence was stretching into things becoming awkward the server arrived to take their order. Unfortunately, that only lasted a minute before they were once again alone at their table.

What to say? What to say? Aiden thought frantically. He felt completely intimidated and nervous and... like this was a first date.

He'd had job interviews that were less scary.

"Shit, I don't know why I'm so nervous," Aiden admitted. "Maybe I need Lucy here to help fill the silence." He knew he was only half joking.

This was hardly his first time having lunch with another gay man. Hell, he'd been on a ton of dates, even a bunch of first dates.

Not that this was a date.

Or even that Wren was interested in him.

"I'm glad I'm not the only one," Wren admitted softly.

Aiden felt his head jerk up in surprise at the comment. Aiden looked at Wren. He really looked at him and took in his expression, his body language, everything. Maybe Wren was just as nervous. The idea blew Aiden's mind. Was Wren attracted to him too? Did Wren feel just as desperate to not screw this up? Whatever this was.

"I gotta explain something," Aiden said. "I need to address the elephant in the room. I know Lucy told you I have a crush on you but that's not really it—or at least not only it. You are completely hot and I wouldn't say no to a date—a real date—if you were interested but really, I just want to be your friend. I always thought you were cool when we were younger but the three-year age gap seemed too big to overcome. Now we're adults I really want to get to know you better as your own person and not just as Lucy's best friend."

Wren had smiled and relaxed while Aiden was talking and by the time he finished, Wren was nodding and appeared as though a weight had been taken off his chest.

Ouch. It looked like just the idea ofdating Aiden stressed Wren out. Oh well, he hadn't been lying. Aiden was happy to just be friends with Wren.

"I'd like to be your friend too," he confided with a grin.

Then they actually talked. Now that his cards were on the table Aiden finally felt free to talk. Wren even answered questions first using full sentences and then even paragraphs. By the time their food arrived the conversation flowed and Aiden had to force himself to shut up long enough to take bites to eat.

Wren was funny. Aiden had forgotten that about him. He told funny stories about his coworkers and the weird people he saw at the hospital.

"So, the guy walks into the emergency room," Wren recounted. They'd finished eating and their plates were sitting waiting to be cleared but for once Aiden was happy their server was mostly ignoring them since he was in no rush to leave. "He's got a needle he used to give himself something still hanging out of his arm but according to him that's not the problem. According to him, the problem is that he must have something going on with his memory because he can't find his wallet anywhere. But see, he's sure he gave it to his friend so the real problem is he can't find his friend. What turned it all from tragedy to comedy gold is that he was convinced his friend is Dr. Dre and he's Eminem. During the entire process he keeps insisting everyone refer to him as The Slim Shady."

They both laughed and Aiden felt a bubble of warmth spread through him. This was really nice, really fucking nice.

Their plates were finally cleared and they paid their bills. They each paid for their own food since this was not a date.

He reminded himself it was not a date.

Then Aiden asked Wren about his time in Toronto and what made him come back to Edmonton. It was like the question stole the joy out of Wren. He could practically see him becoming increasingly tense. Aiden immediately regretted the question and wanted to pull it back into his mouth but that was impossible.

"I was missing my mom, and I wanted to get a job in a hospital to help with my med school applications and I decided it would be easier to get a job at a hospital here where the job market is a bit less competitive." Wren answered his question before Aiden could apologize.

Aiden didn't want to push after Wren's reaction but there was something false about his answer. Or rather, maybe not false but incomplete.

"Well, I'm glad you came back. It is nice to see you again."

The smile came back into Wren's eyes and his shoulders relaxed when it was clear Aiden wasn't going to push that topic. "Me, too."

* * *

Aiden made an effort to avoid mentioning anything about Wren's time in Toronto or his move back to Edmonton for the rest of lunch. The effort payed off and conversation flowed. They were both surprised when they realized it was already two o'clock. They got up and let a somewhat relieved looking server clear their table but continued talking while standing outside of the restaurant.

Eventually, the conversation wound down and there were no more excuses to continue standing there. Aiden felt conflicted because he wanted to keep talking but he needed to pee, and the sensation had been increasing over the time they had been talking outside and now he was feeling desperate. He was relieved they were close to his home. He could get to the bathroom within about five minutes—if he rushed.

"Well, I need to go but this has been great. It might just take a year off my life saying this but I'm actually grateful to Lucy for her meddling."

Wren laughed and smiled shyly.

"With that in mind—umm, do you want my number so we can maybe do this again sometime? Maybe this time without Lucy's involvement," Aiden asked, feeling himself blushing. And once again this felt like more than it was. He'd been less embarrassed and nervous the last time he'd asked a guy out.

To make everything worse, Wren didn't immediately answer. Aiden had to clench his hands to avoid the almost reflexive desire to grab at the air to snatch back the question. It was presumptuous, wasn't it?

God! Why was he so nervous?!

Then, like the question had been harder than it really should be, Wren finally smiled and said, "Ya, let's trade numbers. I had fun too. Give me your phone, I'll put my number in."

Aiden suspected Wren heard his sigh of relief but he couldn't bother caring. He could feel himself grin as he exchanged their cells. He entered his name and number into Wren's contact list then felt lame when he got his phone back and saw Wren had put his name in as 'Lucy's hot sidekick'.

He smiled as he put his phone back into his pocket.

"Call or text me whenever you want to do this again," Aiden encouraged as he turned to head back to his car while giving a small wave over his shoulder.

Three days later Aiden wondered whether leaving the ball in Wren's court had been a good idea. He hadn't figured they would have gotten together again this soon, but he had hoped he would hear from Wren at least. They could text or talk on the phone....

Except it hadn't been a date.

Fuck! He'd never had this problem before. He'd never struggled to think about a friend as just a friend. Well, at least not when they hadn't even kissed or done anything remotely sexual. Wren had come with his sister to his family's Sunday dinner and then they'd had lunch together. That was it.

So why did it feel like more? Why was he so disappointed Wren hadn't gotten in touch yet? He'd given his number to Wren as a friend, not as a potential date. So why did it feel like he'd just been rejected?

# Chapter 6
## Wren

"Hey, eyes up here!" Lucy jokingly chastised. Wren jerked his eyes from his cellphone in his hand up to Lucy's face. He could feel the guilty look pass over his face. He might not be staring at her chest like she was joking, but he was still being rude ignoring her.

Especially, since he was ignoring her to stare at the blank screen of his phone, wishing he had the guts to send a message to Aiden and knowing he wouldn't do it—just like he hadn't acted on his desire to get in touch with Aiden any time over the past two weeks.

He felt like a dick for not getting in touch with Aiden. Wren knew Aiden had given his number as an offer to be a friend beyond just having lunch together randomly when Lucy set them up.

The problem was that Wren knew Aiden liked him, 'like' liked him and Wren really, really wasn't sure how he felt about that.

Sometimes the thought of it gave him butterflies. Sometimes it just made him feel sick.

Unfortunately, when he thought about Aiden, most of the time it made his dick harden. Wren had never had someone he wasn't having sex with do that to him before.

And wasn't that something he was utterly uncomfortable with?

"What has you wool gathering today?" Lucy asked.

"Umm, I don't know," Wren lied.

"Liar."

They both laughed. Lucy always could read Wren better than anyone else.

Maybe that was why he hadn't wanted to talk to her during the last few years he was living in Toronto. He'd even been nervous to get in touch with her when he'd first come back but his mom and Lucy hadn't let that last. Lucy had always been willing to meddle in Wren's life when she thought he needed it.

God, he wished she had been around to keep him from making some bad choices. Too bad half a country had kept her from knowing what was going on in his life and made it so easy for Wren to avoid her or convince her everything was all right even when he needed her more than he ever had before.

"I don't know if I want to tell you what's going on," Wren said with a smile trying to keep the mood light. "I mean, it wasn't that long ago that you stood me up and abandoned me to your brother."

"Ahhh," Lucy said with a knowing tone and smirk. "So, this is about my brother. You like him, don't you? I was just hoping you guys could hit it off and become friends. He has a bunch of awesome queer friends you'd probably fit in with if you gave them a chance. But that face isn't because you hit it off and made a new friend.

"So, either you had the worst time ever and have decided you hate my brother and you are feeling too nervous to admit it, or—and this is what I think it is—you realized Aiden has grown up to be awesome and you are too nervous to admit you are crushing on my baby brother."

Wren opened his mouth to deny but couldn't force out the lie so he had to close his mouth without saying a word. Lucy just laughed harder.

"Oh ya, you like him. I will tell everyone at your wedding I set you up. You will both owe me forever," Lucy gloated.

Wren could laugh with her because he couldn't even imagine it.

Married?! In what future?

Sure, Aiden was attractive. Okay, he was fucking hot, but that didn't mean they should date. He was still Lucy's little brother. And okay the idea of Aiden and Wren dating didn't upset her but it was still weird. Wasn't it?

Plus, what would happen to his friendship with Lucy if they dated and then broke up?

No, it wasn't worth the risk.

"I think you are getting ahead of yourself."

"Why? You didn't have fun during your lunch with Aiden?" Lucy asked. "And think carefully about your answer. I've already spoken to Aiden about it and he said something about a two-hour lunch."

Wren had thought they'd spent closer to three hours together, but he wasn't going to correct Lucy since it wouldn't help his case any.

"Okay ya, we had fun, but that hardly means we will get married," Wren pointed out. "I mean, he is like three years younger than us."

"Wow, you must have really liked him if your excuse why it wouldn't work is how young he is. You know he has his shit together more than you do, right? I mean he has graduated from school and has a well-paying job and is at the start of what promises to be a very successful career."

Wren tried to deny what she was saying, but he knew she was right. Their age difference didn't matter at all now they were both adults. The difference between twenty-six, almost twenty-seven, and thirty was nothing, especially since, as Lucy pointed out, Aiden was hardly coasting through his twenties. He had his shit together.

"If you don't want to date him, then don't," Lucy said seriously when Wren didn't immediately respond. "I'm not really trying to push you to date him despite the jokes. I really do just think you guys would make great friends. Aiden is an awesome guy and so are you. It would be fun for the three of us to hang out. I also think it would be good for you to hang out with other gay men. I've been paying attention and, Wren, it isn't just that you haven't been dating since you came back. You aren't even spending time with anyone in the community. You used to be so involved when you were in high school and at university in Toronto. I want you to have that here again."

Wren had nothing to say. She was right. He wasn't talking to anyone from the LGBTQ2+ community. More than that, if he was honest, he missed it. It was just that he wasn't sure if he was ready to get back into it and he didn't just mean dating.

Lucy took hold of Wren's hand from across the coffee table and squeezed his fingers. "Look, you don't need to do anything you don't want to but at least know you have another friend if you want it."

Wren glanced up from the coffee cup he'd been clutching but had barely drunk and looked into Lucy's eyes. She looked so sincere. He nodded. "I know and I'll—I'll call him." Lucy smiled, and she looked so happy. Not like she'd won an argument but like she was happy he was going to do something she was certain would make him happy. "But Luce, I need to do this at my pace."

"Fine, no more meddling. I'll leave you two alone," Lucy reluctantly agreed with a grin. She knew she'd gotten everything she was going to. "But if you end up dating Aiden, I reserve the right to gloat."

Well, she was still Lucy. Maybe backing off completely was asking for too much—not that he'd have it any other way.

Just don't tell her that!

* * *

Wren sent the first text the evening after he met with Lucy. He hated when Lucy was right. It happened far too often.

WREN: *Hey you want to do something this weekend? Maybe lunch again?*

He wouldn't admit under torture how many variations of the text he had gone through before he had come up with the final, rather boring version he sent.

Wren felt like he was in elementary again asking if someone wanted to be his friend. Except it was worse because somehow the fear of rejection was combined with the butterflies and anxiety of asking someone out on a date.

Even though he wasn't even asking Aiden on a date.

Wren had decided he wasn't going to pursue whatever was between them. At least not for now.

It was stupid for him to date someone now, anyway. He had just finished applying to five different universities across the country in his efforts to get into medical school. Only two of those schools were even in Alberta. How was he supposed to date anyone if he would be immediately moving away? Wren wasn't sure if he wanted to do long distance but he definitely didn't want to try it out with someone he had just started dating.

And okay, he might be accepted into the University of Alberta and would stay in Edmonton—but that was the point. He wouldn't know where he might be accepted into school, if anywhere, for a few months yet.

Plus, who said Aiden even wanted to date him? Just because Aiden thought Wren was hot didn't mean he wanted to become his boyfriend.

All right, fine. Aiden had said he wanted to date but that had been before two weeks had passed without Wren getting in touch.

Wren jumped in surprise as his phone made a swooshing noise indicating a text was coming in. He took a deep breath before looking down at his screen.

AIDEN: *That sounds great! Why don't you come to my birthday party Saturday evening instead of meeting for lunch? We're going to be playing laser tag then going clubbing.*

Wren froze.

Aiden invited him to his birthday party. Shit. That seemed huge. Well, maybe not. Wren admitted he didn't know how many people were being invited. Maybe Aiden had invited everyone he knew and inviting Wren nothing special. Then again, that might be worse.

Either way, there would be other people there. People Wren didn't know. Wren really, really didn't know how he felt about that.

No, that wasn't true. Wren did know how he felt. He was petrified of going to a party with a bunch of Aiden's friends, none of whom Wren had met before. Well, Lucy might be there, but he wouldn't know anyone else.

No, joining the party wasn't a good idea. Plus, he didn't like going to clubs anymore. He was too old to go out dancing.

Except, Aiden had invited him. If he wanted to be friends with Aiden, he should go. Saying no now might make Aiden angry and ruin things before they really got started.

Reluctantly Wren looked at the calendar on his phone and sighed in relief when he realized he was working Saturday night. He was going onto shift at six that evening.

He couldn't go.

He had to say no. He wasn't available.

WREN: *Thanks for the invite but I work that night. I'm still good for lunch on Saturday or Sunday or maybe next weekend would be better?*

Wren stood transfixed by his phone in the middle of his room, laundry completely forgotten. He waited for the response.

In that moment he was so nervous about seeing Aiden again that he almost wanted him to say he couldn't make it this weekend because of his party and suggest the meet-up next weekend.

AIDEN: *Lunch Saturday sounds great! Where do you want to meet?*

Wren sighed in relief again and felt the butterflies in his tummy start up again. Okay, maybe he would have been disappointed if they couldn't have made something work this weekend.

WREN: *Uhh, not sure what's good in town anymore. Where would you suggest?*

AIDEN: *I have been craving Po'Boys. What about going to Dadeo's?*

WREN: *?*

AIDEN: *You've NEVER been to Dadeo's? And you call yourself Edmontonian!!!*

Wren laughed and sent a shrugging emoji.

AIDEN: *We are definitely going there. Meet me at my apartment at eleven thirty. There is no parking near the restaurant anyway so we can walk there together.*

Wren couldn't keep the grin off his face as Aiden sent him his address, which he saw was just off Whyte Ave.

Wren's grin lasted three days before the anxiety of going out and meeting Aiden again caught up with him.

Shit! What was he doing again?

# Chapter 7
## Aiden

Aiden was so excited he was having trouble standing still. He had been pretty disappointed after waiting two weeks without a word from Wren. Then the entire conversation over text had been like a roller coaster. Happy that he'd texted, sad that he couldn't come to the birthday party tonight and then happy that he still wanted to get together. Aiden had been extra happy Wren had wanted to do something just the two of them. Aiden hadn't wanted to put any pressure on Wren. The last time they'd spent time together it hadn't been a date and the two weeks of silence sent a clear message that Wren wasn't interested in anything romantic so Aiden had tried to treat Wren like he was any other friend. Secretly, he was delighted they got to spend time alone again instead.

Did the fact they were doing something just the two of them mean it was a date after all? Wren had reached out to him and asked to get together for lunch alone. He didn't think so but...

Either way, Aiden was just happy to be spending time with Wren however he could get him. Really, he could hardly believe this was happening. Part of him felt he must be dreaming and he had to keep pinching himself all week to make sure he wouldn't wake up. Even if this didn't lead to them dating, Aiden was okay with that.

Maybe it was better that way, actually. Friendships can last forever. There was much more of a risk that everything would end badly if they dated. It would be awkward for everyone if they dated and then broke up, especially since Aiden just knew if he ever got a taste of Wren, he would never want to let him go. If they dated then broke up, it would likely leave Aiden broken hearted.

Aiden knew he was a bundle of excitement and nerves but couldn't help himself. The almost complete radio silence since they had planned this—whatever it was—didn't help.

Aiden had sent a message yesterday to make sure Wren was still coming and Wren had responded with a single word, "Yes." Aiden couldn't help wonder if this was further proof that Wren wasn't really that interested getting together.

Either way, Aiden found himself alone in his apartment, dressed and ready to go, and needing to waste another thirty minutes before Wren's expected arrival time. And that was assuming Wren was on time.

Aiden took a deep breath. He needed to get a handle on himself. It was just lunch between friends.

No matter how much Aiden wished it could be more.

Plus, there was always the chance that everything was as he remembered, their chemistry was off the charts, and this would be the start of something great. Even if today wasn't a date, maybe next time could be.

Lucy had been calling and texting him all week. Somehow, she seemed to know Wren had texted Aiden before Aiden could tell her even though she denied Wren told her. Aiden wondered if Lucy's not-so-subtle manipulation was still at play. He was tempted to be annoyed, but it was hard to argue with the results. Well, so long as Wren actually wanted to get together. Aiden didn't want to be a chore.

Oh god! What if Wren was only meeting with Aiden because Lucy talked him into it? What if he didn't even want to get together?

Yesterday, Lucy had tried to convince Aiden to go shopping with him after work to get him a new outfit. Aiden reminded her being gay didn't make him magically enjoy shopping. He had also pointed out he had several perfectly suitable outfits to wear and since they had only just been reacquainted Wren had no way to know what clothes were new. Plus, this wasn't a date, no matter how much Lucy and Aiden wanted it to be. Therefore, they should save any date related shopping trips for an anniversary or something special after he and Wren had been dating for a while—if they ever got together.

This comment had made Lucy lose her mind since, apparently, it was "incredibly telling" that Aiden was already thinking about their anniversaries. Aiden had tried to argue the point, but he knew she was right. He wanted this to be a date. He was more interested in going out with Wren than he had been with any other man. That was truly the scariest part of all of this. What would he do if Wren just wanted to be friends?

No, he knew the answer. It would disappoint him, but he'd get over it. He would be happy just to have Wren in his life even if it was just as a friend because somehow after only two meals together, Aiden already couldn't imagine his life without Wren in it.

He kept having to remind himself to calm down and not turn into a crazy creeper. Maybe that was why he was so worried it was all in his head. He wanted this to be something so badly. Let them become friends at least. Please!

Aiden also had to admit Lucy might have been right about doing pre-lunch shopping because when he was getting dressed that morning, he had spent more time picking out his outfit than he had ever spent getting dressed before—or at least since the last time he'd dressed up for Wren. While he enjoyed looking hot and knowing he looked good, he wasn't that interested in fashion.

Lucy had called him at ten in the morning to ask him about what he intended to wear. It was earlier than Aiden usually got up in the mornings on the weekend but Aiden had already been up and showered for over an hour. Unfortunately, instead of calmly getting dressed he had been standing in front of his closet for over ten minutes gripped by indecision.

"I decided on the dark jeans with the interesting stitching around the pockets," he had answered. "They make my ass look good."

"Hmm, okay, a hot ass for your first date is a good idea. What about for your top?"

"This isn't a date, and I was thinking of the blue plaid button up. It fits well in the shoulders and if I roll up the sleeves my forearms look attractive in that shirt. Or at least that is what Bobby always said."

"Bobby may have been a cheating asshole, but he was correct about that shirt. Plus, Wren has always been into muscular guys. Your shoulders looking good would likely be almost as much of a turn on as your hot bubble butt. And don't mention Bobby when you're talking to Wren."

"First, I know how to conduct myself on a date. Although, again, do I really need to remind you this is not a date?" Aiden retorted. "Second, I never want to hear you to describe me as hot or as having a bubble butt. Jeez, Luce, you're my sister."

"What? I can appreciate the artistic beauty even if I am not interested in sampling the goods."

"God! Just stop talking already."

The phone line was quiet for a moment and Aiden had been worried that Lucy had listened to him for once when she continued, "I just want this to go well. I totally can see you and Wren together. And it would be awesome to have him as my brother."

"Okay, Lucy, maybe slow down. This is just lunch. I don't even know if he is interested."

"Oh, he's interested all right. Something has him nervous, but he's interested. You are both hot, gay and even I could feel the chemistry over dinner the other day. Make it happen, all right. I know you've been dreaming about this since you were a kid."

"Luce, if you ever tell him I had a crush on him when I was younger, I will put toads in your bed. Also, how did you even know I had a crush on him in high school? I wasn't even out then."

Lucy laughed maniacally without answering before saying goodbye and hanging up. Her laughter was unsettling.

Now, here he was pacing his apartment anxious about the date. He was almost tempted to call Lucy if only because bantering with her would distract him and help pass the time.

He picked up his cell phone, desperately trying not to look at the time. A watched pot never boils so maybe a watched clock never moves.

The apartment buzzer sounded.

# Chapter 8
## Wren

Walking up to Aiden's apartment Wren froze and had a moment of panic. He could have sworn he recognized the driver of that grey car which just passed him on the street. Except that wasn't possible as there was no way that person was here in Edmonton so he shook off the fear and panic that had gripped him.

He was just nervous. The happy butterflies in his stomach had turned into galloping elephants over the past two days and Wren wasn't sure whether he was about to laugh hysterically or vomit.

Why was he even nervous? This wasn't even at date. It wasn't even at night. They were having lunch. Just lunch between two friends. That's it.

Maybe if he repeated it often enough, he would believe it.

Wren took a deep breath to steady himself and pushed the buzzer for apartment 12. He waited a few seconds before hearing Aiden through the speaker. "Hello?"

"Hey, it's—ah, Wren."

"Come on in. Up the stairs. Second last door on the left." Buzz. Click. The door unlocked.

Wren slowly entered the building, taking his time to look around at the stark white walls before preceding up the stairs. The hall was clean for an older apartment building and fairly well maintained. He also noticed how quiet it was in the hallway and wondered if it was unusual or if this was just a quiet building.

Standing in front of Aiden's door Wren hesitated a moment then knocked. Aiden had obviously been waiting for him to arrive because he immediately opened the door with a huge smile.

God, that smile. It lit up Aiden's entire face and took him to a whole new level of attractiveness. It was like watching the sun come out. Wren could almost feel the heat of it on his face.

"Welcome to my humble abode," Aiden invited Wren in as he stepped back into his apartment and gave an over-dramatized arm wave.

"Thanks," Wren said with a laugh and looked around curiously. "Seems like a nice building."

"I moved in right after I graduated from high school when my old roommate left me to move in with his boyfriend. I like it enough here to not bother moving."

Aiden patted his pockets as though he was looking for something then when his search was unsuccessful, he said, "I'm just going to run upstairs to my bedroom to get my wallet, then we can get going."

Wren nodded in acknowledgment and Aiden started up the stairs to the loft. "You still okay with walking to Dadeo's for lunch?" Aiden called down the stairs.

"Yep," Wren responded distractedly. "I'm just going to snoop around your living room until you come down."

Aiden just laughed.

Alone in the living room of Aiden's apartment Wren looked around curiously. The suite was a relatively small loft style apartment. The door had opened into a small living room with a small couch and a large television. There was a Play Station below the television, a bookstand beside the television with video game boxes, DVDs, and fancy board games he'd never heard of with names like Dominion, Race for the Galaxy, and Exploding Kitties. The other side of the television had another bookcase. Books, both novels and engineering textbooks, were overflowing the shelves. There was even, Wren noticed, a technical manual for the Starship Enterprise and a toy model of an X-wing.

On the walls, there was a large poster of the blue Tardis with David Tennant as Doctor Who. Another poster showed Chris Evans as Captain America. There was a photograph of the night sky over the ocean lit up by lightning. Then there was a collection of framed photos of Aiden, his family, and what Wren assumed were his friends. Wren's gut tightened at the picture of Aiden with a group of guys, two of whom were in full drag. They had clearly taken the picture at a Pride event. Everyone had huge smiles on their faces and all looked so open and proud. Wren hadn't attended Pride the last few years and added it to his long list of regrets.

The place was nice. It felt like a home even if it was a nerdy bachelor pad. He felt comfortable here and noticed even the dancing elephants had settled down. This was a place he could spend a lot of time.

Wren felt conflicted about moving out of his mother's house. She wasn't pressuring him to leave or anything, but he felt like a bad cliché, the almost thirty-year-old who had been forced to run back home after a bad breakup. It felt like he had suddenly returned to high school. To make things worse, his mother was trying but she couldn't help babying him, especially after everything that happened.

The thumping of Aiden hopping down the stairs pulled Wren from his musings.

"Your neighbours must hate you," Wren said with a smile. Aiden just shrugged in response. "Also, you are a total nerd!"

Aiden responded with a smile and a shrug. "What did you expect? You used to play video games with me when I was a kid."

"Ya, but you aren't just a guy who continues to play video games occasionally as an adult," Wren pointed to the Dr. Who poster. "You've embraced your inner nerd."

"What? I grew up to be an engineer. It's one of the nerdiest professions out there. Plus, David Tennant and Chris Evans are hot."

Wren shook his head and laughed. Then with a conspiratorial wink, he said, "Chris Hemsworth is hotter."

Aiden laughed. “All right, now that you’ve snooped through my stuff and are done judging me, you wanna go?”

“While I’m happy to leave, I won’t promise to stop judging you.”

“I suppose that’s fair,” Aiden agreed with an eye roll.

It wasn’t far to walk, but with each step they took their hands brushed against each other. Wren wondered if he was standing too close. He wondered if people could peg him and Aiden as a gay couple going on a date and he should back off. Except, he liked the contact. He wanted to take Aiden’s hand.

But that would be weird because this wasn’t a date.

Maybe he would have just done it anyway, but he wasn’t sure if Aiden was comfortable holding hands casually in public or even if they were safe in this area of town.

So instead of taking Aiden’s hand Wren made fists and stuck his hands in his jacket pockets. It kept them warmer anyway.

When he was younger, before he left Edmonton, Whyte Ave could be dangerous for gay guys at night. It had always seemed sort of weird that during the day it was all about independent stores, arts and crafts, and theatre and rarely there were any issues at all. At night, everything changed. The funky stores closed and bro culture and bars took control.

He’d had gay slurs yelled at him a few times and once a group of guys had followed him and hadn’t stopped until he had walked up to one of the police officers that were always hanging around at night.

Aiden didn’t look nervous so maybe things had changed. Hell, ten years ago, gay marriage had only just been legalized nationally. Now there were more liberal governments both nationally and provincially. Maybe the Texas of Canada was ready to live and let live—or at least as much as they were in most of the rest of the country.

Plus, this was the middle of the day during late winter when it was still cold enough to keep the crowds indoors.

They were ambling along, not bothering to rush. Aiden mentioned he had made a reservation, but it wasn’t for another twenty minutes and the walk wasn't nearly that long. It was also nice out, only about zero degrees and barely a cloud in the sky. Wren loved the transition from winter to spring in Edmonton. It might take forever to arrive and stayed cold by the standards of most places, but each warm day really felt like a reward after surviving the everlasting frozen winter.

Aiden was in the middle of reminiscing about their adolescence when he suddenly stopped talking and they both watched in silent shock as a grey Honda Civic followed them around the corner, going the wrong way down the one-way street, and almost hit another car. The Civic ended up having to reverse and back onto the two-way road to get out of the way to the sound of honking and shouting.

Wren couldn't see the driver because of the angle and the light of the setting sun reflecting off the glass but he wondered who was driving so dangerously.

He wondered if it was the same driver he'd seen before. The car looked the same. He shivered in fear but shook it off with a laugh. There was no way.

Wren and Aiden shared a look of amused shock at almost witnessing an accident.

"I guess you can't stop stupid," Aiden joked, shaking his head. "I hope whoever was driving wasn't drunk. I'd hate to think someone might die today because of that idiot."

Wren hummed in agreement. They continued, walking in an oddly comfortable silence for a moment before Wren picked up the conversation where they'd left it before being interrupted, "You know she taught me how to knit?"

"Who?"

"Your mom," Wren explained. "That winter she was knitting hats and scarves all the time. I was over hanging out with Lucy and got chatting with your mom about her amazing knit tuques and commented I didn't know how to knit. She told me everyone should know how and suggested I learn so I could knit some nice guy a scarf and then taught me how to knit. Gave me my first set of needles."

"Do you still knit?"

"Not for a few years now."

"I won't tell my mom," Aiden laughed. "She tried to convince me I needed to know how to knit. I told her I already knew how to cook. After some thought, she decided food was the way to a man's heart, so it would do."

"I can't argue with that," Wren said, glancing pointedly at the restaurant now in front of them.

Aiden laughed before saying, "All right, let's get you fed."

"I still can't believe you've never been here," Aiden said, starting in on Wren after they had been seated. "This restaurant is practically an institution. It's the best. I know you were out of town for a long time, but still."

The server arrived and took their drink orders then left while they looked at the menu.

"I hope you're hungry because the portions are big," Aiden commented as he looked over the menu.

"You warned me, so I ate a small breakfast," Wren said, looking over his own menu. "So, what do you suggest?"

"Okay, so everything is fantastic but their Po'Boys are classic. And their sweet potato fries are the best I've ever had. They have been making them here since before sweet potato fries were popular everywhere else. It was their sweet potato fries that taught me to enjoy sweet potatoes since I never liked them as a kid."

The food was delicious. Wren wondered whether it would be as good as he remembered if he ever came back since the company more than the food made lunch so enjoyable.

Much like during their shared meal two weeks earlier, Aiden made him laugh and got Wren talking more than he was used to. These days he was quiet and kept to himself. It had felt awkward talking to other people, like he was rusty and had forgotten how to engage in small talk.

With Aiden that was completely gone. He felt comfortable like he usually only felt around Lucy and his mom. Not that there weren't any pauses in their conversation, but the pauses didn't feel strained. Aiden kept a up stream of conversation without steamrolling him the way Lucy sometimes did.

Aiden also asked questions without pressing him to talk about things he didn't want to talk about.

"You wanna get dessert?" asked Aiden as they finished their entrees.

"Yes, and no," replied Wren. "The food was amazing. So, I want to see what they do with dessert but I'm full."

"You wanna share a Banana's Foster? They flambé it at the table. It is pretty cool to watch."

"Fire at the table," Wren said with a big maniacal smile. "That sounds like a disaster waiting to happen, and therefore not to be missed. Let's go for it."

The waitress brought out the dessert, poured the brandy over the banana and toppings, then lit the liquor with a small cooking torch. The beautiful blue flame ran over the banana and lit up Aiden's and Wren's faces with a soft glow. Wren watched Aiden watching the flames die down. His heart did a little pitter patter.

Wren knew even though this wasn't supposed to be a date, it might be one of the best he'd ever had.

# Chapter 9
## Aiden

Walking back to his apartment after lunch was bitter sweet. Aiden wasn't prepared for their time together to end, but he also was almost giddy with how well things had gone. His worries about them not getting along and everything being in his head had been unfounded.

While he enjoyed the walk, Aiden wasn't sure what would happen once they got back to his place. He knew what a southern part of his anatomy wanted but Aiden was trying his best to avoid thinking about that. He knew that wasn't going to happen.

What was harder to ignore was his heart, which kind of loved the idea of having a stupidly romantic kiss. That would be weird, though.

Right?

When they were standing in front of his apartment, Aiden stopped and looked at Wren.

Wren had been talking but his voice trailed off. He looked back at Aiden. Aiden felt his breath catch as the air got heavy and electricity seemed to pass between them.

There was no way this was all in Aiden's head. He wasn't that bad at reading people.

Aiden saw Wren's eyes glance down at his lips and Aiden felt his heart speed up in anticipation of the kiss he could practically feel in the air.

Wren's hand twitched up like he wanted to take hold of Aiden but stopped himself first. It felt as though that small movement took control of

Aiden. Without consciously deciding to do so he took a small step forward, closing the gap so only a few inches were left between them.

"I'd really like to kiss you," he said. "I know you didn't ask me for lunch as a date but... can I kiss you, anyway? I mean, you can say no. I won't be mad but—"

And then they were kissing.

Aiden wasn't even sure who started it. He was pretty sure it was Wren but their height difference meant he must have leaned down for Wren to reach his lips. Which meant he must have moved, but he had no conscious memory of doing so. All that he could absorb, all that he could experience, was the feeling of Wren's lips pressed against his.

Aiden found his hand against Wren's cheek, supporting his face. He felt Wren's fingers in his hair then the kiss deepened and Aiden felt Wren's tongue seeking entrance and Aiden happily obliged. Wren tasted like heaven. There was the sweetness left over from dessert but mostly Aiden relished his first taste of Wren.

The kiss went on for moments, years, decades until they both had to pull away to catch their breath. Aiden looked down at Wren and felt wrecked by the look in Wren's eyes. He didn't look like someone who had been merely kissed. No, Wren looked like someone who had lost himself in something amazing. There was also a look of surprise and almost awe on his face which Aiden could completely understand since he was feeling the exact same thing.

"Wow," Aiden wasn't even sure which one of them said it. Aiden rested his head against Wren's forehead and ran his fingers through Wren's hair. It was so smooth. The feeling of the strands running through his fingers felt better than silk. He never wanted it to stop.

"Was this a date?" Aiden asked softly.

"I don't know," Wren answered equally softly, like they existed in their own bubble and talking any louder than a quiet whisper would break the spell. "But—it felt like a date."

Aiden couldn't help but press his lips to Wren's again. The sweet taste of his lips threatened to consume him once again.

Then a car honked, and they both jumped in surprise. Aiden saw a weird look cross Wren's face. It was almost like a cross between sadness and fear.

"I should go," Wren said. He sounded both disappointed and determined and Aiden wasn't sure what was going on. What had gone wrong? That kiss had been perfect.

Aiden took a deep breath and forced himself to take a step back so he was further from Wren. Maybe Wren was right about going. Aiden reminded himself that this wasn't a date or at least hadn't been one.

"Can I text you?" Aiden asked, knowing the answer he wanted and dreading he might be turned down.

Wren smiled as he took another step back, moving toward his car.

"You'd better." Wren smiled as the look of sadness disappeared. "Or I might track you down. I know where you live after all."

# Chapter 10
## Wren

Wren wasn't sure what to think after their first date—or whatever that lunch should be called. No, he needed to stop pretending. The only way it would have been more of a date was if they'd admitted that was what it was going to be before the lunch started. Wren just hadn't been able to admit what he wanted.

The kiss had changed all that. As soon as Aiden's lips had touched his, Wren had felt as though his entire world had shifted. Suddenly, nothing was more important in his life than seeing where this thing might go. The thought had been completely and utterly terrifying. He wasn't ready to lose himself in another relationship. He didn't trust himself enough for that.

So, he'd run.

Except his world had changed and he couldn't hide behind denial anymore. All the excuses he'd used before their kiss rang hollow. If he walked away now, he'd know it was because he was afraid and he didn't think he could live with himself if fear was controlling him that much.

That might be the thing which finally breaks him.

So, he'd run, but he hadn't run far; and when Aiden sent him a text on Sunday morning, he'd answered right away instead of pretending he was still asleep after working a night shift.

That first text had broken the dam. One of them called the other each night before bed, they texted random questions and jokes throughout the day, and suddenly after being mostly isolated for over a year, Wren didn't feel so alone.

He laughed aloud at jokes and had tingles of anticipation every time he saw the three little dots showing Aiden was responding to something he'd said. Like every time they'd been together in person, their conversations were easy and comfortable.

On Monday they'd made plans to get together for dinner on Friday. Wren spent the rest of the week wishing the week would pass more quickly.

On Tuesday, Aiden had suggested they meet on Wednesday for a drink after he finished work. Wren had been disappointed when he'd had to decline because of work again, that was despite Aiden having suggested they go to a bar.

In response, he'd almost suggested Aiden take an extra long lunch so they could meet up for another lunch date, but he'd decided against it because he worried it sounded desperate.

Plus, things were already moving so quickly. Maybe too quickly?

It was scary but in an exciting way, a what-will-happen-next sort of way. But scary exciting wasn't worth worrying about when he had actual scary things happening to get worked up about. Earlier in the week he had gotten two weird voicemails from the same strange number.

The first one he had dismissed as a wrong number. He could hear distant voices in the background but couldn't understand anything being said. Instead, all he could distinguish was someone breathing. Not even hard. Just... breathing. It was creepy.

He'd thought the first one was weird but the second call from the same number had been even creepier. There had been no background noise at all. It had been silent except that same soft breathing.

Wren hadn't told anyone about the messages. They scared him. The weirdness of them sent chills up his spine but he worried people would think he was a wuss if he made too much of them. When he didn't get any more, he figured what was the point in scaring his mother, or worse, having her thinking it was a product of PTSD and telling him to go back into therapy. He didn't want people to think he was delusional.

Even if they were right because the calls hadn't been the only thing freaking him out recently. He kept seeing someone who just couldn't be there. It was like he was seeing a ghost.

He was tired of feeling crazy. That was worse than dealing with everything alone.

The result was that instead of completely scaring him, his blooming relationship with Aiden was a welcome distraction to his otherwise paranoid thinking and he threw himself into it with both feet.

Despite Wren suggesting the date, Aiden invited Wren over to his apartment for their Friday night dinner. This time, instead of going out, Aiden wanted to show off his culinary skills.

He cooked a delicious pan-fried steak, and served it with roasted cheese and broccoli and freshly bought French bread. Aiden hadn't been exaggerating when he'd bragged earlier. He really was a good chef. One more point in his favour, not that Wren needed more reasons to like Aiden.

Even without mood lighting or a fancy table setting, the dinner had been romantic. Wren was no longer surprised when they just seemed to click and his normal stress seemed to disappear. He could even stop over-thinking everything and relax and enjoy the moment.

That was until dinner drew to a close and Wren realized he would have to decide what would happen next. He was paralysed between his anticipation of what was to come, and his fear that nothing would happen at all.

Somehow, Aiden knew what he needed, or maybe he was just that easy to read but either way his relief was a physical thing when Aiden suggested they enjoy the unseasonably warm spring weather and go for a walk through the woods down in the river valley.

They ended up going on a long walk, down to Kinsmen Park, across the river and up to the Legislature grounds. They had stopped at a bench looking over the river. The view was beautiful. Even though it wasn't that late, the sun was setting which left the sky awash with colour. The pink and orange streaked across the sky, to merge into purple and navy. Although spring had not yet brought the leaves back onto the trees, the evergreens ensured the undeveloped river valley was still full of green.

Wren leaned his head against Aiden's shoulder and they sat in silence. Wren felt at peace. He felt Aiden looking down at him. Wren moved to look at Aiden's face and was struck again by his beauty.

"You are so gorgeous," Aiden said, breaking the silence. Wren blinked as his thoughts came out of Aiden's mouth.

Aiden leaned forward, then paused a hair's breadth from Wren's lips. Wren closed the distance and felt Aiden's soft lips against his. The second kiss was no less powerful than their first, the week before.

As with their last kiss, when Aiden's lips touched Wren's, his world changed. Except this time instead of rocking his world, everything fell into place and Wren knew there was no need to be afraid.

Aiden's lips were slightly cold from the cooling evening air. Wren felt Aiden's warm breath against him as he opened his mouth slightly and deepening the kiss.

Wren felt Aiden's tongue slide against his as it entered his mouth to explore, then withdraw, tempting and teasing him into trying to catch his tongue. He bit down and caught Aiden's lower lip in his teeth then felt himself smiling. He pulled away a little and let Aiden's lip go as he opened his eyes and caught Aiden already looking at him.

"That was amazing," Aiden breathed. Wren smiled. He stood up and took Aiden's hand, pulling him up off the bench.

"Although I agree that was a great kiss, I think we can do better," Wren said with a cheeky grin. "Let's go back to your place and see if we can reach amazing."

Wren watched as Aiden's smile grew even larger. Then he pulled Wren forward on the path.

After their first amazing kiss—of course, he was lying and both kisses were absolutely amazing—Wren had walked away because it had scared him. He was sure the good times he'd experienced so far wouldn't last. Everything had gone well over lunch, and with the kiss he hadn't wanted to risk more.

This time was different. Today may only be their second date but it felt like they'd been together longer. They'd spent all week talking and because they'd known each other when they were younger, they could skip so much of the get-to-know each other part of a new relationship.

Or maybe it was because Wren couldn't ever remember being attracted to anyone as much as he was to Aiden.

After all his time alone, he was finally ready to do something that required them to get naked. And god, oh, god, was he ready to get off.

They walked back toward Aiden's apartment, playfully alternating between rushing forward and pulling each other off the path to stop and kiss.

By the time they made it back to Aiden's apartment they were both tired and almost desperate for each other. As soon as they were inside and the door was closed, Wren and Aiden were on each other. Stumbling backward, Wren allowed Aiden to push him onto the couch in the living room. They fell with Aiden on top. Wren moaned at the feeling of Aiden's body pressing against him.

With their mouths still connected, Wren pushed his hands between their bodies. He pulled at Aiden's pants, opening his button and fly, and slid his hand into Aiden's pants and briefs. He felt himself moan again as his hand closed around Aiden's hard silken cock. Or maybe it was Aiden who moaned into his mouth. It didn't matter. All that mattered was that he finally had his hands on Aiden's cock.

Wren moved his mouth and kissed his way to Aiden's ear to nibble his earlobe while he stroked up and down Aiden's cock. He felt the foreskin slide back and forth over the head. He revelled in the smooth silky texture. He felt it twitch as he squeezed on the downstroke. He heard Aiden's breath become shallow, felt the hot breath on his neck as Aiden buried his face in Wren's shoulder and moaned. Wren felt himself hump his hips against Aiden's leg in an effort to increase the friction against his aching cock.

Then Aiden was suddenly gone, leaving Wren feeling bare and stranded.

"Off," Aiden instructed. "Clothes off. I need to see you naked."

Wren looked over at Aiden. His eyes tracking Aiden's hands as they pushed his shirt over his head revealing a nice muscular stomach. God, he was fucking gorgeous. And strong. And...

Fuck.

Aiden's thumbs were now hooked onto his pants and underwear in an obvious precursor to removing the rest of his clothing. Wren salivated in anticipation of seeing Aiden's cock for the first time. He just knew it would be amazing.

"Babe. I gotta see you. I need to see you naked," Aiden begged, reminding Wren he was supposed to be getting naked too, not just ogling Aiden while he disrobed. Wren ripped off his shirt, not bothering to unbutton all the buttons, instead pulling the shirt and the undershirt over his head in one go. He then struggled out of his tight jeans, his battle made harder by his complete distraction watching Aiden push down his pants and reveal his beautiful, amazing penis.

"I knew it," Wren whispered in awe. "I knew you would have a fucking perfect cock."

Aiden's cock was long and thick with a slight curve to the up and left. It was uncut with short trimmed hair above it and darker, medium-sized balls below it and was leaking precum. Wren salivated. He wanted to lick those balls. He wanted to taste that cock. His hand twitched. He wanted to feel the hard, velvety member in his hand again but this time while he watched as his fist closed around it.

# Chapter 11

## Aiden

Aiden stood before Wren unable to speak, practically unable to breathe. He was in heaven. No, he wasn't there yet because he wasn't touching Wren yet, but he was closer than he had ever thought he would be. He stood, completely naked before Wren and could barely remember he wasn't wearing clothes he was so focused on Wren and Wren's beautiful body.

Wren was narrow but his clothes had hidden the full impact of his wiry muscles. Aiden remembered from when they were kids that Wren had always had a fast metabolism. He seemed to have to eat a ton of calories just to keep muscle and weight on. This didn't seem to have changed based on how much Wren had eaten at dinner during their past two dates. But Wren obviously worked out as well because this was not the body of someone who was coasting on good genes. This was someone who worked for it.

Aiden had already been fascinated by the play of muscles on Wren's arms but now, without his clothes, Aiden could practically feel his legs collapsing as his body unconsciously prepared to crawl toward Wren and lick his way down Wren's stomach, along the muscles, to his dark treasure trail, and toward the straining cock.

Aiden figured Wren's cock was shorter and slightly wider than his own but was perfectly straight. His foreskin was being pulled back by the length of his erection and his dark pink head was gleaming with precum. The veins along the shaft were full and provided a texture Aiden wanted to explore with his hand, with his tongue, with his throat, anything as long as he could get that cock inside him.

"You are so beautiful," Aiden said reverently. "Can I please touch you?"

"Yes. God, yes."

Aiden stepped forward and fell to his knees before Wren, who was sitting on the couch. He wanted to worship him. He wanted to worship this amazing man who somehow kept exceeding his expectations; wildly exceeding the dreams he had had about him when Aiden was still a child learning about what he wanted and what sex meant to him.

Aiden slowly trailed his fingers from Wren's shoulders to his pecs, to his navel, to his wild pubic hair, then finally to his cock. He wanted to see how much of it he could fit into his mouth but knew there would be time for that later.

As he slowly, gently stroked his hand up and down Wren's shaft he groaned and heard his voice in stereo, only to realize Wren was groaning too. He watched as Wren's cock jumped in anticipation, in eagerness. Aiden felt himself smile. This was pure fantasy made real.

He groaned again as he felt Wren's hand slide down to grip his cock. Wren grabbed Aiden by the back of the head, his fingers twisting into his hair, holding him back from sucking his cock. Wren pulled his head up and to the side so Wren was talking into his ear.

"I want to feel your cock against mine," Wren breathed into his ear. "I want to rub up against you. I want to fuck our cocks against each other as I feel you shudder. I want to feel groans rumble through your body as you get closer and closer to coming. But before I let you come, I want to make you wait while I suck your balls. And then, I want to suck on your cock while I drink you down when you finally come down my throat."

Aiden felt himself shudder with excitement and desire. He had to consciously hold himself back from coming right there like some kind of overly hormonal teenager.

“God, yes. Yes, please,” Aiden moaned. Wren nibbled on Aiden’s ear and pulled Aiden on top of him so their pelvises were almost touching and their cocks rubbed up against each other as Aiden humped his hips back and forward unconsciously.

Aiden wrapped his hands around their cocks and stroked them together. But before he got more than two strokes in, Wren wrapped his legs and arms around Aiden and flipped them over so Aiden was lying back along the couch and Wren was on top of him. Looking down at him, Wren took over.

Then Wren did exactly what he had said he would do. It was the sweetest and most excruciating torture. Aiden started begged for mercy but even he didn’t know if he was begging for more or for the torture to never end.

“Oh, god,” Aiden moaned. “Wren, baby. I can’t hold it. Wren, I... ohhh. Wren, I’m gonna. Fuck. Fuck! I’m gonna come.” Aiden threw his head back into the couch cushion and his cock shot come into Wren’s mouth. Wren continued to gently stroke and lick as he swallowed while come and spit dribbled down his chin.

“That was so fucking hot,” Wren commented, smiling as he looked down at Aiden who was slowly recovering.

Aiden felt like his muscles had turned to jelly and his brain had melted out his ears, maybe it had blasted out his cock along with the week's worth of come that had been building up since they had shared that first kiss. Not that he hadn’t been jacking off in between but he couldn’t make himself orgasm that hard on his own.

After a moment, Aiden looked down at Wren who rested his chin on Aiden’s pubic bone. He smiled up at Aiden as his eyes fluttered and his body twitched with the force of his orgasm. He looked content.

“Your turn,” Aiden said with a predatory smile. He sat up and pulled Wren onto his lap and gave him a kiss.

“Oh, you don’t have to.”

“Oh, I absolutely do. I misspoke. I should have said, my turn.”

Aiden jackknifed and flipped himself and Wren over so he was on top of Wren.

"I want to suck your cock until you forget your name and your brain leaks out your ears like you did to me." Aiden explained while holding Wren's hands in one of his and using his other hand to stroke down Wren's chest and tweak his nipples. "But, if when you said you don't have to, you meant you don't want me to, I will stop."

Aiden then released Wren's hands and sat back, showing this decision was completely up to him.

A look of sadness, or maybe regret passed over Wren's face before a smile and a laugh replaced it. Aiden wondered what thoughts had caused that look but let himself become distracted when Wren shook his head and said, "Yes. Of course, you can suck my cock. I would never say 'no' to you about that."

Wren's emphasis on the word 'you' made Aiden pause and wonder again what was going through Wren's head. Except Aiden had his answer. It was his turn now.

Aiden paid attention to each of Wren's reactions, each shudder and gasp, each moan and twitch as he stroked and licked and nibbled his way from Wren's mouth to his ear, down his neck to his collarbone and down to his nipples. Each sound, each quiver was a jolt directly to his groin, and he felt his cock twitch in a valiant effort to get hard again.

Aiden continued trailing kisses and nibbles along Wren's ribs to his stomach and down his beautiful, enticing treasure trail over to his hips and along his pubic bone. He skipped his cock and balls to nibble at his inner thigh and slowly licked and sucked on Wren's balls as he ran his hands down Wren's legs to the back of his knees and down to the top of his feet and the sensitive skin on the arch of his foot.

This time it was Wren who was moaning and panting and begging. Wren gasped when Aiden finally closed his mouth over Wren's wide cock. It stretched his mouth and lips and he pushed his tongue up into the spongy area on the underside of the head. Then he slowly, oh so slowly, pushed down, pushing Wren's cock into his mouth and held his breath as he pushed Wren's cock down his throat.

"Fuck!" Wren exclaimed.

Aiden hummed and elicited squirms and moans from Wren as the vibrations moved from his throat up Wren's cock.

"Oh, shit!" Wren exclaimed again and his hands buried themselves in Aiden's hair. "Fuck! So ghaaa."

That's a start, Aiden thought as he pulled himself back up enough to breathe then sucked Wren's cock in earnest.

It was difficult since Wren was thicker than anyone else he'd done this to, but every moan made the discomfort worth it.

Wren's speech lost even more meaning as even swears became groans and meaningless moaning. Every time Aiden suspected Wren was getting close Aiden would pull back or slow down until the moans gained a begging quality about them.

Aiden could feel himself getting hard again as he encouraged Wren to fuck his face. Aiden slid a hand down to his shaft and stroked himself while the other hand joined his mouth and worked on Wren.

The feeling of Wren in his mouth felt amazing and Aiden felt himself clench in anticipation of Wren fucking him, filling him up somewhere lower down. Aiden sped up his hand, loving the sounds Wren made as he increased the suction of his mouth on Wren cock.

The moaning gained an urgency to it before Wren suddenly moaned, "Fuuuuck!" and released into Aiden's mouth.

Aiden continued to suck Wren's cock gently as he came down from his orgasm. Aiden could feel his own orgasm approaching. He rolled his eyes up and watched Wren. His beautiful face, flushed with orgasm, looking relaxed and happy brought Aiden ever closer to his second climax.

Releasing Wren's cock, Aiden took the hand that had been holding Wren and licked his fingers before inserting them into his own anus and came again, shooting come all over himself and onto Wren's stomach and chest.

“Fuck!” Aiden exclaimed before collapsing onto Wren, with his face buried in Wren’s neck.

After a bit, Wren stirred. “Shit, I’m probably squishing you,” Aiden said as he rolled off Wren, falling onto the floor beside the couch.

“Smooth,” Wren laughed. Aiden stuck his tongue out at Wren as he sat himself back on the couch. Wren leaned his head on Aiden’s shoulder. They sat there is silence, enjoying the contact and the post orgasmic glow. Wren played with Aiden’s hair, running the strands through his fingers. Aiden felt the soothing tug on his hair down to his toes.

Aiden felt Wren sigh in relaxed contentment and Aiden smiled, enjoying the moment. They stayed like that, silent but content for a while longer, and Aiden was so happy to be able to enjoy the silence with this man.

“This is great,” said Wren, breaking the silence. “But I should go home. I’m working tomorrow.”

“Oh,” Aiden’s voice let a hint of disappointment peek through. Had he done something wrong? He understood they couldn’t stay like this forever but he didn’t want Wren to leave. “Okay. Ya, of course.”

Aiden stood up and pulled Wren up beside him. He gave Wren a light kiss and felt relieved when Wren pulled him in to deepen the kiss. Maybe it was nothing. Maybe Wren just had to go to work.

# Chapter 12
## Aiden

The next morning, Aiden was sitting around his apartment messaging back and forth with Wren when there was a knock on his door. Aiden wasn't even dressed yet. He was sitting in his underwear with his half-eaten breakfast laid out in front of him.

Aiden had woken up in a fantastic mood and decided to try to make it better by seeing if he could convince Wren to come over to hang out, maybe watch a movie with him after Wren finished work. After messaging off and on for an hour or so, Aiden's day got even better when Wren agreed to a second date—or was it third? —after work despite being tired from not sleeping much the night before.

"Be right there," he yelled at whoever was waiting on the other side of the door. Aiden ran upstairs to grab a t-shirt and a pair of pants before running back to open the door.

He opened the door. Aiden found himself facing one of his neighbours, he couldn't remember his name but Aiden thought the guy lived in one of the basement suites with his girlfriend.

"Oh, hello," Aiden said. He wondered what this was about. He'd never done more than say hi to this guy before.

"Hey, umm, you drive a blue Subaru, right?" the man asked.

"Ya?" Aiden answered with a clear question in his voice. He was even more confused. His car was parked in his parking spot behind the building. He couldn't see any reason another tenant would have an issue with that.

“Did you know your car has scratches all over it? I think someone keyed your car.” The guy looked nervous enough that it took a moment for the words to penetrate Aiden’s head.

“What?!” Aiden exclaimed when he realized what he’d heard. “No, I did not know!”

“Umm ya, I figured if you didn’t know you’d want to be told as soon as possible.” He looked more confident now that he could see Aiden wasn’t yelling at him.

“Ya, umm, thanks for telling me,” Aiden said mostly to fill the silence when really all that he was thinking was ‘What? Why? Huh?’ “Are you sure it’s mine? The blue Subaru WRX parked in 110?”

The guy nodded. “Ya, I noticed it went I was taking out my garbage just now.”

Much later, Aiden was back sitting in front of his abandoned breakfast feeling much less excited about his day. He had completed an online police report about the scratches on his car. It required him to take a bunch of photos of the damage but otherwise hadn’t been too difficult to do, at least not physically. Emotionally, it had been a different story.

He’d also looked at his insurance policy and now he had to decide whether it would be worth getting his car repainted and repaired professionally or.... He didn’t know if this was something he could do himself.

God.

He had money saved up, he could pay for it out of pocket, and maybe he should so he didn’t have to make the claim and see his insurance premiums shoot up. Except there were marks all down the passenger side of his car and because they were on the passenger side, he couldn’t be sure when it had happened. It wasn’t like he did a full walk around his car every time he drove. He usually just walked straight to the driver’s door and got in.

Fuck, this sucked!

It wasn't just about the savings. Aiden's WRX was the first big purchase after getting his first adult job. It was his baby. He took care of it and cared about it. Why would anyone hurt his baby?

Aiden looked around not sure what to do now since everything he had planned for the day had gone out the window. He was starving. He had lost his whole day to this mess and still hadn't even eaten his breakfast—or lunch or whatever the hell time it was now. He was feeling positively cranky but could barely think clearly enough to get out of his chair and force himself to make dinner.

His door buzzer rang, and he wanted to scream in frustration. What now?!?

"Hello?" Aiden answered with significantly more bite to his voice than normal.

"Aiden? Umm, it's Wren."

# Part Two

## Things come back to haunt

# Chapter 13
## Wren

“Wren, Wren!” Aiden said, breaking Wren from his memories. “What’s wrong? You spaced out there for a bit.”

He blinked and took in what was on the television screen, no idea what was happening. He had been thinking about….

No!

“Sorry,” Wren apologized. “Umm just wool gathering. I guess I’m tired. I promise to stay focused now.”

“It’s okay,” Aiden shrugged. He didn’t even look angry.

Wren couldn’t believe it. Wasn’t Aiden annoyed he had been ignoring the movie?

“I’m sorry. You wanted me to watch this and I will pay attention now.”

“All right, if that’s what you want but we can do something different if this isn’t working for you today.”

They turned back to the movie and Wren tried to focus and pay attention but he'd clearly missed some important plot points because he didn’t understand what was going on. Plus, the movie was a science fiction film and while Wren enjoyed those occasionally; he preferred romantic comedies.

He didn’t want to tell Aiden that though, it might disappoint him.

When the movie ended Wren felt a sense of dread because he knew he wouldn’t be able to say the first thing about the movie he’d just watched.

He'd tried, but it hadn't made sense and the ending was completely confusing. What would he say when Aiden asked him about it?

Except he never did. When the credits rolled, he leaned forward and gave Wren a kiss then asked if he was staying or needed to go home. Wren knew he'd be going home, but as he packed up his bag, he wasn't sure what to think. He didn't want to leave Aiden. He liked spending time together. But it was a relief to leave and go home where he didn't need to second guess everything he did or try to pretend to be something he wasn't.

Not that Aiden ever demanded he behave differently. In fact, Aiden rarely made any demands, and even the few he had made seemed to be negotiable if Wren objected. It was strange. Nice, but strange.

He was so distracted that it wasn't until he was halfway home that Wren realized he had forgotten to kiss Aiden good night. The realization made him sad. What was going on with him? He finally had something good with a guy and it was like he was losing his mind and trying to destroy it. They'd only been going out for a few weeks. With no history to hold them together, how long before Aiden got angry and decided he'd had enough.

A horn honked, and he glanced into his rear-view mirror and saw a grey sedan behind him and felt himself freeze for a second in fear when the driver looked familiar. Then realized he must be imagining things when he looked forward and realized the car had honked because the light was green. He put his foot on the gas and continued driving home.

Despite knowing he was likely being paranoid, Wren was relieved when the grey sedan finally turned off onto a different side street two blocks from his mother's house.

What was going on with him these days? He was so inside his head he could barely function. He went straight upstairs as soon as he got home and fell into bed, feeling the exhaustion from not sleeping well the night before weighing him down, yet he could tell it would be hard to fall asleep.

His phone rang, and he answered it without looking at the display, assuming it was Aiden making sure he got home all right like he always did.

"Hey,"

No answer. Just heavy breathing.

"Hello?"

Still no answer.

"Look if you aren't going to say anything I'm going to hang up."

More breathing without words.

Wren hung up the phone then almost jumped out of his skin when it rang again in his hand. He looked at the screen this time and was glad to see a picture of Aiden's smiling face.

"Hey," Wren could hear the smile in his own voice and he felt himself relax.

"Talk until I fall asleep," Wren begged. "You chase away the nightmares."

# Chapter 14
## Aiden

Aiden laid out the dinner plates and spent a few seconds reorienting the cutlery so the forks were aligned with the knives. It was just dinner with Lucy but if he was cooking, he enjoyed having everything done right. As he went back into the kitchen, he admitted he might be going overboard tonight but he felt antsy and couldn't sit still. Preparing an amazing dinner gave him something to do. He'd already tidied the house this weekend and anything was better than scrubbing the bathtub, the next thing his list.

He knew what the problem was. He was nervous.

Not about Lucy coming for dinner. That was no big deal. If only every part of his life was as easy as seeing his sister.

No, he was nervous because he had been going out with Wren for over a month and sometimes, he couldn't even be sure if Wren liked him—or at least liked him as much as Aiden liked Wren. Aiden didn't think Wren disliked him. No, Wren liked him, it was just that something—something Aiden couldn't put his finger on—was off. It was almost like Wren was running hot and cold. Sometimes everything would be great and then other times... not so much. Aiden just wished he could figure out why. Was it something he was doing?

They talked all the time and got together for dates a few times a week. Mostly, when they were together everything was great. Wren laughed at his jokes, which Aiden loved, and they could get lost in conversations and talk for hours.

Physically, there was no question they were compatible. Since they'd started dating, Aiden had had some of the best orgasms of his life. They hadn't had anal intercourse because Wren didn't seem into it but that was fine.

Sometimes Aiden missed anal sex. He was a switch and enjoyed the intimacy of being totally connected to another man but he only wanted to do it if Wren wanted it too. The sex they had was so hot he knew Wren would satisfy him even if they never did anything more than they were doing now.

No, the weirdness wasn't the lack of anal sex after a month of dating. No, it was other things.

Everything would be good between them until out of nowhere it was like the shutters came down and he was suddenly a closed book. When they were apart, it was worse. They talked on the phone and suddenly Aiden would feel like he was talking to a puppet, or a robotic imitation of Wren. He would talk and laugh but everything sounded wooden and false.

It had come to a head when Wren had started and laughed the first time Aiden had suggested they be exclusive. Aiden had been devastated and tried to hide his pain, but must not have succeeded because Wren had explained it hadn't occurred to him they wouldn't be exclusive. The explanation had helped, but the laughter made him nervous. Bobby had always thought the idea of exclusivity was funny too. Look how that turned out.

Aiden's history with Bobby was worse than he'd even revealed to Wren. Bobby hadn't just cheated on him and ruined their two-year relationship. He had maintained his somewhat laissez-faire attitude toward condoms when he was fucking other men. Aiden had always insisted they used them when they were together but Bobby hadn't told Aiden about his risky sexual behaviour, even after they'd had a condom break. It has been Aiden walking in on Bobby barebacking another man that had finally awoken Aiden to the type of man he was involved with. The weeks and months that had followed that discovery had been one of the scariest times of Aiden's life. Nightmares about HIV, hepatitis, and other less deadly sexually transmitted diseases had kept him up at night until his test results had finally come back with a clean bill of health.

Aiden knew Wren wasn't Bobby, but it was hard not to wonder what Wren's secret was since there was so clearly was a secret. Aiden just wished Wren would talk to him about the things that were going on in his head. Then his imagination wouldn't be going into overdrive trying to fill in the gaps.

When he had asked Wren if anything was wrong, he'd said, "I'm fine, just having some trouble sleeping lately. I've been stressed about school applications." Wren seemed to be placating him with or at least the answer sounded incomplete.

Aiden tried to be understanding. Maybe he was just nervous about where he might get into university in the fall. Depending on what happened, their relationship might end. It was hard to really commit to someone when the relationship might be doomed. This had to be even harder for Wren who was the one waiting on acceptance letters.

Or work was stressing him out...

Or his father was being a jerk....

Well, Wren's school applications were stressing Aiden, too. Aiden wanted him to get into med school. He knew how important it was to him, but if he got in somewhere other than Edmonton, what would that mean for them?

Wren wouldn't even talk to Aiden about school, something that would affect them both. Aiden wondered if maybe they didn't have a future together, anyway. Maybe Wren didn't really like Aiden, and all the chemistry and everything was all in Aiden's head. Was it a case of 'he's just not that into you'?

It wasn't just not talking. Wren refused to sleep over. He had fallen asleep in Aiden's bed a few times but would get up and leave when he woke up, even if there was no good reason not to stay. They were exclusive and had been dating and sexually active together for a month and they'd never, not once, shared breakfast together. Aiden wanted to spend a whole night in Wren's arms. He wanted to wake up and see him rumpled from sleep and kiss him when he still had morning breath. Aiden wanted to make Wren pancakes and walk around the block for morning coffee.

But he couldn't do any of those things because Wren wouldn't stay the night and his excuses sounded weaker and weaker every time. In some ways it was the worst part of their relationship. Wren's insistence on leaving in the middle of the night cheapened their relationship and made Aiden feel used. It made everything feel like a hook up rather than the increasingly intense relationship Aiden sometimes thought it was.

It didn't need to be all the time or every night or anything like that. He understood that some people couldn't sleep as well when they were sharing a bed. He knew Wren had other commitments and responsibilities. But once in a while, it would really be nice.

But then, when they were together and awake things were usually so good, Aiden would forget about everything and would feel like his whole body was glowing with happiness.

Until Wren said goodbye or something set him off.

During dinner with Lucy, Aiden had admitted his fear to Lucy, saying the words out loud for the first time.

Lucy had laughed at him but then sobered when she realized he wasn't joking.

"He likes you," she assured him and although the words were nice to hear, they didn't convince him.

"How do you know? You've never seen us together," Aiden pointed out. And she hadn't.

That was weird wasn't it? Lucy was Aiden's sister and Wren's best friend, yet whenever they tried to have all three of them meet up, Wren wouldn't be able to come. Wren spent time with both Lucy and Aiden individually. The three of them hanging out together should be natural and easy. So why didn't they?

"Something is going on with him."

"Have you talked to him about it?"

"Of course," Aiden confirmed with exasperation. "He says it's because of work and worrying about school. He also says he is having trouble sleeping but it can't just be that, can it?" Aiden was so scared that this thing, which felt like it was the start of the most important thing in his life, might in reality, be completely one sided.

"Look. You're right. I haven't seen you guys together yet," Lucy agreed and Aiden felt his heart sink. "But I have spoken to Wren since you started seeing each other, and I can say with certainty he is happier than I've seen him in a long time."

Aiden couldn't help but smile. He felt himself start to successfully fight off the fear that had been growing inside him. "Really?"

"Yes, really, you doofus!" Lucy said with a playful smack on his shoulder.

"Well good," Aiden said before changing the subject to ask about Lucy's work but his mind was still on Wren for the rest of the evening.

If Wren wasn't acting weird because he was trying to deal with the fact that he wasn't that into Aiden and was trying to figure out how to break up with his best friend's little brother; then what was going on? Could it really just be stress and trouble sleeping?

Aiden thought back to all the times Wren had apologized, often over the smallest things. It was like he was worried he had angered Aiden. Aiden thought about the flashes of dread he sometimes saw in Wren's eyes. He thought about how Wren had told him Aiden made him feel safe. Aiden had worried when Wren had said that, concerned safe meant boring and it was Wren's way of saying he wasn't interested in Aiden. But what if instead Wren meant it as a compliment because Aiden made him feel physically safe in a way others hadn't?

This time when Aiden felt his heart grow heavy and his stomach feel queasy it wasn't because he worried Wren would break his heart and leave him. It was because what he was thinking may have happened to Wren horrified him.

Had someone hurt Wren? Was it his dad? Was it his ex?

# Chapter 15
## Wren

*Wren lay in front of the television enjoying a rerun of Breaking Bad. He had already seen all the episodes on TV but loved the show so he'd gotten sucked into watching rather than coming to bed.*

*"Aren't you coming to bed?" Tyler asked, startling Wren from his television trance.*

*"Jesus, you scared me," Wren said with a laugh putting the show on mute and turning to look at Tyler. He was standing with his arms crossed and a scowl on his face.*

*"Shit, was the sound too loud?" Wren asked. He knew Tyler had an important meeting the next day and didn't want to keep him up. Wren had nothing to do tomorrow. He wasn't scheduled to work at the lab and so he was looking forward to relaxing around the condo but he didn't want to be keeping Tyler awake just because he got to sleep.*

*"You said you would come to bed," Tyler said, completely ignoring Wren's question and the implied apology.*

*"Ya, but I'm not working tomorrow so I figured I'd maybe watch some television before coming to bed," Wren tried to explain but Tyler scowled harder and he knew the argument fell on deaf ears.*

*Tyler hated it when Wren stayed up late. Moving in with Tyler had been a shock. Suddenly after almost ten years of living on his own, he was back to having a curfew. Except it was worse. When he'd been living with his mom, it only mattered what time he got into the house not when he went to bed.*

*Tyler wanted the best for him and he always said going to bed and maintaining a strict sleep schedule was fundamental to living a successful life. He pointed out how much easier it was to focus after having had a good night's sleep. Tyler also insisted on eating healthy for the same reasons. "A healthy body is a healthy mind," he'd say and Wren knew Tyler was right. How could he argue when he knew Tyler was telling the truth? He functioned better when he was sleeping right and eating healthy. He just wished it felt more like his choice.*

*Sometimes he had to remind himself that he had done pretty well for himself long before Tyler had come along. He had managed to complete his masters in microbiology with good grades and land a coveted job at a medical research lab. He knew how to function as an adult.*

*"I'd like you to come to bed," Tyler responded, scolding him like a five-year-old. Then his voice softened as he admitted, "It would be easier for me to sleep if you were there."*

*"Babe, I'm not tired," Wren tried to explain. "I'd just keep you awake tossing and turning if I come to bed right now."*

*"You had coffee today, didn't you?" Tyler accused. Although Tyler drank coffee regularly, he never liked it when Wren drank it because Wren had trouble sleeping if he had any caffeine too late in the day. Wren felt guilt eating at him. Tyler was right, Wren knew he felt better if he avoided caffeine. And he had been cutting back. It was just that Wren enjoyed the taste of coffee. Didn't he deserve to have fun and indulge himself once in a while?*

*"Ryan bought one for everyone in the lab this morning but that isn't why I'm not tired and even if it is because of the coffee, I don't work tomorrow so it isn't that big of a deal," Wren snapped. He knew he was getting defensive but he couldn't help it.*

*"Wren, you know how I feel about you drinking coffee. It completely ruins your sleep schedule and makes you both cranky and antsy. It isn't*

*good for you," Tyler said with exasperation. "I care about you and I want you to be your best."*

*Wren felt himself melt as guilt consumed him again. Tyler was right. He shouldn't have had the coffee and he shouldn't be so upset with Tyler for caring about him. It was nice to have someone care about him, especially since he never saw anyone outside of work other than Tyler.*

*"Now, please come to bed. It's bedtime," Tyler said, motioning for Wren to get up.*

*"You're right. I'm sorry but Babe, I'm not tired right now. We finished the project today and I want to stay up, watch some television, and relax," Wren tried to explain, but he felt himself become whiny. Why was it that whenever he argued with Tyler, he felt their age difference like it was in decades instead of less than ten years?*

*"My name is Tyler not Babe," Tyler snapped. "You know how I hate infantile nicknames. And I said to come to bed right now. Now turn off that fucking television and get to bed before I have to come over there and make you."*

*Shit, Wren thought. Now Tyler was angry.*

*Shit, shit, shit. Wren had just wanted to stay up and watch the episode of Breaking Bad which, Wren realized as he glanced at the television, had ended while they were arguing.*

*"I'm sorry. I didn't realize this would upset you so much," Wren apologized, trying to appease Tyler. He turned off the television and got up, heading to the bathroom to brush his teeth and prepare for bed.*

*"Why do you do this every time?" Tyler asked, exasperation evident in his voice once again. "It is not that hard. I'm not asking for anything unreasonable. I want you to take care of yourself. I love you and I worry about you."*

*Tyler was clearly still angry. Wren felt that saying this happened 'every time' was pretty unfair because usually he was in bed by ten pm every night. He had to get up in the mornings to go to work. Hell, recently he had been in bed closer to nine o'clock, exhausted from how hard he had been working at the lab as they worked to finish everything on the experiment's strict time line. But Wren knew not to argue further. Anything he said now would just make Tyler angrier.*

*Fifteen minutes later Tyler and Wren were in bed. Wren wasn't tired, and he was struggling to lay still. Wren admitted silently to himself that it was probably because of the coffee. His tolerance had gone way down since he had stopped drinking it and the single cup he'd had this afternoon appeared to be preventing him from sleeping just as Tyler had predicted. He couldn't stop fidgeting and he could tell he was annoying Tyler—and they'd only been in bed a few minutes.*

*"If you can't calm down, I will fuck that energy out of you," Tyler said. It felt like a threat.*

*"I'm sorry. You're right. I shouldn't have had that coffee. I'm sorry. I'm just not that sleepy. But..." He was about to say he didn't really feel like sex but thought better of it before the words left his mouth.*

*Tyler was already annoyed, and he always hated it when Wren didn't want to have sex. He had explained it felt like Wren didn't love him when he refused. Wren sometimes worried because he loved Tyler. Right? Because sometimes when he didn't want to have sex with Tyler, especially when he got angry, he wasn't sure if he did.*

*No, he did love Tyler. That's why he'd moved in with him. That's why they had been together for over a year now. He wouldn't still be with him if he didn't love him.*

*Right?*

*Tyler exhaled in exasperation. "Fine," he said. "I wanted to go to sleep but I have an important client meeting with a possible new client that needs to go well tomorrow. If this is what I need to do that's what I will do."*

*Tyler rolled over and grabbed a condom and lube from the bed-side table. He grabbed Wren by the leg. Wren didn't fight him. He knew everything would be easier if he did what Tyler wanted. Maybe he would even be able to fall asleep. He didn't really want to have sex but...*

*everything was so much worse when he fought Tyler than if he just went along with what he wanted.*

*A short while later Wren lay awake, forcing himself to lie still. He hadn't orgasmed, not that Tyler had noticed. Tyler kept telling him he loved him. Wren was trying so hard to make them work but despite all his efforts it felt like he was always one step behind. They felt out of sync and Wren couldn't help wonder if it was all his fault. Maybe he was broken somehow? What was wrong with him when he couldn't even have sex right any more?*

*Wren rolled over trying to get comfortable.*

*"Go to sleep," Tyler admonished and Wren felt himself freeze in fear.*

Wren woke with a gasp. His heart was racing in his chest and cold sweat covered him. He frantically looked around then sighed in relief when he realized he was alone in his bedroom. The room at his mother's house where he had been living since he moved back to Edmonton. It was just a dream—or rather a nightmare.

Too bad it had really happened.

The flashbacks were coming more and more often. For a long time after he'd moved back to his mother's he'd been able to focus on moving forward and, mostly, avoided the memories of what had brought him back there. He could pretend none of his past was real.

But over the last few weeks a name had echoed inside his head despite having sworn never to even think it again. It seemed to increase in volume the closer he got to Aiden.

Tyler.

Tyler.

Tyler.

NO!

He would not think that name again. That asshole had haunted his life enough. Wren had felt enough shame and guilt during those two years that he didn't need to spend another second thinking about that man.

When Wren had left Toronto, he'd promised himself he would not think about his time there anymore. Wren was determined to leave that part of his past behind him and move forward. He'd finally escaped, and he wasn't going to let his memories destroy his life.

Except the memories wouldn't leave him alone.

He suddenly couldn't keep the memories of Tyler at bay. His ghost crept into his head. It whispered in his ear while he slept and woke him up terrified and drenched in cold sweat. Even staying awake didn't keep the memories at bay. They made him freeze up or run in fear.

Spending time with Aiden was such a contrast to the memories. Aiden was sweet, and funny, and unbelievably kind. But with the memories haunting him, Aiden's kindness was just making him nervous. How could anyone be that perfect?

For over a month, the time he spent with Aiden was full of laughter, joy, and kindness. Aiden never seemed to get angry and instead would shrug when things didn't go his way. But this couldn't be real, could it? It couldn't last. So, Wren felt himself gripped with fear and heartache.

Every moment spent with Aiden—which were frequent—resulted in Wren finding himself caring more and more about Aiden and where their relationship was going. Yet, there was the constant drum of fearful questions. Where was this relationship going? What if he got into school somewhere else and had to leave? What if the things he liked so much about Aiden weren't real? What would happen when he got angry? What if Aiden left him?

Wren constantly felt as though he was holding his breath, waiting for the other shoe to drop.

Sometimes Wren just wanted to run away and hide, avoid even thinking about everything that scared him ever again. Unless he was with Aiden, then his worries seemed to float away. He felt at peace and safe and happy. Being with Aiden or even talking to him on the phone had become Wren's haven. But it was simultaneously forcing him to confront his hell because once he was alone again, the fear came rushing back. In the silence, he couldn't escape the nagging voice in the back of his head or the memories which wouldn't leave him alone.

So, what was the point of even trying?

Except, the asshole had already taken so much from him. He had already stolen his life in Toronto. Was Wren willing to let the fear he had developed during those years control what happened now?

Once again, Wren felt like laughing at Aiden's initial concern Wren might cheat on him. Not only was Aiden a catch—his cheating ex- was obviously an idiot—but Wren could barely wrap his mind around being involved with anyone after what he'd gone through.

Really, Wren knew the only reason he could trust Aiden enough to date him at all was because Wren had known Aiden since he was pre-pubescent. Even then, he could barely fall asleep around Aiden and he panicked at the very idea of intercourse instead of just the blow jobs and frotting they'd done so far.

Wren was really glad there hadn't been any pressure in that area so far because the memories of last time he'd been having sex regularly were invasive and terrifying.

Wren wasn't sure why, but he couldn't bring himself to tell Aiden about what had happened to him. It wasn't that he thought Aiden wouldn't be supportive. Aiden had been great since their first date. He always encouraged Wren to come to him when he was ready. In truth, Aiden hadn't pressured Wren on anything, not even sex, despite over a month of dates without any anal sex.

But what if Aiden learned about Wren's past and thought Wren was weak for letting it all happen to him? Wasn't he supposed to defend himself? Shouldn't he have been able to prevent the bad things from happening? How could Aiden not judge him for his inaction? Wren judged himself half the time, and he had learned so much about domestic violence from his therapist.

And who would want to date let alone have sex with someone that weak?

Wren tried to shake off his morose thoughts. He got up and drank a glass of water before settling back into bed. He hoped he'd be able to fall back to sleep but knew he probably wouldn't. He had been having nightmares almost every night for over a week and fairly frequently before that. Between the night shifts and the nightmares, he was becoming a zombie.

With each sleepless night, Wren felt more and more like his brain was unraveling. Everything was so much harder to deal with, even the good things like Aiden.

His phone buzzed indicating a call was coming in. Wren glanced at the display saw the same mysterious number and silenced the call without answering it. He closed his eyes a moment in frustration wishing he could be anywhere but here, awake at two am.

If the nightmares and fear about starting a new relationship weren't enough, there were also the strange phone calls which had not stopped and instead seemed to increase in frequency—still without a word spoken. Three days ago, Wren had stopped answering, hoping whoever was calling would get the message and stop calling.

It hadn't worked so far.

# Chapter 16
## Aiden

Aiden felt content as he drove home from Wren's house. Wren hadn't been able to borrow his mother's car so Aiden had offered to pick up and drop Wren off from their date. While he was once again disappointed Wren refused to stay the night, he couldn't be anything but happy about how the date had gone.

They had spent most of the evening at the Muttart Conservatory drinking wine and looking at flowers during the adult only evening. It had been relaxing and fun to visit somewhere Aiden hadn't bothered to go since he was a kid.

When Wren had first suggested they go to look at flowers for their date, Aiden had been skeptical but willing to go wherever Wren wanted. Aiden hated seeing the look of surprise on Wren's face which suggested he hadn't expected Aiden to agree. After they had been there for a little while, Aiden knew he'd made the right choice if only for the frequent looks of joy Wren was giving him.

Things were going so well. Aiden felt as though many of the concerns he had with his relationship with Wren had evaporated over the past two weeks. Aiden wasn't sure what to make of it. It was amazing how everything could seem so different with a small change in perspective.

The first time Aiden had seen Wren after his revelation, it was as though a blindfold had been ripped off. Suddenly all these hints and signs that Wren was struggling with something were obvious and impossible to miss. It was so clear in the looks of fear which sometimes passed over Wren's face. It was obvious in the moments when he would freeze, flinch, or stop himself from saying something right as he was about to speak. But most obvious of all, Aiden could see Wren's past in the questions Wren continued to avoid answering. It was the words not given voice which spoke louder than anything Wren could say.

Aiden had realized Wren had an ex-, and not just a cheating asshole like Aiden's. No, the ghost of Wren's ex-boyfriend haunted him and had chased him across the country. Aiden didn't know what happened exactly, but he'd figured out a few things and every time he learned something new, he wanted to cry or maybe just find Wren's ex-boyfriend and tell him how much of an asshole he was.

The first thing Aiden had figured out was that whatever Wren had survived had left scars, and not just the physical ones Wren brushed off. Sometimes when there was a loud nose or if Aiden unexpectantly moved too quickly Wren would flinch. He also would get lost in his head thinking about something he didn't want to talk about. After that he usually would get distant and often want to go home.

Before Aiden had figured it out, he had thought Wren was bored or disinterested. Now he understood it had nothing to do with him. This was about something or someone from his past. Suddenly Wren's behaviour stopped bothering him. Aiden saw Wren's silences for what they were, something bad had happened and Wren didn't want to think about it. And because Aiden reacted with understanding instead of frustration, Wren had started to relax and seemed to stay longer instead of rushing off.

Instead of being afraid he was alone in his affections, he could finally see all the things Lucy had talked about, all the indications Wren liked him too. And it wasn't just the physical stuff, which was great. Instead, it was Wren's comments about Aiden being safe. It was in the looks of tentative hope. Wren also did this thing when they were sitting still for a while. He would scoot so far onto Aiden's lap he was practically sitting on him. Then he would run his hand through Aiden's hair. Aiden loved the sensation of his hair being gently tugged and played with. It had quickly become one of his favourite sensations.

So, yes, instead of being scared they were at the beginning of the end of their relationship, Aiden was finally seeing Wren clearly. What he saw made him increasingly certain Wren would be part of his life for a very long time.

Finally home, Aiden pulled into the alley to park in the parking lot behind his apartment Aiden saw a grey Honda Civic driving erratically down the alley away from him. Aiden wondered if the owner of the car lived around here. He seemed to have seen the car all the time over the past couple of months and the driver was an idiot. Aiden had seen him drive the wrong way down one-way streets and make dangerous turns. And the car had almost hit him twice while he'd been crossing the street. He knew it was the same person because he'd caught a look at the person both times and it was the same tall, brown-haired man. He shook his head. He hoped whoever it was figured himself out or moved away. He was a menace.

As he walked into his apartment building, Liz, his neighbour from across the hall, stopped him.

"You just missed your friend. He stopped by and seemed flustered when I came out to tell him you weren't home."

"What? Just now? What friend?" Aiden frowned in confusion. "I wasn't expecting to meet anyone."

"I don't know, bud. I was coming home about fifteen minutes ago and this guy was standing there playing with your doorknob like he was trying to get in. I don't know how he got in the building but you know it isn't the most secure. So, I figured he hadn't bothered to buzz you because he followed someone in. He said you were supposed to meet. I told him I knew you weren't home tonight since you were out on a date with your boyfriend. He seemed pretty upset but then left."

"What did he look like?" Aiden asked, totally confused since he was sure he hadn't double booked himself.

“Big guy. Attractive but looked serious. Short brown hair. Cut looked expensive. I think he had blue eyes,” Liz said.

Aiden paused to think, not sure who she could be describing. “Well, whoever it was, I’m sure they’ll call me or come back if it was important.”

# Chapter 17
## Wren

Wren walked through the door to his mother's house—his house too, he supposed—and just wanted to fall into bed. He was exhausted. He'd just finished a twelve-hour night shift after working four back-to-back day shifts. He was really looking forward to having a few days off, although he figured he would likely sleep for the first full day first.

Much like every other shift worker he'd ever spoken to, Wren hated switching back and forth between night and day shifts. He felt as though he lost track of himself. He often joked he should invest in coffee stocks since he was single-handedly boosting sales.

Not that he wanted to think about much of anything at the moment given how tired he was, but before he could go to bed, he needed to have a shower. He had changed his clothes at the hospital and left his scrubs behind but his hair and skin still smelled like disinfectant and sickness.

He enjoyed being in the hospital and his dream of becoming a doctor had only intensified after working there for the past year. But he really could do without the smell following him home.

He climbed into the shower and turned on the water, only to yelp and hop out when a stream of freezing cold water hit his chest.

Now he was awake.

And... still partially clothed.

Fuck!

Wren pulled off his sopping wet underwear and socks before moving back under the stream of the now reasonably warm water. He washed himself quickly, hurrying to finish and get into bed as fast as possible. He already felt the hit of adrenaline waning and knew the crash was fast approaching.

Despite that, Wren felt himself growing hard. He'd been using the shower to masturbate so much recently that he associated it with coming. The problem was that although the sex with Aiden was good—no, it was fantastic—they still hadn't had anal sex and Wren was realizing that was something he wanted to do.

Wren had been thinking about anal sex a lot recently. It had almost become an obsessive preoccupation. Between his fear of taking that step again and his desire to do so, his brain felt like it was running around in circles.

Aiden had a perfect ass and sometimes when they were naked, he just wanted to eat it. Then he definitely, absolutely, wanted to stick his cock in it. He hadn't topped in a really long time and Wren missed it.

Wren wanted to fuck Aiden. But he wasn't sure if Aiden would go for that. And he was terrified that if he brought it up, then Aiden would demand Wren bottom and he just couldn't, not after how he'd been treated. To make things worse, he couldn't explain to Aiden why not. It wasn't like he didn't enjoy bottoming. It wasn't like he hadn't done it before, so how could he explain why he wouldn't do it now?

So instead of doing anything to make it happen, Wren spent a lot of time fantasizing.

And jerking off in the shower.

He was so tired today that he didn't do anything. Wren was pretty sure if he managed to stay awake long enough to orgasm, he'd immediately pass out. Given the location that would probably mean falling and cracking his head open.

Once he was out of the shower, he brushed his teeth and walked down the hall to his bedroom with only the towel around his waist. He'd remembered his phone but left his dirty clothes in a pile on the bathroom floor. His mom and step-dad didn't use that bathroom, anyway. He would deal with them tomorrow, or later today or.... In his exhaustion Wren had lost track of what time of day it was or even what day it was. He only knew he didn't need to go to work for over forty-eight hours. He was allowed to sleep until the world made sense again.

Wren walked into his room, closed the door and dropped the towel into the laundry hamper before walking naked toward his bed. He flopped down with a groan of exhaustion. Then moaned in frustration when he felt something poking his chest. He rolled over and picked up the offending object.

It was an envelop. A large one white one. The kind someone uses to send a package of information or a document with a lot of pages.

The return address indicated the envelop was from the admissions department of the University of Alberta.

Holy shit!

Wren jerked up into a seated position. He was suddenly wide awake, sleep the furthest thing from his mind.

Holy shit!

He looked at the envelop and fear of what was inside and what it could mean overwhelmed him until it paralyzed him.

What if this was an acceptance letter? That meant he would stay here in Edmonton. What would that mean for him and Aiden?

But what if it wasn't? What if it was a rejection letter?

He'd applied to seven different medical schools in Canada, everything outside of Ontario other than McGill as that had still been too close. He really wanted to be a doctor. He'd come to this realization later in life than some people but that didn't make him any less committed. He'd argue he was more determined because this wasn't a childhood dream that followed him into adulthood. It was a decision he'd made fully understanding what he was getting into and what he might need to make.

Yet...

Over the past few months he'd been forced to truly accept what achieving his dream might cost, what he would need to sacrifice if he got into university anywhere but Edmonton.

Aiden and him were just getting started, but he felt like they were finally in sync. He wasn't sure what had done it, but recently being with Aiden had released something inside him and he felt like he could really be himself for the first time in a long time. Aiden was safe.

Things had been going so well with Aiden that he was pretending he hadn't submitted school applications because if he didn't get into the University of Alberta, and instead got in somewhere else, then he would be stuck deciding between his personal and professional happiness. In that case, no matter what decision he made he feared he'd always regret it.

For the first time, Wren wished he had never applied to medical school.

Wren looked back down at the letter.

Maybe he wouldn't have to make that choice after all.

His hand shook as he moved to open the letter. Then he stopped.

No, he shouldn't do this alone. Aiden needed to be part of this too. They hadn't talked about it. He'd been afraid to talk about it but Aiden was almost as much a part of this as Wren.

Wren put the letter back down on the bed and picked up his phone from the charger.

# Chapter 18
## Aiden

Aiden was just coming home from a run through the river valley when his phone rang.

He huffed in frustration, knowing his running app would likely get all confused and wouldn't track the last half a kilometre before he reached his apartment.

He glanced at the screen through the case on his arm, trying to decide if it was worth answering before slowing to a walk and finally stopping as he scrambled to get the phone out of the case so he could answer it.

"Hello," he gasped. He resumed walking. He could feel sweat dripping down his face from his hair. He tossed his head to shake it off.

"Umm, Aiden?"

"Hey, Wren, sorry. I'm just finishing my run," Aiden tried to explain, although he could hear his voice was still somewhat strained as he tried to slow his breathing enough to speak normally.

"Why aren't you asleep? Didn't you just come off a night shift?" Aiden asked after a few more deep breaths.

"I got a letter," Wren said. He paused like that was important but Aiden didn't understand. "From the Admissions Department of the University of Alberta."

Aiden stopped in his tracks. He practically stopped breathing before he realized Wren was waiting for him to speak. "What does it say?"

Aiden felt his heart speed up. Oh, man. Please, please, please let this be good news.

"I don't know," Wren admitted. He sounded small and quiet. "I'm scared to open it. What if it says no?"

Aiden could understand. While the suspense was almost killing him, Aiden was almost afraid to hear what the letter said. As long as it remained unopened there was still a chance the answer was yes.

But waiting wouldn't change anything. "You want me to come over or is having me on the phone enough?" Aiden asked.

"You're willing to just come over?" Wren asked, surprise evident in his voice.

Aiden suppressed a sigh. He hated it when Wren acted surprised when others put him first. "Of course. If you need me, I'll come. Always."

There was silence on the other end then a sniff, like Wren might be crying.

"You know what? I'm coming over. Just hang on fifteen minutes. I'll be right over."

* * *

Aiden bounced on the balls of his feet as he stood waiting for Wren to answer his front door. He was still in his running gear and was feeling the uncomfortable sensation of cool, drying sweat on his body since he hadn't bothered to shower before heading over.

The second he'd hung up the phone he'd picked up his pace again, run home, dashed inside to grab his car keys and wallet, and headed over to Wren's house. He was careful to watch his speed since this wasn't an actual emergency and there had been a bunch of crazy drivers on the road recently.

He'd still made it to Wren's house in less than half the time he'd predicted.

When Wren opened the door, he looked like death warmed over. His hair was sticking up a bit at the back and he had dark circles under his eyes. He was also wearing a... was that a shirt from their high school track team?

Wait. Wren had never been in track in high school.

"Is that my shirt?" Aiden asked as he pulled Wren into a hug. Wren clung to him tightly and Aiden had to walk him backward into the house to close the door with them on the inside.

"I stole it last week when I couldn't find my shirt," Wren mumbled into Wren's chest.

"Keep it. I didn't even realize I still had it. It hasn't fit me for years."

Wren chuckled because that was evident. It fit him pretty perfectly.

"You came fast."

"You needed me," Aiden stated in a matter-of-fact tone. He moved himself back so he could look down and see Wren's face. "Where's the letter? Let's get this over with, like ripping off a Band-Aid."

Wren led Aiden back up to his room and handed Aiden the letter. Aiden didn't argue, although he wondered whether it would be better for Wren to do it himself.

Aiden looked at Wren in the eyes, took a deep breath, "You ready?" Wren nodded, although it lacked conviction.

He slipped his finger under the flap of the envelop, ripped it open and pulled out a stack of papers, including what appeared to be a file folder. He offered it to Wren without looking at it but Wren just shook his head. "You do it."

Reluctantly, Aiden kept the stack and looked down at the letter that lay on top. He started reading and felt his heart race. Before finishing the first paragraph he looked up at Wren and met his scared eyes.

"What does it say? Did I get in?"

Aiden nodded and said 'yes' but before the word had even been formed, Wren had leaped onto him and knocked the air out of him. Once he had caught his breath and his balance, Aiden put the papers down as gently as he could and grabbed Wren with both hands and hugged him as tightly as Wren was already hugging him.

"I got in?" Wren asked again. His words muffled by Aiden's neck.

"You got in."

"I got in!" Wren jumped out of Aiden's arms and ran madly around the room in his excitement. He repeated the words that he got in as though he could barely believe it was true. Aiden understood. There had been so many bad possibilities, he could barely believe the best possible outcome had come true.

Wren had gotten into medical school at the University of Alberta!

Aiden wouldn't have to pick between letting their relationship end or following Wren across the country to god knows where, just so they could stay together.

Wren wouldn't have to choose between following his dream and staying with Aiden.

No one was moving. No one was making any big sacrifices. They got to just be together. And Wren got to attend medical school at one of the best universities in Canada.

Suddenly, Aiden felt light-headed. His vision tunnelled, and he realized he was hyperventilating. He leaned forward to put his head between his knees and tried to focus on his breathing. In, pause, out, pause. In and out, in and out. God, he'd been so worried. He'd tried not to think about it but the weight of the unknown had never been far from his thoughts.

He hadn't even known where Wren had applied, only that he had applied to the University of Alberta and a few other schools, all within Canada. Wren hadn't said anything else and Aiden hadn't wanted to ask. He hadn't wanted to admit aloud that any other school was possible, at least not when everything was going well and they were together. So, instead of asking, he'd researched every place in Canada with a medical school to see what work might be available for him, just in case.

"What's wrong, Aiden?" Wren asked, kneeling in front of him. Aiden looked up and found he could sit again without fainting.

"You aren't going to be moving away."

"Isn't that a good thing?" Wren asked, sounding concerned.

"So good," Aiden said, taking hold of Wren's hand. "I'm just so relieved. It's a bit overwhelming."

"Ya. I—uh, I feel like a huge weight has been lifted off me. I had actually started thinking about not accepting if I got in anywhere else."

"Oh my god, no!" Aiden said, concerned even though that hadn't happened. "You need to go to medical school. It's your dream. I'd have followed you. I mean—I had been thinking about maybe following you, if you had to move for school. That is if you had wanted me to."

Wren leaned up and caught Aiden in a kiss. It seared him, burning him up from the inside. Then Wren pulled back and laughed. "We were both so worried about school breaking us up, but if we'd talked about it, we would have known there was no need to worry. We were both ready to make sure we stayed together."

"Well, now it isn't a problem. You can accept the offer and I don't even need to move for us to stay together."

"No," Wren said, looking more serious. "No, there isn't anything in the way of us being together now."

He pulled Aiden in for another kiss. This time he deepened the kiss. He pulled Aiden down off the bed and they ended up kneeling before each other, doing their best to devour one another. This was not a soft, gentle kiss. This was a relationship affirming kiss. This was the first kiss of the rest of their lives together.

When the kiss ended, they stared at one another, panting. Aiden felt himself smile. This was good. The future was looking really great.

Wren, however, still looked serious despite his kiss-swollen lips. "Can I ask you a question?" Aiden could hear the trepidation in his voice.

"Always."

"Do you want to... I mean, can we... can I... do you want to have anal sex?" Aiden felt himself blink in surprise. Anal sex had seemed off the table. Aiden had suspected either Wren just didn't enjoy it or wasn't interested in it anymore. Given what Aiden suspected about Wren's past he hadn't wanted to question it.

Wren ended the silence caused by his silence by continuing frantically, "Maybe not right now if you don't want to. I meant maybe sometime. Now I know I'm not leaving, we have time. Or, it's okay if you don't want to. I mean, do you ever bottom? Is that something you do? Because I would very much like to do that."

Wren's voice petered out, and he looked away from Aiden. Aiden brought his hand up to cup Wren's cheek. Looking into Wren's eyes Aiden felt a wave of emotion hit him and he thought he might be falling in love with Wren. Maybe he already had.

For the first time since they got together, the thought of falling in love didn't scare him.

"Yes," Aiden breathed. Wren's head whipped back, so he was staring into Aiden's eyes. "To everything."

"Like right now?"

Aiden nodded and Wren launched himself at him. He knocked Aiden onto his back and kissed him.

"Great, let's do it now," Wren gasped between kisses. "I want to do it now."

"Thank god," Aiden moaned as Wren kissed his neck and nibbling on his ears. Aiden knew he would have continued being patient, waiting forever if that was what Wren needed. Their sex life had been good without intercourse. Except, now that Wren had brought it up, waiting even a moment longer just might kill him.

They made out some more, and Aiden found himself with one sock on and his shirt on the floor beside him. He wasn't exactly sure how it had happened but he was pleased to find that Wren had also lost his shirt and his pants were undone. That was when Aiden realized one hand was gripping Wren's hair and his other was pushing into Wren's underwear, almost as though it was acting on its own, desperate to get to Wren's cock.

They were also still on the hard floor, beside Wren's bed.

"Stop!" Aiden interrupted, breaking both himself and Wren out of the moment.

"What? Why?" Wren said, lifting his head off Aiden's chest where he'd been sucking Aiden's nipples. "Oh god! You didn't actually want to do this? I'm going too fast. Oh, god, oh god!" Wren frantically pushed off Aiden, elbowing him in the shoulder in his effort to move away as quickly as possible.

"Wow, yes," Aiden said. Then he realized what he had said and connected it to Wren's stricken expression. "No, wait! No, I mean, yes. I mean... FUCK!" Aiden paused to take a deep breath and get his brain functioning well enough to connect back to his mouth. "I want to have sex with you. Everything we were doing was great. I just meant let's stop and get onto the bed. I would prefer we don't have anal sex for the first time on the floor. Plus, we need to grab the supplies from your bedside table. I just meant, let's have sex in your bed."

Wren's face softened with each word Aiden spoke and was chuckling by the time Aiden finished speaking. "Maybe we should slow down and yes, let's get into the bed rather than risk carpet burn on our asses."

Wren stood up and offered his hand to Aiden and helped him up. He looked down at himself and seemed to take in his state of partial undress for the first time. He laughed again. "Maybe we can also take the time to undress properly."

"That might be a good idea."

# Chapter 19
## Wren

Despite their mutual ridiculous state of semi-undress, Wren could feel the anticipation consuming him again. There was still fear. It had never really gone away but, like when he'd suggest sex earlier, the anticipation and desire overwhelmed him until he was barely aware he'd ever had a reason to fear.

Aiden stood before Wren, just barely touching the side of the bed with his legs and ran his hand gently along Wren's jaw before cupping his cheek and head and leaning down for a slow kiss.

Wren felt consumed.

He raised his own hands up to run through Aiden's hair, tugging his head closer to deepen the kiss. He needed them closer.

He pulled on Aiden's pants, unable to manage the button when so much of his attention was focused on Aiden's mouth pressed against his.

"Slow," Aiden reminded him, pulling back from their kiss and stopping Wren's hand. "We have time. There is no rush."

"Speak for yourself," Wren argued. He felt desperate. He needed to be with Aiden. They needed to get naked and have intercourse before he lost his nerve and the fear overwhelmed him like it had for so long.

He reached for Aiden's pants again. Intent on undressing Aiden as quickly as possible. Except Aiden stepped back, preventing Wren from touching him.

"Let me take care of you first," Aiden said. Then he slowly, carefully kissed every inch of Wren's body while peeling each piece of clothing off one at a time. Wren lost himself in the attention. He begged Aiden to go move faster but received chuckles of satisfaction and even more leisurely kisses for his efforts.

And when Aiden finally finished, Wren stood before him naked, swaying, barely able to keep himself standing and unable to think about anything beyond his desperate need to touch Aiden. Aiden was still on his knees before him, still waiting to touch the one part of Wren they both wanted most of all.

Wren pulled Aiden to his feet and then fisted his cock, squeezing it for a second because he needed some stimulation. He let go quickly though because he had other plans for his cock.

"My turn," Wren announced before switching their positions so Aiden's back was to his bed and then Wren pushed. Aiden toppled over, landing on the bed with his legs over the side. Wren made quick work of the single remaining sock, tossing it over his shoulder before he, too, worked on Aiden's pants.

Wren lacked Aiden's patience and pulled Aiden's jogging pants off in one swift move, making Aiden laugh at Wren's obvious excitement. Wren felt his cock twitch in response to the joyful sound.

Wren found himself laughing too. He felt light and happy. Sex had never been this playful with—

NO! Wren shook his head, refusing to let his mind go there. Not now.

Instead, he focused on the man before him. Aiden lay gloriously naked. He was unashamed, with one hand resting on his stomach and the other folded behind his head like a pillow. His cock was straining straight up making Wren's mouth water. Aiden looked at Wren with such hunger that Wren wondered what Aiden was thinking. How could he possibly deserve the man lying before him? "You are gorgeous."

He gripped his cock again for a second before letting go and climbing onto the bed. He took hold of Aiden's free hand and encouraged him to move so they both lay side by side. Wren looked into Aiden's eyes and despite Aiden being naked and Wren being desperate to touch and taste him, there was a moment when it felt as though the world took a breath and everything stopped.

*I could fall in love with this man*, Wren thought, but could barely cope with those feelings, so he leaned forward and rolled himself on top of Aiden for an intense scorching kiss. This one consumed them both until the need to breathe asserted itself and forced them apart. But Wren wasn't finished. It was still Wren's turn. Now they were naked Wren intended to explore.

Wren had Aiden lie on his stomach with a pillow propped under his hips. Then starting at his knees, he explored every inch of Aiden's body. Wren already knew the insides of Aiden's knees were sensitive but he didn't stay there for long before he moved on, looking for other sensitive spots he may have missed before.

He refused to stick to one area of Aiden's body and instead of slowly progressing toward their final destination; he jumped around, keeping Aiden on his toes and unable to predict what was coming next.

Aiden had spread his legs without Wren having to ask and had humped his hips into the pillow. The sounds that were coming out of his mouth were amazing and Wren felt his own erection fighting against his determination to take this slow and make their first time together special.

Finally, when Wren felt both he and Aiden had had enough, Wren moved his tongue up and licked along Aiden's testicles and up toward his anus. Wren used his hands to pull Aiden's cheeks apart. What he saw was beautiful.

Aiden's anus was clenching and relaxing, a sure sign he was desperate for something to be put inside him. Wren was happy Aiden was so eager because he couldn't stand waiting much longer himself.

His eagerness scared him and for a moment Wren was almost paralyzed with fear. He was so desperate to be with Aiden, wanted this to happen so badly it was terrifying. What if something when wrong? What if he hurt Aiden?

Aiden wiggled his ass greedily and groaned, “Please.” The word broke through the fear. Wren needed to stay in the moment. He had to focus on the here and now. He was with Aiden. He cared about Aiden and Aiden cared about him.

Wren leaned forward again and brought his tongue down onto Aiden.

Aiden was begging again, asking for more, begging for more. Wren would give it to him but he intended on taking his time. So slowly, ever so slowly, Wren pushed his tongue inside Aiden. He licked him and loosened him gently. He used his free hand and grabbed the bottle of lube which he had already tossed on the bed and went back to licking Aiden’s balls.

Aiden groaned in frustration, then in relief when Wren dribbled lube onto his hole and gently pressed one finger inside him, then another. Now Aiden was begging and groaning incomprehensibly, which turned Wren on more than even the feel of Aiden’s hole wrapped around his fingers.

Finally, after what felt like ages but was really just long enough, Wren pulled his fingers out to put on the condom and added more lube. The moment his fingers moved out of Aiden’s body Aiden chanted, “No, no, no. Please, please, no, please!”

Wren tried to sooth him but Aiden was beyond words. So instead of trying to explain, he lifted Aiden’s hips, and the positioned his cock so it pressed against Aiden’s hole. Then he pushed inside.

It was like a switch flipped and the begging turned into a long, slow, steady moan of appreciation. Except Wren wasn’t sure which of them was making the sounds since he also felt like this was the best thing he’d ever experienced his entire life.

He continued to press inside, slowly but steadily, until he was seated completely inside Aiden’s body. Then he held still, waiting for Aiden to adjust.

After only a moment, Wren felt Aiden relax. He pleaded again and moved his hips, fucking himself on Wren’s cock. For a moment Wren stayed still, allowing Aiden to control the pace and the movement. When Wren couldn’t hold back any longer and he grabbed Aiden’s hips with both hands and pulled himself out almost all the way before pushing himself back in, faster and faster.

Feeling his cock slide in and out of Aiden's tight hole was beyond anything he thought he would experience again. He was wordless and could hear himself groaning and moaning along with Aiden.

When he saw Aiden slide one hand underneath himself, Wren leaned forward and moved Aiden's hand out of the way so he could stroke Aiden's cock in time to his thrusts. He couldn't control the increase in his speed as he felt himself approaching his climax.

Knowing he needed to make Aiden come more quickly or else he might shoot first, Wren repositioned himself and Aiden so he was hitting Aiden's prostate with each trust. He knew he'd achieved his goal when Aiden cried out louder and louder.

Then, just as Wren was feeling his cock tingled with his rapidly approaching orgasm, Wren felt Aiden's cock swell briefly before his anus clenched down on Wren's thrusting cock and Aiden was coming all over the pillow and Wren's hand.

Wren wasn't even able to finish enjoying the feeling of Aiden's orgasm before his own barrelled through him. The world disappeared and fireworks shot off behind his eyes.

Some time later—he wasn't sure how much time had passed—Wren worked up enough energy to kiss Aiden on the shoulder before grabbing hold of the condom to pull himself out and roll over to collapse on his back beside Aiden.

"Holy fucking shit!" Aiden gasped as he, too, rolled over to cuddle into Wren and move off the wet spot he had made.

"Ya," Wren agreed. "I think my brain may have exploded. You see it anywhere?"

"Can't move to look."

Wren just huffed a laugh. He could honestly say that had been the best sex, the most powerful orgasm of his entire life.

He could barely move but, despite that, found himself rubbing his hand up and down Aiden's back. It felt as though his hand and fingers were working on their own, unable to keep themselves from touching Aiden.

Wren could relate.

Holy fucking shit, indeed.

* * *

Buzzz, Buzzz. Buzzz. Wren's phone vibrated, signalling an incoming call. Wren jerked awake, not having intended to fall asleep. He felt Aiden stir awake beside him.

Wren glanced at the screen and silenced the call. He felt himself go cold seeing the same mysterious number that continued calling. They were coming with increased frequency despite Wren having stopped answering almost a month earlier. This was already the fifth call today. He decided right then, he would block the number as soon as Aiden had left. This was getting ridiculous.

"Who was that?" Aiden asked with his eyes still closed.

Wren rubbed his fingers through Aiden's hair as he answered. "No one, just another call from that same number."

"Again?" Aiden asked sounding concerned. He opened his eyes and peered up at Wren.

The calls were coming in so often it had become impossible for Wren to pretend they didn't exist. Wren had been happy when Aiden had agreed they were weird and hadn't done anything in word or deed to suggest Wren was over reacting or crazy to be worried. In fact, Aiden had seemed more concerned by the calls than he was.

"Ya, I'm gonna block the number. They aren't stopping and frankly that in it of itself is really freaking me out."

"You should. You don't need to put up with that crap. If it was someone important or even someone that actually wanted to talk to you, they'd have said something by now. Or left a message or, anything a normal human being does when trying to reach someone."

"Ya, I just wish I knew what they were about and why I keep getting them."

Aiden said nothing more but snuggled himself around Wren and hugged him tighter. Wren felt himself relaxing. He felt his eyes drift close and the little part of his brain that still knew what was going on was amazed he could relax so easily in Aiden's arms and he almost started awake when he realized why.

Aiden made him feel safe. It wasn't just that Aiden didn't make him feel unsafe like... well, never mind. Wren realized he felt even safer with Aiden than when he was alone.

He felt tears drop down his face onto the pillow and tried to keep silent as he cried with relief that he finally had that. For so long Wren had thought he'd never feel safe again. After asking what was wrong once with no answer, Aiden just hugged him closer and periodically whispered, "I'm here. You're safe."

Somehow, Aiden knew exactly what to say and for the first time in a long time Wren knew those words were true.

# Chapter 20

## Aiden

“They know I’m coming, right?” Wren asked as the car stopped in front of Aiden’s parents’ house.

“Nope, I thought I’d let it be a surprise,” Aiden said with glee.

“Aiden!” Wren yelled. “What if there isn’t enough food? What if your mom gets mad?”

“I’m just fucking with you. I called my mom to let her know this morning. Although, were you seriously worried my mom might be mad that you're here?”

Wren mumbled sheepishly because even though he was nervous, he knew it was ridiculous to think Lillian Walker would ever, in any universe, be upset to see him.

“Well, okay, maybe not but it’s still polite to let someone know before showing up,” Wren grumbled but laughed when Aiden just knocked his shoulder and laughed at him.

“Actually, Mom has been pretty disappointed you haven’t been coming every week since you came the last time. When she discovered we were dating, she almost cried.” Aiden rolled his eyes at this. “I think she’s more excited about this thing between us working out than Lucy and she told me last week she’s already started drafting an ‘I told you so’ wedding speech.”

“So, no pressure.”

"Ya... I try not to think about it. But the point is, ever since my mom found out about us, she's been bugging me to get you to come for dinner again."

Wren grunted and looked out the window, not looking entirely convinced.

"I don't know what you're so nervous about anyway," Aiden continued. "It's me who'll get it. Everyone will be super nice to you and just happy that you showed up. Me, I'll get in trouble for missing last weekend, never mind I was hanging out with you and celebrating that you got into med school. Then Lucy will make fun of me like she always does, and she won't censor herself like she might around someone she didn't know."

"Lucy would censor herself?!" Wren asked with incredulity.

"Maybe if I was lucky," Aiden laughed. "She won't for you, though, since you're one of her best friends."

"Well, she sort of has a reason to gloat. We might never have dated if she hadn't forced us on our first quasi-date."

"Don't your dare tell her that!" Aiden begged, continuing his lament about how horrible things would be for him over dinner. He was mostly just talking to distract Wren. Aiden loved his family, and he was definitely used to their... quirks. Ya, let's call them that. "Then, my mom will probably get in on it and say something horribly embarrassing. Gahhh!" Aiden let out an exasperated noise to make Wren laugh. It worked.

"Okay. So... nothing has changed?"

"Ya, basically everything is the same. You'll fit right in."

Aiden wondered if Wren was so nervous because this was the first time they'd done anything with other people since they were a couple. It felt like a big moment even if Wren already knew everyone there. Tonight would be the first time they would be a couple outside their little bubble. Aiden had to admit, he was a bit nervous. What if Wren started acting weird, or Aiden said the wrong thing or...

Before today, whenever Aiden had suggested a date or activity involving other people, Wren had gently shut it down. The fact they never did anything with his friends or even either of their families had annoyed Aiden before he'd understood something horrible had probably happened to Wren. Then he'd realized this had nothing to do with logic or Aiden. This was about whatever Wren had gone through and whatever was going on in his head because of it. Aiden would be patient and let Wren have the time he needed to feel safe. Even if that meant he skipped family dinner to hang out with Wren after Wren got the admissions letter last weekend. Then he went home alone to sleep in his own bed.

Being accepting didn't mean he never pushed.

Last night when Wren suggested they get together after he finished work, Aiden had jumped on the suggestion and was able to convince Wren to join him for the Sunday family dinner.

He may have promised sex after.

Although he intended on follow through, he didn't really think it was why Wren finally agreed to come. Something had changed between them. It was like getting into school here had finally let Wren fully commit to their relationship. It wasn't just having intercourse either. They talked more when they were apart. Wren laughed more and seemed more relaxed and free.

Aiden paused, took a deep breath, then with a grin for Wren said, "Okay, let's get this party started."

They exited Aiden's car and walked up to his mother's front door. She opened the door before they got there.

"I was wondering if I would have to come out and get you. Welcome, Wren. It is great to see you again, dear. You really have grown into such a handsome young man. Aiden, dear, I can totally see why you asked him out."

"Mom!" Aiden pleaded with a blush.

Wren smirked and wiggled his eyebrows at Aiden as his mom gestured for Aiden and Wren to come inside. "Well, come in, come in. Don't stand around outside." They looked at each other, Aiden winked and proceeded inside.

"Thanks for inviting me, Lillian," Wren said, as he walked into the house and handed her the bottle of red wine he had been carrying.

"That is generous of you. You didn't need to do that. You're practically family. Although, it has been much too long since you've come for dinner."

"Mom, let us finish coming inside before you harass him," Aiden pleaded. "Is Lucy here yet?"

"Of course, come in, come in. Don't mind me, Wren. I'm just so pleased to see you." His mom looked at Aiden. "Your sister called earlier saying she would be late but wasn't going to miss seeing Wren."

"You told her we were coming?" Aiden asked with disappointment showing in his voice. He'd wanted it to be a surprise because sometimes Lucy said hilarious things while entering a room before checking to see who was there. Aiden was hoping she would say something embarrassing before she realized Wren was there.

"Oof," Aiden exhaled as Wren elbowed him. Aiden just smiled impishly not the least bit contrite.

"Of course, dear," his mother answered, ignoring the antics between Aiden and Wren. "Your sister agreed to bring an appetizer, and I wanted to make sure she brought enough. She promised to make sure Wren got extra spanakopita to celebrate his return to Sunday dinner since you started dating. She admitted she might take Wren's portion from yours but we were both sure you wouldn't mind." His mom had a twinkle in her eye as she spoke and Aiden knew his mom knew exactly what he'd being trying to do and was enjoying the heck out of Lucy getting one on him instead.

"That's okay mom," Aiden agreed. "I'm sure Wren will share."

Wren stood still and put his finger to his chin like he was thinking really hard. "Umm, nope. I don't think so."

Aiden felt his heart melt. It was so wonderful to see Wren being playful. It was crazy to think of how quiet and reserved Wren had been during his last dinner with Aiden's family. The changes had mostly happened so slowly Aiden had hardly noticed. Yet today, even as nervous as he was, Wren was relaxed and having fun.

If that meant he didn't get to have one of his favourite appetizers, so be it. Completely and utterly worth it.

Man, that was sappy. Aiden shook his head, laughing at himself. Maybe he really was in love. The idea was exciting and terrifying. He really hoped he didn't get his heart broken because it was too late to walk away.

His mom led Aiden and Wren into the kitchen. "Sit here, boys. I could use the company while I make a salad," she said as she gestured to the two empty chairs at the kitchen table.

Wren and Aiden sat down while she started putzing around the kitchen, picking things up and putting them back down again, all while continuing to talk. "Your father is outside searing the steaks on the barbecue. The weather has been fantastic. Probably due to global warming but we can enjoy it, anyway. I was thinking we could eat outside. Although, I haven't had a chance to clean the deck furniture off yet, so maybe we should just use the dining table."

"Here, Aiden, dear, come here and help me cut vegetables for the salad," she continued with barely a pause. "No, not you, Wren, you stay seated. Would you like anything to drink? We can open your wine or we have beer in the fridge. There is also water and milk, of course, but I suppose you are too old to want a glass of milk."

Aiden stood up and moved his mom into his chair to get her out of the way while he took over preparing the salad. Or rather, started making it since all his mom had done was take the ingredients out of the fridge, and looking around, he saw that nope, she hadn't even got everything out while she was talking.

"A beer would be nice. What do you have?" Wren responded.

Aiden looked in the fridge and answered for his mother. "They have two Yellowhead Brewery beers: a Pale Ale and Saison Tête Jaune."

"How about the Saison," Wren responded.

"What about you, Mom?" Aiden asked, looking at his mother as he reached into the fridge to get Wren and himself a beer. "You want me to get you something, maybe open the wine?"

"No, thank you, dear. We should save the wine for dinner. Anyway, I have a glass of water somewhere around here," his mom responded, waving her hand around distractedly. "So, Wren, honey, what have you been up to? Any updates on the school admissions? Or is that taboo?"

"No, not taboo. Actually, miraculously I got word a week ago that I got into the U of A med school and will start in September here in town."

"That's great! Aiden, isn't that great?"

From behind his mom's shoulder, Aiden caught Wren's eye and rolled his eyes at her exuberance but answered with sincerity, "Yes, Mom it's really great," while he continued preparing the salad.

Aiden was still amazed Wren would go to school here. Not because he didn't think Wren deserved to be admitted but because it had seemed too good to be true. He'd kept having to pinch himself all week to make sure he wasn't dreaming. Well, okay he wasn't really pinching himself because he didn't want to be covered in bruises but metaphorically, he was black and blue.

Wren and his mom continued to talk and update each other on the past couple months of their lives. Aiden listened in, not saying anything, just occasionally catching Wren's eye and smiling. Aiden felt content. It was wonderful spending time with two people he cared so much about at the same time. It was especially great watching them get along.

Not all of his partners over the years had, not that he'd introduced that many men to his parents. Derek and Lucy had always rubbed each other the wrong way. Aiden wondered if he should have seen that as a sign of what was to come. Well, not that Derek was a cheating asshole but that they'd never work out in the long run.

With Wren it was different. No matter what happened for them as a couple, Wren would always be a part of the family. He and Lucy just had so much history. In many ways, Aiden didn't remember a time when Wren hadn't been hanging around.

*"Why are you always here?" Aiden asked Wren. He wasn't complaining. He liked Wren, unlike some of Lucy's other friends. Wren was at least cool and never talked down to Aiden just because he was younger and wasn't popular and didn't have a million friends like Lucy. Wren laughed at the question and Aiden blushed when he realized how the question sounded. "I mean, it's cool you're here but don't you have your own home? Don't your parents get sad that you're never home?"*

*"I think they are just as happy to have me out of their hair right now," Wren answered honestly. It appeared his answer made him sad so Aiden didn't push anymore but he was kind of confused. Why wouldn't Wren's parents want him around?*

*"Oh well, I guess it's good you can come here then," he said instead.*

*Wren smiled, "Ya, I'm lucky Lucy and your parents are so awesome."*

*"Not me?" Aiden asked. He was mostly joking but he also kind of meant what he said. He wanted Wren to like him. Wren was so cool and Aiden often wished he could be Wren's friend too rather than just Lucy's baby brother.*

*Wren smiled again, this time looking directly into Aiden's eyes. "Ya, you are pretty awesome, too."*

*Aiden felt something stir in his tummy. It was like his tummy had filled with pop or something. He felt bubbles had filled him. He couldn't help but smile back and once again he felt his face heat and redden with a blush.*

*"Ya, you're awesome all right," Lucy said. "Awesome at being a twerp. Now go away and stop bugging Wren. Don't you have homework to do, or like your own friends to play with?"*

*Aiden felt himself blush more. He hated that Lucy would put him down and treat him like a baby in front of Wren. He wasn't a baby anymore. He would enter grade eight this fall. He was only three years younger than Lucy and Wren.*

*"Aww, leave the kid alone Lucy, He is pretty awesome. You could have a little brother like Sandra's," Wren defended. Aiden almost wished he*

*hadn't. He really didn't want Wren calling him a kid. Sure, he was still short and hadn't started going through puberty yet like some of the kids in his class but that didn't make him a baby.*

*Aiden hated being short for his age and hated even more that there were no indications that he had started going through puberty. Lucy had been late to start, not having to wear a bra until she was in grade eight, but it was like she had a selective memory. She still treated him like he was a baby while he was going through the same thing. His dad said he had been a late bloomer and he shouldn't worry but Aiden couldn't help worrying. He was shorter than almost all of the other girls and boys in his class. There were only a few other guys in his grade whose voice hadn't changed and here he was looking like he was still eight years old rather than in grade eight.*

*Later that night, after Wren had gone home, Lucy pulled Aiden aside. "Don't ask Wren about why he's here all the time or what's going on at his home, 'kay?"*

*"Why?" Aiden asked. He still didn't really understand.*

*"'Cuz I said so,"*

*"But why? I'm just trying to get to know him."*

*"Look, things are shitty at home for him, all right. His parents are getting divorced and his dad has gone mental and his mom is too busy dealing with everything to pay attention to Wren. It just sucks for him there. That's why we never go there anymore." Lucy explained. She sounded completely exasperated that she was having to talk to Aiden about this.*

*"Oh, that sucks," Aiden said after an awkward pause. "Thanks for telling me."*

*"Ya, well. He doesn't like talking about it because it is totally horrible so don't ask him any more questions. All right?" Lucy sounded stern and annoyed with him. Aiden nodded because she didn't seem like she would leave until he acknowledged her but he wasn't a complete idiot.*

*She'd sounded like that a lot recently. Well, really since grade nine when she really hit puberty and started dating boys. Before that Lucy had been cool. Sure, they didn't play together all the time or anything because of how much older than him she was, but at least when they hung out, she was nice. These days it was all sass and exasperation. She was nice to Wren, he'd seen her being nice to him but she never seemed to have any patience for Aiden anymore. Their mom had said it was hormones but Aiden just thought she was turning into a bitch and hoped it wasn't permanent. He hoped when he finally hit puberty it didn't turn him into a moron. Since he wasn't a moron yet, he'd been smart enough not to say that out loud.*

*He knew sometimes he had a tendency to stick his foot in his mouth, usually with unwanted questions but he had some tact. Well, he wasn't completely tactless at least. It was just that he was so curious. He wanted to know how everything worked and why they worked that way.*

*These days he'd been especially curious about one boy in his class, Liam. And Wren. Aiden had been very curious about Wren recently, too. He'd wanted to know everything about him, even what he smelled like and especially what made him smile. But most of all Aiden was curious about what it would be like to kiss him. Well, maybe not him specifically but some boy. Kissing Liam would be cool, too.*

*Last week at dinner Wren and Lucy had been arguing about whether Colin Sheppard, a boy in her class, would ever go out with either one of them. Wren and Lucy disagreed about whether he was gay and the fact that he could be gay seemed to matter to Wren.*

*At first Aiden was confused. As far as he knew Wren was straight like everyone else Aiden knew. He'd always figured that was why he hung out with Lucy so much. He knew they'd never dated, but he'd figured Lucy at least thought Wren was hot. Aiden could understand that.*

*His mom had clarified everything when she had asked whether Wren was having any troubles with bullying after coming out. Wren had said he and Lucy had joined the gay/straight alliance and he was getting a lot of support there. Aiden had almost choked on his milk and Lucy had shot him the stink eye and called him a freak.*

*Aiden wondered if Lucy thought Aiden was homophobic or something. Maybe that was why she was being so defensive.*

*Aiden wasn't homophobic, but he had been so curious. Throughout the rest of dinner, he's divided his focus between keeping himself from asking questions by eating and listening to every word that came out of Wren, trying to pick up as much information as possible.*

*Wren was gay.*

*He was also the first person Aiden had ever met who was gay, at least that he knew of. He'd heard the statistics that about one in five people were gay or something like that so, he guessed he probably had met others without knowing it.*

*Either way, Wren was gay and Aiden wanted to know more. He wanted to know everything. Most of all he wished everyone would stop treating him like a baby so he could ask some of these questions because Aiden was starting to suspect he was gay, too.*

Aiden smiled thinking about the first time he'd realized he was gay. He hadn't come out to anyone, not even his parents, until years later after Wren had moved to Toronto, but Aiden knew his realization that he was gay was intertwined with learning about Wren's sexuality.

At the time Aiden had known the chances of Wren ever liking him were basically nonexistent. Wren was completely out of teenage Aiden's league. Once Wren left, the almost nonexistent chance went down to zero, and he thought he'd gotten over his crush.

Then Wren had shown up at their family dinner and it all came flooding back. It made him wonder if Wren was the unconscious reason none of his other relationships had ever gotten serious. As if he'd been waiting for Wren the whole time. Aiden smiled. The romantic in him liked the idea even if he knew it was fanciful thinking.

It was strange for Aiden knowing he was back in the same place where he'd spent so much time fantasizing about kissing Wren, except now they were dating. Instead of going upstairs to daydream about Wren after dinner, Aiden and Wren would leave together and go back to Aiden's place to make some of his old fantasies a reality. Not the teenage fantasies. Young Aiden had ever been able to imaging sex as hot as he and Wren shared.

Aiden smiled to himself. His junior high self was shitting bricks right now. That and popping a giant teenager boner and dying of embarrassment.

# Chapter 21
## Wren

While Wren chatted with Lillian, he watched Aiden move confidently around the kitchen, chopping vegetables and putting ingredients together for their salad. Occasionally he would pause for a moment to turn and look at Wren and smile or wink.

Everything about this felt right.

Just like last time he regretted not coming sooner. After dinner at the Walkers' two months earlier he'd promised himself he wouldn't hide at home so much, and he'd come to these dinners again, even if it wasn't every week. Then everything with Aiden had started, and the plan had fallen by the wayside. Suddenly coming had seemed overwhelming and scary again.

No, that wasn't entirely true. Being here wasn't scary; it was that by coming, suddenly everything would be about him and Aiden instead of reconnecting with Lucy's family. Coming to dinner with the family was the equivalent of meeting the parents even if he'd known them forever. Wren had worried he wasn't ready for that.

Now he was here, he felt like an idiot.

"What's that smile about?" Aiden started Wren out of his thought tangent by tweaking his ear then leaning down for a quick kiss.

"Just happy to be here." Wren got a wicked smile. "Different than the first time I came over."

"You mean when you were first introduced to the crazy?" Aiden joked.

"Well, I was a bit confused by everything after this tiny kid, who I figured had to be like seven years old, knocked me on my ass before I even rang the doorbell."

"That just means even when I was nine—not seven, asshole—I could already make an impression."

"Make an impression by making me fall on my ass," Wren said with a smile before pulling Aiden down for a kiss.

"You can pay me back by making an impression on my ass anytime you want," Aiden whispered onto his lips. Aiden pulled back and smiled at the blush on Wren's cheeks. He went back to lean against the counter. Wren saw Aiden had finished the salad.

Lillian's eyes flicked back and forth between Wren and Aiden with a soft, happy smile. "You boys are so sweet. You have both grown up so well and it's wonderful to see you finding a life together."

Wren couldn't help but agree. If someone had told him back in high school that he would end up being insanely attracted to Lucy's little brother, Aiden, and would enjoy a happy and increasingly intense relationship with him, Wren would have laughed in their face. Especially since Aiden still looked about twelve when Wren moved away even if he'd had actually been fifteen years old.

Well, he was still Lucy's brother but now he was all grown up and, after nine years apart, their age difference didn't seem weird in the way he knew it would have had they dated when he had been in high school and Aiden in junior high.

"Hello, everyone! I'm here so the party can start!" Lucy yelled from the front entry as she entered the house.

"We're in the kitchen. Come on back, dear," Lillian responded. "Aiden and Wren are already here and I believe the food is just about finished."

Lucy entered the kitchen, handed off a ceramic container to Aiden then gave her mother a quick one arm hug and a kiss on her cheek before plopping herself on Wren's lap.

"Hello, stranger," she said. "So, you lose my number when you got my brother's or are you dedicating all your phone energy to him now? I haven't heard from you all week."

Aiden threw a piece of carrot at her. "Couldn't even wait until we sat down to eat before you bug us."

"Nope," Lucy said, popping the p. "I have to do double duty here. I have to bug you both as your best friend and my brother's boyfriend. So, is he a good kisser?"

"Eww, you really want to know details about my kissing skills?" Aiden said with a grimace. "Mom, I made the salad. I used my honey mustard dressing. It's just waiting over here until we are ready to eat."

"Thank you, dear," Lillian said to Aiden. She then turned to Lucy, "Honey, leave the boys alone. They just shared a beautiful moment and I want to bask in it. Also, I want them to come back for dinner next week."

"Sorry, Mom but I can't make any promises. This is too good to be true."

"Exactly. Don't ruin it."

Wren laughed. Yes, he really shouldn't have waited so long to come back.

Wren decided he agreed with Lucy. He had to do double duty here. He'd been coming to the Walker home as Lucy's friend long before Aiden was anything special to him. He decided he'd give her the same details he'd give about any of his other boyfriends.

"He's the best." Wren deliberately said it loud enough to know Aiden would overhear. He knew talking about it would make Aiden blush and squirm and that just made sharing gossip with his best friend even better. God, that blush. It made him want to do nasty things to Aiden, he wanted to....

Wren shifted in his chair to get more comfortable but stopped because Lucy was sitting on his lap. He glanced at Aiden who smirked at his trouble, making the situation worse. The asshole knew what that smirk did to him.

"So, not another Colin Sheppard?" Lucy asked with an almost identical smirk. God, they really were related even if their smiles didn't have the same impact.

"God, don't remind me. That was the worst kiss of my life. Totally destroyed my crush. Although, now that you remind me, I think you still owe me for the bet we made. I sooo called it. You always said he was straight, but I knew. He used to check out guys' junk when we were changing for gym class."

"You cheat! You never told me that," accused Lucy.

"And they're off," Aiden said to his mother. "I figured by bringing him here tonight there would be a fifty percent chance that I would lose my boyfriend to my sister."

"He was mine first."

"Don't worry, dear, he's still going home with you," Lillian responded. "He isn't interested in her parts. He told me all about it when he was fifteen years old."

Everyone laughed.

"Meat's done," announced Steven as he entered the kitchen carrying a plate of steaks in one hand and roasted potatoes in the other. "Should I put everything in here or on the table in the dining room? Wren, nice to see you, son."

Wren felt his heart clench and felt Aiden slid his hand into his and squeeze it. Wren squeezed back before letting go to stand up and taking the food from Steven's hand to give him a hug. Wren loved it when Steven called him son even if it made his heart squeeze with useless regrets.

The conversation flowed around him. Wren spoke up, arguing with Lucy or joining forces with her to rag on Aiden. He felt so free in this moment. Even if just peripherally, it was nice to be part of such a beautiful, amazing family who so clearly loved each other. Although, maybe it wasn't peripherally after all. Wren looked around the room and saw his face in many of the photos decorating the walls. Wren glanced between Lucy and

Aiden and felt the connection between himself and both siblings, and knew he was already part of this family.

# Chapter 22
## Aiden

Dinner was delicious; made better by his salad if Aiden did say so himself. It was the sort of good food that everyone enjoyed but didn't distract from conversation. Instead, everyone was talking, arguing, and joking. People were talking over one another. Laughter was bouncing off the walls. Aiden could practically feel himself glowing he was so happy. He loved watching Wren chat comfortably with his parents and joke with his sister.

Wren fit in with Aiden's family.

In fact, Wren already had his own relationship with Aiden's parents. This was never more evident than when his mother brought out pie for dessert.

"I can't believe you remembered how much I like your strawberry rhubarb pie, Lillian," Wren said excitedly after Lillian admitted she had picked that specific pie for dessert after she learned Wren would join them. "The whole time I was in Toronto I raved about your pie. I told everyone that would listen they were the best. When we were in University, a friend of mine and I used to get strawberry rhubarb pie whenever we could. We looked for one that was as good but we never did. Elliott decided I must have built yours up in my mind. I was starting to wonder if it was true but nope. This is amazing. The best."

"Ya, this is great, Mom," Aiden agreed.

"Thank you so much, dear. What a beautiful compliment," Lillian had said. "We have extra, which Steven and I don't need. Why don't you take a few pieces home for you, your mother, and Jim?"

"I'm sure they would love that, if I don't eat them all myself first," Wren said with a cheeky smile. Aiden loved that smile and rubbed his leg up Wren's under the table where they had already hooked their legs together.

"Hey, what about some for me? I rely on your leftovers for lunch on Mondays. It is my only reason for coming," Lucy joked.

"What, my thrilling company wasn't enough of an exchange?" joked Aiden.

"Hmm, your company or mom's pie..." Lucy said, pretending to think about it.

"I'd take the pie," Lucy and Wren decided in unison.

"Ouch," Aiden's dad joked.

Because he was his father's son, Aiden put his hand to his chest and pretended he was dying. "You wound me! I thought you cared about me?"

"Oh, I do," Wren said with a smile and a quick peck on the lips. "I just love this pie more."

Everyone laughed. Even Aiden laughed, but he felt his gut clench... 'I love this more'. Did that mean Wren loved him too? Aiden knew it was a joke but had that been a slip of his tongue?

"While I love your pie, Mom, I'd pick Wren," Aiden said with a wink at Wren.

"Ahhh," yelled Lucy. "That is too sweet. After that, I don't think I will be able to have dessert for a week."

"Good," laughed Wren. He grabbed her dessert plate and pulled it toward him. "That leaves more pie for me." A laughing struggle ensued between the two friends before Wren relented and gave Lucy back her pie.

Ding, dong. The door bell rang. Everyone exchanged a look of confusion.

"You expecting anyone, Steven?" Lillian asked.

He shook his head but pushed himself to his feet. “You start eating. I’ll see if I can get rid of whoever’s at the door.”

The conversation at the table resumed as his mom and Wren playfully fought over whether all the leftover pie was Wren’s or whether he would share it with the rest of the table. Aiden smiled at the exchange but kept an ear on his father and whoever was at the door. He couldn’t hear anything at first, just the quiet murmur of his father and at least one other voice, but he felt himself stand with no conscience thought when he heard his father ask, “What?” loudly.

He wasn’t the only one.

The entire group converged on the front door. Aiden, who was at the front of the group, saw his father talking to two police officers. “What’s going on, Dad?”

His father turned to look at him and looked at Aiden sadly. “These officers got a call about a suspicious person in the neighbourhood. They were doing a drive-by and noticed a car in front of our house had all the tires slashed.”

Aiden heard a flurry of voices behind him but barely paid attention as he continued to stare into his father’s increasingly sad eyes.

“I’m sorry to bother you during dinner but in the course of our patrol, we found a blue Subaru WRX parked out front of this house with four flat and damaged tires.” The officer spoke with a calm and matter-of-fact tone but Aiden had to take a few deep breaths before he could speak.

“Ya, ah, that’s my car.” He wanted to cry. What were the odds? He had had the car for two years and nothing had happened except an easily patched flat tire from driving over a screw. Now, suddenly, in the past two months or so he had the car keyed and all four tires slashed. Fuck.

FUCK!

“Wait, what?” Wren said coming up beside him. “Your tires were slashed? By who?”

“We are not sure of that at the moment,” the officer answered Wren’s question, although Aiden suspected Wren hadn’t been asking the officer but, rather, the world in general. “The reporter admitted they did not get a clear view of the suspicious individual. The suspect was described as a tall male with short, dark, hair. I know it is not much to go on but does that description sound like anyone any of you know, maybe someone that might want to harm to anyone here?”

Aiden couldn’t think of anyone that matched that description, well no one or everyone. Hell, he was a tall, dark-haired male. He glanced around and he saw a flash of... something, pass across Wren’s face before he too glanced at Aiden and seemed to have the same realization Aiden had just had. The description matched him.

“That description is pretty generic,” Lucy pointed out what they were all thinking,

“I can’t think of anyone that would want to do this to me,” Aiden continued. “I mean, I’m sure I know a hundred or more tall dark-haired men.” He waved his hand in front of himself to point out he matched the description, “But I can’t think of anyone that would want to damage my car.”

The officer nodded his head. “It may not have anything to do with you specifically. It could be a prank or some kind of hazing activity.” He then put his hand into his pocket and handed Aiden a business card. “I’m Constable Jordan Dean. If you think of anything, call me. I would also like you to come into the station or use the on-line incident report to write up your statement. Mention my name and badge number,” he pointed to a number on the card under his name. “Make sure to include your contact information. You may be eligible for victim services financial aid to help pay for the damages. If not, if we track down the person who did this, you may be eligible for restitution. I will take photos of the damage before I leave and then will put a little sticker on your window with the occurrence number. You will need to include that number in your report.”

Aiden took the card but just nodded. He wasn’t sure what to do now. How was he going to get home? How was he going to get to work tomorrow?

Lost in his self-pitying thoughts, he was barely aware of the police officer leaving. He noticed when Wren wrapped his arm around him. Aiden felt himself lean into Wren and wanted to burst into tears. His poor car. His poor baby.

They sat back down at the table and ate dessert but Aiden could barely pay attention. All he felt was confusion. Once had been difficult. Once had been weird. Once had felt like bad luck. But twice? How was it possible to have this happen to him twice? It was like there was someone out there trying to get him but he knew that was just anger and paranoia talking. He was boring. He didn't have any enemies. He didn't have a vindictive ex- or even any recent exes. His last relationship had ended over a year ago because Bobby hadn't cared about him enough to stop himself from having sex with other people. He definitely wasn't the type ofperson who would try to come after him now.

Plus, the damage happened in two different locations. No one even knew he was at his parents' house today except for the people at the table with him. Well, Zane and Rachel could probably guess this is where he was but that was only because they knew him well enough to know he spent most Sunday evenings at his parents'. It wasn't like he had told them where he was going tonight specifically.

"All right, son. I'll drive you home," his father said and Aiden looked down at his plate and was surprised to discover it was empty and everyone finished dessert while his mind was elsewhere. He was holding Wren's hand, and he didn't remember doing that either but he didn't let go. He felt almost as though Wren's hand was the only thing keeping him bursting into tears.

He knew he was overreacting. It was just a car. It was just damaged tires. It wasn't even the two thousand dollars he would have to pull from his savings to pay for new tires after only just getting his car back from spending another two thousand dollars repairing the previous damage.

No, his car really was important to him, even if it was just for sentimental reasons.

“I drove Wren,” Aiden responded. Aiden really didn’t want to leave Wren, not at his parents’ house or in the more general sense. He never wanted to let him go. Wren squeezed his hand, and it was like he knew. Maybe he did.

“Dad, why don’t I drive them home,” Lucy suggested. “I have to drive home anyway and then you don’t have to go out.”

Aiden just looked at Wren. He didn’t care who drove him home. He knew he wouldn’t be the one doing the driving, at least not today and maybe not even tomorrow.

# Chapter 23
## Wren

"Do you work tomorrow?" Aiden asked softly while they both sat in the back seat of Lucy's car. Despite the soft music Lucy was listening to in the front seat Wren felt like he and Aiden were alone in the dark of the back seat. Wren had offered Aiden the front seat so he would have more room for his long legs but Aiden had gripped Wren's hand harder.

"I have an afternoon shift tomorrow so I don't start work until two."

"Can you please stay at my house tonight?" Aiden asked. "I know you haven't before and I don't want to pressure you to do anything you don't want to but...." Aiden's voice trailed off like he didn't know what to so. He sounded so small. Wren didn't entirely understand what he was going through. Wren had never owned his own car. When he finally got around to buying one, he didn't think he'd care much about it beyond its ability to get him from point A to point B.

He knew it was different for Aiden. Aiden loved his car. He had tried to explain why he cared about it so much after their second date when someone had keyed his car. Aiden had talked about how much time and love he'd put into picking just the right car for himself shortly after he got his first full-time job after graduating from university. He'd nerded out on the technical specs and engineering of the car. Then he'd talked about how much time he'd put into making sure he kept it well maintained. He'd even done some modifications to the car himself, spending weekends and evenings painstakingly removing and installing new and better parts.

Wren hadn't understood everything. Understanding why didn't really matter, anyway. In the end, it didn't matter why Aiden cared about his car, only that he did. He cared, and the car had been maliciously damaged for no apparent reason. It wasn't a car accident or even mother nature. No, it was a deliberate attack that took time and effort by someone. And no one knew why.

Wren had to admit he was feeling somewhat tender as well. When he had walked up to the door behind everyone else to see what was going on and seen the uniform, he'd had a moment of panic. He could almost feel the phantom pains from his assault. Injuries which had long since healed had flared up in pain for a moment before he had blinked and realized what was going on. His past had tried to pull him back under when the policeman had given the generic description of the suspect, a description which fit almost anyone, including Wren's ex. Wren had been panicking, wondering if the worst had happened before he had looked at Aiden for reassurance and realized the description matched Aiden just as well.

"It's okay if you don't want to," Aiden started talking again but Wren cut him off. It wasn't okay for Aiden to be alone tonight. It wasn't okay for either of them.

"No, I'll stay. I want to stay."

And if he had nightmares... so be it.

Aiden released a breath of relief and leaned his head on Wren's shoulder. It was awkward because Wren was shorter but they made it work. Wren felt himself release a breath of relief. He'd have to let his mom know he wasn't coming home tonight because she would worry but he'd just text her. He could call tomorrow to tell her what happened. Tomorrow could be about moving forward and finding solutions. Tomorrow he could help Aiden look into repairing the damage. Tonight, tonight would just be about them comforting each other since that was what they both needed. Things might feel bad now but nothing could be really, truly bad as long as they were together.

# Part Three

## Things get serious

# Chapter 24
## Aiden

"So, give me the deets," Zane demanded as he and Aiden sat across from each other drinking coffee. "I already know things are going pretty well because you have fallen into the dark zone."

"Dark zone?" Aiden asked with a laugh.

"Yes, honey, the dark hole, the wonderful place where people disappear when they start a new relationship and forget they have friends. It's all right, Sweetie. It happens to the best of us."

"Right. I know what you are talking about," Aiden laughed. "I recall this happening when you met Derek. Even though we lived together, I barely saw you more than once a week."

"Yes, that's what I said. It happens to the best of us," Zane gloated with a laugh before scowling when Aiden kicked him playfully under the table.

Aiden was laughing, too. He had to admit Zane was right. He was feeling pretty good. The weather was great, and he had managed to snag a great deal on a new set of tires so he wasn't as broke as he'd thought he'd be.

Oh, and things with Wren were going great, which meant they had been spending a lot of time together. Not that they didn't see other people, it was just they usually hung out with each other instead, usually in bed.

"Ooh, what sexy things are you thinking about?" Zane asked, causing Aiden to blush. He'd been thinking about sex with Wren again. So, what?

Sue him. It was damn good sex. The feeling of Wren pushing himself inside Aiden's body made him feel full and complete in a way he missed whenever they were apart.

"Blushing, okay now I know it's good. My little Aiden. I'm so happy for you. It's been too long since you've being able to give a good pounding."

Aiden felt himself blush more while Zane wiggled his eyebrows at Aiden. "Who says I'm not getting a good pounding." He shifted positions to get slightly more comfortable and blushed even more. The quickie they'd had this morning had left him nicely tender.

"Ahh," Zane said looking scandalized. "Who's a hungry bottom now? You do your sensei proud."

Aiden laughed at Zane's antics and threw a small piece of the table bread at his gloating face.

When he and Zane had first met during first year university, both of them had been relatively new to the whole being out and sexually active thing. Aiden had been out for most of high school but had only had sex a handful of times with his first and only one semi-serious relationship before university.

Zane hadn't come out of the closet until he'd moved out of his small conservative hometown for university. "Although how anyone could believe I was straight is one of my life's greatest mysteries. I've known I was gay since I was five years old and I had a crush on Gabriel, the prettiest boy in kindergarten. My parents still don't know I'm gay. A fact which truly is evidence of the lengths people will go to in order to delude themselves into believing even obvious lies so they can maintain their world view."

When a professor randomly partnered them for a class project, Zane had been desperately looking for a friend who could show him that being gay could be no big deal. Aiden had been happy to be that friend. Between their close friendship and the fact they were both going through their first real sexual awakening at the same time meant they both knew way more about each other's sex lives and sexual preferences than was probably normal for two men who were not, and never had been, romantically involved but Aiden liked that. What else were best friends for?

Aiden couldn't help but let his thoughts drift back to Wren and the sex they'd had this morning. He'd been happy when Wren had showed up for their date last night with a backpack full of stuff. He knew Wren had to work today and had expected him to have to leave early to get home to bed. Instead, they'd stayed in and watched a movie before settling into bed together at a reasonable hour. Aiden had barely kept the smile off his face as he went to sleep with his arms wrapped around Wren.

The smile had returned immediately when he'd woken up with Wren's mouth around his morning wood. Oh, god, the feeling of Wren's mouth on his cock was second only to the feeling of Wren's cock sliding inside him. Something that had happened soon after. They'd been in a rush since Wren had needed to leave, so they had taken as little time to prep as Wren was willing. Aiden hadn't complained one bit.

He loved the feeling of Wren claiming him as he pushed his way inside his body. He loved how his senses were heightened and every stroke felt a million times more intense than normally until his body accepted Wren and relaxed. They both orgasmed so hard Aiden had practically seen stars. Most of all he loved how, hours later, he could practically still feel Wren inside him. He wanted to squirm so he could feel it more.

Zane laughed at him when Aiden squirmed again.

"So, it's going well?" Zane asked in a more serious tone.

"Ya, it's..." Aiden let his voice trail off as he thought about how to describe his relationship with Wren. "It's amazing. Wren is amazing. He is crazy smart, and funny, and caring, and generous, and he gets along with my parents and Lucy, and... and—"

"And fucking hot."

"And fucking hot!" Aiden agreed with a laugh. "And humble." Aiden voice trailed off again. This time he was thinking about how Wren never seemed to know how to accept a compliment and how Wren would deny any compliment related to his looks. It was as if he had this giant blind spot. He just couldn't see how awesome he was. Wren would talk about how great Aiden was but he couldn't see that he was even more amazing.

"I think I'm falling in love with him," Aiden said simply. That wasn't strictly true. He was pretty sure he already had.

"Honey, if you *think* you're falling in love with someone it's already too late," Zane said with a smile and Aiden knew he was thinking about Derek. "But I won't push. You'll realize that when you're ready. Do you think he loves you too?"

"I don't know. We haven't talked about it but I'm patient."

"Well, I'm glad he makes you happy. You deserve it," Zane said and got a determined look on his face. Oh, no, Aiden thought, what's he up to now? "Since everything is going so well, no more excuses, no more hiding him away. You need to bring him to hang out with the rest of us."

Aiden thought about how Wren hadn't even wanted to hang out with Aiden's family until recently. He thought about how Wren seemed to only really relax around people he knew well and seemed to avoid crowds. Aiden wasn't sure it was a good idea to force Wren to hang out with too many people. "I don't know, Zane. Wren is—I don't know. I think something happened to him while he was away."

"So, you going to hide him away forever? You'll hide away forever?" Zane asked with a knowing look.

"No, I mean, I'm just not sure throwing him in with too many people is a good idea. What if we just had dinner with you and Derek, maybe eased him into it?"

Zane smiled like he'd won. Aiden realized that was all he was looking for in the first place. Somehow Zane always knew just what to say to make Aiden do exactly what he wanted. Aiden shoved Zane's foot under the table again and they both laughed.

A little while later they wandered back to Aiden's car. He'd parked in a few blocks away and had agreed to drive Zane to his dance studio for the dance class he was teaching soon.

"The car looks good," Zane commented as he pranced ahead and grabbed a paper off the windshield as Aiden unlocked the doors.

"Ya, I should hope so after paying close to four thousand dollars over the past few months." Aiden felt his heart sink a moment, thinking about everything that had happened to his car recently. Zane whistled at the amount in sympathy, but more had happened than Zane knew about. Just in this week alone he'd been almost side swiped and rear-ended. He'd had to do some serious driving to avoid both collisions. He was feeling like the universe had it in for his car.

"YOU AREN'T WANTED," Zane said in a playfully ominous voice.

"What?" Aiden asked as he started the engine.

"That's what this note says. It isn't signed or anything. In big block letters it just says, 'You aren't wanted.' That's totally weird." Zane waved the piece of paper he'd grabbed off the windshield.

"Not another one," Aiden said with an exasperated sigh.

"Another one?" Zane asked. "What do you mean another one? You know who this is from?"

"No, none of them are signed. But it's the third one I've gotten this week," Aiden explained. The first one had been waiting on his car the morning after Wren had stayed over for the first time. He had found it when he had driven Wren to work. The note had said, "GO AWAY". Then the second had been in the same place after he'd gone for dinner at Wren's mom's and step-dad's house. That one had said, "BACK OFF." Now this one. Aiden told Zane about the other two.

"Third one and you aren't worried?" Zane asked. Aiden could tell Zane was worried enough for both of them. The truth was, they unsettled Aiden. He was just trying to stay calm.

"No—I mean, yes—they are completely weird and insane. I don't know who they are from and who would do something like this. But what can I do? They aren't really threatening. I don't even know what they want me to back off from. So, really what can I do about it?" What was the point in freaking out when there didn't seem to be anything he could do?

"I think you have a crazy ass stalker or something." Zane did an exaggerated shiver. "Maybe I don't want to hang out with you. What if he comes after you with a knife or something?"

"Shut up," Aiden said with a forced laugh but he didn't really think it was funny. "You're freaking me out more. I'm going to start having nightmares or something."

"Uh, oh. What's Wren's number? Maybe I should let him know he needs to come over to hug you when you cry."

Aiden shook his head at Zane's playfulness but quietly hoped Wren would come over tonight in case he had nightmares. Zane's concern about the notes had made it harder for Aiden to discount them as a prank or something he should just throw away. Except really, it wasn't like they could be anything serious. They were just some weird ass notes from some weird ass person—some kid pranking him.

A prank from someone who knew where he was when he'd been at three different places in the city.

Because that made sense.

Fuck!

# Chapter 25
## Wren

"Uhh, yes. Can you grab me a refill of this, please?" Wren answered the hostess before turning his focus back to Zane and Aiden who were arguing about the merits of the colour purple.

Yes, the colour purple. The argument might be the most meaningless argument he'd ever heard.

"It signifies royalty and many Roman emperors banned their citizens from wearing it. Furthermore, it was revered in the Byzantine Empire," Zane argued.

"Okay, Google, if you want to go with that, then that further supports my point. It's elitist and you shouldn't be wearing it."

Wren shared a look with Derek. "Are they always like this?" he asked.

Derek nodded, then laughed as he caught the fries both Aiden and Zane had thrown at him.

"Yummy," he responded cheekily as he ate the fries. "They are like siblings. They'll argue about everything but never about anything that matters. If anyone else joins the argument, they immediately join forces to gang up on whoever dared to get in the middle. They will deny it but they only argue because they enjoy it."

Both Aiden and Zane interjected with a "Hey!" when he said they were the same but neither disagreed in any other way.

"I noticed Aiden is arguing against the colour while wearing a purple shirt," Wren said.

Wren laughed as he saw Aiden look down and blush. "I never said I didn't like purple. I just said it wasn't the best colour."

"Sure, whatever, you are such a liar," Zane laughed. "You know you love it and your shirt just proves it."

"Just because I'm wearing a purple shirt doesn't mean I think it's the best," Aiden argued but even Wren could tell he was just joking around now.

"Oh, it's not your favourite? That's weird. Didn't you say just yesterday that this was your favourite shirt?" Wren asked with a grin.

"Hey, who's side are you on?" Aiden said with false indignation.

"Ummm, Zane's?" Wren joked. "You told me he was your best friend and so I wanted him to like me."

Wren watched as Zane got a smug smile on his face. Then he was momentarily distracted by his phone buzzing in his pocket. Wren glanced down at the display and saw a number he didn't recognize. He ignored it with a sigh.

After he'd blocked the number of the weird caller, Wren had had two blissful weeks with no strange calls. Then suddenly, three days ago the calls had started again, except they were from a different number. He'd blocked that one but almost immediately the number had changed again. Then again.

Wren didn't bother answering or blocking them anymore. The number seemed to change every few hours. Even though he'd stopped answering his phone for anyone not in his contact list, the phone calls kept coming with increasing frequency. Since he never answered anymore, the person had started leaving strange messages, filling up his voicemail box. He'd stopped even deleting them. If it was full, he couldn't get anymore messages. Wren sighed in frustration but was determined not to let these calls destroy his night.

He looked back at Aiden and Zane. Aiden was glaring at Wren playfully while Zane gloated. Wren could sense a slight question in Aiden's expression despite the playfulness.

"You should side with me anyway. He doesn't need a bigger head than he already has," Aiden said returning Wren's focus to the conversation.

"Too true," Derek agreed then laughed again when Zane threw another fry at him.

"Aren't you supposed to be on my side, too?" Zane asked Derek, batting his eyes.

"Oh, Zee, I'm always on your side," Derek said, pulling Zane into a crushing hug which caused Zane to flail his arms. Wren couldn't help laugh and felt the weight of the calls and general nervousness float away.

He was having a good time which surprised him. God, when would he be able to just enjoy himself and move on?

*Wren felt uncomfortable in his black suit and boring navy tie. Not that he didn't like dressing up. He thought he looked fantastic in a nice suit. He liked to wear his navy one with his fun green bow tie that had dancing monkeys on it. He especially liked the way his dress pants hugged his ass in just the right way and the suit jacket emphasized his trim waist and broadened his shoulders. He always felt attractive, like a gay James Bond.*

*Well, that was normally how he felt when he wore his navy-blue suit. But today he wasn't wearing HIS suit. Instead, he was wearing a black number Tyler had insisted on buying for him. Tyler had said he looked too immature and young in his normal suit. Wren was only twenty-six. He was young. But he wasn't eighteen anymore. Plus, who cared if he looked immature? He wasn't. He had his Masters and a good job which had paid his rent before he had moved in with Tyler. He was proud of everything he had accomplished in his relatively short life. When he wore his navy-blue suit, he felt he looked like a successful, young, attractive, gay man.*

*Sometimes Wren suspected the gay part of that was the real issue for Tyler. Tyler really didn't like to advertise his sexuality. He wasn't in the closet per se. Wren was going to the party as Tyler's boyfriend. His colleagues and close friends were all aware that Tyler and Wren lived together and were a couple but Tyler always said, "You do not need to advertise." Well, Wren didn't really feel as though he could hide, nor did he really want to. When he'd come out in high school, it had surprised no one. Recently, Wren had started to wonder if, maybe, being so open was wise. Normally, when he was in his own clothes, he was confident and happy but somehow whenever he picked out clothes to go out with Tyler and his friends, Wren felt self conscious and inadequate. Maybe his sexuality was holding him back. Maybe, if he could play it a little straighter, things would be easier.*

*Except, Wren wasn't sure this was better. Instead of feeling merely inadequate, now he felt like he was back in junior high—misplaced, inadequate, and immature in an ill-fitting suit he'd borrowed from his father. And sure, the boring black suit let him pass as straight—if he weren't on a date with his boyfriend—but he didn't feel at all like himself either. He felt like a big giant lie.*

*Wren wasn't entirely sure how it had happened because Tyler always dressed so sharply. Somehow the suit he'd insisted on Wren wearing was just all wrong. It wasn't only the boring colour. No, it was also the fit. It wasn't loose around his waist, so he guessed technically it fit, but it was baggy around his ass in a way that made him look like he didn't have one. And the jacket was cut oddly, or something, because he looked shorter and almost fat—well, maybe not fat because it wasn't padded—but like he was hiding a paunch.*

*And wearing this god-awful suit wasn't helping with how people treated him. Tyler's best friend, Ryan, was at least trying to be nice, but it was in this condescending way that made Wren want to scream. Or maybe cry. Everyone else just ignored Wren like he was just arm candy and not very attractive arm candy, at that. Wren had even seen a few pitying looks. What was the point of even being here?*

*People surrounded them and Tyler kept a hand on Wren almost the entire time. Wren felt about two inches tall and completely alone. He wasn't part of this suave, fast talking, know-it-all marketing and consultant group. He was just a nerdy scientist who worked in a lab.*

*Wren was relieved when Tyler wanted to go home after about two hours. It felt like the longest two hours of his life.*

Wren tried to shake off the memory which had briefly sucked him under. No, this was different. So far Wren loved hanging out with Zane and Derek. He'd only just met them, but Zane and Derek seemed to be kind and caring people. Zane had already shown he possessed astronomical levels of snark but beneath it was clear how much he cared about both Derek and Aiden. Plus, they were all going out of their way to be nice to Wren, including him in the conversation and never ignoring or talking over him like his ideas didn't matter.

Mostly Wren was staying quiet, but that was his choice. It was funny watching Zane and Aiden interact. Aiden was different around Zane. For one thing, he talked more. He also had gotten this adorable excited energy that Wren rarely saw. Zane seemed to bring out the adolescent inside Aiden, and Wren recognized some of his behaviours from when Aiden was a kid. It was very clear by how they spoke and all the inside jokes that popped up without their even noticing that Zane and Wren were very, very good friends.

Wren was almost jealous that he still hadn't gotten to know Aiden that well yet. Except he was glad Aiden had such a good friend. Zane had Aiden's back. Wren knew what that was like. His friendship with Lucy had kept him sane when life was trying really hard to make him lose his mind.

"So, Wren, a little birdy told me you are staying here?" Derek asked. Wren nodded with a smile. Aiden grabbed his hand and squeezed it.

"Which is fantastic!" Zane exclaimed. "If you left, I would have had to deal with mopey Aiden, and no one wants that, least of all me."

Aiden said nothing and Wren realized belatedly that was because he agreed. Aiden would have been miserable if Wren had left him behind. Good, that made two of them.

On their way home a while later Aiden grabbed a piece of paper from under his windshield whipper. He glanced at it scowled then crumpled it up.

"What was that?" Wren asked as he climbed into the car.

"Nothing, or well—just some stupid note from someone." Aiden looked uncomfortable and Wren wondered what was going on.

"From who? What did the note say?"

"I don't know who's leaving them. They just show up on my car. They are never specific, instead just telling me to stop doing something or go away. I have no idea what they're talking about. I wonder if it is a case of mistaken identity." Aiden ran his head through his hair, something he did when he was stressed or nervous.

The street lights flashed across his face and Wren realized Aiden was being deliberately casual with his words, or at least trying to be. He was really not okay with this note—or rather these notes. "These notes? As in, more than one?"

"Ya, there's got to be close to ten now. They are always sitting on my car and telling me to back off, or go away, or something like that." Aiden's hand ran through his hair again. "They show up everywhere. Honestly, I'm completely freaked out. I think someone is stalking me. It's the only possible way to know where to find my car in all those different places."

"Why didn't you tell me?"

"Because I'm trying not to think about it. And what am I supposed to do?" Aiden sounded so lost and hopeless.

Buzz, buzz. Fuck his stupid phone again. Wren grabbed his phone out of his pocket, glanced at the screen and swore. New number again. This was eight calls and three numbers tonight alone.

"Who is it?" Aiden asked but Wren didn't answer. He wanted to know the same thing.

Suddenly, he'd had enough. He was done. He was done with the calls and Aiden's notes and whatever else was fucking with them.

“Hello,” Wren answered briskly. He was trying not to be rude, but he really wanted to yell, ‘What do you want?!’into the phone.

At first it was the same breathing, the weird-as-fuck, almost horror movie level breathing.

“Please stop calling me. I’ve told you to stop calling me. If you don’t stop calling me, I will report you to the police,” Wren said after a few seconds of listening to the breathing.

“You are mine. He can’t have you,” the voice said, speaking for the first time. It was muffled or distorted. Wren didn’t recognize the voice but, if he was honest, he wasn’t sure if he’d recognize his own mother through whatever was messing with the sound.

“I don’t know who you are,” Wren almost shouted into the phone.

“You’re mine,” the voice repeated before it clicked and the call disconnected.

“What the fuck?!” Wren shouted. He wanted to throw his phone in frustration but refrained. The call had really freaked him and he could practically feel himself losing his cool.

Aiden took hold of his hand and the contact startled Wren. He’d forgotten for a moment he wasn’t alone.

He looked around and saw they were waiting at a red light. Aiden was looking at him with concern while periodically glancing back at the light to confirm it was still red.

“I thought you weren’t answering them.” Aiden said without judgment.

Wren just shrugged then he decided that this really was crazy, and he told Aiden about the call. Wren was upset and could tell his voice was rising and tried to calm down but he wasn’t able to manage it completely. He found himself going back to the same point, “I don’t know who they are from and I’ve done everything I can to make them stop. Why won’t the weirdo who was doing this leave me alone?”

Aiden, being Aiden, just drove and listened, holding his hand as much as he could while still driving safely. Luckily the drive to Aiden’s apartment wasn't long and once Aiden pulled over, Wren took a deep breath and tried to let all his frustration go.

"Sorry, I didn't check if you wanted to go home with me," Aiden said after a moment of silence. Neither of them made a move to get out of the car but Wren waved off Aiden's implied question. He wanted to stay here. Wren knew the only reason he was so angry about the calls was because he was scared. This was not normal, and he didn't know what to do.

"What's going on with us?" Wren whispered.

"I don't know but maybe we should do what you threatened, maybe we should talk to the police. Not just about your phone calls but about my notes too. It's weird they are both happening and I'm wondering if they're connected, especially after hearing what the creep said to you just now."

Wren didn't really want to go to the police. He'd made the threat to scare the guy off but hadn't really intended to do it.

His phone rang again in his hand and he immediately dismissed the call when he saw the number. Make that ten tonight. Looking down at his phone Wren couldn't come up with a single reason not to go to the police, at least not a reason that made any sense whatsoever.

# Chapter 26
## Aiden

Aiden wasn't exactly sure what he expected to happen when he went to the police but this certain wasn't it. He and Wren had decided to go in together. Wren had been worried about showing up together. He worried they might be ignored or discounted because they were gay but Aiden had argued the police could hardly be expected to properly respond to the calls or the notes unless they knew they were likely connected.

Plus, Aiden had argued, the police are super involved in the pride parade. They can't be that bad.

Aiden was now starting to reconsider. Maybe the pride groups across the country were making the right choice when they banned uniformed officers from the parade.

Well, maybe that wasn't fair. He wasn't getting a homophobic vibe off the old and bored looking officer working the front counter. He was getting more of a 'I don't know why you guys are freaking out, this is a giant waste of my time' sort of vibe. Aiden wasn't sure that was much better.

Aiden and Wren had decided to go in-person to one of the stations instead of making a report online. Aiden had worried that without one of the notes in front of them or a look at the call log of Wren's phone their story wouldn't be believed. So, they'd walked in and waited for their turn to speak to someone. When their turn finally arrived, the officer had listened, not so patiently, to their story before interrupting Aiden to ask for the notes. Aiden only had three of them. He hadn't been keeping them until recently. The officer hadn't been impressed.

After glancing at the notes, he'd stated, "There is nothing threatening about these." The officer then asked for Wren's phone. He'd gone through the call log and commented that the calls were from different numbers. Wren agreed, explaining again that the number the calls came from seemed to change a few times a day and had been doing so since Wren had blocked the first number.

The officer had just grunted and, again, he didn't seem impressed. He looked at the phone again for about a minute before giving it back to Wren. "You say the voice only spoke once and you couldn't identify it," he confirmed.

Wren nodded but then elaborated, repeating things both he and Aiden had said before, "But I heard the breathing loads of times before I stopped answering and my voicemail box is full of messages with the breathing."

The expression of boredom was briefly replaced by a flash of sympathy before it was gone again. "Look guys, I'll make a report but there is nothing we can do. You don't know who is leaving these messages or making these calls. You don't even know for sure all of these calls are from the same person.

"I'm gonna be honest with you, because there is no clear threat, even if we knew who was doing this, the most I could do for you is call the person up to tell them to cut it out."

"So, we just need to let it keep happening?" Aiden asked in frustration.

"No, keep the notes you get and when and where you get them. If any of the notes are signed or somehow identify who sent them, bring them all in and bring this card in with you." The officer handed Aiden a business card with a number on it. Aiden took it but still felt as though he was really being told to just keep living with this until whoever was doing it either stopped on his own, which didn't seem likely as things had been getting worse not better, or wait until things got worse.

“As for the calls,” the officer continued. “My suggestion would be to change your number. Only give it out to the people you want calling. If the calls start up again, that might give you a hint as to who's behind them.”

Wren was also given a card with the same number on it and then they were encouraged out the door with a simple, “Come back if you need anything else.”

Back in the car Aiden felt upset and out of sorts. “Why did we file a police report again?”

“Because you were right, sure we got a brush off, but at least now there's a police report out there that shows this is going on. If they find our hacked-up bodies they will know where to start looking.”

“That’s not funny,” Aiden scolded Wren with a frown. He felt a shiver go up his spine. Sure, that cop could say there is no clear threat but Aiden sure felt threatened.

“I'm not sure I was joking,” Wren responded with a frown of his own. “Even though that cop didn't seem overly worried, there is something really sinister about these messages we've been getting. Aiden, I'm scared.”

Aiden took hold of Wren’s hand and squeezed it before releasing it to go back to driving. What more was there to say? He was scared too.

“Well, let’s take his advice and get you a new phone number. Then at least the calls should stop.”

“What about you?” Wren asked.

Aiden wasn't sure how to answer but he took a deep breath and said, “Well, I’ll do what the cop suggested. I'll keep all the notes and track where I get them. If I'm still getting them a month from now, I'll go back and maybe I’ll get a more enthusiastic response.”

“If not?”

“Let’s not borrow trouble. One day at a time. So, with that in mind, why don't we stop and grab some food on our way home from getting your cell phone. Then we can hole up and watch a funny movie so we can stop worrying about this crap when it doesn't seem as though there’s much we can do.”

Wren nodded and Aiden felt relieved. He just wanted to stop thinking about this, stop worrying, and have some fun. Maybe have some sex after the movie to cheer them both up even more, maybe even before the movie, now that it was on his mind.

A few hours later when they arrived back at his place, he noticed another note on the glass door, "Reminder: Please do not let anyone inside the building you do not know. There have been several recent reports of an unknown individual in the hallways who appears to be attempting to get into apartment units. Preventing crime is everyone's responsibility!" There had been one like this last week as well but it had been taken down less than twenty-four hours after being put up so Aiden had dismissed it.

Here was a new reminder notice. Another shiver run up his spine. What the fuck was going on?

# Chapter 27
## Wren

Wren snuggled up to Aiden on the couch. He wanted to think both he and Aiden had put their afternoon out of their heads but he had to admit they might not have, given their movie selection.

Wren watched as two uniformed officers pulled a man over for speeding and then played a game to see how many times one of them could say, 'meow' during the traffic stop. *Super Troopers* might be a movie about a bunch of police officers but at least it was a comedy and Wren knew the good guys won in the end. He felt he needed a bit of ridiculous escapism.

When the movie ended, they both went up to Aiden's loft to go to bed. Wren looked up after taking off his shirt and saw Aiden had stopped and was staring at his naked chest. Wren immediately felt blood pool in his groin despite the sex they'd had before the movie.

Wren felt sexy. Aiden's eyes on him made him feel sexy. Then Aiden's eyes lifted until they were staring at each other. Time froze. Suddenly Wren felt as thought they were not just the only two people in this room but possibly the only two people in the universe. No one had ever affected him like this before.

"I love you," Wren thought. Then he had a moment of panic because he thought he'd said those words out load but he luckily hadn't. So instead he leaned down and kissed Aiden until they both had to come up for air.

Their sex was slow and loving. It was passionate and intense. It wasn't just sex. When Wren entered Aiden, they stared into each others eyes and

Wren felt as though his soul was merging with Aiden's. For a moment Wren lost himself. He was no longer Wren Evans. Instead, he was just part of the whole that was both he and Aiden together. He felt whole and complete in a way he'd never experienced before.

"Look at me. Don't look away," he ordered Aiden. Aiden nodded and, in his eyes, Wren could see Aiden was feeling the same thing he was. The amazing connection that always seemed to between the two of them had solidified and in this moment, they didn't need words, they didn't need actions, they didn't need anything to communicate because they were one.

He thrust down as hard and as fast as he could. Suddenly Wren was coming. Somehow despite practically blacking out he kept his eyes on Aiden's. Aiden's hand in his hair tightened to the point it almost hurt, then Aiden, too, was coming.

Wren came back to himself a moment later. His head was on Aiden's shoulder. They were both breathing hard and Wren realized at some point he had moved his hand so it was tangled in Aiden's hair. Wren could still feel Aiden's hand in his own hair and Aiden's legs now slumped on top of Wren's. They were completely tangled together, sticky from lube and Aiden's come, and Wren wasn't sure he could move to separate them. He wasn't sure whether he wanted to.

"Wow," Aiden groaned.

"Ya," Wren had to agree. Wow indeed.

Wren knew what he'd just done was make love. Because—because he was in love with Aiden. He didn't just care about him as Lucy's brother, or as a good boyfriend. No, this was fallen-down-the-well, head-over-heels in love.

Fuck!

Wren pushed himself up with more difficulty than normal, grabbed hold of the used condom and gently removed himself from Aiden. Both Aiden and Wren sighed with some regret when he removed his cock from Aiden's body before he collapsed, half on top, half beside Aiden.

Wren's brain was swirling and his heart continued to beat erratically, even as he could hear Aiden falling asleep. He was in love with Aiden and more terrified than he'd ever been in his entire life. Because if this was love? Then everything he'd ever experienced up to now was nothing, maybe even less than nothing.

He'd barely walked away after his ex. If something bad happened between him and Aiden...

That would destroy him. No, destroy wasn't a strong enough word. It would obliterate him.

A little while later Aiden spoke up again, "We should get up and get cleaned off. I'm a bit worried we're going to fuse together."

"Ya, in a moment. Still not sure I can move." Wren also didn't want to move even if it meant a more painful shower later. He was scared, but he wasn't going to pull away.

He didn't want to lose their connection. It might kill him, but for now, it felt amazing, an extension of something that was always there but more powerful. Powerful, yet fragile, like maybe with the right attention, the right support, maybe, just maybe, it would become something truly amazing that would last for all time.

* * *

"So, how are things going with my brother?" Lucy asked. They'd already been hanging out for almost half an hour and this was the first time Lucy had mentioned Aiden. He was grateful. Wren didn't want to lose his friendship with Lucy just because he was dating Aiden. Maybe that was why he had been so hesitant to have the three of them hang out. Some part of Wren had worried he couldn't be Aiden's boyfriend and Lucy's friend at the same time. Having dinner with their family had helped him see that his relationship with one didn't negate his relationship with the other even when they were all together.

He didn't want to talk about Aiden all the time but that didn't mean they couldn't discuss him. Aiden was important to both of them. It made sense that Lucy would be curious, and they'd always talked about the people they were dating before.

Well, almost always.

Wren thought back to the sex he and Aiden had had the night before. It had been close to perfect. He'd slept over and like every other time he'd slept held in Aiden's arms, the nightmares had stayed away. He still felt haunted by memories but somehow Aiden's arms wrapped around him lessened their power.

Lucy bumped him to bring his attention back to the present. Wren shot her a look asking her if she really wanted to know the answer. There was one difference between Aiden and Wren's past boyfriends. Lucy hadn't been related to any of his exes.

"I don't need to know how big his cock is but, yes, tell me how things are going. Are you happy?" Wren felt himself get hot when Lucy referred to Aiden's cock—which was large and nice—but he knew what Lucy meant.

"I'm happy." Wren smiled. He was happy. Happier than he'd been in a long time. It wasn't entirely Aiden. It couldn't be. If it was just Aiden making him happy it wouldn't last, it wouldn't mean anything when they weren't together. No, it wasn't just Aiden but having Aiden around helped.

"It's not just Aiden," Wren explained to Lucy, putting his thoughts its words for the first time. "Getting into medical school here in Edmonton has finally let me see my future as something real rather than some unpredictable fantasy. I'm also enjoying my job, and I've saved up a bunch of money which will be useful when I'm paying big tuition and I've moved out of my mom's.

"Really, things have been going so well for me recently that my mom hasn't being trying to helicopter parent her thirty-year-old son for the first time since everything happened with Tyler."

"You know, that's the first time you've mentioned your ex- since you moved back here," Lucy pointed out. "If it wasn't for the fact that you told me about him while you were dating, I wouldn't even know who Tyler is."

Wren jerked in surprise and felt his mind swirl. It was strange to hear that name on someone else's lips. It was even weirder that he'd said the name first without even realizing. He'd been avoiding talking about or even thinking about Tyler for so long it was odd to hear the name out loud.

Wren couldn't look at Lucy and instead looked around the mostly empty coffee shop where they were meeting. The dessert display looked delicious and the vintage furniture was unique, but in the end, nothing was enough to distract him from thinking about Tyler.

Yet, the name seemed less heavy. It opened fewer wounds. Maybe it wasn't just being in Aiden's arms that was keeping the nightmares away. Wren wondered if he was finally ready to discuss what happened.

"Ya, I guess I wasn't ready to talk about him," Wren admitted. The 'before now', hung in the air as Wren decided whether he had the courage to tell his oldest and best friend the story of what had happened to him and why he had decided to move back to Edmonton after living in Toronto for nearly a decade.

He still couldn't look at Lucy, so instead he stared at the table, tracing his fingers along the black-and-white tiles spread unevenly across the middle of the table, like a chessboard on acid. "I told you when Tyler and I got together. I told you when we had moved in together but I wasn't really talking to you when things started to fall apart. Or maybe it wasn't so much that things fell apart as I was falling apart and that was what I was trying to hide from you. Even across the country you would have been able to tell."

Lucy said nothing. When Wren finally glanced up, he saw that she was staring at him, listening with such intensity that Wren could practically feel the heat of her focus. He looked back down and told her everything.

"Motherfucker!" Lucy said when he finished up his story.

When he'd explained why he'd moved back to Edmonton Wren felt... lighter. But also exhausted, like he'd run a marathon or done some crazy physical feet.

They sat in silence for a moment both absorbing everything Wren had said. It was a crazy story. Something that felt like it should only happen in the movies or, at least, to other people. Except if it happened to other people, then Wren guessed there had to be someone—some unlucky person like him—who was the 'other person' everyone pitied. Maybe that was why he never wanted to talk about it.

"I'm glad you told me," Lucy said breaking the silence. At some point during the story she'd taken hold of his hand and squeezed his fingers, almost like she couldn't bear to be separated from him while he told her of his pain. There had been no pity in her eyes and the touch had comforted him so Wren hadn't pulled away.

That was something Aiden was helping with without even knowing it had become a problem. After Tyler Wren had found himself less and less comfortable being touched. It was like his personal bubble had expanded to protect him and no one was allowed inside. Except Wren was so incredibly attracted to Aiden he constantly wanted them to be touching. If he was honest, Wren would happily hold Aiden's hand forever or they could just become permanently attached at the hip. Well, maybe not the hip, that might make certain activities particularly complicated...

"You're the first person—well, first friend—I've told," Wren admitted to Lucy and saw by the slight smile on her face that this had been the right choice. Lucy and he may have drifted apart for a short while but she would always be his best friend. She was the first person he'd come out to, the person he'd confided to about his difficult relationship with his father. It seemed right she was just about the first person he'd talked to about Tyler. Really, there were things he'd said to Lucy that he'd only ever told his therapist, things he hadn't been able to tell his mother.

"I haven't even told Aiden yet," Wren admitted quietly. "Don't tell him. I want to tell him myself—when I'm ready."

Lucy nodded and squeezed his fingers again. Then something flashed in her eyes. "Uhhh, I may have told him something already," she admitted, looking embarrassed. "I mean I didn't know any of this, obviously, at least not how bad it was or any of the details, but after that first dinner at my parents, before you even got together, Aiden commented how different you seemed—how sad. I said I wasn't sure but I wondered if something had happened that made you come back to Edmonton.

"Wren, you were so different when you first came back. It was like you had become this puppet pretending to be you. It wasn't until after you and Aiden started dating that I felt you came back to me."

Of course, she'd known something had happened. Of course, being the best friend that she was, she'd told the first guy he'd dated since leaving his last relationship to be gentle with him. Lucy looked so nervous, so worried that she'd done the wrong thing and made things worse, but how could he be mad? Wren knew exactly who Lucy was. They'd been friends since they were twelve years old. Lucy was caring, observant, and incredibly kind. But she was also bossy and would stick her nose into other people's business if she thought it was for their own good. Hell, if it weren't for her interference he and Aiden may never have gotten together, or at least not as quickly.

Sure, part of him was embarrassed. What had become of him that, even without knowing the full story, Lucy felt that dating Wren needed to come with a warning label? Except they hadn't been dating at the time and, well, maybe he did. Maybe Aiden would have been as patient with him no matter what. Maybe he would have been satisfied with a simple kiss on their first date and no anal sex for two months, even without Lucy's warning. But Wren was fairly certain the warning had helped.

"I'm not mad," Wren said with a laugh. "A bit embarrassed but I should have known you'd done something like that. Aiden was—is—incredibly patient with me. I had figured it was just Aiden being sweet and caring but I know you. I should have figured you'd done something like this."

"Honestly, I didn't say much. I didn't know enough to say a lot. So, it probably is just Aiden," Lucy confirmed. Wren could tell she wanted to make sure Wren didn't think badly about Aiden because of this. Wren was pretty sure there wasn't much Lucy could tell him at this point which would adversely affect his opinion of Aiden. "I'm pretty sure Aiden would find a way to walk on water if that is what he needed to do to care for you. He is completely gone for you."

Wren didn't know what to say to that. After last night, he could no longer pretend he wasn't completely gone for Aiden too. But he wasn't sure Aiden felt that strongly about him. He hoped but... Aiden was just so nice and caring that sometimes Wren wondered if that was what he was seeing.

Wren voiced his concerns and Lucy just scoffed. "Wren, Aiden isn't a pushover. He isn't a saint either. Trust me, I know. I'm his sister. What he is, is completely in love with you."

Wren waved it off, not ready to hear those words from her. Except at the same time he could feel his heart filling and couldn't help hoping Lucy knew what she was talking about.

"Whatever you think, the question isn't whether Aiden loves you because I'm sure the answer to that has been yes since he was fifteen years old. No, the real question is whether you love him. Wren, are you going to break my brother's heart?"

Wren looked at Lucy and then looked back down at the table. He knew she wanted him to say he loved Aiden too. He knew that was what Lucy wanted to hear. Part of him knew it might even be true, but it terrified him. And when he finally got the courage to say those important words aloud, they shouldn't be test driven with Lucy first.

"I'm scared, Luce," Wren admitted softly. Now that he'd told her about Tyler, he could finally talk about what he was feeling to someone who might understand. "I care about him. A lot," he conceded. "But last time I thought I was in love everything went so wrong. How can I ever trust anyone that much again?"

"No," Wren corrected before she could speak. "How can I trust myself? How can I know I'm making good choices when I have made such royally fucked up choices in the past? I ignored all the signs with Tyler, Luce."

Wren took a deep breath and finally revealed his deepest darkest fear, “Maybe after that—after proving I’m a complete failure—I don’t deserve to find someone or be happy.”

These were the questions that plagued Wren. Aiden was so great. How could Wren possibly deserve him after everything he’d done wrong in the past? And if he didn’t deserve Aiden, how could what they have be real?

“Oh, baby, Wren, honey. No.” Lucy got up and moved around the table so she was beside Wren then she pulled him up so she was hugging him and holding him in her arms. “No, no, no. Wren you deserve all the happiness in the world. You aren’t a failure or an idiot, or any of the other things you are thinking right now. Tyler was a monster, a real wolf in sheep’s clothing. And you got away. Here you are with me having coffee at our favourite coffee shop while he is rotting far away.”

Wren felt tears fall down his cheek and knew his nose was running. He laughed at the picture he was sure he made and the laugh came out halfway between a giggle and a sob which made him laugh more.

Wren knew that Lucy’s words, the same words his mother and his therapist had been repeating to him, wouldn’t be enough but it was still nice to hear. And somehow, they sounded more like the truth today than they before. Maybe he’d start to believe them.

# Chapter 28
## Aiden

The following Sunday, Aiden went to Wren's house to pick him up for a date. Susan and Jim were heading out just as he was pulling up.

"Where are you two off to?" Aiden asked Susan and Jim.

"We are going to a BBQ to celebrate Canada Day and the end of the school year. All the teachers at my school throw a big party every year," Susan answered.

"Sounds like fun," Aiden commented.

"Oh, it is," Wren said wryly. "Last year Mom drunk dialled me at four AM trying to convince me to find her a cab. When I tried to reason with her, saying it was the middle of the night and she could do it herself, she started singing."

Susan tried to deny it while Jim nodded his head behind her back.

"Oh, stop. It is my one night to have fun," Susan justified. "And where are you off to?"

"We decided to keep it quiet, just hang out at my place and watch a movie. Maybe we'll order a pizza," Aiden responded.

"If we are feeling adventurous, we might walk down to Kinsmen to watch the fireworks," Wren added.

"Well, have fun, boys," Jim encouraged.

They said their goodbyes before heading off in different directions.

Aiden enjoyed their homemade thin crust pizza and the secret chocolate coconut dessert he had waiting for them in his fridge.

"Yum, that was good," Wren said, rubbing his tummy after they finished eating. "The only problem with dating you is it has upped my food game. If you ever leave me, I might need to actually spend time cooking."

"You can cook?" Aiden asked in mock shock.

"Ha, ha! Laugh it up Mr. Amateur Chef. Why do you think I let you do all the cooking?"

"I guess it's a good thing I'll never leave you," Aiden said as he leaned across the table to give Wren a quick kiss.

After dinner the negotiations about which movie they would watch started.

"This movie is fucking classic!" Aiden exclaimed when he won the rock, paper, scissors battle they'd used to decide which movie to watch tonight. He'd been possibly a little too excited when he got to tell Wren they would watch a Star Trek movie together.

Aiden knew Wren wasn't as interested in science fiction as he was but this movie was pretty entry level for a classic Star Trek movie. Plus, on Wednesday it had been Wren's turn to pick the movie, and he'd forced Aiden to sit through a rom com. To be fair, Wren had brought over *Warm Bodies*, which at least had zombies in it. So, they were both taking the other into account, somewhat.

Their tastes weren't always overlapping. Wren's choice for tonight had been some musical. Wren really like musicals and knew most of the words to the more famous productions. Aiden wasn't a huge fan. It wasn't that he hated them but... they weren't his favourite. A few weeks ago, Wren had tried to make him sit through *La La Land* and Aiden had been forced to entertain himself by using his hands to distract both of them.

"I can't believe you'd rather watch *Star Trek* than my movie. How do you not like musicals?" Wren joked as he settled down on the couch while Aiden put *Star Trek* into the DVD player. Wren sang the theme song to... something. Aiden could only guess it was from whichever musical Wren had wanted to watch tonight. "It's like you aren't even gay."

"I'm pretty sure what makes me gay is the fact that I love having your cock inside my ass," Aided had retorted while snuggling against Wren. Wren had grabbed Aiden and pulled him in tight for a kiss as the movie started.

"I have to admit I actually like this movie," Wren admitted with a grin after they'd been watching for a little while. In a fake Russian accent, imitating Chekov, he continued, "Can you direct us to the nuclear wessels?"

Aiden smiled. Maybe he had recognized the cover and some of the songs from *Mamma Mia!* Not that he'd admit it out loud.

They laughed and snuggled while watching the movie. By the time the movie ended it was raining, so they decided to forgo the fireworks. Instead, they moved up to Aiden's room. Aiden got to see fireworks anyway which made him decide they'd made the right decision.

Once they finished and cleaned off, both Aiden and Wren passed out, snuggling in each other's arms.

Several hours later, well after the fireworks had ended, Aiden woke when Wren suddenly sat up in bed.

"Fuck! I need to head home," Wren said with immense regret. "I have to work tomorrow—or no, today, it's today now—and I forgot my scrubs at home." Aiden blinked up at Wren, trying to let his brain wake up enough to absorb what he was being told.

"You want me to call a cab?" Wren asked.

"Wah...?" Aiden groaned. Wren was leaving?

"I have to leave," Wren repeated. Why, Aiden wondered. He thought they were past that. Oh wait, he'd said something about work and no scrubs....

"Umm, okay." Aiden sat up. "Okay, let me just throw on some clothes and I can drive you home."

"I'm sorry. I swear I can get a cab. I really wish I could just stay in bed but all my stuff is at my mom's and I'm on shift at six." He glanced over at Aiden's bedside clock. Four twenty-seven in the morning. "Which is in two hours. So, I'd need to leave now to get to work on time."

“No, no, of course,” Aiden dismissed the idea of Wren using a cab. He turned in circles looking for his shorts and a shirt. “I can take you home. I knew you had to go to work this morning. Plus, you’d never find a cab. It’s Canada Day—or was,” he added, rubbing the sleep off his face. “But do I have time to make a coffee? Not sure I can drive safely without some coffee.”

“Of course. Why don’t I make us both some while you get dressed?” Wren suggested. He clearly felt guilty and Aiden didn’t want that. Yes, this was much earlier than he had intended on waking up but it was hardly the end of the word. It was a statutory holiday so he could just go back to bed or have a nap this afternoon.

“Thanks, I really appreciate this,” Wren said with a shy smile as they were walking out the door.

“Anytime. Well, hopefully not... it would be great if you’d remembered your scrubs so we could both get the extra hour of sleep and snuggles,” Aiden said with a smile and a gentle push on Wren’s shoulder. He was relieved to see Wren laugh.

Aiden felt a warm happiness spread, helping the coffee wake him up, when Wren grabbed hold of his hand and took the lead toward Aiden’s car.

“Huh,” Aiden grunted to himself as they left the building.

“What?” Wren asked, glancing back at Aiden with concern.

“The sign by the door reminding everyone not to let strangers into the building is gone again. Someone keeps pulling them down shortly after they are put up.”

Although the roads were virtually empty because of the early hour, Aiden drove carefully on the still wet roads. They drove to Wren’s home in relative silence, both drinking their coffee. The radio was playing music softly and occasionally Wren hummed along with a song he liked. Aiden was too self conscious of his bad voice to sing unless he was alone but he sure enjoyed listening to Wren.

Wren had a beautiful clear voice. When they were kids Aiden had thought Wren was good enough to act and sing professionally. Now he was older, he knew it was more complicated even if that was what Wren wanted to do with his life, which it wasn't.

Wren was still one of the best singers he knew in real life. It was nice that Wren seemed to be unconsciously singing again. When they'd first started dating Aiden had noticed Wren would sometimes stop himself from singing but that hadn't happened for a while now. The goofy grin Aiden couldn't keep off his face whenever he heard Wren singing probably didn't hurt.

When they arrived at Wren's, his mother's car wasn't back. Instead, Aiden noticed a grey Honda civic parked where she usually parked. He briefly wondered when he had started noticing that particular make, model, and colour combination. It wasn't an uncommon vehicle. He noticed someone was sitting inside the car and felt sorry for whoever it was that had also been forced to be awake and out of bed at this ungodly hour.

"Looks like Mom and Jim aren't home," Wren commented as he got out of the car. "Those two don't drink often but they sure go crazy at this BBQ. I wonder where they ended up."

"Probably someone else's couch," Aiden said, then winked. "Or maybe someone else's bed... and not alone."

"Eww! I do not want to think about my mom and Jim involved in some kind of drunken orgy."

"You said it."

Wren closed the door to the car loudly singing nonsense to block out anything else Aiden might say. He paused for a second to lean down into Aiden's window for a goodbye kiss.

Once the kiss had finished, Aiden took advantage of Wren's silence by continuing to bug him, "Maybe it's one of those parties where everyone puts their keys in a bowl at the beginning of the party and you go to bed with whoever's keys you get."

Wren laughed as he ran toward his front door. "La, la, la." Right before closing the door he stopped singing to say "Bye! I love you, I'll talk to you tomorrow."

Aiden laughed, then froze for a second after the door was closed. Had Wren just said that? Did he really mean it?

He waited another moment as hope bubbled up in his chest before he turned the engine of his car back on and pull out. The grey Honda pulled out behind him. Aiden was just about to turn out of the neighbourhood when his phone rang. “Hey, Wren. You want me to keep talking about your mom and Jim’s imaginary sex life.”

“Aiden,” Wren said seriously. “Can you please come back?”

“What?” Aiden blurted, immediately matching Wren’s serious tone. “What’s wrong? I just have to turn around. I’ll be right there.”

“Ya, okay. That’s good.” Wren took a deep calming breath. “Aiden, someone was in my house—in my room.”

“What!” Aiden exclaimed. “What’s going on? Is anyone there now?”

“No. I mean, I don’t think so. I don’t know. Do you think someone might still be here?” Wren’s voice quivered and was so much more timid than Aiden was used to. Aiden quickly shoulder checked. The roads were empty and he took advantage of everyone else being asleep to swing a U-turn in the middle of the road. Then he was speeding back to Wren’s house as fast as his car could safely take him.

“They’re probably gone but call the police,” Aiden instructed. “I’ll be right there.”

# Chapter 29
## Wren

After the call disconnected Wren stood unmoving in his bedroom. Aiden had told him to do something but he couldn't think clearly. He was frozen in place, stuck like a statue, staring at the wall above his bed.

"HE CAN'T HAVE YOU. YOU ARE MINE!"

The words were spray painted in bold, black letters spread across the entire wall, easy to read from across the room. He felt his body shake. He felt like he was breaking from the inside out. He could barely breathe and realized he was hyperventilating, but he was having trouble catching his breath. He felt waves of cold and hot run through his body and felt faint.

*Beep.*

*Beep.*

*Beep.*

*Beep.*

*The noise of the heart monitor echoed in the soft room. It invaded Wren's dreams and became background noise during his waking hours. It was never ending. His world had become timeless. Day and night meant nothing, minutes, hours, days meant nothing. All that was left was the oscillation between floating numbness and pain. And the beep.*

*Beep.*

*Beep.*

*Beep...*

It wasn't just the words painted across his wall. His sheets had been pulled from his bed and torn into strips. There were clothes strewn across his room. Everything except his underwear had been cut up almost beyond recognition then dumped onto his bare mattress.

*Wren wasn't sure whether he was awake or asleep. Was the pain and hospital his nightmare or his reality? When he woke up and opened his eyes, would he find himself in bed next to Tyler? Or was this a different kind of nightmare? Would he wake up in the bedroom of his new apartment, alone and missing Tyler.*

*He was almost afraid to open his eyes. He didn't even know what he wanted to be true.*

Pictures of him with friends had been taken off the wall but could be found strewn around the room. Broken glass and damaged picture frames lay in various places around the room. Wren could barely see his floor. He'd had a framed picture of Aiden and him on his bed-side table but Wren couldn't see it anywhere. It was impossible to tell whether it had been taken or was just lost in the mess.

The word 'MINE' was also written across the mirror by the door and above his desk, written in the same bold black marker.

*He'd been having a dream, a dream where he had been back in Edmonton spending time with Lucy. It was a good dream.*

*Maybe that was reality and the rest was just a horrible nightmare?*

*No, it must have been a dream.*

*Which mean this was reality. Except, he didn't want to open his eyes and see where he was because the more awake he became, the more he realized he was too hurt, too uncomfortable for it all to have been a nightmare.*

*What if he hadn't escaped? What if he was still lying on the floor waiting for Tyler to come back and kill him?*

Wren heard a sound downstairs and almost jumped out of his skin.

"Fuck, fuck, fuck, fuck," he muttered silently to himself. He realized he was crying; tears and snot were running down his face. He'd only been this afraid once before in his life. What if he wasn't alone? What if the person that did this was still here?

*He tried to focus on his memories of Lucy. He tried to remember the high school play they'd acted in together. He focused all his energy on trying to remember the lines he had spent hours memorizing. But the harder he tried, the less he could remember. Instead, a voice kept interrupting his thoughts saying he was stupid and didn't try hard enough; whispering that he was a disappointment and calmly assuring Wren he wouldn't be angry of only Wren didn't make so many mistakes.*

*Wren wanted to scream and drown out the voice but found himself mute, unable to respond.*

Wren looked frantically for a place to hide when he heard the noise downstairs again. It sounded like it was coming from the front door. But was it someone trying to get in or out?

*But that same smooth voice also whispered 'I love you' and 'I'm sorry for the things I have to do.'*

*It sounded so sorry. It sounded so sad.*

*How could someone loving you be a bad thing?*

His phone rang, startling him again. He frantically shut off the sound. What if the person heard and came upstairs?

*Wren wondered if he was back with Tyler except—except maybe that was where he was meant to be? Maybe everything that happened really had been his fault?*

He looked down at his phone to shut off the sound properly when the display lit up and rang again.

Aiden.

*That voice was bullshit.*

*Right?*

"Hello," Wren whispered.

"I'm at the door but it's locked. Come let me in," Aiden asked. "Hey, hey, hey," he continued and Wren realized he was crying loudly now, almost hysterical in his relief that the sounds he'd been hearing downstairs were from Aiden not from some psycho who was going to kill him.

*Maybe he really was in a hospital room because of Tyler, someone who was supposed to love him, someone he had thought he loved.*

"I'm right here. Please just come let me in," Aiden repeated. Wren nodded, then realized Aiden couldn't see him so he said he would. Although, he wasn't sure how much Aiden understood through the sobs.

*But the voice kept whispering in his head.*

*Maybe he had died and this was his punishment for—for being so weak and useless. He deserved everything that happened to him.*

# Chapter 30
## Aiden

Aiden guided Wren into the living room. He sat down on the couch and pulled Wren onto his lap. Wren's body shook and his breathing was shallow. When Wren had first opened the door, Aiden had tried to ask him what was going on but Wren had been hysterical. He could barely form sentences and was as white as a ghost. So, Aiden tried to be patient has he hugged Wren to his chest and rubbed his hand up and down Wren's back.

Wren's shirt rode up and Aiden took advantage of this to rub his hand along Wren's bare skin. He hoped having skin to skin contact would help ground Wren into the here and now. Or maybe it was for himself. Maybe it wasn't just Wren who needed reminding they were both here and safe.

At least for now.

What the fuck was going on?

Aiden wasn't sure if he'd ever been as scared before in his life. The call from Wren had been scary but those moments when he'd stood outside Wren's house with the door locked and Wren not answering the phone had been worse. He'd waited just long enough for every worst-case scenario to play through his head.

What if he had been attacked? What if he was hurt? What if he was dead?

Aiden continued to hold him quietly until Wren pulled away looking embarrassed but still so lost.

“Shhh,” he said to Wren, pulling him back against him. “You were there for me when I needed you. Let me be here for you now.” Wren nodded and hugged himself back into Aiden’s body.

They sat in silence in the living room, without even turning on the lights for over fifteen minutes before Wren sat up again and turned his body to look at Aiden.

“I’m sorry,” Wren whispered. “I’m not sure why that scared me so much.”

“Because someone invaded your home!”

“I was already scared but when I heard you trying to open the door, I thought someone was still here. I thought they were going to come upstairs and kill me.”

“Have you called the police yet?” Aiden asked. Wren confirmed his suspicions when he shook his head. “Let’s do that,” Aiden suggested gently. “Then we can distract ourselves while we wait for them to arrive.”

Momentarily, Wren looked like he wanted to say ‘no’ but took out his phone and dialed 9-1-1.

The call to the police took a long time. The operator seemed to ask Wren a million questions but eventually Wren was allowed to hang up.

“She didn’t think anyone was here still since we haven’t heard or seen anything since we got home, but she’s still sending officers over right away, just in case. If anything else happens I’m supposed to call back immediately.”

Wren had gotten off Aiden’s lap to pace while he was on the phone with the 9-1-1 operator. Now he stood up defiantly with his hands on his hips.

“Someone destroyed my room, Aiden,” Wren stated. Aiden had overheard a pretty detailed description of what was done while Wren was on the phone, but Aiden let him talk. “All of my things were thrown around everywhere, even my clothes, and there was stuff written on my wall. Half my stuff is destroyed and the other half was touched and tossed around. I haven’t looked around the rest of the house but even if that’s all the damage—maybe especially if that's all the damage—it's freaky. They spray painted 'YOU ARE MINE' on my wall."

"Who would do this?" Wren demanded and as he spoke his voice rose in both pitch and volume. "The only person who has ever said stuff like that to me was... It can't be him. It just can't. I left my entire life in Toronto to get away from him. He ended my life there. I'm just getting my life back, making friends again and moving on. It can't be him. I can't deal with him, not again."

Aiden felt his body stiffen as Wren spoke. Aiden wanted to cry as Wren confirmed so many of his suspicions about Wren's past in a short few sentences. He wanted to hit the man, whoever he was, this person who had taken a confident and sociable person and somehow turned him into someone nervous and shy.

Wren wasn't broken. But he was different and he should never have had to change. Aiden couldn't be upset that Wren had moved back to Edmonton, but he wished he'd come back because he wanted to instead of to escape someone who was so horrible Wren felt he needed to give up everything just to get away.

"I don't know, honey. Let's wait until the police gets here. They can check out the house and maybe answer some of your questions."

"Ya, okay." Wren took a deep, calming breath. He sat back down onto the couch, took another deep breath and then relaxed himself back against Aiden's body. Aiden felt himself breathe out in relief as he felt Wren calm down and start to relax. They sat in silence for another moment while Aiden rubbed Wren's back soothingly.

"I'm totally freaked out but also really comfy. We didn't sleep much and I'm still tired. I'm worried I'll fall asleep before the police get here if we stay like this," observed Wren.

"You can go to sleep if you want. I'll wake you up when the police arrive or..." Aiden paused as Wren shook his head. "Okay, how about this? I go into the kitchen, get you a glass of water, then..." Aiden looked around the living room, trying to figure out what they could do, spotted a deck of cards. “Then we can play cards.”

“Ya. That sounds good. While you do that, I should probably call work to let them know I’m not coming in…”

Aiden shifted Wren off his lap, stood up and walked into the kitchen. As he looked around, he had a shiver of fear. From what Wren had described, this room wasn’t as bad as Wren’s bedroom, but it was still a mess. They had broken the large window on the back door, probably with the rock which was now sitting on the kitchen floor. There was glass all over the floor and a small puddle of water by the door from the rain earlier in the evening.

The asshole who’d broken in had definitely had it in for Wren because they had ignored the china cabinet by the door to the dining room. But the framed pictures of Wren, Susan, and Jim, which had been decorating the wall, were ripped off and thrown around the room, or at least the ones with Wren in it. They had left the other pictures where they were.

In fact, they had systematically destroyed everything that was obviously associated with Wren. The old programs from school plays and amateur theatre productions Wren had acted in over the years, which had been attached to Susan’s fridge, were shredded all over the floor. They had even ripped up the birthday card Wren had given Susan three weeks earlier.

Based on what he had said, Wren had gone straight up to his bedroom earlier so he probably wasn’t even aware of the damage to this room. Aiden was not looking forward to him finding out.

If Aiden was honest with himself, this entire thing was really freaking him out. The notes and calls had been weird and scary. This—this was a serious escalation from that. Aiden knew he couldn’t be certain everything was related but there was a similarity between the messages. Aiden couldn’t imagine they weren’t all being sent by the same person.

Someone was trying to tell them that Wren was taken and Aiden needed to back off.

Aiden knew he wasn't an expert, but it sure seemed as though some random thief hadn't done this. Nothing had been taken. Or at least nothing that was worth any money. On the coffee table near where he and Wren had been sitting was an iPad just sitting out, and they hadn't touched the nice television. Even in Wren's room where so much had been destroyed, Wren had mentioned his laptop was still on his desk.

No, this was personal. This was a targeted attack on Wren after weeks of vaguely threatening notes and phone calls. Aiden was just grateful no one was home. Although, part of Aiden—the terrifiedpart of him—suspected that hadn't been an accident. The police had minimized it but the thing that had always bothered Aiden the most about the notes on his car was they were showing up at different places around town, including places no one could know he'd be unless he was being followed. Aiden suspected this wouldn't have happened if anyone had been home because whoever did it knew exactly where Aiden and Wren had been.

Aiden didn't know what happened to Wren exactly but the fact he'd even mentioned his ex- in connection to this scared Aiden. He had a bad feeling this was just the beginning and it would still get worse.

After getting a good look around the kitchen Aiden had briskly walked back to the front door to grab his shoes. Wren looked at him as he passed the living room. He paled when he saw Aiden had gone to get his shoes.

"What's going on?" Wren asked, fear in his voice as Aiden walked by. Aiden said nothing, but he knew Wren could tell something had happened to the kitchen.

Aiden went directly to the cabinet, got out a glass then went to the fridge and opened the door. There was milk, almond milk for Jim, who was lactose intolerant, orange juice, and a jug of water being kept cold. Aiden pulled out the juice and the water. He poured a glass of juice and then got another glass and filled it with water. He put both the water and the juice back in the fridge. He took both glasses and went back into the living room.

"Here, I brought you some orange juice. I thought the sugar would help. I have water too. You can have it instead or as well if you want," Aiden said as he placed both glasses on coasters on the coffee table in front of Wren.

“Thank you,” Wren said as he picked up the juice and took a sip. “It’s bad in there too?”

“Ya, but don’t worry about that now. It can wait for the police. In the meantime, we are going to play an epic game of cards.”

Aiden turned around and went over to the bookshelf where he grabbed the deck of cards. He took them out of the package. He quickly flipped through them, noting they were in order and all the cards were there. He shuffled them as he walked back toward Wren. “Okay, so here is what I’m thinking. We can either play crazy eights or speed.”

“Those are my only options? Not poker or any of the many other more adult oriented games.”

“Yep. We are limited to games you and I used to play together with Lucy back when you guys were in junior high.”

Wren laughed. After laughing for a moment, he looked at Aiden with a small smile and gave him a grateful nod, acknowledging Aiden’s effort to cheer him up. “Okay. I can accept that but I might need some reminding how to play speed. It’s been a long time.”

“I can do that. I used to play speed at lunch with my engineering friends between classes so it hasn’t been too long for me. Is that the one you pick?”

“Well, you clearly have an unfair advantage if you’ve played it in the last ten years, but sure.” Wren shook his head at Aiden’s silly rule.

Aiden knelt on the floor in front of the coffee table across from where Wren was sitting. Aiden laid out the cards and quickly reminded Wren of the rules before starting a game.

Wren seemed to be getting into the game. He reacted slowly, stopping frequently to think about the rules. Although he was smiling a little, Aiden could still see tension around his eyes and in his shoulders. There needed to be a bigger distraction. Aiden lay down cards more quickly to make it harder. He let Wren put a few cards down before he suddenly put four cards down at once.

"Wait, wait. You can put more than one at a time?" Wren asked, glaring at Aiden. "I think you're cheating."

"I'm not cheating! You can put down as many as you want. They just have to work." He went back and showed Wren he had put a two, a three, a four, and another three down on top of an ace.

"Hmmm... right, cheater. I'm watching you."

Aiden just laughed and was relieved to see Wren stare more intently at the cards and happy to watch some of the tension disappear.

They continued playing, shuffling and restarting each time the game finished. Aiden was much faster and Wren kept groaning and exclaiming, "Stop, wait. No! I had that," each time Aiden placed a card on top of the card he wanted to use and kept him from winning.

"Okay. Let's play again. I can do this," Wren said after losing three in a row, now totally focused on the game. Aiden smiled to himself. This was a good choice. It was hard to think of anything else while playing speed. The game was so fast-paced you had to focus if you wanted even a shot at winning.

"All right, old man, if you think you are up to it," Aiden goaded Wren on.

"Old man. I'll show you, 'old man'. Hurry up and deal already."

Aiden laughed out loud and did as directed. He dealt the cards and, with a nod to Wren, they were off and playing another game. This time Wren finally won. If Aiden slowed down a bit to let Wren win, he'd never say.

"Ya, that's right, who's the best?" Wren celebrated, standing up and doing a little dance. Aiden casually adjusted himself. He knew now was not the time or the place but watching Wren be carefree and happy was a turn on. Especially right now when he had every reason to be scared and sad. Wren was so strong. Aiden just wished Wren could see how truly amazing he was.

They played a few more games, each winning a few—Aiden may have gotten distracted by Wren's growing smile and laughter—when the doorbell rang. Wren stopped and got a confused look on his face before his face fell as he remembered what was going on and why someone would be at his door at almost five in the morning.

Yep, Aiden wanted to hurt whoever had done this.

"You stay here," encouraged Aiden. "I'll go let them in."

"Ya. Ya, okay," Wren agreed and cleaned up the cards they had abandoned mid-game.

Aiden watched with a heavy heart as Wren visibly curled back in on himself. God, he really hoped the police were able to do something or say something to help make all this seem more manageable and less like the scary personal violation it seemed to be right now.

Although, Aiden knew no matter what, Wren would cope because he could handle anything. Plus, he wasn't alone. Aiden was with him every step of the way.

# Chapter 31
## Wren

Wren had been trying really hard to stay calm ever since the two officers had arrived. Aiden had convinced him to play cards again while they waited but the game had been much more subdued. Despite slowing down, Aiden had won all the games because Wren couldn't focus. His eyes kept swinging toward the door to the kitchen where he could hear the officers work.

How was this possible? What was going on? Who would do this to him? What was it about him that attracted these crazy people that wanted to hurt him?

The officers had introduced themselves as Constable Johnson and Constable McDougall. Johnson was a young, not entirely Caucasian woman. Her hair was a lovely dark brown. She had pulled it up into a tight bun at the back of her head. She was relatively short—shorter than him for sure—but Wren got the sense she wasn't someone to be overlooked in a fight. Or anywhere else. Not that he had any interest or intention in fighting either officer.

McDougall, on the other hand, was a middle-aged white guy. He looked so much like the stereotypical cop Wren was disappointed he had a clean-shaven face. The classic cop moustache would have completed the look. Well, that and a potbelly. In reality, McDougall was taller than Wren, although not quite as tall as Aiden. He was also physically imposing. The obvious muscles suggested he didn't let his age become an excuse to get out of shape.

Both officers had arrived with a no-nonsense attitude and a ton of questions. No, Wren hadn't looked around the whole house. No, they hadn't heard anything. No, no one had been home when this had happened. No, he wasn't the owner of the house. He was living with his mom and step-dad, who were out for the night, and they hadn't answered their phone when he had tried to reach them earlier.

Aiden had told the officers he'd gone to the kitchen to get Wren a drink, and he'd found the back door broken. Wren hadn't been able to repress a shiver of fear when he thought about yet more damage to the house.

The officers had just nodded and told them to wait where they were while they looked around.

*Thoughts swirled around in Wren's head like a mouse on a wheel, going around and around, not stopping, not going anywhere. He should have seen what Tyler was capable of. He should have left sooner, he never should have left home. If he was a real man, he should have been able to fight back. If he were smarter, he should have been able to say something to keep Tyler from getting angry. He should have—should have been able to prevent it from happening.*

When Johnson and McDougall finally re-entered the living room Wren dropped his cards on the table and quickly stood up. They didn't matter. He didn't even know which cards had been in his hand.

"Hello," Wren said to the officers. "So... what are your thoughts."

"Let's start with what we can discern from what was done here. Then we'd like to get some more information from you two."

"Okay," agreed Wren. Aiden was standing behind him and holding his hand. Wren was so grateful he had Aiden here for support.

"I will start with things we know to be true," McDougall said. "The perpetrator entered the property through the back gate. He probably walked down the alley to get to your property. It is unlikely anyone saw him entering your property—few people notice anything going on in their back alleys. We will canvas to confirm in case there are any especially curious or nosey neighbours but I'm not expecting anyone to have seen anything.

"After entering your property, he walked straight to the door and broke the window in the back door by throwing a rock through the window. He entered the house and walked through the kitchen. It appears he went straight upstairs and left the way he entered. Your bedroom was obviously his target. You or your parents will need to confirm but as far as we can tell, the only room with any damage upstairs was the room you identified as yours, Wren."

McDougall gave Wren a meaningful look; although, it wasn't necessary since the words already felt like bullets. Each hitting him harder than the last. Wren didn't want to listen anymore but forced himself to keep taking everything in as the officer continued to speak. "Based on the water on the floor in the kitchen and the lack of water or mud in the rest of the kitchen or hallway, we strongly suspect the perpetrator broke the window before the rain started at around nine o'clock this evening. You said everyone in the house left at around seven o'clock so they probably broke in shortly after that.

"The next thing we know is this was not random or motivated by theft. There is no doubt in my mind this was a targeted attack on you, Wren." McDougall paused and looked at Wren, giving him a chance to process this piece of information.

But, how could he? This was a nightmare.

Hadn't he endured enough nightmares to last a lifetime?

*How could he have spent two years with a man without knowing he was capable of this level of violence? How could anyone do this to someone they love? How could he not have known? How could anyone do this to anyone? How could he have not recognized that Tyler was a monster? How—how could this have happened? He should have seen this coming.*

Wren could feel the shock that this whole thing was an attack on him personally. He had suspected it. Maybe he had even known it on some level. The message on his wall was pretty clear, but he hadn't wanted to admit it to himself because, really, this was crazy. What was it about him that attracted people that wanted to attack him?

"Now we need to figure out who would do this and if this is an isolated incident or if there has been other stuff going on you might not have noticed," Johnson said to Wren gently into his stunned silence.

*Or was it something Wren had done? Did he cause this monster to develop in Tyler? Did he destroy Tyler's life and his?*

*It must be all his fault.*

*There must have been something he could have done—should have done—to prevent this from happening. There must have been a way to stop it before it started.*

"I don't believe this is an isolated issue but I really can't say who's doing this," Aiden said, filling the silence.

Wren knew they needed to answer the police questions and work with them but he was too overwhelmed to talk. His mind was caught in memories from his past.

"You see, this is hardly the first weird thing that's happened to us recently." Aiden continued. "We've even made a few other police reports."

*Maybe he should never have tried to leave. He wondered if maybe Tyler was right and they were meant to be together. He wondered if he should have tried harder to make the relationship work, make Tyler happy. When Tyler was happy, things were pretty good.*

*Wren recalled times, especially at the beginning before they moved in together when they'd been great together. Or even times later, especially after a fight, Tyler could be so sweet and caring. Sometimes they had been so in sync it felt like they were just two halves of one whole. He needed Tyler. Why he hadn't tried harder to fight for him?*

Both officers nodded in a sort of go on type of way so Aiden did. Neither officer seemed surprised when Aiden told them Wren had only changed his cellular number last week and that it had taken the number change for the calls to stop. They made Aiden go out to his car to get the notes from his glove box that had accumulated over the past few weeks. They hadn't stopped since they'd gone to the police, if anything, they were showing up even more often. They had also taken on a threatening tone even if there hadn't been any explicit threats yet.

The officers looked at the notes in silence for a moment before whispering something Wren couldn't hear to each other. "You say these have been showing up on your car when it's parked at different places around town?" McDougall confirmed.

*Sure, things hadn't been great near the end. He hadn't been happy but sometimes relationships were hard. Who just leaves? What did that say about him that he had never tried to fight for Tyler? At least Tyler hadn't just given up on them.*

"Ya." Aiden nodded. "Even sometimes when I hadn't planned to go somewhere ahead of time. Like last week, traffic coming home from downtown was bad because some truck tried to drive over the High Level Bridge and got stuck. At the last second, I stopped to get dinner downtown before trying to make it the rest of the way home. When I came out of the restaurant, one of the notes was waiting for me. No one could have known I'd be there.

"And that's not the only thing. Things have been happening to my car. In the last few months my car has been keyed at my apartment and had the tires slashed in front of my parents' house." Aiden proceeded to tell the officers about the details of both incidents.

*The ever-present heart monitor continued.*

*Beep.*

*Beep.*

*Beep.*

*No, that was wrong. Tyler had hurt him. That wasn't okay. No matter what he might have done.*

Johnson looked more and more concerned as Aiden continued to talk and Wren felt a sinking feeling grow in his chest watching her face change. He didn't like that she wasn't maintaining her serious cop face. There was just no way that wasn't a bad sign.

"The thing is that since all this started Wren and I have been trying to figure out who'd do this and we can't think of anyone," Aiden continued.

*Beep.*

*Beep.*

*Beep.*

*Wren slowly forced his eyes open and looked around him and felt tears slide down his cheek because he was in the hospital. It hadn't been a dream. His tears were tears of relief but part of him knew they were also tears of sadness because he wasn't with Tyler. He tried to roll over onto his side to curl up into a ball.*

*Tyler didn't like to see him cry, and he had learned how to hide his tears. But he couldn't roll over to hide. Everything hurt.*

"What about past boyfriends?" Johnson asked.

Wren laughed weakly. Wren liked her for just being straight up with the question and not acting weird. She wouldn't ignore their case just because they were gay. He was happy there was at least one officer that was taking this seriously.

*It was like the pain pushed the reboot button on his brain. Suddenly everything seemed crystal clear.*

"I don't really have any recent ex's," Aiden said shaking his head again. "The last guy I dated was over a year ago and he was an asshole but he wouldn't do this. The reason we broke up was because he was cheating on me… with more than one guy. I'm pretty sure he couldn't care less that I had finally started dating again."

*Yes, he still didn't fully understand why this had happened to him but the why didn't matter. Not really.*

"Don't worry about whether you think they'd do this to you or not, just go through anyone, girl or guy, who was interested in you and might have felt rejected. This might not even be someone you have dated," McDougall interjected.

"Then how am I supposed to know who it could be?" Aiden said throwing his arms in the air in exasperation. Aiden was willing to talk about everything or least everything Aiden knew about—he didn't know about Wren's past.

Guilt gnawed at Wren. He hadn't had the courage to tell Aiden about Tyler, yet.

*He was just so sad. And not because he wasn't with Tyler. No, he was sad because everything he thought they'd had hadn't been real—couldn't have been real. That hadn't been love, not for either of them. No matter how many times Tyler had said the words.*

*Love wasn't hurting the person you claim to love. Love wasn't constant apologies and forgiveness. Love wasn't selfish or blind devotion, or even always putting the other person's happiness above your own.*

"What about with you?" Johnson said to Wren, bringing Wren back into the conversation. "Any ex-boyfriends or guys who are interested in becoming a boyfriend and might be jealous of your relationship with Aiden? Given the note upstairs, I think it's more likely someone from your past than from his."

*Love wasn't about control or giving up more and more parts of yourself. No, if Tyler could do what he'd just done, then that wasn't love. And Wren couldn't love someone who wanted to change him and would beat him down with words and actions until he hardly recognized himself anymore.*

*Love didn't make you feel as though you had lost your soul.*

"Umm, no, or none I think could have caused the problems here." Wren gripped Aiden's hand.

Wren wanted to cry. Was the break-in his fault, too?

He took a deep breath. Guilt and terror consumed him. What he was about to admit, what he was about to tell Aiden next might change everything. He also felt guilty because he hadn't said anything yet. Even worse, if his worst fears were true than all of this, everything that had happened to them was his fault. "I have a crazy ex- that I could totally see doing something like this. I mean, I can't really because it seems absurd that anyone would do this but I've been horribly surprised by him before, so.... But he lives in Toronto. Plus, I think he is still in jail."

*Wren was also angry, angry, angry with himself. How had he given so much of himself up without a fight? He'd always been willing to fight the good fight, unwilling to put up with crap from anyone. And yet, here he was in the hospital and he still didn't even know what sign or signal he had missed. How could he possibly trust himself with anyone again when he didn't even know how he could have avoided things going wrong with Tyler? Maybe he needed to be alone forever.*

*Beep.*

*Beep.*

*Beep.*

# Chapter 32
## Aiden

Of course, the police asked questions.

Aiden wanted to ask questions but he let the police take the lead and just sat there and listened while Wren used an almost unnaturally calm voice to tell the officers about how he had spent almost two years in a romantic relationship with Tyler Rose. He explained Tyler had seemed like a good boyfriend; however, in retrospect, Tyler exhibited controlling behaviours, which isolated Wren from his friends and family. Within a year of starting to date Tyler, he had completely stopped talking to everyone else in his life. He had quit everything but work and spent the rest of his time with Tyler.

Aiden thought about the period, a few years ago, when Lucy had complained she never heard from Wren anymore and couldn't ever seem to talk to him for more than five minutes when they did manage to connect. Suddenly that made so much more sense.

Wren admitted he hadn't returned to Edmonton the entire two years they were together despite being close to his mother. He also had discouraged his mother from visiting, explaining he was too busy. It hadn't been a lie, per se, he had felt like he was too busy. It was only after he realized he was only busy with Tyler.

Wren told the police officers about how they had started fighting more and more. It started with Tyler storming out of the apartment. But their fights had quickly progressed to Tyler yelling and then throwing things.

Wren talked about an argument when Tyler had thrown Wren's favourite coffee cup against the wall near where Wren had been standing. The cup had exploded and pieces of the cup had hit Wren and cut his arm. It wasn't until after everything was over that he realized Tyler never broke anything of his own during the fights. Instead, seeming to react in blind frustration, he would destroy Wren's favourite things, especially those things Wren had received from other people in his life.

Wren explained how things were always better for a while after Tyler got really upset, but then, something would set him off and Tyler would get angry again. Looking back, he could see it was a cycle but while it was happening to him it had seemed both completely normal and totally insane.

Aiden felt his heart breaking. With every word Wren spoke Aiden's heart broke more and more. He could barely breathe through the pain of hearing Wren's words and he wondered how someone who'd lived through this could ever think he was anything other than incredibly strong.

After a moment of silence, Constable Johnson asked, "When did he start hitting you?"

Wren took a deep breath. "When I tried to leave." He paused again. "Looking back, knowing all the stuff I know now about domestic violence, I think it was inevitable. Except maybe I would have been so conditioned to letting him get away with everything and so dependent on him that it wouldn't have been the deal breaker I always thought it would be.

"Instead, I'd been missing my mother for about two weeks. It was fall and I was thinking about how much my life had changed in the last while—really, since Tyler—and realized I used to be happy but I wasn't anymore. I was sad and lonely. I didn't like my life.

"I realized a big part of the problem was that I was accommodating Tyler too much and it wasn't making me happy. The problem was, I didn't really think he could change to give me the freedom I needed. And really, even if he did, I couldn't trust him anymore. So, I decided to leave." Wren took a shuddering breath and Aiden pulled him closer to him. Aiden practically hurt with the need to make sure Wren knew he wasn't alone anymore, he wasn't back in the clutches of that asshole.

"I figured it might upset him, and I didn't want to be stuck living with him after we broke up," Wren explained after a second to recuperate. "So, I made a plan. I found a new apartment and rented it in secret. I took a day off work without telling him and spent the day packing up all my stuff while he was at work. Then I moved everything into the new place. All that was left was for me to say goodbye.

"The fact that I thought I needed to leave in secret to get away should have warned me it wasn't going to go well but we'd been together for two years. It seemed important to end it in person. I wanted to say sorry and look him in the eye.

"I was waiting for Tyler when he got home. My bag was waiting by the door with my jacket on top. My cell phone was in my jacket pocket. I just planned on telling him I was leaving then walking out the door. I was trying to avoid an argument." Wren looked like he was begging the police officers to understand, to believe him that he wasn't trying to put himself at risk or to cause problems. Aiden wondered if Wren blamed himself, if he thought this was his fault because he didn't somehow know what would happen.

Aiden knew that whatever was coming next would be horrible. He wanted to scream and cover his ears. The impulse was so strong he felt himself start to lift his hands. It was almost as if part of him believed if he didn't hear about what Tyler had done, then Wren wouldn't have had to go through it, but he knew that wasn't true. And Aiden wanted to know everything about Wren, even the times when things went horribly wrong.

"He came home from work at his normal time," Wren continued his story. "He noticed right away my stuff was gone. I told him I had decided to end our relationship and was moving out. I tried to explain I didn't think I could be what he needed. I apologized and said it was my fault.

"That was when he yelled that I couldn't leave. He told me leaving was a mistake I would regret. I stayed calm, said I didn't want to fight. Then I tried to walk out the door. Before I even made it to the door, he grabbed me by the arm and dragged me into the bedroom. He is bigger and stronger than me. I mean, look at me, I'm not tiny but I'm by no means a big guy. He probably had at least fifty pounds on me and most of that was muscle.

"I tried but I couldn't get free. I asked—begged him to let me go. Then he hit me. I ended up on the ground and tried to crawl away. That is when he kicked me. He kicked me in the head once and I put my arm up to protect my face. He kicked me again, and I heard my arm crack. While I cradled my arm to my chest, crying in pain, he kicked me in the head again."

Aiden couldn't breathe. It hurt to just listen to the story. How could this happen?

"The next thing I remember he was standing over me wearing a new shirt. He was completely calm, as if nothing had happened. He explained he was going out to eat dinner. He instructed me to clean myself up so I was presentable. He said when he got back, I should apologize to him for saying I would leave and tomorrow we would go get my things. As he was walking toward the door he turned, looked at me, and without raising his voice or even sounding angry, he said he would kill me if I tried to leave him again. I believed him."

The room was silent as Wren finished speaking. Aiden felt himself gripping Wren's hand. He was desperate to hold on to him. He knew this had happened a while ago but he could have died. Wren could have died right there, alone on the floor, and Aiden never would have reconnected with him. They never would have gotten to know each other or shared their first kiss. They never would have made love.

He could have died.

Wren looked over at Aiden and wiped a tear off his cheek and that was when Aiden realized he had been crying. And why not? That was possibly the worst story he'd ever heard.

Aiden looked at Wren in amazement. He'd just had to hear the story. Wren had lived through everything.

And he'd thought Wren was strong before.

# Chapter 33
## Wren

Wren took a deep breath. That hadn't been so bad. Every time he told the story it got easier. Admitting what a failure he had been wasn't ever easy. He didn't think it ever would be, but this time had been both better and worse.

It was worse because he was telling police again. They had helped him but they had been there when he was at his worst.

But it was better because Aiden was there too. Once he'd started talking Aiden pulled him into his side and held him tight. It was hard to get pulled into memories of Tyler when he could feel Aiden's arms anchoring him in the present.

Knowing Aiden was hearing these words for the first time made him feel conflicted but not necessarily bad. He felt guilty because he was only telling Aiden now and under these circumstances. But it was also such a relief, especially since Aiden wasn't pushing him away.

Maybe Aiden didn't understand it was possibly all his fault?

Instead, Aiden kept pulling Wren in, holding on to him like he might never let go. Wren wanted to laugh. He knew he was already crying but suddenly Wren felt certain he could handle anything because he really wasn't alone anymore. The weight of Tyler's actions didn't seem so heavy now that Wren knew he could share that weight with Aiden.

"I know it is difficult to talk about but since it may relate to the current situation, I need to ask, what happened next?" McDougall asked.

"Tyler left. I was alone in the apartment, finally, but I was in more pain than I had ever been in before. I was nauseous and dizzy. I couldn't stand and crawling seemed impossible because my arm was on fire. But I also figured it was life or death and I needed to get to my phone—which was by the door—and call for help or I was dead. I'd die of my injuries or shock. And if I somehow survived the night and didn't escape; Tyler would kill me, maybe not that day, but someday.

"So, I crawled, dragging my broken arm back to the door and called 9-1-1. I told the operator what happened. They sent out an ambulance and the police. The ambulance took me to the hospital and a group of officers stayed at my apartment to catch Tyler. I was later told they caught him when he came back to our apartment. When he walked in, he was whistling like he didn't have a care in the world."

Wren pauses for a second. That always got to him. How could Tyler have cared so much about him staying and yet, cared so little about his welfare?

Wren realized Aiden was almost growling under his breath and Aiden had pulled his body even closer. Wren turned his head into Aiden's neck, breathed in his warm familiar scent and felt himself calm down again. He gave Aiden a quick kiss on the neck before pulling back to continue his story.

"Of course, he denied having done anything wrong. He said I was lying when they told him the charges but he was still taken into custody. It was hard to argue nothing had happened when there were so many bruises and broken bones. They even denied him bail because the severity of my injuries convinced the judge he would be a danger to me if he was released. I never attended court. So, I haven't seen him since he walked out the door to get himself dinner.

"I stayed in Toronto for a while after that but moved to Edmonton at the end of June last year. I haven't been back since."

"Sounds like he's worth looking into even if you last saw him in Ontario," Johnson commented.

Wren shook his head. “I can’t see how this could be him. I mean, he’s in Toronto and, sure he could move, but I never told anyone in Toronto I was returning to Edmonton. I deleted all of my social media accounts to make sure nothing accidentally got to him that way. Plus, the Crown told me he got eighteen months of jail. I don’t see how he could be out yet. He should still be in jail.”

Wren snuggled into Aiden. Now that he had finished telling his story he was exhausted, relieved but exhausted.

McDougall interrupted the quiet that followed Wren’s story. “We can’t say for sure who did this. We will do an investigation but, Wren, if Tyler knew your mother lives in Edmonton, guessing you would come here wouldn’t be too difficult. Just in case this somehow involves Mr. Rose, we will find out where he is. Maybe he’s still in custody like you think but in case he’s not, we will still look.”

“One of us will call you when we know more,” McDougall said as they both stood up. “No matter what, I want you both to be cautious. Until we catch whoever is doing this, you should both be cautious. What happened in this house is serious and might signal whoever is behind these acts is moving to more aggressive behaviour. If this is Mr. Rose, he has already demonstrated a willingness to harm you. Do not give him another opportunity.”

McDougall handed Wren and Aiden each one of his business cards. The cards were somewhat worn and soft to the touch. Wren idly wondered how long they’d been in his wallet.

“My cell phone and my office number are both on the card. If anything else happens, call me directly. You know what? Even if you just notice something odd, call me. Let’s err on the side of caution from now on.”

# Chapter 34
## Aiden

At first, he wasn't sure what woke him. They hadn't gotten back to his house and then back into bed until approaching nine o'clock. So, still groggy from having not slept enough and then having to deal with—everything, Aiden didn't register that anything was wrong for a few moments. He lay quietly in the shaded room wondering what time it was. Had he slept at all?

They'd gotten into bed so late that they had discussed whether it was worth trying to go back to sleep or whether they should just drink more coffee and get up for the day. They decided with nothing else to do and the exhausting emotions of the early morning jumbling around their heads, sleeping or at least resting seemed like a good idea.

Wren had been antsy and tense when they had first gotten into bed. He'd tried to apologize for not telling Aiden about his asshole ex- sooner but Aiden wouldn't hear it. Wren had done nothing wrong.

Eventually Aiden had told Wren to roll over and he'd given him a relaxing massage until his muscles were pliant under him and Wren had finally drifted off to sleep.

Except, Aiden realized Wren wasn't sleeping calmly now. He rolled over and rubbed his hand up and down Wren's back as he registered that the noise that had woken him was Wren whimpering.

"No, no, please," Wren begged in a tiny terrified voice. He was still asleep but his body was shaking and he'd curled up in on himself.

"Wren, baby, please wake up," Aiden whispered, rubbing Aiden's arm and back. "Please Wren, come back to me. You're safe."

At first Wren didn't react. He continued to shake and beg for mercy. Aiden felt tears well up in his eyes.

He wanted to rage and scream in anger. How could life be so unfair that not only had Wren had to live through that nightmare but now he had to relive it in his dreams?

Aiden wondered how long it had been going on. Was this the first time? Or had he just been lucky that this hadn't happened any of the other times Wren had stayed over?

Aiden thought back to all of the times when Wren had said he couldn't stay the night and had looked so sad. Was this why? Was he afraid of the nightmares?

The courage it must have taken Wren the first time he agreed to stay over astounded Aiden. Wren amazed him more every day.

Suddenly, Wren's arm shot out, hitting Aiden across the face. The sudden pain surprised a shout out of Aiden and he fell backwards, landing on the floor with a thud and a grunt of surprise.

Wren lurched into an upright seated position. His eyes were blown wide, and he was panting.

"What?" he said before looking around and noticing Aiden, standing beside the bed with his hand to his cheek where Wren had struck him. "Oh, my god! Did I hurt you? Are you okay? Aiden, I am so sorry. Oh god!"

Wren pushed himself back away, which was the last thing Aiden wanted. He moved to follow Wren who scrambled away until his back was against the wall, as far away from Aiden as he could get.

"Oh, god! I hurt you! I shouldn't be here. I need to go. I need to get away from you! I—"

"No, no, no," Aiden interrupted. "It's my fault. You did nothing wrong. You were having a nightmare, and I was trying to wake you up. I shouldn't have been so close. I should have realized I'd scared you."

Wren hugged his legs into his chest. It took a moment for Aiden to realize Wren was shaking and sobbing quietly.

He couldn't stand this. He needed to be touching Wren. Aiden moved across the bed. He crawled slowly to make sure Wren had a chance to tell him to stop or move away but he didn't. Instead he kept crying, these soft muffled sobs which broke Aiden's heart even more.

Why had Wren learned to cry so quietly? Who was he hiding it from? Was it Tyler who taught him this to do this? Or had he learned earlier from his father when he was a kid?

When he was within touching distance, Aiden whispered, "Can I hug you?" Instead of answering, Wren threw himself at Aiden, knocking them both over onto their sides.

Aiden wrapped his arms around Wren and held him tight. Wren's body shook harder as he surrendered to the tears. Aiden whispered comforting nonsense and swayed back and forth.

He was happy that they were together and he was able to help Wren through this. What would Wren have done if he'd been on his own? The question haunted Aiden.

Aiden never wanted Wren to be alone again. He didn't want him to have to suffer through this, through anything else alone.

That was when Aiden knew he couldn't pretend this was anything other than it was. He was completely, irrefutably in love with Wren. He didn't just care about Wren. He wasn't falling in love. No, he was already there, the fall was over. The question was answered.

Aiden loved Wren—was in love with him.

Part of him was shocked by the force of this realization. The rest of him knew this wasn't anything new. Aiden had loved Wren for a long time, maybe as long as he'd known him. Zane was right. Once you wonder if you are falling in love, you already have.

But he couldn't worry about that right now.

Wren needed him so he would do everything he could, everything in his power, to help him.

"Shh, you are all right," Aiden murmured into Wren's hair. "It was just a dream."

"He was hurting you," Wren gasped between sobs. "Normally, he is just hurting me. I'm just remembering what happened—or maybe I'm back there because I never got away, or—or maybe he finds me. But this time he was hurting you, too."

"It's okay I'm here. I'm safe. You're safe."

"But you're not safe. I hurt you. And what if he is the one that is doing this? I thought I got away but what if I didn't? What if he is coming after you now?"

"We don't know who is doing this," Aiden pointed out. He moved them both to sit up. He wanted to look at Wren in the eyes. "We need to let the police do their job."

"If he hurts you. I'll never forgive myself." Wren grabbed onto Aiden and pulled him in for a kiss. The kiss deepened until they both needed to breathe, except breathing wasn't as important as their kiss. They were both here. They were both safe and this connection between them was the most important thing in their lives.

# Chapter 35
## Wren

Wren broke off the kiss. Panting he stared into Aiden's eyes. He could see the same desperation he felt reflected back at him. And compassion and—and something else, something more.

But the guilt and fear he had been feeling since the moment he had woken up hadn't disappeared. It wasn't just the nightmare. It wasn't just the fear because of what had happened the night before. Whether it was Tyler or someone new, someone was after him and there was apart of him that wasn't sure whether he could deal with this again. The fear was there even through the numbness of his tears.

But nothing could take away his shame because he knew he had to live with the fact that just like before, he had ignored all the signs and let this happen to him.

How many times had Tyler hurt him in little ways before he'd even tried to get away? He'd willingly destroyed friendships and lost opportunities without even thinking. He'd stayed. He'd chosen to stay for so, so long.

Now, here he was back again, sitting around waiting for the other shoe to drop after ignoring the notes, the calls, and all the other strange things that were happening to them. How many things had he missed? How much sooner could this have been stopped if only he had paid attention? If he was not such a fucking idiot?

He pulled Aiden back in for another kiss, this one even more desperate than the one before. He tried to inhale Aiden. He tried to consume him. He wanted to take Aiden inside his body and hold him there so he would never be alone again.

"I need you," Wren moaned into Aiden's mouth.

Aiden moaned his agreement. He pulled Wren even tighter against him, grinding their pelvises against each other as they continued to make out. But it wasn't enough for Wren.

"I need you," he repeated before moving to pull down Aiden's underwear. Aiden was mirroring his movements and pushing Wren's underwear out of the way as well.

Quickly, and yet still so slowly, they knelt on the bed, naked before one another. They stayed like that for a few seconds, just staring at each other, Wren could see Aiden's chest moving up and down as he panted. He was so gorgeous. How could anyone be so gorgeous?

Aiden's cock stood straight ahead, ready for whatever they would do next. Aiden's arm muscles flexed as if he was preparing to move them, to pull Wren into his arms. But he didn't move. While his eyes were hot with desire, Wren saw patience too and something else, something more. Aiden would wait and take Wren's lead.

Wren didn't deserve this amazing and beautiful man. How could he possibly deserve to be here after everything he had done, after all the mistakes he had made?

Patience was not what Wren needed right now. Wren was desperate for Aiden to consume him, to fill him.

"I need you."

Aiden shifted forward and wrapped his arms back around Wren and pulled him back in for another kiss. His arms moved up, so his hands were in Wren's hair, pulling him in closer, holding him in his arms and keeping him safe.

Wren wrapped his arms around Aiden and held him tight. He never wanted to let him go. He might not deserve Aiden but he wanted him anyway.

Aiden moved his hands to play with Wren's nipples and run up and down Wren's spine. Wren moved his hips, rubbing their naked cocks together. He spit into his hand and fisted their cocks together. Continuing to move his hips back and forth, he stroked them against one another. Precum leaked from them both, adding lubricant to his fist. He felt as much as heard Aiden groan in excitement.

Except it was still not enough.

"I need you. Please," Wren begged into Aiden's mouth.

"I'm right here," Aiden said as he moved to grab the lube and a condom out of the bed-side table. He fell onto his back and looked up at Wren. Aiden put lube on his fingers and moved his hand to prepare himself.

Except it felt wrong. Wren needed something else. He still felt so alone. He still felt so empty.

Wren needed something more.

"No, I need YOU." Wren said, and he moved so he was on his hands and knees with his ass facing Aiden. "I need to feel you. I need you to fill me up and make me feel not so lost," Wren begged. *I need you to take away this guilt that I cannot escape, even if it is just for one moment,* Wren continued silently.

# Chapter 36
## Aiden

Aiden felt a groan escape him as the blood rushed south and, somehow, he became harder. He sat up and stared at Wren. His ass, his beautiful hole was peeking out from between his ass cheeks. He was on display for Aiden and it was most definitely the most gorgeous thing Aiden had ever seen. If you could go blind from beauty, then this would surely do it for him.

Aiden had been dreaming of fucking Wren since... possibly forever. Not that he was complaining about their sex life to date because he wasn't. He loved having Wren top him. Wren knew exactly how to make him beg for it.

But this—this would be really good too. God, did he ever want to feel the grip of Wren's anus around his cock. He wanted to fill Wren up and feel him stretch around him. He wanted to pound into him and force the same pleasure on Wren that he had received.

But only if Wren was certain. Aiden wouldn't be able to live with himself if there were any regrets.

Wren had never seemed to want this before. He'd, in fact, shied away from even having Aiden even finger or play with him.

"Are you sure?" Aiden asked. "Maybe we should wait until another day, wait until the shock and scare of having your house broken into was more than a few hours ago."

Aiden didn't want Wren doing this for the wrong reasons. Aiden never wanted Wren to regret any part of their relationship, especially now that he'd heard about Tyler.

Wren sat back up and wrapped his hands into Aiden's hair and held him steady and explored his mouth. Aiden opened himself up to Wren and gave him everything. The kiss continued and Aiden took everything Wren had to give him and gave just as much in return. Their tongues met and explored each other's mouth. Wren pulled on Aiden's lip with his teeth before pushing his tongue back into Aiden's mouth.

As they lost themselves in the kiss, Aiden felt torn open. He felt exposed. He felt as though every part of him was out there for Wren to see, to explore. Except instead of making him scared this made him feel cared for. It made him feel loved.

Except this wasn't supposed to be about Aiden. This wasn't about caring for him or making him feel loved. This was about Wren, and Aiden would make sure he felt all the love Aiden had to give.

Aiden took control of the kiss. He slid his hand up to support Wren's cheek and battled with Wren's tongue. He entered Wren's mouth and explored before pulling back, then pushing back in. In and out, mimicking the movements his cock would make soon.

Some time later—maybe it was only moments, maybe it was hours—Aiden pulled back and looked down into Wren's eyes. Wren blinked slowly, drunk on his arousal.

"If you want me to stop, if you need me to slow down. No matter what, you let me know and I will stop. Even if I'm already inside you," Aiden said seriously once Wren appeared to have regained some of his brain cells.

Wren nodded his understanding and Aiden felt the leash he'd been keeping on his desire slip.

Aiden felt a slow predatory smile spread across his face. Yes, this would be fun. He leaned forward to whisper in Wren's ear. "I've imagined sliding my cock into your tight ass. I've been stroking myself off imagining my hand was your hole for years. Are you excited to be finally giving that to me? Do you want that? Do you want me to push my cock into your tight hole?"

Wren wriggled against Aiden in anticipation. "Yes," he breathed out.

Aiden used all the tricks he'd learned during their time together to make Wren go out of his mind with pleasure. Using his mouth and fingers he touched Wren everywhere, until Aiden was sure Wren was open and ready to accept him without pain or discomfort.

"Now I get to make my dreams reality," Aiden whispered as he removed his fingers from inside Wren and moved down so he was right above Wren's straining cock.

"Yes, please, please, please," Wren repeated in a husky, almost incoherent voice.

"So polite." Aiden smiled before leaning down and engulfing Wren's cock in his mouth.

"Yes," Wren moaned. "Oh, yes, but more—more, please. I need you," he begged, jumping his hips up and splaying his legs wide to give Aiden access to his ass but Aiden continued to only suck Wren's cock. Every time Wren came close to coming Aiden would back off or slow down.

Wren's groans of frustrated disappointment were music to Aiden's ears. Aiden released Wren's cock, licked his lips and looked down at Wren. He was spread out before him like some kind of sexual sacrifice. His hair was messed and sweaty. His eyes were glazed, and his lips were red and swollen from their kisses. His nipples were angry and red, and moved up and down with each panting breath. His cock was as hard as granite, swollen and wet from Aiden's mouth. It looked so good Aiden was almost sorry he wouldn't experience that amazing cock in his own ass this time.

Aiden grabbed the lube off the bed where he'd tossed it earlier. With the lube still in his hand he leaned forward and kissed Wren one more time, his lips too inviting to ignore a second longer.

Wren hugged Aiden tighter and kissed him back fiercely. He then pulled back, grabbed the lube and condom out of Aiden's hand.

"Please fuck me," he begged once more before putting on the condom on Aiden and liberally drizzling lube over it. "I want you to open me up and stick your cock inside me."

"Eager, are you?" Aiden asked with a laugh, leaning forward and kissing and biting Wren's nipples again.

"Yessssss!"

"Don't worry. I've got you. I'll take care of you." Aiden grabbed the lube from Wren and added more to the entrance of Wren's asshole. He laughed again when Wren breathed out a sigh of relief.

But the sighs turned to frustration when Aiden continued to circle Wren's hole rather then pushing his cock inside.

"Just stick them in!" Wren shouted at him after a few more moments of this. He was almost sitting up as he glared down at Aiden. "I'm not a virgin. Please. Enough teasing."

Aiden looked up at Wren and smirked. Now he knew Wren was ready. While Aiden knew Wren was hardly a virgin, Aiden suspected it was worse for Wren than if he was a virgin. Although his body knew the pleasure that could be found in sex, it also had experienced the pain that came with neglect and force. Aiden would never do either of those things. He would never do anything to make Wren doubt he was safe.

He pushed Wren back onto his back. "Put your legs on my shoulders," Aiden instructed.

"Yes, yes!" Wren panted, doing as he was told. "Please. Faster. I need you."

"I'm here," Aiden soothed rubbing his hand up and down Wren's chest. "I'm not leaving."

Aiden locked eyes with Wren and thought, "I love you." Then slowly, ever so slowly, Aiden seated himself into Wren. He held himself there for a moment, panting, enjoying the feeling of Wren's muscles grip his cock.

"You okay, Wren?" Aiden panted.

"Yes, more than. Please, please, please, baby, please fuck me already!"

Aiden thrust his pelvis into Wren's ass as Wren fucked himself back against him. He started slow but sped up moving with more force until their skin slapped together with each stroke.

"You feel so good," Aiden breathed as he leaned forward and gripped Wren's cock in his fist and stroked the leaking cock in time with his thrusts.

"Oh, god, Aiden. I'm gonna come," Wren warned, pulling his mouth away from Aiden's. "I'm gonna come. Fuck! Make me come!"

"Come for me, Wren. Show me how much you love it," Aiden instructed as he sped up his thrusts and the hand on Wren's cock.

Almost on command, Wren came, shooting come all over the bed. As Wren orgasmed Aiden sped up and felt his own orgasm coming as Wren's ass clamped around his cock. Wren slumped back against the bed just as Aiden's orgasm ripped through him. And he came and came and came.

Aiden fell forward on top of Wren. After a few breaths he realized Wren was shaking. He looked at Wren's face and saw tears silently sliding down his face. Aiden shifted his weight and kissed away Wren's tears.

"What's wrong?"

"Nothing, ignore me. It's just..." Wren sobbed, having difficulty breathing enough to speak through his tears. "It's just that I wasn't sure I'd ever be able to do that again."

"But it was okay? We never have to do it again. We can go back to you topping every time," Aiden said with concern. Shit, did he hurt Wren after all?

"No," Wren said as his tears slowed. "No, it was perfect."

Aiden pulled Wren close and hugged him and after a few moments Wren's tears stopped. Aiden secured the base of the condom and gently withdrew his penis. He took the condom off, tied it, and tossed it into the garbage. It landed on the rim, then slid out onto the floor.

"And fail," Aiden said with a tired laugh as he fell onto his stomach, snuggling into Wren's side.

"No part of what we just did can be called a failure."

"I love you," Aiden said looking over at Wren. He was right. It had been perfect. Wren was perfect.

Suddenly, looking into Wren's eyes, Aiden's emotions became too much to hold back. Even if Wren wasn't there yet, Aiden needed him to know how loved he truly was. "I love you, so much."

# Chapter 37
## Wren

Wren blinked at him then sat up and stared at Aiden in shock and amazement. “You what?” he whispered. Had he heard that correctly?

“I love you. I know you might not be ready to say it back but I needed you to know you are loved.”

“You love me?” Wren whispered again. Feeling the words on his lips. They felt true.

“I am in love you.”

“I—I love you too,” Wren said, looking Aiden directly in the eyes, hoping he could see how sincere he was. “I’ve known for a little while actually, but I was so scared.”

“Of what?”

“I’m terrified that this isn’t real like—like it wasn’t real before. Or maybe it’s even worse if it is real because then something could happen and something could take away you from me.”

Aiden hugged Wren into his body and Wren felt himself relax.

“You aren’t alone anymore,” Aiden said, somehow able to understand what Wren was really afraid of. He’d been alone for so long and now he wasn’t anymore. He was terrified of being alone again.

“I’m sorry,” Wren responded, looking over at Aiden.

“For what?” Aiden asked, cupping Wren’s face in his hand and gently kissing him.

"For bursting into tears after sex, for being a spaz," Wren shrugged. "For not admitting I loved you sooner."

"You aren't a spaz and I won't let you apologize for saying you love me. The timing doesn't matter. Nothing else matters when we love each other."

It sounded good but Wren had to admit he was still scared. He had a bad feeling their love alone wouldn't keep them safe.

* * *

It was early afternoon before Wren and Aiden finally got out of bed. They spent the day lazing around watching bad television. Wren tried to avoid thinking about what had happened to his house. Instead, he enjoyed his time with Aiden as much as possible.

And enjoy each other they did. It was as though they had broken a dam when they admitted they were in love. They couldn't get enough of each other, constantly wanting to touch and repeat the words over and over again. Wren felt himself relax into the joy of being in love with someone worthy.

Yes, Aiden was definitely worthy of his love.

The only time he was really forced to face reality was just before dinner time when his mother called and asked him whether she needed to clean his room so he could return home to sleep in his bed that night.

Wren couldn't even imagine going back to his mother's house. He was having trouble thinking of it as his home anymore. That, too, had been taken from him.

So, he told his mom he wasn't ready to go back but promised to come by at some point, maybe on the weekend, to help clean the room. He mused aloud that he'd probably find a hotel room somewhere. His mother wasn't thrilled with that solution. Wren figured she probably wanted him to stay with her where she could keep him safe, but there was no way he would feel safe again in that room, no matter how hard his mom worked to clean it.

"You should just stay with me," Aiden said, as soon as Wren hung up the phone. "You've been spending almost half of your nights sleeping here, anyway. A hotel would be a waste of money.

Wren had to admit Aiden wasn't wrong but still he hesitated. "What if I have more nightmares?"

"Then I definitely want you here." Aiden said the words which such confidence Wren had to believe him.

Wren wanted to stay with Aiden. For about a million reasons he would prefer staying with Aiden over having to stay in a hotel. Except...

Moving in, even if it was because he had nowhere else to go, felt like a much bigger deal than when he was just sleeping over. They hadn't been dating that long. Wasn't it too early to be moving in together?

Aiden was right, he had been staying over more than half the time over the past few weeks. And it had been wonderful. He loved spending his nights cuddled in Aiden's arms. Things were great between him and Aiden. Their relationship felt more solid and more real than just about anything else in his life.

What if having Wren living with Aiden, even temporarily, ruined that?

What if he put Aiden's seemingly infinite patience to the test living together? What if Aiden decided he couldn't handle Wren's crazy work schedule and his ongoing neurosis? His life right now could drive anyone crazy.

What if Aiden got angry?

No! Wren stopped that thought in its tracks. Aiden is not Tyler. Aiden will never be Tyler. Aiden is NOT Tyler and never will be. Wren repeated this thought to himself over and over until he felt the fear of history repeating itself leave his body.

He trusted Aiden. Trust wasn't really the problem. He knew Aiden would be great to live with but that didn't mean they were ready. It didn't mean he was ready.

Wren agreed to stay. It made the most sense. What reasons could he use to explain paying money he didn't really have to stay at a hotel? But

Wren decided he'd have to look for an apartment to rent right away. That way it would be temporary, and he might even be able to get out of Aiden's hair by the end of the month, maybe even sooner if he was lucky.

After all, there was no way Aiden would want him around longer than that.

Also, he didn't want to impose. What if Aiden had only offered because he had nowhere else to stay and didn't really want him here, at least not yet? Maybe living together for real was something they could consider sometime in the future. Sometime… later, when they were both ready.

Four days later, Wren had to admit most of his fears hadn't materialized, at least not yet. He really enjoyed living with Aiden and he would be very sad when it was time for him to leave.

Wren was comfortable being around Aiden. They were always so in sync. Even after a stressful or long shift at work, it was really nice to come home to Aiden or even his empty apartment.

The apartment building was also fairly quiet, which was great for sleeping during the day and catching up after a night shift. He couldn't complain about the location since it was central and close to the university where he'd be going to school starting in September. Maybe he could consider moving in with Aiden sooner rather than later… but not yet. A few more months on their own was a good idea.

Right?

That evening after Wren's morning nap, run through the river valley, and shower to wash off the sweat; Aiden returned home from work to suggest they go out for dinner.

"I had a super stressful drive home from work today and I absolutely don't want to have to go get groceries or cook," Aiden announced. "Let's walk to Whyte Ave and find something to eat. It would be nice to go for a walk anyway. I spent all day behind my desk today looking at the sunshine and wishing I could go outside to enjoy it."

Wren had agreed, despite being tired from his run. He knew the more active he was after a night shift, the more likely it was for him to sleep through the night. He wanted his schedule to flip back around so he could work days again.

"What happened?" Wren asked as they were exiting the apartment.

"This fucking car must have been driving a similar route to mine because I kept seeing him and he was a complete menace on the road. He almost hit me at least three times before I could get away from him. Even then I could have sworn I saw him again just as I was pulling into the lane at the back to park my car. Except, I can't be sure it was the same person or just the same type of car since I didn't get the license plate when I was pulling in to park."

"But you got it before?"

"Ya, after he almost caused an accident when he practically stopped in the middle of the road and forced me to slam on my breaks to avoid hitting him. I memorized the license plate so I could report it to police if something happened. He almost side swiped me and nearly rear-ended me, too. Luckily, I was watching out for him like a hawk for the rest of the drive after he'd almost caused the first accident or we would've gotten into one later for sure. Some people shouldn't be allowed to drive."

"You said he. You saw the driver?" Wren asked, wondering, fearing this latest thing might be connected to everything else.

"I don't know for sure if it was a man," Aiden admitted. "I think I saw short dark hair but it could have been a girl. I didn't see a face."

"You think this is connected to everything else?"

"I don't know, but if it is, they've upped their game again because if I was a worse driver or hadn't been paying as much attention, I'd definitely have been in a car accident today. We weren't going fast enough for any serious damage but it still would have hurt."

Wren shivered. For the past few days he'd been able to forget all the creepy and weird stuff going on. He'd still remember when he thought about why he wasn't staying at his mother's but it wasn't constantly on his mind or anything. It was scary to think whoever was doing all this was still out there and might become more aggressive.

During dinner, Wren knew he wasn't the only one thinking about what this all could mean. He felt like there was a black cloud hanging over both him and Aiden and he wasn't sure if it was an ominous prediction of what was to come or just a reflection of their sour mood. Either way, they were both pretty quiet, and they ended up taking home most of their food—neither had much of an appetite.

Wren hated it. He didn't want his bullshit to be raining all over Aiden. He didn't want him hurt or even having to deal with this shit. Whatever the fuck it was. Whoever the fuck it was.

"This is bullshit," Wren yelled aloud when they were only a couple blocks from the apartment.

"What?" Aiden asked, completely confused. He blinked a few times, obviously also caught up in his own thinking.

"All of this—it's bullshit." Wren was gesticulating wildly and knew he probably looked like a crazy person but he'd had enough. He'd discovered his line in the sand and this was it. It was not acceptable for Aiden to get hurt. "The notes and calls were bad enough. What happened to my room at my mom's was completely insane but some dickhead trying to drive you off the road or hit you with their car is too much. That's it. I'm done."

"Face me like—like a fucking man!" Wren shouted at the empty street. "If you want me, you've got to actually talk to me!"

"Oh, honey," Aiden whispered, wrapping his arms around Wren. Aiden had looked upset before but as Wren spoke devastation consumed his face. "It's okay. I'm okay."

They stood there, hugging each other for several moments, just feeling the comfort of being together, before continuing their walk home. The mood was once more subdued. Wren felt exhaustion consume him. He didn't have the energy for this. His run earlier, the nightshift, everything else was easy compared to the emotional toll of the mysterious threat that was hanging over them.

Right before they got back to the apartment, Wren's phone rang in his pocket. He pulled it out and glanced at the display, fully prepared to ignore whoever was calling him since he didn't really feel up to talking. Except it wasn't a random friend or his mother as expected. The call was from McDougall, the police officer they'd met after the break in. He stopped and showed Aiden the display on his phone before answering the call.

"Uh, hello. This is Wren speaking."

"Hello, Wren. This is Constable McDougall. We met July first after someone broke into your mother's house."

"Ya, yes. I remember. What can I do for you?"

"Well, I was hoping you and Aiden, if he is available, could come down to the Southwest Police Station. Constable Johnson and I obtained some information about your case we would like to share with you."

Wren felt himself break into a sweat despite the cool evening breeze. The weight he had been feeling ever since Aiden had come home felt immeasurably heavier. Somehow, he knew this would be bad news.

"Aiden's right here with me. Can we come by right now?" Wren asked, catching Aiden's eye and seeing him nod to confirm he was willing to go talk to the officers right away.

McDougall agreed they were free to meet Aiden and Wren immediately and would be around for at least an hour, giving Wren and Aiden plenty of time to get to the station. As soon as he was off the phone Wren relayed the conversation. Aiden asked what McDougall had wanted to tell them and when Wren had to admit he had no clue, he felt himself becoming increasingly concerned. Why would they want to meet in person? If it was good news or telling them they didn't have any new information, they could've just passed that information on over the phone.

Wren wasn't sure if he wanted to hear what the officers had to say. The exhaustion from before felt increasingly heavy. He knew living in ignorance wouldn't keep him safe but sure felt easier and less scary. He really didn't want to know the boogie man was real.

Too bad pretending nothing was wrong wouldn't keep him and Aiden safe.

While they were cutting through the alley and passing the parking lot in the back on their way to the door, Aiden suddenly stopped. “Fuck!” Aiden let out an exasperated sigh and turned on his heel to walk toward his parking spot where his car was parked as usual. Wren looked at the car and didn’t see anything wrong at first and wasn’t sure what Aiden was going on about. Then he saw the piece of paper which someone had tucked under the windshield wiper.

Fuck, indeed.

# Chapter 38
## Aiden

'THIS IS YOUR LAST CHANCE. HE IS MINE. LEAVE OR I WILL KILL YOU!' The writing was the same as the writing on Wren's bedroom wall and all the other notes. Aiden was certain they were connected. The only difference was the threat was clear this time.

Aiden glanced at Wren and he looked stricken. Aiden put the note back under the windshield wiper, trying to touch it as little as possible. Then he wrapped one arm around Wren before pulling out his cell phone and dialling Constable McDougall.

"I got another note on my car and this one is clearly threatening," Aiden explained as soon as he had identified himself.

"Bring it with you when you come," Constable McDougall instructed before saying goodbye and hanging up.

They were on their way to the police station within five minutes of ending the call.

*I will kill you. I will kill you.* The words repeated inside Aiden's head and he could see them reflected in Wren's eyes. He'd thought the notes were scary before, and they had been, but this was worse. *I will kill you.*

Maybe it wasn't just being threatened. Knowing the police wanted to talk to Wren and him made it worse. What did they want to tell them? The sinking feeling that this was just the start, that Aiden had felt before, had returned but was ten times worse. The call from police, this threat, and his scary drive home—all of it signalled things were getting worse. Aiden worried how much worse it could get.

Aiden glanced at Wren and saw he'd clenched his hands into fists and his skin was pale. Wren didn't deserve this. He'd already gone through enough. Why did he have to go through this again?

"It is not fucking okay whoever is doing this is coming after you!" Wren suddenly broke the heavy silence in the car, reflecting Aiden's recent thoughts. "This is clearly about me. You shouldn't be mixed up in all this."

Aiden didn't agree. He didn't want any of this and he didn't deserve it. But neither did Wren. This wasn't Wren's fault, no matter what the police had to say. Wren was as much or more of a victim than he was. At least this was a first for Aiden.

"Let's wait and see what the officers have to say. Maybe this is all about me and you're the innocent bystander," Aiden pointed out as he took Wren's hand and led him into the station. Wren snorted like he didn't believe it. Aiden said nothing further. There wasn't any point. They were on their way to talk to the police and it sounded like they had information.

Despite having called ahead, Wren and Aiden were forced to wait around for nearly twenty minutes before Constables McDougall and Johnson were available to meet them. They were at least courteous enough to apologize for the wait.

"I left the new note in the car. I didn't want to touch it more than necessary without talking to you. I don't know if it is just Hollywood but on TV, they always use stuff like paper and notes to get fingerprints," Aiden said once they settled into a small conference room after going through a security door and up a set of stairs.

Constable McDougall nodded his head then said, "We can go get the note once we've told you what we've learned so far."

Wren took hold of Aiden's hand and Aiden had to admit he was feeling nervous, more now than before they'd seen the officers. Aiden thought Constable Johnson, especially, did not look like she was about to give them good news. Aiden prayed he was wrong.

Constables Johnson and McDougall exchanged a look. Then Constable Johnson spoke for the first time since they arrived. "When we met a few days ago I said I would look into where Tyler Rose is living. Wren, you thought he might still be in jail in Ontario. It took a while to find the right person who could tell me where he is at the moment."

Constable Johnson paused and took a deep breath. Aiden knew this would be bad. He could feel it in his bones. Aiden glanced over at Wren and saw the blood drain from his face. Obviously, he was having the same premonition Aiden was having. Aiden squeezed Wren's hand to make sure he knew he wasn't alone in this. "Wren, earlier today I learned Tyler isn't in jail or even in Toronto anymore. He followed you and is living in Edmonton."

Constable Johnson told them she hadn't been able to location Tyler to discuss the current situation yet but given the history between Tyler and Wren, he was their prime suspect for the break in at the moment. Constable McDougall added that despite having no clear evidence to tie Tyler to the crimes, they felt they had enough circumstantial evidence for a warrant and were in the process of getting one issued.

Aiden looked over at Wren and watched as Wren's face became increasingly pale. He immediately wrapped his arms around Wren. Holding him close, Aiden felt Wren shake with fear. He was hyperventilating causing him to wheeze, each breath a struggle. Aiden pulled Wren onto his lap and squeezed him with his arms. Aiden could feel Wren's pulse galloping along with his breathing. He tried to show Wren he wasn't alone. When that didn't work, Aiden looked at the officers and asked, "Can you give us a moment?"

Constables Johnson and McDougall nodded. Constable Johnson raised her hands and showed all ten of her fingers before standing up to leave. Aiden nodded in acknowledgment but didn't wait to watch them leave the small conference room before he kissed and whispered to Wren, "You're all right. You are safe. You are not alone. He can't hurt you. You are safe. I have you."

Aiden hugged Wren tightly while he rocked and repeated Wren was not alone and he was safe. It took a while but eventually, his words or his presence penetrated Wren's fear. Wren's breathing slowed.

"Take a deep breath," Aiden instructed, breathing deeply to demonstrate. "That's right. Now, again."

Aiden breathed with Wren, occasionally reminding him he was safe and he was not alone. After a few minutes, Wren was through the worst of his panic attack. He sat up but did not move off Aiden's lap. Aiden continued to rub Wren's back but stopped murmuring in his ear.

"How're you doing?" Aiden asked after a moment of silence.

"Scared," Wren responded. "But better. Thanks. I got caught in my head and for a moment I was back to right after Tyler hurt me."

Wren paused. He looked around the room as if just now noticing the police were no longer there. He gave Aiden a questioning look. "They stepped out when you started to panic. They should be back in a few minutes."

Wren nodded. There was another moment of silence while Wren continued to look around the small interview room. Aiden suspected he was not seeing anything in front of him.

"Tyler promised he would kill me if I tried to leave him again. That was the last thing he told me before he walked out the door to get dinner like it was any other day of the week and he hadn't just threatened me—like he hadn't just broken my arm, or knocked me out and given me a concussion. He said it seriously but without heat as though he was telling me what the weather was outside. The air was full of the coppery smell of my blood and every breath brought me pain. My arm hurt so badly my vision kept blurring and yet, he just looked at me like it was any other moment, any other day, and told me he was going out to get dinner. Then, like an afterthought, he turned around and told me he would kill me if I ever tried to leave him again. How do you not believe that?

"And now he's threatened to kill you, too!"

Aiden hugged Wren to his chest again, let him hear his heart beating and feel the rise and fall of his breath but said nothing. He let a moment of quiet sit between them before Wren continued to speak, “In that moment I was sure I would die. I was sure he would kill me. But I knew I needed to get to a hospital and decided I would rather die because I left him than die because I stayed.

“But after he went to jail and I recovered physically, I thought maybe he would move on. I mean, sending him to jail was pretty final. I didn’t talk to him again. Although, he tried to call me once, in May of last year, two months after being sentenced to jail.

“I was sitting in my kitchen in Toronto. It was bright and sunny—a beautiful spring day. I had been out walking earlier, enjoying the beautiful weather, and for the first time since he had hurt me, I was feeling really happy. It was spring, and I felt hopeful, as though my life was about to have a rebirth too. I suppose I was right but not in the way I thought.

“So, I’m standing in my kitchen, drinking water and looking at a bird outside my apartment window when the phone rang. I answered it. An automated voice told me there was a collect call from an inmate by the name of Rose, Tyler, calling from the Ontario Correctional Institute. The call would be subject to recording and I should press 1 if I was willing to accept the call. For a moment I stood frozen in shock. The voice asked me again to press 1 if I accepted the call. I snapped out of it and hung up the phone.

“That is when I decided to move back to Edmonton.” Wren took a deep breath, then climbed off Aiden’s lap and walked around the small room. He moved like he couldn’t sit still any longer, like he had too much energy and not moving was impossible.

“My mom had been trying to get me to return to Edmonton since she first visited me in the hospital. It had taken her two days to get out to Toronto and she was frantic. I was still in the hospital because they were worried about internal bleeding. Once she arrived, she didn’t leave my side until a week after they released me. I had to beg her to go. I felt caged in and needed space.

"She agreed to leave but repeatedly tried to convince me to come back to Edmonton. What did I have left in Toronto? she asked. I told her I was working. I told her I had the apartment. I told her I was in therapy through victim services in Toronto and if I left that would end. I was also registered into an MCAT prep course in May and June and needed to take the course and write the exam in July. She tried to convince me I could do everything in Edmonton. But I felt that by moving back home to my mom's I would be admitting I'd failed—or was running away. It would be as though he had won. I really didn't want him to win. I couldn't stand letting Tyler control me anymore. And I felt safe. He was in jail.

"Or at least I felt safe until he calls me out of the blue. From fucking jail! So, I ran. It took a month to get everything figured out. Then I packed, shipped everything, and returned to Edmonton. Really, by coming back so suddenly, it screwed everything up. I quit therapy against my counsellor's advice, and I missed my original MCAT writing date. But my mom was right. I didn't bother getting another counsellor, but I had no problem rescheduling my MCAT course and test date. Things were so much better once I got here.

"While I was in Toronto, I thought I wanted to stay there. I kept telling myself 'this is where my life is now and I want to stay' but I was lying to myself. Tyler had taken my life in Toronto away from me while we were dating and then he had killed any last remaining reasons to stay when he had hurt me.

"I didn't have any friends left, or at least none I spoke to regularly. So, I didn't tell anyone where I was going. I just quit my job in Toronto, broke my lease, and left. I disappeared from Toronto. I was scheduled to go back to court to testify at his trial but he pleaded guilty at the last minute so I cancelled my plane tickets and stayed here. I had to call the crown prosecutor to find out what his sentence was.

"I was in Edmonton and he wouldn't know where I was. I felt safe again. I couldn't see why he would still want me. I was clearly done with him. And he had already had all that time in jail to get over it. We were only together for about two years. That is a long time, but it has been almost that long since I left him. Who hangs on like that?"

"Some people get obsessed," Constable Johnson said from the doorway. She and Constable McDougall moved into the room and sat down across from Aiden where they had been seated before. "Some people's actions don't make sense. Maybe he has some kind of diagnosable mental disorder and he is obsessive or experiences delusions. Maybe he was abused as a child or watched his mother get abused and he thinks this is what relationships are supposed to be like. Who knows? Once we catch him and stop him, the psychologists can try to figure him out. But really, for you, right now, it doesn't matter why. What matters is he somehow figured out where you were and followed. What matters is he hasn't given up on having a relationship with you. What matters is, based on the information we got from his previous Probation Officer in Toronto and his current Probation Officer in Edmonton, he is still obsessed with you."

Constable McDougall continued where his partner left off, "We believe he is likely following you, probably both of you. He might just be watching the house but the notes Aiden has been getting suggests he is aware of where at least one of you is most of the time. We think it is why he knew no one would be at your residence on Canada Day."

Wren froze and got a panicked look again. Aiden rushed over and held him. He whispered he would be okay. Wren took a deep breath and did not panic this time. "If he's following me, what do I do?"

"Unfortunately, at this point, there is only so much you can do," Constable Johnson said. "Although we will issue a warrant for Tyler's arrest, it is important you do not get complacent. The fact of the matter is that we went out earlier today to arrest him at his apartment and he wasn't there. I cannot say how long it will take to locate him."

"Until then?" Wren asked. His eyes and voice were pleading for a quick resolution. Aiden could practically feel him begging for some way to make this all stop.

"Unfortunately, until he is located and arrested, there is not much you can do that you are not already doing," Constable McDougall said with regret. "I cannot promise to make his arrest my top priority. There are a lot of criminals, some of whom are much more violent and pose a more immediate threat. Despite his history of violence against you, there is no clear evidence tying Tyler to the current issues you are having. He is just our prime suspect."

"But you think he did it?" Aiden confirmed.

"Yes," Constable McDougall stated clearly. "We think this was Tyler, and we think he is dangerous. We want you to be prepared."

"So, what do we do?" Aiden asked, repeating Wren's earlier question.

"Wren, where are you staying right now?" Constable Johnson asked.

"I don't really feel comfortable returning to my mom's place after the break in, so I've been staying with Aiden while I look into finding my own apartment. I'm hoping to move on first of the month."

"After the note you both received this morning, I would suggest you consider staying at a hotel or finding somewhere else to stay where Tyler will have more difficulty finding you. Try not to go anywhere alone until Tyler is arrested and if you see anything suspicious contact Constable McDougall or myself." Constable Johnson instructed. "I believe you have our numbers already?" Aiden and Wren nodded.

"I could stay with my dad. Barry is an asshole but he would let me stay, at least under the circumstances," Wren suggested thoughtfully. "Wait, what about my mom and Jim? Are they going to be safe or should they be going to stay somewhere else, too?"

"They should be safe," Constable Johnson answered. "As I said before, the attacks seem to be specifically targeting you."

"What about Aiden?" Wren asked, gripping tightly to Aiden's hand.

"Given this seems to be focused on you, Wren. Aiden will probably be left alone if he is not interacting with you. Tyler seems to believe you and he are still in a relationship, or at least this is what he's been telling his Probation Officer."

Wren took a step away from Aiden and looked back at him in horror. "I'm like the fucking plague! Anyone with me is at risk of being hurt."

Aiden stepped toward Wren and wrapped his arms around him. "You are not alone anymore."

"Ya, well, maybe I should be," Wren said, pushing Aiden away. But Aiden was having none of that and immediately stepped back to Wren and wrapped him in another embrace.

"I won't let some asshole break us up. We are fucking homos! If we let the haters stop us, we won't ever be together. Tyler is just another fucking hater!"

"This is different," Wren argued.

"Ya, it is," Aiden agreed. "But it is also exactly the same. If the wrong person sees us, we could get the shit beaten out of us for just standing too close. Hell, not that long ago forty-nine gay men were killed and fifty-three were injured in Orlando just because they were at a gay club. They just arrested a serial killer in Toronto who was killing men from the gay village. Unless I pretend I'm straight, I will always be at risk of something happening to me. I decided when I was still a teenager, I wouldn't let the haters control me. They want us to be apart. Why let people that hate me, that want to take away my rights, or even want me dead, control me?"

Constable Johnson nodded. "Okay. Just make sure you are careful. Although there is always some risk, this is a little more specific. So, just be careful. Wren, you especially need to avoid going out alone until we sort this out."

# Part Four

## Things Really Start to Go Wrong

# Chapter 39
## Aiden

Aiden smiled after he saw who was calling and felt his body relax as soon as he heard Wren's voice on the other end of the phone. He'd had a hard day at work and he missed Wren. He hadn't been able to see him in person since dropping him off at his father's house a week earlier. They had spoken on the phone and sent a bunch of texts back and forth but after living together for a few days and seeing each other a few times a week before that, a full week apart seemed like a really long time.

"I miss you," Aiden said. "I've never known a week to feel so long."

"I miss you, too." Wren sounded sad. Aiden wanted to pull him into a hug and felt his arms ache from missing him.

"How is it going over there? Your dad behaving himself?"

"I managed to pick up some extra shifts at work for the next two weeks so I won't be at home much," Wren said instead of answering Aiden's question. Or maybe that was his answer.

Aiden ground his teeth and held in a cutting remark about Barry.

Wren's dad, Barry, had only reluctantly agreed to let Wren move in with him because his son was in need, but Wren still had to constantly convince him to help. Wren hadn't said anything outright, but it was pretty clear that since moving in, Barry had been dropping subtle and not-so-subtle hints that if Wren was a real man—in other words, if he wasn't gay—then Wren wouldn't be in this situation.

Wren was pretty resigned to the whole thing but Aiden was livid. How could anyone talk to their child that way? How could a person say they love someone and then put conditions on their affection? Real love was unconditional.

Aiden hadn't had the best opinion of Barry before this but hearing how he treated his only son over the past week had made Aiden want to punch him in the face.

If there was anything Aiden could do to make the situation better, Aiden would do it. If only he could just move Wren back into his place but Wren refused to even consider the idea. Not only because it was against police advice but because Aiden hadn't received any notes since Wren had moved in with his father. With every day that passed without a new note, Wren was more and more certain he was making the right choice.

Aiden would respect his choice but if Wren never wanted to see his father again after this was over Aiden would support him one hundred percent.

So instead of calling Barry the asshole they both knew him to be, Aiden asked how work had gone. They chatted about their days and work. They both avoided discussing the fact they hadn't heard from the police yet, which mean Tyler still hadn't been arrested.

"I want to see you," Aiden said when they were wrapping up their conversation. "I know we're supposed to limit how much we see each other but I don't want to go another week without seeing you. I could come get you. We could get dinner. Maybe you could stay the night at my place—just for one night."

"I want to see you too. But—but I don't think it's a good idea. Tyler has been leaving you alone. Plus, I just came off a double shift and I have to work again at six a.m. tomorrow morning."

"I miss you," Aiden repeated. "Okay, not tonight. You're tired so you should sleep. But—but... when?"

"I don't know, Aiden. I thought the police would have arrested him by now. I hoped we'd be safe."

"Wren, honey, I know Tyler is still out there and I know he is dangerous but are you really expecting us to wait until they catch Tyler before we see each other again?"

"Maybe," Wren responded in a quiet and hesitant voice. "I—I'm really scared Aiden. I know that probably makes me weak and an idiot or something. But he almost killed me last time when I tried to leave him. What is he going to do after I had him arrested, left town, and then am dating you? And he isn't just after me. You're the only one he's directly threatened since he started all this crap in Edmonton. What if he follows through with his threat and kills you? Seeing us together could tip him over the edge."

Aiden tried to soothe Wren. He hated, hated not being able to wrap his arms around him. It really truly sucked not being able to comfort Wren the way he wanted to. "Honey, I'm safe. You're safe. You are not weak or an idiot or any other shit other people have said about you. You're scared. I'm scared too. This is completely crazy. I'm just saying—I'm just wondering—what if he isn't arrested for a long time? It's already been a week. What if he is hiding somewhere and they can't find him for weeks or even months? How long are we going to wait?"

"I don't know," Wren admitted softly. He sounded so defeated. Aiden wanted to make it better, but he didn't know how. He worried that pushing this was just making it worse. It was just pressuring Wren to do something he didn't want to do and forcing one more thing onto his already overflowing plate.

"Let's leave it then," Aiden suggested. "We can't do anything today. Let's wait and give it another week or two. Maybe something will have changed. We can decide then."

Wren sighed into the phone and Aiden could hear the sadness in the sigh. Both of them knew there was a good chance even two weeks wouldn't change anything. This had been going on so long already. If it was easy to solve, something would have happened already.

"Why don't you get ready for bed and call me back. We can talk while you fall asleep. It will be almost like I'm right there with you." Aiden suggested into the silence. It was only eight o'clock but if Wren had worked a double, he must be exhausted. Aiden knew Wren usually got up around four when he was starting work at six. So, even going to bed right now, he wouldn't be able to get more than eight hours of sleep.

"Ya, that sounds good," Wren agreed and hung up the phone.

Aiden got ready for bed as well while he waited for the call. He was tired. It was amazing how much energy waiting for the police to call seemed to take out of him. Despite the fact that Tyler was still at large, nothing much had happened all week. That in it of itself seemed to further confirm that Tyler and his jealousy was behind everything and he was only upset with Aiden because Wren and Aiden were dating.

The only interesting thing that he'd been dealing with had been a few more weird encounters with cars. The crazy Honda driver was still driving around the neighbourhood, being a general menace, but Aiden wasn't sure any of that was out of the norm. There always seemed to be people driving who made him wonder how they'd ever passed their driving exam.

* * *

Another week went by with no updates from the police. Aiden didn't find any more notes. There weren't any indications Tyler was even still around. Aiden and Wren continued to talk and text but Aiden could tell neither of them was happy at how long this forced separation was lasting.

"I miss your face," Aiden said to Wren. They hadn't seen each other in three weeks. "How is it going over there?"

"God! I don't know how much longer I can do this. Some of the shit he says..." Wren trailed off. Then he sighed. "If I wasn't worried about you, I think I would just leave.

"I don't want to be ungrateful. I know he didn't have to let me stay. Some parents wouldn't have said yes. Some kids come out to their parents and their parents kick them out and forced to live on the streets or with friends or relatives because they're too homophobic to love their kid if their kids aren't straight.

"I know that I'm lucky that when I needed him, when I was looking for a place to stay, he let me move in even though I didn't know how long this would last and even though I'm thirty and normally fully capable of living on my own. I'm lucky because he didn't have to help me. But there are all these little jabs. Little things he says about me not being strong enough, not being manly enough—just not enough. I know it is him, not me, but it sucks hearing it from my dad."

Aiden huffed in frustration. "Letting you stay with him doesn't make it okay for him to be mean to you. I know you don't like it when I say shit, but Barry is a fucking asshole. And I refuse to call him your dad. Fathers—real fathers—don't act like this to their children." Aiden could feel his blood boiling. Fucking asshole. Fucking asshole! Wren was already dealing with Tyler—or whoever—being a complete psycho. How could his father sit there and try to make him feel worse? God. Asshole!

"I don't remember him being like this before. When I was a kid, he wasn't this bitter, at least not to me. He used to say stuff about my mom during the divorce. My mom tries to never say anything bad about Barry but sometimes she lets it slip that he was kinda verbally abusive to her, especially near the end before she kicked him out. But having him say shit about me, to my face..."

Aiden held his tongue, biting back the further insults against Barry that were at the tip of his tongue. He couldn't hold back the growl but Wren didn't seem to mind.

"Especially now, like how can he think it is okay to be attacking me when I'm already down? It isn't like having Tyler stalking me isn't enough. What does he think this will accomplish? I will suddenly become straight, then 'man up' and kick Tyler's ass?

"Which would only accomplish having me go to jail because Tyler would absolutely go to the police and report the assault. That, or just kill me. Let's be honest, killing me is probably the option he would choose. And he would win since he is so much bigger than me. Except maybe in my dad's world changing fantasy I'm suddenly built like Dwayne Johnson or can suddenly fight like Jet Li."

"I'm so sorry you have to deal with this. Although, I gotta say, I'm thrilled you don't look like Dwayne Johnson." Aiden joked. "I mean, I guess he's hot but I definitely prefer my men to not make me feel like I'm small. You're fucking hot and I wouldn't change a thing about you.

"Well, maybe I'd transport you to my bed where I could kiss your soft lips and lick down your chest while I grip that adorable bubble butt... ah hem," Aiden interrupted himself. He could feel himself getting hard just thinking about that and Wren wasn't really in his bed. "Enough about that. Anything I can do about your dad?"

"You're doing it," Wren said with the smile back in his voice. "Just talking to you helps."

"I know we agreed to stay apart for a while but it's been two weeks, and he still hasn't been arrested. I don't want to do anything dangerous, but could we go out next Saturday night?"

"That sounds like heaven but... I'm really not sure. Maybe he is only backing off because we aren't together."

"I'm not trying to suggest we go on a quiet secluded walk in the river valley where anything could happen. How about going out for dinner in a crowded restaurant followed by dancing at Flitter with a bunch of people we know? It is almost a week away, so if we're lucky the police will arrest Tyler before then."

"What's the occasion?" Wren asked, but he sounded more positive. Aiden hoped that meant he'd agree to go.

"Dinner would be just us because I miss you. But the dancing is for Zane's birthday. He likes to pretend he is still twenty-one, so he is going to Flitter for his birthday. He invited us. In fact, he specifically told me to invite you."

"Didn't you play laser tag for your birthday?"

"Yes, then we went dancing after."

"So, if he is twenty-one, what are you? Eighteen?" Wren asked.

"Shut up," Aiden said with false seriousness. "I am a mature seventeen with a fake ID. Don't add on years."

They both laughed. Although he knew it was more because of the stress than because of his joke, Aiden still felt more of the tension leave his shoulders. It felt like forever since he'd laughed.

"So, you going to come?" Aiden asked after they had stopped laughing.

"Ya, that sounds great," Wren agreed. Aiden felt his heart skip at the prospect of finally seeing Wren again. They wouldn't even ever be alone, at least not completely. They wouldn't be idiots and ignore the police advice. But they would be in the same place again, sharing the same air, and able to touch each other again after what would be almost three weeks apart. Even without having a chance for sex, it felt like he was being offered food after a long fast.

"You're right. The police never said we couldn't see each other at all until after they arrested Tyler," Wren agreed. "They just said to try not to be alone together and to try to stay safe. Let's go out and dance. I need a night to look forward to. I need a chance to shake my ass and maybe we can sneak into the bathroom together and be alone, even if we won't be alone for real."

"God, I love you," Aiden responded. And he meant it. His feelings only intensified over the next few days the more he thought about Wren's suggestion for how they could have time alone.

# Chapter 40
## Wren

Wren sat on his front porch outside his father's house. There was at least forty minutes before Aiden was supposed to arrive to pick him up but he was already ready and waiting outside. Since his outfit included a pair of dangerously tight skinny jeans and eye liner, he thought it best to avoid his father. He didn't think his father would be a fan of his magenta button-up shirt either. He was pretty sure the only item of clothing his father wouldn't complain about was his dark grey vest.

No, that's a lie. Wren was sure Barry would find something wrong with that too. Luckily, he wasn't dressing for his father. He was dressing up for his date with Aiden and Wren was positive Aiden would salivate before Wren even got into Aiden's car.

As excited as Wren was, part of him still wished he could go back to Aiden's apartment to have sex and cuddle on the couch until it was late enough to go up to the bedroom to pass out for the night. Unfortunately, quiet evenings alone with Aiden were off the table until the police got off their asses and arrested Tyler. After four weeks of waiting, Wren wasn't holding his breath for it happening anytime soon. Maybe this was his life now. It almost made him want to go look for Tyler himself, just say, 'Fuck it,' and do anything he could to end this situation.

At this point, the only thing that was holding him back from behaving irrationally was that anything stupid he did could hurt Aiden as much as it did him. Wren wasn't willing to see Aiden get hurt.

Well, that, and he really didn't want to become one of those stupid characters from a teen slasher movie that ignores good advice and causes bad things to happen. If he was smart enough to get into med school, he really hoped he was smart enough to avoid being classified as 'too stupid to live.' Yet, every day that passed made it harder to be patient.

The wait had been hard and, at the moment, Wren felt like complete shit. He was running on fumes, both mentally and physically. It wasn't just the forced isolation from his friends and family. It wasn't even entirely because of his asshole of a father who had agreed to let Wren move in, but only after calling Wren a pussy and suggesting if he was a real man, none of this would have happened. It wasn't even missing Aiden so much he could barely breathe sometimes. It was all of that on next to no sleep.

Shortly after he moved in with his father, Wren picked up extra shifts at work. His biggest motivation was so he could save money more quickly to make sure he had more than enough to move out at the end of the month. Moving out had gone from something he thought he'd do eventually, to something he should do soon, to an urgent, absolutely must-do action.

There was no way he could stay here any longer than necessary. Moving into an apartment where he'd be alone might be riskier than living with his father, but his mental health had to count for something too. He couldn't stay any longer than necessary with a man who showed him through every interaction that he wasn't good enough. If he'd been okay with being treated like that, he never would have broken up with Tyler.

He had managed to find a cute bachelor apartment near the university, not too far from Aiden. Rent was higher than he'd hoped and the lease was only for three months but he didn't care. He just had to make it through one more week and then he could move out and Barry and he could go back to pretending they didn't talk because they were too busy, and not because they had nothing in common and Barry couldn't accept that he had a gay son.

Working all of those extra shifts didn't just make him money. It had the added benefit of getting him out of the house more often. His favourite shifts were evening or night shifts. When he worked evenings, he was at the hospital when his father got home after work and didn't get home until shortly before his father when to bed. When he worked nights, he left for the hospital shortly after his father returned from work and could sleep all day and avoid his father on the weekends. Unfortunately, he still had a few day shifts which had completely confused his sleep schedule. Between the nightmares, his work schedule, and all the coffee he was drinking to survive, he was barely sleeping.

It didn't help that somehow after only three nights in a row sleeping with Aiden, Wren had somehow forgotten how to sleep alone.

God, he missed Aiden—and his mother, and Lucy, and just about everyone else in his life. The idea that Tyler would pay attention to other people in his life terrified Wren. It was bad enough that Aiden was being threatened. He didn't want Tyler threatening anyone else too.

He hadn't even seen his mother because Wren worried she might lead Tyler back to him. The only good thing about living with his father was that Tyler couldn't know where Barry lived. Until this happened, Wren hadn't visited him for over a year.

Fuck, he missed Aiden.

He couldn't even work out properly because he didn't have a gym membership, and he'd been told not to be alone. So, he couldn't exactly go out for a run. The result was he was lonely, exhausted, and antsy. And horny.

And he really, really missed Aiden.

Since he'd started dating Aiden, Wren's sex drive had come back with vigour. Three weeks apart with no sex, not even a rushed hand-job or blow-job was killing him.

As though his thoughts had conjured him, Wren let out a whoop as he spotted Aiden's car come around the corner and head toward Barry's house. Wren was up and walking toward the car before Aiden could even stop.

As Wren climbed into the car, he was pleased to see his outfit had hit the mark. Aiden had to blink a few times and licked his lips before he turned on his blinker and pulled the car back onto the road.

"As soon as we're out of sight of Barry's house you need to pull the car over so I can kiss the ever-loving shit out of you. I can't do it in front of his house or I might not be allowed to come back again," Wren said once the car was moving. Aiden just blinked again before nodding.

Two blocks and a left turn later, Wren was undoing his seatbelt and climbing over the centre console onto Aiden's lap. He grabbed Aiden by the face and wrapped one arm around his head until he could weave his fingers into Aiden's soft hair. God, he missed running his hands through Aiden's hair. He hadn't even realized he did that until he couldn't do it for three weeks. He stared into Aiden's eyes for a few beats, enjoying being with him and touching this man whom he loved more than words.

"Hey," Aiden whispered with a smile. "It's good to see you."

Wren just nodded slowly before lowering his head and kissing him.

The kiss started out slow and soft but neither of them could maintain that. They were both too desperate for each other. Wren was pulled in by the taste of the chocolate and minty favour of whatever Aiden ate last combined with the indescribable taste that was simply Aiden. He felt himself falling into the moment and lost track of time as their mouths became reacquainted.

After a while a passing car beeped its horn, startling them out of their moment. Wren reluctantly pulled back and climbed back into his seat. He looked over at Aiden and had to almost physically stop himself from going back over for a second kiss—or maybe something more. Aiden's lips were pink and swollen from the force of their kiss. He looked stunned and his pupils were blown wide.

"You look hot," Wren said, staring at his face and eyes. He rubbed Aiden's hair back into a semblance of style before trailing his fingers back down his cheek. He couldn't help but brush his fingers over Aiden's swollen lips and Aiden rewarded him with a light nip to his fingertips.

"I don't know, I feel under dressed next to you. That shirt and vest... and those pants... god!" Aiden adjusted his pants trying to get more comfortable and Wren could practically feel himself salivating as he saw Aiden's erection growing in his pants. "Are you sure you want to go for dinner then go to the club? Maybe we could find someplace where we could be alone and I could peel those amazing pants off to see what else I can do with that gorgeous ass."

Wren could feel himself getting hard too, which was a problem given how tight his pants were. He was sorely tempted to throw caution to the wind and do what Aiden was suggesting. God, he was so horny. Getting pounded into a bed, or a couch, or anywhere sounded perfect.

Aiden laughed, breaking the silence left by Wren's hesitation. "No, we need to keep being smart. We have suffered through the past four weeks and I'm not wasting that sacrifice on one night of sex."

"It would be great sex," Wren whined, his need overriding his common sense.

"Yes, it would be. But—" Aiden said forcing himself to be responsible. "It would still be a stupid decision."

"Fine," Wren grumbled. He agreed with Aiden, reluctantly. They needed to keep being smart. But sex!

With only a few grumbles of disappointment which were echoed by Aiden, Wren managed to buckle himself into his seat and move his hands back onto his lap. They had somehow ended up rubbing against Aiden's cock and balls.

As they drove toward 124$^{th}$ Street where they intended to go out for dinner—at a nice busy restaurant—Aiden and Wren chatted about their day and other random non-sexual topics. No matter how frequently they talked on the phone and texted it was just not the same as sharing the same physical space. It wasn't even really about sex, despite how horny Wren was feeling, it was about the feeling of togetherness.

While chatting, Wren could feel the weight of their separation returning. They were together now but at the end of the night they would return to their own places, with no end in sight. Getting his own place wouldn't help him and Aiden. It wasn't as though he could invite Aiden over. They were still not supposed to be alone together.

This wasn't fair to Aiden. How long could this continue before Aiden rightfully said, 'enough' and walked away? Wren wouldn't even blame him. Who wanted to stay with someone you weren't allowed to see? Someone who brought a crazy psycho into your life?

Their conversation petered off and after driving in silence for about ten minutes, Wren looked over at Aiden and said seriously, "You sure you want to stay with me?"

"Yes!" Aiden exclaimed.

"No, wait. You need to really think about this," Wren said even more seriously. "This is the first time we've seen each other in a month. Tyler is deranged and it doesn't look like he is going to stop. He is threatening you. His last note said he would kill you if you didn't leave me. This isn't just about scary notes or him destroying your stuff. He almost killed me for trying to leave. As long as you stay with me and he thinks you are standing in his way, he might kill you.

"Aiden, this is serious. He is violent and wants you dead!"

Continuing, Wren pleaded, desperation evident in his voice, "You said earlier that you need me to be safe. Well, I need you to be safe too. I'm not worth it, Aiden."

Wren wanted to cry, maybe he'd already started. He loved Aiden. Aiden had brought sunshine and true happiness back into his life but he would cut off his own arm in order to protect Aiden.

Aiden said nothing as he pulled the car over into a gas station. Turning off the engine, he turned his body so he was facing Wren.

"First off, Tyler isn't going to kill me. I will be careful. We will be careful. And even if he does, it wouldn't be your fault. I can't promise I will always be safe. But then, neither can you. I could die while driving to work on Monday. Hell, statistically I'm probably much more likely to die driving to work than doing just about anything else, even with Tyler around. So, let's take dying off the table.

"Second of all, I can't just walk away. Wren, you are absolutely worth getting hurt for. I'd risk everything to stay with you. I'm fucking in love with you."

By this point, Aiden was almost shouting. His arm waved in excitement but never came anywhere near Wren. Almost like he realized how upset he was getting, Aiden stopped and took two deep breaths before continuing at a regular volume. "I was half in love with you when we were kids. But after really getting to know you as an adult and after seeing how strong, brave, and funny you are—now that I know how fucking amazing you are—I love you. Wren, I will say it again, I love you.

"If you want to leave me because you don't like me any more or you can't do this anymore, fine. That's one thing. You can go live your life. You'd take my fucking heart with you but I'd let you go. But as long as you love me and want to be with me, I'm not leaving you. And I'm definitely not going to end something as amazing as we are together because some psychotic ass-hat has threatened me."

Wren's eyes widened in surprise but he took Aiden's hand. *So, this is what Aiden's like when he gets upset and yells,* Wren thought to himself. He'd spent all that time fearful or expecting Aiden's anger, and this was it; a little exuberance and then deep breathing. He wanted to laugh with relief but also cry because he'd finally found someone that really cared about him, someone who would truly love and support him, and maybe they needed to end it.

"I love you too. But I'm scared. No, I'm terrified—I'm terrified that this time Tyler will make me watch while he beats you or kills you, instead of just sending me to the hospital. And it will be my fault. I know you don't think so but you would be dead because of me. It would be my fault because I'm the one that thought it was a good idea to get into a relationship with this psychopath. I didn't see him for what he was because

I was blind and stupid. I got involved with him and now he is making me pay for my mistake.

"And Aiden, this last month has been so fucking hard. I miss you with every breath I take. I'm terrified and my father is spewing bullshit at me constantly and all I want to do is hug myself into your body and I can't. I can't." By this point Wren was openly weeping, not pretty tears but big ugly wreck-your-face tears. He was certain his eye liner was running down his face making him look extra disgusting but he couldn't make himself stop. It was like the dam had been broken and everything he'd been holding back for the past few weeks was coming out through his eyes and nose.

This time it was Aiden who unbuckled himself and awkwardly leaned over the centre console, wrapping his arms around Wren. He didn't speak, he just hugged him and showed Wren that he wasn't going through this alone even if it felt that way sometimes, even when the short fifteen-minute drive to Aiden's apartment could have been a trek across the world, for all the good it was doing him.

Eventually Wren calmed down. He laughed as he wiped tears from his cheek and came away with black smudges on his fingers. "God, I'm a mess."

Aiden took Wren's chin in one hand and used the other to gently wipe away more tears. "You are still the most beautiful man I know."

Wren laughed as he took a Kleenex and used the mirror to help him clean the results of his meltdown from his face. "I won't tell Zane you said that. Somehow, I think he would be offended," Wren joked.

"Nope. He'd understand. He'd call me biased and say I was wrong but he would understand," Aiden said with a smile.

Wren took a deep breath and squeezed Aiden's hand. "I would do anything to keep you safe, including giving you up."

Aiden squeezed back, then let go and turned to start the car and resume driving.

"Well, it's a good thing you don't have to because we are staying together. If you still love me, then I'm not giving you up. This is not your fault and you do not deserve any of this. You agreed to date him, not to become his property.

"But he is right about one thing. You are absolutely worth fighting for," Aiden stated calmly. "Plus, self-sacrifice is for idiots."

"Isn't that what you are doing? Sacrificing your safety to be with me?" Wren asked with a small laugh.

"No. I'm being completely selfish. Believe me, being without you would be the much bigger sacrifice. If there is one thing these past weeks have taught me, it's that being apart might be the hardest thing I'll ever have to do."

"You fucking, sap," Wren shot Aiden a happy and teary grin.

"You love it," Aiden responded with a grin of his own.

"Maybe," Wren agreed grudgingly but he couldn't keep the happy grin off his face.

# Chapter 41
## Aiden

"Maybe we shouldn't go," Aiden suggested after remembering there was no parking at the club. "We will have to park a few blocks away and walk. That seems like a bad idea. I'll just text him and say we can't come after all. I'm sure Zane would understand."

But Wren was already shaking his head. "No," Wren said firmly. "You are not missing your best friend's birthday party because of me. We can walk. It'll only be a few blocks."

"It wouldn't be because of you. It would be because of Tyler or whoever is doing this. I'm sure Zane would let me make it up to him when this is all settled." They had just left the restaurant and if that was all they did together it would still have been a good evening.

"The only reason Tyler knows about you is because of me, so it's my fault. And you aren't going make it up to Zane because we're going to go to the club and dance our asses off tonight. I've been looking forward to tonight since you told me about it last week. If I can't do this, then I might as well just offer myself up to Tyler because there is no point in trying to keep him from killing me. I'd already have done it to myself."

"All right, all right," Aiden reluctantly agreed. He still wasn't sure it was entirely a good idea, but he had to admit he felt the same way as Wren. He was stir crazy and needed tonight to let off some steam. "At the end of the night I'll see if one of the other guys will walk us to the car just to be on the safe side. That way it's just walking to the club where we'll be alone."

Wren nodded and Aiden manoeuvred the car onto the road. They drove in companionable silence for a few blocks and Aiden was enjoying the soft blues playing on the radio. The music clearly wasn't working for Wren though, because after less than one song he grabbed Aiden's phone and flipped through his play list to pick something more up tempo. Suddenly, the first song from the *Queer as Folk* season 2 soundtrack blared, completely changing the mood in the car. Aiden felt a smile grow across his face.

"Man, this brings back memories from when I first came out," Wren said.

"I know. You and Lucy used to watch it. After you left, and I came out, Lucy gave me the entire show on DVD. She called it educational and demanded I not be anything like Ted but said I could be as fabulous as I wanted."

Wren laughed. "That sounds like Lucy. So, what did you decide?"

"I decided I could never be as fabulous as Emmitt. Zane is the Emmitt in my life, although I didn't meet him until later. She was right that Ted was a loser. Michael is annoying until he gets together with Ben, who was just too sane and rational to be me when I was seventeen, and I wasn't enough of a slut to be anything like Brian. Plus, I was in love with an older man who barely looked at me. Clearly, I was Justin."

Wren laughed. "So true! Plus, you are a complete romantic at heart, even if you say you don't like romantic comedies."

Aiden shrugged. "There is that."

"Well, much like Justin, you got your older man to love you back eventually," Wren said with a cheesy smile.

Aiden laughed and felt the tension and stress fall from his shoulders. Ya, tonight was going to be fun. He just knew it. He was finally with Wren. What could go wrong?

Aiden hoped he hadn't just jinxed himself but shook off his concern. He hoped it was all in his head. Aiden turned up the music and let himself get into the groove.

A second ripple of apprehension travelled through Aiden when they weren't able to find parking any closer than four blocks away.

Once again Aiden was struck by the changes in his life since learning Tyler was after them. When he'd come to this club a few months earlier, he'd walked there and taken a taxi home. It was about a thirty-five-minute walk and his only concern had been braving the April cool spring weather. He hadn't even considered whether the walk was safe. Now, walking four blocks with Wren in the well-lit road seemed intimidating.

Stepping out of the car, Wren and Aiden shared a look of trepidation and Aiden knew Wren was feeling the same way he was. But there was nothing they could do unless they wanted to turn around and go home. Wren made the decision for them when he closed his car door, came around the car and took Aiden's hand. "Like you said before, we can get someone to walk us back to the car so we aren't alone more than we need to be."

The walk was uneventful. After all the anxiety and build up, Aiden was almost disappointed nothing happened. Not that he wanted Tyler to show up or anything, it was just he wanted everything with Tyler to be done. The anticipation was killing him. He was sure it must be worse for Wren.

"You're amazing, you know that?" Aiden said as they walked in through the doors to the club.

"What?" Wren shouted over the music.

"You are amazing!" Aiden shouted back.

"WHAT?" Wren shouted again. The music really was loud.

Aiden waived Wren off. When he continued to look curiously at Aiden, he just mouthed, "I love you." Wren smiled and mouthed the words back before turning back toward the main area and leading Aiden into the club.

# Chapter 42
## Wren

"You're still putting up with his ugly mug, I see," Zane joked, talking loudly over the music.

"It has its perks," Wren said back. It was hard to have a real conversation even though it was quieter here in the back compared to the area near the door.

Zane laughed before continuing seriously, "How are you doing? I heard about what's been going down with your ex-. That's some crazy shit."

Wren wasn't sure how to respond. It was weird to have people other than Lucy and his mother care about him—besides Aiden. Wren was getting used to Aiden caring.

"Umm, it sucks but I'm managing," Wren finally answered.

"Good. You tell me if you need anything. Derek and I are here for you."

Wren was touched. He and Zane were only starting to get to know each other. He wasn't sure if before this he would have called Zane his friend, more like an acquaintance, but maybe he needed to give Zane more credit. Maybe they were friends after all.

"I appreciate it," Wren responded sincerely.

"Enough about that. It's a party," Zane said shaking his ass and laughing when Derek gave him a gentle slap on the ass. "Birthday boy privilege: You have to dance with me tonight. You can't let the giant monopolize your time."

Wren laughed and nodded, "Sure."

Aiden and Wren sat down at the table with the others. They sat around the table talking loudly to each other. Zane told the group a few funny stories from his work. After a few songs, more people arrived. More hugs were exchanged. Even Wren joined in, despite not knowing everyone. Everyone was friendly and before long Wren realized he was relaxing and having a good time. It had been a long time since he'd interacted with this many people at once. It was... nice.

After about twenty-five minutes, Aiden stood up and pulled Wren up behind him. He leaned into Wren and told him, "We're dancing now."

Wren smiled, nodded, and followed Aiden onto the dance floor. This was what he'd been looking forward to. It was exactly what he needed to let go and really have fun.

They danced together, grinding their bodies then moving apart and coming back together. They danced for each other and for themselves. Sometimes other people from their group of friends came up and danced with them. Other times they were the only ones dancing, surrounded by equally sweaty strangers. The world shrank down to just the two of them.

Wren laughed. He laughed with joy because he was dancing. He laughed because he was with Aiden and he laughed at the irony of being less afraid now, when Tyler was definitely stalking him, than he had been before Aiden had entered his life—when everyone had been telling him he was safe.

Aiden looked at him and he smiled. It was not the smile he seemed to have on his face all the time, or the smile he gave to his friends or family. It was a special private smile, a smile that said 'I'm happy you're here with me and I'm happy you're happy.' Wren hugged Aiden close and yelled into his ear so he could be heard over the music which was much louder on the dance floor, "I love you."

Aiden hugged him back and yelled, "I know."

Wren jokingly pushed him away but pulled him back to yell, "Fucking nerd!" then pushed him away again. They continued dancing.

After what felt like no time at all but was probably over an hour, Aiden stepped back grabbed Wren's hand and pulled him back to the table. A few other people were dancing but Rachel, Zane, and Derek were sitting at the table again. Aiden pulled Wren in and shouted, "I need some water. You want some?"

Wren nodded and gave a thumb up before sitting down beside Zane. Wren didn't bother listening to the conversation as he caught his breath and enjoyed the feeling of the warm muscles. After a few minutes Zane grabbed his hand.

"We'll be back. I'm taking my dance," Zane shouted to the rest of the table. Derek smiled and put his face up for a kiss which Zane gave him before pulling Wren onto the dance floor.

It was weird but also fun dancing with Zane. He was shorter than Wren and it felt weird since it had been a long time since he had danced with anyone shorter than him. Both Tyler and Aiden were a few inches taller than him, close to the same height, actually. But Zane was fun. He danced extremely well, as expected from a dance instructor. Zane was so good he made him dance better than he ever had before. He imagined they looked fucking hot together and glanced around looking for Aiden but couldn't see him through the crowd. He saw a few other dancers giving him and Zane some speculative looks but was relieved that no one approached them.

Wren was quickly sucked back into the dance. Zane's skin-tight bright pink pants and white and yellow striped tank top, which glowed on the black-lit dance floor, accentuated Zane's fluid and extravagant style. Wren laughed and couldn't help agree with Aiden. Zane was pretty fabulous in every sense of the word.

They danced a few songs together but Wren was thirsty and wanted to get back to Aiden. He mimed drinking and headed back to their table with Zane behind him, shaking his hips to the music.

When they got back to the table, Aiden wasn't there. He leaned into Rachel and asked her, "Aiden come back then leave?"

"No, I haven't seen him since you left," Rachel responded, turning back to her discussion with Derek.

Wren frowned. He didn't know why it was taking Aiden so long to get their water. Then a friend of Zane's named James came back to the table with a tray of shots. He placed them on the table and handed two to Zane and one to everyone else. Wren shook his head. He hadn't wanted to drink before but definitely didn't want to drink until he found Aiden. Where was he?

The rest of the group did a round of shots and talked more. Aiden still wasn't back. Derek got up and went to the bathroom. They talked some more and the others did another round of shots. Aiden still wasn't back. Derek came back from the washroom. Aiden still wasn't back. By now Wren was starting to quietly freak out.

"You'll be pleased to hear I declined getting my cock sucked by some drunk guy in the bathroom," Derek said to Zane. Zane just smiled and shook his head.

"Hey," Wren said to Derek. "You see Aiden in the washroom?"

Derek shook his head, looking confused.

"You see Aiden when you were at the bar?" Wren asked Jamie. Jamie shook his head.

"What's wrong?" Zane asked. "You look totally freaked out?"

"Aiden has disappeared," Wren said, feeling increasingly frantic.

"Shit," Zane and Derek said together, looking as apprehensive as Wren felt.

"I'm sure he has just gone out to get a breath of fresh air or found someone else to dance with," Jamie suggested.

"No," Wren shook his head. "He wouldn't do that. Not right now. Not with everything that's going on. He'd tell me where he was."

By now everyone at the table was listening.

"What do you mean? What's going on?" Rachel asked.

"My psychotic ex- has been stalking me and threatened to kill Aiden," Wren tried to explain.

"What?" Jamie exclaimed with a laugh of incredulity, thinking this could only be a crazy joke.

"It's true," Zane confirmed. "I don't know all the details but Aiden said he might not even make it tonight because Wren's violent and psychotic ex-boyfriend is stalking the two of them and the police haven't been able to find the guy yet to arrest him."

"Holy fuck!" exclaimed Rachel. "How come he didn't tell me?"

"He's been hiding at home recently. I think he only told me because he wasn't sure if he would make it to the party and he wanted to make sure I understood why."

"And you still came out tonight?" Rachel asked Wren.

"Neither of us has been out for anything except work for a month and the police said we should be okay as long as we stayed in public. We're being careful!"

"Okay," said Rachel, ever the problem solver. "Wren, you stay here and see if Aiden comes back. In the meantime, text him. The rest of us should all look for Aiden, see if he is just lost in the crowd, maybe got caught up with someone else. Everyone has their phone? Let's meet back here in fifteen minutes."

Everyone nodded, confirming they had their phone and would return in fifteen minutes.

Wren felt like he was going to throw up. He wanted to be helping look, but he agreed that someone needed to stay back here in case Aiden was just taking the longest time ever and was unaware of the stir he was causing.

As everyone dispersed in different directions around the club to see if they could find Aiden, Wren texted furiously.

Wren: *Where are you?*

Wren: *Come back to the table.*

Wren: *You have been gone at least an hour to get water. This is crazy. I'm worried.*

Wren: *Just tell me you're OK?*

There was no response from Aiden.

Wren realized maybe he should let the police know what is going on. He couldn't call because of the loud music in the club and he didn't want to go outside to make the phone call. He wasn't sure if it would be okay to text them but, after a moment of thinking, he decided to text Johnson anyway. She'd specifically told him to get in touch if anything happened.

Wren: *This is Wren. I can't call because I am at Flitter and the music is way too loud.*

Johnson: *What's up, Wren?*

Wren: *You didn't arrest Tyler and forget to tell us by any chance?*

Johnson: *Sorry. We still haven't been able to find him.*

Johnson: *He quit his job, hasn't shown up to his Probation appointments recently, and we can't figure out where he is living since he broke his lease a month ago.*

Wren: *Shit.*

Johnson: *Why?*

Wren: *Aiden is missing.*

Wren: *He left to get water almost an hour ago and no one has seen him.*

Johnson: *You sure he isn't lost in the washroom or anything?*

Wren: *Pretty sure. One of my friends was just in there and said he didn't see Aiden.*

Johnson: *Where are you?*

Wren: *I'm waiting at our table but five other people are searching the club.*

Johnson: *Okay. What would you like me to do to help?*

Wren: *Tell me it is okay and I'm overreacting.*

Johnson: *If you're worried, I'm worried. Trust yourself.*

Wren: *Shit.*

Johnson: *Why don't we wait until your friends come back and if no one has found him get someone to speak to security and get his name announced.*

Wren: *Okay*

Johnson: *Then if he still hasn't been found call me and I will get Cst. McDougall and we will meet you there and help you look.*

Johnson: *Technically someone has to be missing for twenty-four hours before we consider them missing but, given the circumstances, I'm willing to start sooner.*

Wren: *Thank you!*

Finally having a plan, Wren felt somewhat calmer. He was still really worried but he no longer felt helpless. He sent off another message to Aiden while he waited.

Wren: *If you don't show up soon you will be completely embarrassed because I'm about to go to security to get your name announced and if you don't come the cops are coming to help me look.*

Wren waited. Still nothing.

Rachel came back first. She looked worried and dejected. She shook her head 'no'. James and Derek arrived shortly after. Then a young man Wren didn't know showed up. He nodded to Rachel, James, and Derek, and introduced himself to Wren, "Hi, I'm Alex. Zane explained the situation. I haven't seen Aiden since I saw him dancing with you. I thought I would see how I can help."

"Thank you," Wren responded, grateful Aiden had so many people in his life willing to help.

By then Zane had arrived with another two guys. Zane shook his head to show he had also had no luck. Wren's gut clenched again.

"Okay, I messaged one of the police officers helping Aiden and I. She told me to speak to the bouncer to get his name announced. If he doesn't show up after that, she will bring her partner and they will come look for him."

Rachel spoke up, "It seems pretty clear he isn't here anymore. Maybe while you speak to security, the rest of us can see if we can figure out where he went after he left our table—see if anyone saw him after that."

Everyone nodded.

Zane looked around, looked at Wren and asked, “You said Aiden drove right?”

Wren nodded.

“Okay, maybe Derek and I should go make sure his car is here. I know he wouldn’t leave without you but I bet the police will take you more seriously if you can say his car is still here.”

“That’s a good idea,” Wren said gratefully. Wren described where they had parked as quickly as possible before Zane and Derek turned to leave the club.

Wren took a deep breath and followed them to the door. It was the only place he knew he could find a bouncer. He walked toward a very tall, large, muscular man in a tight white t-shirt with the word ‘SECURITY’ written on the front and back. The shirt glowed in the lights and Wren wondered if that was why they picked white for the shirts.

“Umm, excuse me,” Wren said, trying to speak loudly enough to be heard without having to get too close.

The bouncer didn’t even twitch. Fuck, the bouncer hadn’t heard him over the music. He moved over so he was standing directly in front of the guy and waved his arm until the bouncer’s eyes locked on Wren. The security guard arched an eyebrow, silently inquiring what the problem was.

“I need your help,” Wren shouted.

The bouncer just shook his head and pointed toward the door. Wren nodded and followed the man outside the door. Once they were through the door, the decibel level dropped significantly and Wren could hear his ears ringing from the noise. The bouncer pulled out an ear plug. He was listening. Wren just hoped he’d take him seriously.

“What do you want?” the man said in a serious voice.

“I need your help finding my boyfriend,” Wren said. He took a breath but the bouncer interrupted him before he could continue his explanation.

“I can’t help you if you lost your date. Sorry, bud,” The bouncer said, already turning to go back into the club.

"No," Wren said hurriedly, trying to keep the man's attention. "A police officer told me to speak to you. I think he has been hurt or maybe kidnapped or something."

The bouncer stopped and shot Wren a look of complete disbelief.

"Please, just listen. It's a bit of a story."

The bouncer shrugged and nodded, although the look of disbelief didn't leave his face.

"This is going to sound crazy but I can give you the name and number of the police officer I'm dealing with if you need to confirm my story. So, please just hear me out."

The larger man nodded. "Okay."

Wren told the bouncer a very condensed version of the events of the past few months which lead led to a warrant being issued for Tyler. "And this is the first time we've been out together in four weeks," Wren said, finishing his story.

The bouncer had stopped looking like he didn't believe a word out of Wren's mouth, especially after he'd been told about Johnson and McDougall.

As Wren finished the story a little sob escaped him. He took a deep breath to calm down. He didn't want to become an emotional wreck. He needed to stay calm so he could help Aiden. Wren knew he could break down once Aiden was safe.

"What do you need me to do?" the bouncer asked. The question helped Wren stay focused.

"I texted the police officer helping us. She told me she can't come out to help look until his name gets announced across the club to make sure we aren't overlooking him. So, I need you to get his name announced. Like maybe between songs or something. I need to get it announced that he needs to come to the front door or something."

"Okay. I can do that," the bouncer agreed, turning to head back inside.

"Oh, thank god!" Wren sighed and followed the bouncer back.

While he was walking back, he checked his phone and noticed he had missed two texts from Zane. He stopped about a few feet from the door to read the texts.

Zane: *Car is still here. Or at least I'm pretty sure it is Aiden's car.*

Zane: *It looks like someone took a baseball bat to it.*

There was a series of photos of a mangled mess that was Aiden's car. The windshield was cracked beyond repair, there were dents all over the car, and someone had knocked both of the side mirrors off. One appeared to be hanging by some wires and the other was completely gone. The driver's side window was completely destroyed and, in the photo, Wren could see glass all over the inside of the car. Shit, shit, shit! This was not a good sign.

Wren looked up and realized the bouncer was already inside and he was alone. Before putting away his phone to go back inside, he decided to update Johnson with the information from Zane.

Wren: *One of my friends went to check for Aiden's car. It's still where we parked but someone damaged it.*

Wren forwarded the pictures from Zane.

Johnson: *Okay. I will get Cst. McDougall and come. Meet me out front. We can look at the car if you find Aiden first and help look for Aiden if not.*

Wren: *A bouncer is on his way to get Aiden's name announced between songs. I will let you know if he shows up or not.*

Johnson: *Sounds good. See you soon. It will probably be about thirty minutes before we get there.*

Wren: *Okay. I will be waiting, hopefully, with Aiden.*

Wren put his phone in his pocket and walked to the door. He was startled when the door opened on its own just as his hand touched the handle. The music blasted. The person coming out was looking over his shoulder rather than ahead of him, saying something to the bouncer, maybe a joke since he was smiling.

Wren felt his blood freeze in his veins. He knew who it was.

# Chapter 43
## Wren

Wren stepped back, tripped down the stairs and fell onto his bum and back. Tyler looked down, caught by the movement. He smiled a big open smile, like he had just found exactly who he was looking for. Wren guessed he probably had. Before Wren could do more than blink in surprise, Tyler stepped forward, leaned down, and grabbed Wren's arm to haul him up. Tyler's grip was punishing as he held him against his body.

"I was just looking for you. I was worried when I could not find you right away but here you are. You are going to come with me now," Tyler said. Just like when he threatened Wren's life, Tyler was completely calm.

Wren shook with fear. He shook his head, unable to form words through the fear.

"You will come with me." Tyler repeated. "See, I believe I have something you want."

"Oh, god," Wren cried, finally able to move and speak. "Why, Tyler? Why can't you just leave us alone?"

"Because you are mine," Tyler explained his tone of voice suggesting this was the most logical thing in the world. "You are not allowed to be with anyone but me. He is garbage. I will show you. He is filth and will be punished for thinking he could have you. You both will be. But that will happen later once we are away from here."

"Oh, god," Wren cried again, more quietly. But he allowed Tyler to drag him away from the club.

Wren felt helpless. He felt the same as when he was sure he would die in Toronto. Except he knew Aiden was relying on him.

Then he remembered. He still had his phone in his pocket. He was no sixteen-year-old girl but Wren was pretty good with his phone. Maybe he could send a message from inside his pocket or when they got to the car because he knew he had to go with Tyler. He couldn't leave Aiden alone at Tyler's mercy.

Wren's mind raced as he walked beside Tyler. He tried to figure out the best thing to say. He knew if he was obvious Tyler would take away his phone and would hurt him worse. He knew he needed to find a way to send the police a message so they knew to come find him. Tyler took them a few blocks in the direction opposite to Aiden's car and they quickly arrived at Tyler's car, a boring, unremarkable few years old grey Honda Civic.

The reality of the situation hit him like a ton of bricks. This was the car he and Aiden kept seeing around the city. It was the one that had almost hit them while crossing the street. Tyler really had been stalking them since the beginning.

"Why?" Wren repeated.

"You are not allowed to decide when we are over. I told you before, we are not done." This time Wren saw the rage in Tyler's eyes, the same rage he'd seen before Tyler had almost killed him the first time.

Tyler opened the passenger door and before Wren could get in and sit down, he felt Tyler's fist connect with his stomach and he grunted as he fell forward and was tossed into the front seat. The door slammed after him. He didn't bother trying the doors. Wren wasn't trying to escape. He knew what he needed to do. He needed to find Aiden. He needed to lead the police to Aiden even if it killed him.

While Tyler went around to the driver's seat, Wren sent Johnson a quick message before hiding the phone under the passenger seat.

Wren: *Going with T—has A.*

Wren: *Rescue us pls.*

* * *

Wren's stomach ached where Tyler had hit him but Wren forced himself to sit up straight in the car and look out the window. Maybe if he watched where they were going, he could tell police where they were. He'd need to get his phone again, but he didn't want to miss an opportunity because he wasn't paying attention.

They left downtown and took a bridge over the North Saskatchewan river. Wren soon realized they were driving near Aiden's apartment, except they didn't stop. Tyler continued to drive, passing houses and other cars. Wren wondered if he were to open his window suddenly and scream for help would anyone come to his aid. It was already close to midnight, but it was a Saturday in the summer. The roads were relatively busy despite the late hour.

But what would be the point? He needed to find Aiden. He needed to make sure he was all right and do everything in his power to keep him safe from the monster sitting in the driving seat beside him.

Tyler was driving calmly with both hands on the wheel. There was no music playing, and he wasn't talking. Wren remembered Tyler preferred to drive in silence so he could concentrate. No music, no talking.

They hadn't driven together often as driving was generally unnecessary in downtown Toronto. Tyler had always been so scornful of people who lived in the suburbs and commuted into the downtown each day. He'd been proud of his high-rise apartment in the gay village right near downtown. He enjoyed showing off his posh address almost as much as he enjoyed showing off the muscles he worked hard to maintain at the gym. He wasn't blatant about it. No, Tyler had too much class for that. Instead, in a posh and sophisticated way, Tyler used every opportunity to show how much better he was than everybody else.

Tyler believed he was better than everyone else.

Like so many other people, Wren had been caught up in Tyler's image and believed Tyler was actually better than him.

When they'd first dated Wren had loved Tyler's confidence and sexy body. Tyler's high-paying job, good address, and the obvious hard work that went into everything he did had impressed Wren. He'd practically worshipped Tyler, and Tyler had accepted it as his due. It wasn't until later, when Wren had gotten to know Tyler better and began seeing him as a real person instead of a superhero or almost-god to worship, that problems started in their relationship.

Wren wondered how Tyler had managed in jail. He wondered how he allowed himself to move to boring middle of the prairies Edmonton or drive the boring grey Honda Civic. When they'd been together, Tyler had refused to even visit Edmonton and instead dragged Wren to New York, San Francisco, and Montreal. He said those were real cities, places worth visiting, placing worth living. According to Tyler, Edmonton was a Podunk town for two-bit wannabes.

For the first time, it occurred to Wren that Tyler had probably, at least in part, been saying that to keep Wren from visiting his friends and family back home. It was frustrating to know, even years later, he was still coming to terms with all the ways Tyler had manipulated him.

As they continued to drive Wren realized they were heading in the same direction as his mother's house. He had to hold in a gasp as he realized Tyler may have been hiding out close to where he had been living with his mother. Easier to stalk him, Wren supposed.

There were fewer and fewer cars around them as they moved further into the residential area. The drive was so uneventful Wren was feeling confident he might make this work out. If they were going close to his mother's, then maybe he could escape. Or maybe when they got out of the car, Wren could send another message to the police telling them he was near his mom's.

Then, out of nowhere, the silence suddenly disappeared and everything went to shit.

Ping. Buzz, buzz, buzz.

"Was that your phone?" Tyler asked. His voice was cold but quiet, and Wren knew there was more menace to it than if he was yelling.

Ping. Buzz, buzz, buzz

"Umm, I think so," Wren answered. He could feel himself sweat. *Shit! Shit, shit, shit, shit!* Wren shouted silently in his head. "Maybe someone I was with at the club is wondering where I disappeared off to."

"Let me see," Tyler demanded, holding out his hand.

Wren put his hands in his pockets and made a show of looking for his phone without finding it. "It's not in my jacket pocket."

"It's here. We just heard it." Tyler pointed out. "Find it."

Wren ran his fingers under his legs along the seat, looked between the seats and then his phone helpfully showed him where it was hiding when another text message came in.

Ping. Buzz, buzz, buzz.

*Fuck! Fuck! Fuck!* Tyler would lose his shit when he found out Wren had used his phone to message the police and then deliberately hidden the phone in the car.

Wren had to undo his seatbelt to retrieve the phone. He reluctantly handed it over to Tyler. Wren didn't know how Tyler would react to the text messages but he knew how he'd react to being refused. There were no good options, only terrible and deadly.

"Good choice," Tyler said as he pulled the car over and stopped beside a dark house. He looked at the phone a moment before looking back over at Wren. "'Stay where you are. I'm coming,' from Johnson and, 'where are you?' from Zane. Who are they?"

"They are friends. Johnson was coming to meet us and Zane is just someone from the club," Wren lied.

Tyler sneered. "Was Zane the skanky twink you were grinding against earlier? Does your boyfriend know you are a whore? Maybe he doesn't mind sharing, but I told you before I will not accept that behaviour from you!" Tyler was yelling by the end. He lifted his hand and suddenly back handed Wren across the face. “No one else is allowed to touch you but me!” Tyler continued, hitting Wren a second, then a third time.

Wren wasn’t able to hold in his whimper of pain as he felt his teeth cut into his cheek with each blow. The taste of blood permeated his mouth. He reluctantly swallowed wishing he could spit instead.

“What is the password to access your phone,” Tyler asked, his voice resuming its calm and reasonable tone, as if any part of this situation was reasonable.

“252003” Wren answered. He hated that his voice trembled. He hated even more how scared he was, not just for Aiden but for himself.

As he watched Tyler go through his phone, all Wren felt was regret. He regretted not calling his mother earlier this evening and telling her he loved her. He regretted going with Tyler and not making a bigger stink. Maybe if he’d yelled and screamed, then maybe Tyler would have been stopped and arrested right there. The police could have forced him to say where he’d taken Aiden. Instead, it was quite possible Wren wasn’t going to make it out of this alive. And what would happen to Aiden if Wren wasn’t there to rescue him? In fact, as rage settled across Tyler’s face again, Wren regretted that he might not even see Aiden once last time.

No! He wasn’t going to just sit back and let things happen to him anymore. He was done with sitting back and letting Tyler ruin his life.

Wren slowly and subtly moved his hand, so it was over the door handle and then in a rush of movement he unlocked it and threw the door open and scrambled it of the car as fast as he could. Out of the corner of his eye, Wren saw Tyler lunge toward him and try to grab him, but Tyler was still wearing his seatbelt and Wren wasn’t. He was out of the car and out of reach before Tyler could do anything to stop him.

A rush of adrenaline hit him as he turned and sprinted toward the house. He heard a car door slam behind him.

“Stop!” Tyler shouted emphatically.

Wren just pushed faster running toward the house. He screamed. First, he yelled for help, then remembering advice someone had given him when he was a kid, he yelled, “Fire!”

None of the lights came on in the house.

Wren got to the door and repeatedly pushed the doorbell. Ring, ring, ring. *Please open. Please wake up and see what’s going on!* he begged silently. He could hear the doorbell going off inside the house but couldn’t see any movement or hear any other noise from inside the house.

He could hear Tyler’s footsteps getting closer. He was still sternly telling Wren to stop.

Three houses down a porch line went on. Wren turned his body and ran toward the light except he hadn’t made it more than two steps before his legs were kicked out from underneath him. He fell hard onto his hands and knees.

*No, no, no. Please, I need to get help,* Wren thought to himself as he felt Tyler kick him in the stomach repeatedly. He tried to yell for help but Tyler had knocked the air from his chest and he could barely breathe, let alone speak.

“Sorry about that,” Tyler said with an apologetic, almost joking tone. “My friend had too much to drink and was being stupid. I am taking him inside and up to bed. I apologize for waking you. I promise it won’t happen again.”

Tyler was talking to the people with the porch light. Wren tried to talk again, to say something, but could only let out a soft moan of pain as Tyler moved his foot and stood on his wrist.

Then the light went out again.

“I am going to kill you, you little shit.” Tyler hissed as he kicked Wren again before leaning forward and taking hold of Wren by the now injured wrist. “But before I do that, I will take out my frustration on your little shit of a boyfriend. So, if you want to keep him from hurting more than necessary you better behave from here on out.”

Wren felt the fight leak out of him and sagged into Tyler’s grip.

"That's right." Tyler said, pulling Wren not back to the car but toward the house, which was when Wren noticed the sold sign on the front lawn. "Come with me. If you are good, I will show you around. I bought this house for the two of us. It is exactly what you always wanted. It is a little mundane for my taste, but I wanted to make you happy. I took possession at the beginning of the month. You can not imagine how disappointed I was when you disappeared and I could not share the good news with you."

Wren felt a chill travel through his body. This was Tyler's house? And he'd bought it for Wren? No wonder no one had answered the door.

"I decided I should go stay with my father for a while," Wren explained softly. It wasn't worth lying. At least not about this.

Tyler pulled a key out of his pocket and put it into the lock while he glanced over at Wren in surprise. "Why would you stay there? I thought you hated your father. Does he not disapprove of your sexuality?"

"My room was a bit of a mess."

"Yes, I am very sorry about that. You made me very angry." Tyler's voice had taken on the same apologetic tone which he had used so many times in the past. It was odd hearing it now, knowing how insincere it was or at least how temporary his regret truly was. Wren remembered believing Tyler when he apologized. As though his behaviour had been an accident. Right, accident, like Wren accidentally called the police and ran across the country to get away from him. He still hated how naïve, how fucking stupid he'd been to believe all of Tyler's lies.

But not this time.

A plan formed in his mind. Maybe, if he played his cards just right, he could get both himself and Aiden out of this situation. Maybe everyone would survive because this time he would be the one that used words as weapons and hid truths behind sweet sounding lies.

"No, I'm sorry. I screwed up. You had every right to be angry, but I will make it up to you." Wren said. "I was just scared."

"Scared?" Tyler asked. Wren watched as Tyler used a key to lock the door behind them. He was being locked inside the house. "Why were you scared? How can you not know everything I do is to help make you better?"

Tyler released Wren's wrist. Not that there was anywhere for Wren to go now that they were both inside. He had to consciously avoid rubbing his bruised wrist, both to relieve the pain and to wipe the taint Tyler's touch had left. Instead, he forced himself to turn toward Tyler and tried to look as sincere as he could by pretending he was talking to Aiden and apologizing for getting him into this situation.

"I know but I got confused. My mother kept telling me things about you and I got all messed up in my head and it was almost like I didn't know you anymore. I felt lost. I only spent time with Aiden because she wanted me to. Aiden is my old friend Lucy's little brother and my mom likes him. But it never felt right. Every day I was losing myself more but my mom kept whispering lies into my ears and I didn't know what to think anymore. But after I moved to my dad's I remembered how things really were with you. It was like I was coming out of a fog. I knew you were around and I needed to see you but wasn't sure how. So, I convinced Aiden to go out with me so no one would be suspicious. I hoped you would find me."

Tyler looked skeptical. Wren thought more about how much he loved Aiden. He focused on Aiden's face in his mind. "I love you."

"If you wanted me to find you, why did you run away?" Tyler asked. He took a menacing step toward Wren like he knew how much Wren was lying and was already ready to make him pay for even trying it.

Wren thought about Aiden and his mom. He thought about how ashamed he was that he had just gotten into the goddamn car rather than making a scene and getting Tyler arrested there at the club. "I was ashamed." Wren felt the shame travel through his body and could almost feel it leaving him through his pores. "I was so ashamed of how I had acted, calling the police on you and then listening to my mother. Then seeing you holding my phone reminded me of all the messages I had sent while I was brainwashed. Made me think about everything I did while I was under someone else's influence. I couldn't bear to think about how much I'd hurt you."

Wren was crying by this point. They were real tears. He felt ashamed and so much regret. He didn't have to fake those emotions. He just didn't feel them toward Tyler. No, if he could, he'd throw him in jail for the rest of his life. He was ashamed of how he'd acted while he was with Tyler, ashamed of the people he'd hurt, and ashamed of the things he'd done to lie to himself and the small number of people who stuck around because they still cared about him. He thought about Aiden, stuck somewhere, hopefully in this house, afraid, alone, and possibly hurt.

Tyler watched Wren cry and his expression softened. He wrapped his arms around Wren, hugging him in close. Tyler patted Wren's back and made soothing sounds and Wren felt himself cry harder, in fear and horror at being back in Tyler's arms. He wanted to scream and push Tyler away but he needed to keep playing this game.

After a few moments that felt like torturous hours, Tyler relaxed his hold and offered, "There is a way you can make it all up to me."

"There is?" Wren put all his hope for seeing Aiden soon into his face.

"You will do it for me right? You will do what I ask to show me how much you love me and how sorry you are for hurting me." Wren forced himself to nod but couldn't push the words past his lips. "Good."

Tyler stepped back and Wren took a deep breath. He tried to play it like he was happy Tyler might forgive him; but really, he felt like he could breathe again now that Tyler wasn't touching him anymore. Tyler barely glanced at him though. Instead he turned and walked down the hallway leading them further into the house.

Tyler led Wren to a set of narrow stairs. He turned on the light switch and indicated Wren should lead the way downstairs. Wren could barely make himself take the first step. Even knowing Aiden might be down there, Wren struggled to walk down the stairs. He didn't want to lead Tyler—the fucking bad guy—down a narrow staircase into a dark empty basement.

Despite his every effort, he had become the blond bimbo in every slasher film.

God, he was going to die. He was going to die. He was so going to die.

Shit! He needed to stop thinking like that. He needed to get himself under control. Wren started down the stairs.

# Chapter 44
## Aiden

Aiden tried to flex his arms and move his wrists to pull on the bindings for the hundredth time since he'd been left alone in this room. Just like every other time, his movements were lethargic. He couldn't make any give in the rope which attached his wrists together behind his back. There was also a gag around his neck and mouth preventing him from talking or even breathing properly. The cloth was also drying out his mouth and tasted like shit.

Not that it mattered too much if he talked. He was alone in a dark room.

Looking around, Aiden couldn't see anything in the room except shadows and empty walls and floor. Even that could only be seen because of a small amount of light coming in through a narrow window near the top of a wall. The room smelled dank and unused. There was a closed door on the other side of the room. It was the kind of door he'd seen in many of his friends' parents' houses, the ones that had been built in the 1960s and 1970s. Since he'd heard Tyler leave the house, he had heard no indication anyone else was around. The only noises he'd heard were the quiet sounds of an old house at night. Every so often he could hear the soft click of the furnace turning on nearby and the quiet cracks and squeaks of the house settling.

Aiden realized he must be in a basement room in a house.

Yes, Tyler. Fucking Tyler!

Aiden took a deep breath to keep himself from screaming in frustration and annoyance. Despite being on the lookout for the past month and avoiding Wren that whole time, Aiden had let himself be overwhelmed and taken in by Tyler. Despite having been there, he genuinely wondered what had happened.

*Aiden felt his dick throb after watching the fluid way Wren danced. Wren and Zane made a striking pair on the dance-floor and he wasn't the only one to notice. Aiden enjoyed the show. He admitted to himself he was glad he got to do more than watch because he knew the feeling of Wren dancing and rubbing against him was much better than watching anything the two men could do together. And what he could do alone with Wren was even better than dancing.*

*Which was why he turned away and pushed his away through the crowd toward the bar instead of staying to watch. He was so thirsty. The club was hot with all the sweaty bodies and he needed a drink to cool off. He really wished he could go stand outside in the cool evening air but he figured standing around alone outside was a bad idea. He wondered if he could convince Zane and Derek to step outside later so they could all catch a breath.*

*He sidled up to the bar and managed to flag down the bartender. He asked for two waters. The bartender, clearly a seasoned flirt, was wearing a tight pink tank top with a picture of a frog on it saying "Kiss?". He winked when he caught Aiden's eye and then brushed his fingers against Aiden's hand when he passed over the drinks.*

*"Two, that's disappointing," he yelled as he leaned over the counter.*

*"What can I say?" Aiden joked. "I'm a catch."*

*"That you are!" Another wink. Aiden laughed and shook his head as he walked away.*

*Almost immediately he felt himself being pushed by the crowd around the bar. He glanced to his left when he thought he heard someone yell, "Whore!" but there were so many people he couldn't tell who'd spoken. He looked back at his water and took a big gulp from both glasses, to try to keep them from spilling as he tried to navigate through the mass of dancing bodies.*

*The club had become significantly busier since he and Wren had arrived and he had trouble getting through the crowd. People kept jostling him. After the second time the water sloshed onto his shoes and forced him to stop and look around for an opening to get back to Wren, he decided he had better find a less crowded route to the back of the club where their table was.*

*He pushed his way through the crowd of sweaty bodies. He could tell the liquor was hitting people's systems when he got his ass slapped for the third time and a messy drunk came over and propositioned him. God, even if he'd been desperate the answer would have been no.*

*Finally, after what felt like forever, Aiden reached the side wall. It was far enough away from the dance floor and the bar that it was less crowded. He stopped worrying so much about someone spilling the water down his front before he could bring Wren's back to the table. Aiden stopped to enjoy the relative peace and took another long drink of water from his glass. He was so thirsty the cool liquid felt like heaven as it travelled down his dry throat.*

*He stood and leaned against the wall for a little while watching the dancers from the safety of his spot near the wall. He caught sight of Wren still dancing with Zane and smiled at how much fun they were both having. Since Wren was occupied, Aiden took another moment to finish his water. He drank and watched for glimpses of them through the crowded dance floor. When he finished his water, he stood back up to continue his trek back toward the back table.*

*He had to pass by the washrooms on his way back to the table. Seeing them made him realize he needed to pee, so he joined the line to the bathroom. It was nice to stand still. He was tired. He enjoyed dancing, and it was great to touch Wren after not seeing him for weeks; but it had been a long week. He hadn't mentioned it to Wren because he didn't want him feeling worse than he already did, but Aiden missed him at night and hadn't been sleeping well since Wren had moved in with his dad.*

*God, he missed being able to see Wren whenever he wanted to.*

*Man, he was exhausted.*

*Maybe when he got back to the table, he'd have to suggest to Wren that they cut the evening short so he could go to bed. He felt like a complete wimp but the reality was he wasn't a student anymore. He couldn't stay up all night then sleep all day. He had to get up at seven to get to work on time.*

*He used to get up at six so he could go for a run before work but he hadn't been going for his run since he'd found out about Tyler. The whole being alone in the river valley thing had just seemed like a bad idea. Maybe that was part of his problem, too. He'd had a routine which included regular physical activity, but now he was barely working out and he couldn't sleep at night.*

*He was so tired. Why was this line moving so slowly? He really needed to piss, and he wanted to sit down. Or maybe lay down. He felt himself sway on his feet and leaned against the wall to steady himself.*

*Someone came up to him and said, "There's another washroom this way with no line. Come, I'll show you."*

*Aiden nodded his head. He was grateful to the stranger. He couldn't believe how tired he was.*

*"Thanks, man. You're a hero," he mumbled. His legs were growing heavier, but he needed to go piss. Then he would go back to Wren.*

*That's right. He needed to get to Wren and bring him his water. Then they needed to leave. "Just need to pee, then I'll head home, I think" Aiden added in a great example of over sharing.*

*Why did he even say that?*

*Oh, well.*

*There was a door in front of them. Something about it looked wrong for a bathroom door but Aiden wasn't sure. He couldn't think clearly and he was starting to wonder if something was wrong. But he was too tired to worry about it. He just needed to go pee and get back to Wren.*

*He pushed the door open, stepped forward, and found himself outside.*

*"Wha—?" he slurred. He turned around to go back inside except the door was closed and didn't seem to have a handle. He blinked. What?*

*That's when he noticed there was a man standing outside with him. He was around the same height but seemed bigger because he was more muscular. They also shared similarly dark hair. The biggest difference between them was Aiden had no clue what was going on and the other man seemed to know him and had an angry scowl on his face.*

*"Who—?" Aiden asked. What was going on? Who was this person? He needed to get back to Wren. He wasn't supposed to be alone outside.*

*Aiden turned, not even bothering to wait for the mysterious person to identify himself. He needed to find a different door. He needed to get back inside where Wren was waiting for him.*

*"You are a fucking thief—a slut. I will make you pay for your crimes. They said they were punishing me, you at least deserve what you are going to get." Aiden glanced back at the man. He stepped toward Aiden, following him down the back alley. What was he on about?*

*"What?" Aiden repeated. The man took another step toward Aiden, and instead of answering his face shifted into a menacing sneer.*

*What was this guy's problem? Whatever. It didn't matter. He needed to get back inside to Wren.*

*Aiden turned his back to the man and continued back toward the end of the alley which seemed to be further away somehow.*

*That was when he'd felt the first hit. It had been to his shoulder. He tried to turn but the next one had been to his leg and he fell down. The third had been to the back of the head.*

*He knew he cried out in pain but he couldn't fight back. He felt woozy and sick. Something was definitely wrong, and more than having this stranger attack him.*

*He felt sick. That's when he threw up.*

*Maybe it was a type of defence because the blows stopped and Aiden heard a yell in indignation.*

*"You filthy piece of shit!" the man yelled as he jumped back and out of the away of the pool of vomit. Aiden would have felt triumphant except he still felt weak and woozy.*

*He threw up again. Afterword he didn't feel as sick anymore but a sense of dread was overtaking him. He realized something was seriously wrong. He was pretty sure someone had drugged him.*

*He looked up at the man who was a sending over him with a look of disgust. Aiden realized he could guess who this stranger was.*

*"Tyler," Aiden whispered. He wanted to get up and get away but he was so weak he could barely move.*

*Without saying a word Tyler leaned over Aiden and tied his wrists together. Then he stuffed a cloth into Aiden's mouth.*

*Aiden belatedly realized he should have called for help, but his thoughts were muddy and his body felt like it was pushing through molasses. Unable to fight back, Tyler picked him up and shoved Aiden into a car that must have been parked close by.*

Back in the present Aiden's body twitched in surprise when he heard the doorbell ring a few times. Someone was here. He squirmed and tried to yell again but he could barely move. It was like his consciousness was hanging a few inches over his head.

He jerked again a few minutes later as he heard the door upstairs open and the sound of footsteps coming down the stairs.

# Chapter 45
## Wren

Wren felt his heart break when he opened the basement door and saw Aiden. He was sitting on a chair with his arms behind his back—Wren assumed Tyler must have tied him up—and his mouth was half pried open by a gag made of a blue cloth. Wren wanted to run to him and yank him free but he knew he couldn't, not if they wanted to have any chance of escaping.

Wren glanced between Aiden and Tyler. A week ago, if someone had asked him, he would have reluctantly said they looked similar but seeing them together for the first time, all he could see were their differences. Sure, they were both tall and both had short dark hair but that was where their similarities ended. Wren was pretty sure Aiden was a bit taller but Tyler was more muscular. Tyler had somehow put on even more muscle mass since Wren had seen him last. Wren wondered if he'd spent some of his time in custody lifting weights. Conversely, Aiden had a runner's build. His muscles were long and lean. Aiden was also more tanned. Tyler had always been someone who wanted to spend his time inside, surrounded by luxury. Aiden enjoyed spending time outside in the river valley. He didn't even have a gym membership.

But it wasn't just their physical appearance. Tyler's belief in his own superiority oozed out of his skin. It wasn't just that he had kidnapped Aiden and Wren. It was that he truly believed he deserved to get whatever he wanted. Even hurt and tied up kindness shone from Aiden's soul. When

Aiden had seen Wren enter the room he had cried out through his gag and a tear had slid down his cheek. Tyler was the reason they were even there.

"Now that you have us both here, what do you intend to do with us?" Wren asked Tyler. He glanced at Aiden and tried to silently explain what he was trying to do. Except the message didn't connect. Aiden continued to look confused. Wren realized something was wrong with him. Well, more wrong than being tied up in a basement after being kidnapped.

How was this even real?

Something was definitely wrong with Aiden. Although he looked up when Wren first entered the room, his eyes were glassy and now his head was lulling forward as though his neck wasn't strong enough to support his head.

"Well, that entirely depends on you," Tyler answered his first question, although now Wren had a million more.

"What do you mean?"

Tyler took a few steps into the room, walking toward Aiden. Wren took several steps to follow him, every part of his being wanting to stop Tyler from touching Aiden. It was as though somehow by touching him Tyler could transfer his taint. Except by now, it was pretty clear that ship had already sailed. Now it was just up to Wren to see if he could navigate them out without any further harm.

"If you really love me and were just being brainwashed by this piece of filth, then I will punish him for his actions and only punish you a little for leaving me before." Tyler spoke in his terrifying matter-of-fact tone. As Tyler spoke, he took hold of Aiden's hair and pulled his head up and back until his face was pointing toward the ceiling. Aiden whimpered and Wren clenched his fists and jaw to stop himself from running forward to protect him.

"I do love you," Wren asserted. Then he begged, "But you need to let him go. He isn't worth it. Yes, he confused me but if you hurt him, you could end up back in trouble and I don't want that. I want to live with you again, not have to visit you in jail."

"You are right. I refuse to go back there. Maybe I should make you hurt him—prove you really love me and don't care about him." Tyler tilted Aiden's face to the side, exposing the side of his neck.

Wren felt his stomach turn at the very idea of hurting Aiden but he remained focused. "I love you. I really do. I will do anything you need me to do to prove it."

Tyler didn't seem convinced, but he let Aiden's head go. It flopped forward before Aiden raised it. He met Wren's eyes for a moment before looking away. The moment was long enough. Aiden looked so confused and almost betrayed. Wren hoped that they would both make it out alive so that Wren could spend the rest of his life making this moment up to Aiden. At least he hoped he'd have a chance to tell Aiden why he was doing this.

"That being said, if you don't love me, if this is you trying to play me," Tyler emphasized the word 'play,' like he knew this was a significant possibility. "Then I will do whatever I need to make you understand you are mine. Trying to deceive me is not acceptable. Maybe last time I was not forceful enough. What do you think?"

"I'm not trying to do anything but show you I love you," Wren argued. He wondered what more forceful would look like. He could have easily killed Wren last time. Would Tyler only be satisfied when he was dead?

After a brief pause while Tyler let Wren think about what he'd just said he continued, "In that case I will need to kill this piece of trash to make sure you understand being with him isn't an option." At these words Tyler kicked Aiden in the leg. Aiden let out a grunt of pain and shifted his body as though he was trying to get away but could not because of his bindings.

Wren couldn't help it anymore, he couldn't stop the tears from sliding down his face. He had to make this stop or at least slow everything down. If they were slow enough, maybe the cavalry would arrive before Tyler killed anyone. He'd texted Johnson, and when there was no response Wren hoped she figured out that something was wrong and would come looking for them. Maybe she could find someway to track his phone. He just needed to buy more time. He needed Aiden to survive. He wasn't sure if he cared anymore whether he survived.

No, that wasn't true. He wanted to live but he would happily trade his life for a real chance that Aiden get out safely. He really didn't want his last act on earth to be setting Aiden up to die. He was realistic. Tyler wasn't going to let Wren go—no matter what he said about being nicer if he believed Wren loved him. Wren knew Tyler intended to beat the ever-loving shit out of him and there was a good chance this time he wouldn't survive. He just really, really didn't want to take Aiden down with him.

"Tyler, I love you and I will stay with you. I will call my mom and tell her I'm with you willingly, and I won't try to get away. I will accept whatever punishment you think I deserve. I know that I screwed up and I deserve to be punished. I understand that. But you need to let Aiden go. He has a family that won't stop looking for him. You will get into so much trouble if you don't just let him go. I don't want you to get into trouble." Wren was full on sobbing while he begged Tyler.

"You seem mighty concerned about someone you say manipulated you. Aren't you angry with him?" Tyler asked with a sneer.

"Yes! Yes, I'm angry but I want to protect you." Wren fell to his knees in front of Tyler. *Please believe me*, Wren begged silently.

"Then prove it." Tyler said pointing at Aiden. "He manipulated your mind and made you think you were not mine. He needs to suffer for that. Prove that you love me not him."

Wren was shaking his head before he even realized he was doing it. His body shook and he felt sick to his stomach. But it had been long enough since he'd eaten or drunk anything that he didn't think there would be anything to throw up if he was sick.

"Hit him!" Tyler shouted, back handing Aiden across his face with a loud smack. "Hurt him or I will."

Wren started at the sudden loud noise. He slowly pulled himself to his feet and stood in front of Aiden. Aiden was looking into Wren's eyes and he tried to apologize silently. He tried to show Aiden how much he loved him and how much he hated this situation but he wasn't sure how much of this Aiden had gotten. His eyes were still fuzzy although Wren thought they were starting to clear up. He seemed more alert and was holding his head straighter. Wren wondered if whatever drug or substance Tyler had given him was passing through his system.

Aiden gave a slight nod like he understood and was telling him it was okay. It wasn't okay though. Even with the sign that Aiden understood Wren couldn't do it. He couldn't hurt Aiden. He just couldn't.

"I can't, Tyler. Please don't make me. I just can't hurt anyone. I want everyone to be safe, including you." Wren argued. He added the last part hoping it would appease Tyler but knew it hadn't when Tyler raised his fist and punched Wren in the stomach.

Instinctively, Wren tried to block the hit and get away. All it did was deflect the punch to the left side of his abdomen and make Tyler angrier. Tyler continued to punch him. Wren lurched back to avoid the onslaught but tripped and fell to the ground. That's when it really got bad. Wren couldn't do anything other than curl into the fetal position and cover his head, trying to protect himself from the kicks.

Wren couldn't hold back the tears. With each blow he could hear Aiden moaning and yelling through his gag. He wanted to tell Aiden to stop but he couldn't make the words get past his own grunts and sobs of pain. He rolled over, trying to get away but Tyler just followed him.

Then almost as suddenly as it started, Tyler stopped. Wren rolled and moved himself as far away from Tyler as he could. His back hit the far wall but Tyler wasn't even looking at him. He was looking at Wren's phone—the cell phone Tyler must have forgotten about when Wren had tried to run away and then had suddenly started cooperating.

"'I need your help to find you,'" Tyler read from Wren's cell phone. "Who is Johnson?"

Wren didn't answer, but he didn't need to. Tyler used the code Wren had given him earlier and unlocked the phone.

"'Going with T—has A.' Cute," Tyler sneered. "Rescue us pls." He continued in a high pitch imitation of a damsel in distress. He walked over to Wren, following him when Wren tried to scramble away and then kicked him hard in the side. Wren felt his hip slam against the wall but barely felt the secondary pain. He hoped he'd only be pissing blood was not about to experience some sort of more serious liver damage. Although at this point, Wren would just be happy to live long enough to find out.

"I guess you chose option two. You think you can lie to me?! You think you are smarter than me? You think you can control me?" Tyler was yelling and Wren continued to shrink back as he watched Tyler's eyes develop a frenzied glint to them. "For this, I will kill you both. But first, I have to get ride of this fucking phone so they cannot use it to track us," Tyler's voice was back to being calm, but the glint hadn't gone away and his outward calm didn't stop him from kicking Wren again. He looked over at Aiden. "You probably have one too. Don't you? Fucking FUCK!"

Tyler walked over to Aiden and pushed the chair over. Wren watched as Aiden's chair tipped over and shattered while his head hit the ground and bounced. Wren held his breath. Aiden didn't move. And then he saw blood. Wren got up as best he could and scrambled to him. *Aiden wasn't moving, was he even still alive?*

Wren moved forward, ignoring Tyler who was riffling through Aiden's pockets. He had to make sure Aiden was alive but he shouldn't have ignored Tyler. Before he was close enough to see what had happened, Tyler grabbed Wren by the waist and shoved him back. He felt a crack on the back of his head and then everything went black.

# Chapter 46
## Aiden

Aiden woke up slowly. Before he had even opened his eyes, he realized he was sore. He hurt. His whole body hurt. He couldn't think of why. It felt like a truck hit him. It was like the time he'd been run over by a huge player on one of the opposing teams during the summer he'd played ultimate Frisbee.

What was wrong with him? He wondered if maybe he had been in a car accident. He felt sick and his mouth tasted like he'd thrown up then licked an ashtray or something. His head throbbed and his ribs hurt with every breath he took. Even his shoulders and wrists hurt. Wait, if it was a car accident why did his wrists hurt? He frowned and let out a cry as his face exploded with pain at the movement.

He was confused and disoriented. And his head hurt. The last thing he remembered was walking toward the bar to get a drink of water for himself and for Wren.

Had they gotten into a car accident on the way home? Where was he? Was Wren all right?

Aiden opened his eyes and slowly sat up fighting increased pain and nausea as he moved. He realized he had been lying on a concrete floor. So, not a hospital.

He looked around. It was dark except for a small amount of light coming in from a small window on the other side of the room. It was night and the only light coming in was from street lights or general city nighttime lighting.

The room appeared to be empty. Although Aiden noticed a pile of blankets on the other side of the room.

What happened? Where was he? How did he get here? And where was Wren?

Aiden felt a memory flit through his mind but was gone before he could grasp onto it. No, not even a full memory, more like a sketch of a memory. It felt almost like he'd been here before but he couldn't think of why or where he might be.

Aiden moved to stand up but then had to stop when his head, chest, and stomach revolted. He knelt with his head forward, hoping he wouldn't vomit. Something sticky covered the front of his shirt, sticking the material to his skin. It was only partially dry. When he touched it and examined it more closely, he realized it was blood. His wrists were also scratched up and bloody. He lifted his hands to his head and realized he had something wet and crusty in his hair and on his face and... ouch! his nose! His nose must have been bleeding but it wasn't bleeding anymore which was probably a good sign. Although, now that he was paying attention, breathing through his nose hurt. Maybe it was broken.

He slowly crawled toward the door and pulled himself up on the door handle. Being so close to the door, he recognized it as a hollow core style door like he'd seen in many houses growing up. It confirmed his suspicion that he was in someone's house.

He tried the door. The handle turned but the door wouldn't open. He tried the handle again, he pushed, he pulled, nothing happened. The door shook but it wouldn't open. Somehow it was locked or blocked from the other side.

He was trapped in the room.

Aiden knocked on the door and then listened. He couldn't hear anything. It sounded as though there was no one else around. He knocked louder and yelled. More silence was the only response. He was alone.

Just putting that much effort in was difficult. He's breathing was laboured, and he felt as though he might be sick. He leaned back against the door and slid down until he was sitting. He took stock. He was trapped in the room, stuck in some unknown location. He was covered in blood, breathing hurt and his head hurt with every heartbeat. He was pretty sure—now he had thought about it—he was pretty sure he was concussed.

He decided if he looked on the bright side, at least he had a heartbeat, given his current circumstances he figured he should be thankful he'd woken up at all.

He shivered and knew it wasn't only caused by the cool air. What the hell was going on?

Some time passed. Another thought or memory passed through his brain before he could catch it. Had Wren been here with him? Where was Wren now?

More time passed, enough for Aiden to become chilled and for him to calm down enough to check and see if he still had his cell phone. He didn't. Or some other way to escape or contact the outside. He didn't. His pockets were empty. Even his wallet had disappeared. He wondered if he could squeeze out the window. He'd have to find someway to break it but dismissed the idea almost immediately. It was hopeless. The window was small. It was way too small for someone his size to squeeze out.

He checked his nose and head. They still hurt.

That was when he noticed a dark lump against the wall on the other side of the room. Had that been there before? He thought maybe it had, but his thoughts remained fuzzy. The shadows mostly hid the object but there was definitely something there. Aiden crawled over to the corner. As he got closer, he saw it was large, with a dark-coloured blanket covering whatever was underneath. Very slowly Aiden reached his hand out and touched the blanket. The blanket appeared to be a cheap fleece blanket. It was covering something shaped like a body and felt like it might be a person.

Aiden stopped and took a deep breath. He prayed he had not been locked up with a dead body. He was almost afraid to move the blanket.

What if some serial killer had kidnapped him and this was the last victim's body? Oh, god. Oh, god. Aiden took a few deep breaths as he tried not to panic. Then took a few more deep breaths as he acknowledged he was definitely panicking. He needed to see what or who was underneath the blanket. He was regretting every episode of X-Files he had ever watched because, at this point, part of him wouldn't have been surprised if it turned out to be an alien or a monster. Years of loving sci-fi gave him too many ideas for his fertile imagination to recreate.

Taking a deep breath, Aiden grabbed the blanket and pulled it off as fast as he could. Then stopped cold and heard a soft keen leave his lips.

It was Wren. Under the blanket was Wren. He lay unmoving.

No. No, no, no, no. Wren couldn't be dead. This was worse than an alien. This was worse than even his overactive imagination could have created.

Slowly, with shaking hands, Aiden touched his hand to Wren's shoulder. Wren's skin was still warm. Aiden suspected that was a good sign. If he was dead, he hadn't been dead long.

Aiden shook Wren's shoulder. "Hey, Wren," Aiden whispered. Nothing. He moved his hand over to Wren's throat to check for his pulse. Nothing!

Wait, no—that wasn't where his pulse was. There, there! Yes. There was a pulse. Thank fucking god! There was a pulse. Now, he just needed to wake up.

Aiden cleared his throat and spoke louder. "Wren, baby. Wake up. Oh, god. Wren wake up, baby. Tell me you're okay."

Wren moaned.

Aiden whipped his hand back, startled by the noise in the silent room. Then, realizing what he had done, he put his hand out again to touch Wren's shoulder as he moved his body forward, closer to Wren's head.

"Oh, thank god. Wren, baby, Wren, it's me, Aiden. Please open your eyes." Aiden eased Wren's head onto his lap as Wren moaned again. Aiden watched as Wren's fingers twitched. He gently rubbed his hand down Wren's face. "Wren, please, show me you're okay."

Wren's eyes fluttered. Aiden let out a soft sigh of relief. He continued to gently rub Wren's face and encourage him. He finally opened his eyes. It took a second for his eyes to focus. A look of confusion crossed his face before it was overcome with relief, then concern.

"Oh, god. Aiden. Thank god you're alive," Wren said, as he tried to sit and reached his hand toward Aiden's face. "He pushed you over and you landed so hard so hard. You weren't moving. I was so scared you were dead. Are you okay?"

"I don't—no, stay lying down. You were unconscious," Aiden said, pushing Wren back down onto his lap. "I don't know what is going on, but you were unconscious. You shouldn't be moving. Plus, I already checked. There is nothing here, just you and me. We're trapped in some room. I don't know what's going on, but someone hurt you and I don't know how to get out to get help."

"You're sure we're alone? Oh, god, there is blood everywhere. Are you sure you are okay?"

"I must have hit my face or something. I don't remember. The last thing I remember was being at the club and getting water. Then I woke up here. My nose and head hurts. I think I have a concussion. My nose must have been bleeding because there is blood everywhere."

Wren grabbed Aiden's hand and squeezed. "It was Tyler. I don't know how he got you. You never came back with the drinks. I went looking for you. Everyone was looking for you. And then Tyler showed up. I was outside the club and he grabbed me. He told me he had you and he would do something to you, maybe kill you, if I didn't come with him. I was so scared, so I went with him. I didn't have a choice."

"Tyler? Tyler? Shit yes, Tyler!" Aiden exclaimed, as some of the events of the night came rushing back. There were still gaps in his memories and what he recalled was fuzzy or made no sense. "He hurt you!" Aiden almost yelled as he ran his hands gently over Wren's face and chest. He knew he'd found a tender spot when Wren winced.

"I'll survive but seriously, how are you?" Wren ran his hands over Aiden's body as well, looking for injuries Aiden might not be telling him about.

"He fucking roofied me!" Aiden said before he explained what he remembered of what had happened.

"I did tell him I loved him. I had to or, at least I thought that was the only way to save us, but it backfired. He figured out I was trying to manipulate him and he got so angry. See, I'd texted Johnson after Tyler grabbed me and she kept texting me back. I think she was trying to figure out where we were but Tyler had my phone and he saw the messages. He put two and two together. That's when he hit you again and knocked both of us out.

"He has lost his mind. He said he's going to kill us."

Aiden just looked at Wren in horror. Aiden believed Tyler's threat. If Tyler was willing to go this far why wouldn't he be willing to kill them? It was almost the safest option. At least if they were dead, he could try to hid the bodies. If he kept them alive, he had to know he would end up back in jail almost immediately.

"We have to figure out how to escape." Wren moved to sit up again. This time he made it to a seated position. He stayed like that a moment, leaning against the wall. "We have to get away from here and quickly. I don't know how long we've been unconscious or where he is. He could come back at any minute and we can't be here when he gets back. We can't. I don't know why he even left us for this long. Nothing he does makes any sense."

"What about your text to Constable Johnson?"

"Johnson knows we are with Tyler but she doesn't know where we are. Or at least I don't think so. I mean, the phone was here for a while before Tyler took it but I don't think the police can track everywhere it has been. I mean, I know the real world isn't like on CSI and stuff. I don't think the real police can access the 'find my phone' service without a warrant, if they can at all. Besides, the whole reason Tyler left was to get rid of our phones."

# Chapter 47
## Wren

Wren watched as Aiden looked around. His head hurt. Tyler had locked them in a room with no clear way to escape and yet, all Wren could feel was relief. He was with Aiden again. Somehow, they were both alive. After everything, that was an achievement worth celebrating.

*Yeah, to being not dead and together.* Wren felt like they could accomplish anything as long as they were together.

"Okay. Well, if Tyler has left us alone in this house, then we need to use this opportunity to get away. I'm sure he thinks he has locked us in but he isn't as smart as he thinks. There has to be a way out," Wren mused.

"Well, smart enough to capture both of us," Aiden pointed out.

"Except he wouldn't have been able to capture me if he didn't already have you and he probably only got you because you didn't recognize him. And he still had to drug you to actually make it happen."

"I guess. I still think we shouldn't underestimate him."

"Oh, I'm not but I don't think we should overestimate him either. We can do this, we just need to think."

"With concussions and me coming off of a roofie," Aiden pointed out.

"Hey, I never said it would be easy." Wren joked. He wasn't sure how he could laugh, except he was just so relieved Aiden was alive and Tyler had left them alone that he felt practically giddy.

Aiden slowly stood up using the wall to help support himself. Then he slowly walked around the room, looking to see if there was anything in the room they had missed. “I feel sick. I might vomit but I can walk. How about you? How do you feel?”

Wren took stock. He also felt nauseous and his head hurt, pounding with every movement, but he could bear it if he had to—and he had to. His abdomen and side also hurt and he could tell a bruise was developing which would be spectacular in a few days if they escaped and lived long enough for him to see it. He really hoped he didn’t have some kind of internal bleeding. It would be horrible to suddenly pass out and die while they were escaping.

Not helpful.

Otherwise, though, he didn’t feel too terrible. He just had some other bruises he could ignore. He was grateful Tyler hadn’t kicked him in the ribs and broken or cracked any. He’d done that last time, and it had made doing anything almost impossible for days.

He sat for a while and decided he felt stable like that. He wondered whether he could stand up and decided it was worth a shot. He turned onto all fours and, using the wall for support, slowly stood up. It made the pounding in his head hurt worse but he didn’t think his nausea worsened. He tentatively took a step forward. *So far, so good.* He stood up straight and moved his hand off the wall. He took another step forward.

“I don’t think I could go for a run or anything but I think I can manage walking slowly,” Wren said.

“The room is empty except for us.” Aiden said. Despite moving slowly, Aiden was back beside Wren. It wasn’t a large room. “Oh, and the blanket Tyler used to cover you. He must still have a soft spot for you because he didn’t leave me with a blanket.” Aiden added with a small ironic smile.

“I could do without his affection.”

Aiden gave a small laugh then winced when the laugh and smile made his face hurt worse.

“We have no weapons or tools and no phone to call for help,” Aiden summarized. “What do we have? How are we supposed to get out of here?”

Wren looked around. "It looks as though there are two options: the door or the window."

"Something is blocking the door from the outside," Aiden said. "And there is no way I can fit through the window. You might fit, maybe, but it is too small for my shoulders."

"Ya," Wren nodded, looking at the window critically. "It'd be tight. I think I might fit but you certainly wouldn't. I think we should focus on the door. I really don't want us to separate unless we absolutely have to. It might not be logical but somehow it feels like we are safe as long as we are together." Wren slowly walked over to the door and rattled the handle. "Maybe we can break the door down."

They looked at the door carefully. It was a cheap plywood door. It seemed to be the type door made of a thin, hollow plywood. Wren figured they should be able to break it down.

Aiden groaned. Wren knew exactly what he was thinking. Breaking down a door, even a flimsy one like this one appeared to be, would absolutely suck donkey balls with a concussion.

"Ya, I don't want to either but it's this or I crawl out the window and leave you behind which I want even less."

"Ya," Aiden agreed. He looked so resolute, like he was ready to do anything even though he was hurt and likely still had drugs in his system. Maybe the drugs were dulling the pain? They could only hope for small favours.

Wren looked at the door again and grimaced. Glancing back at the window, he confirmed what they needed to do. That window was too small for Aiden. The excitement about waking up together and alone was wearing off and a desperate determination was taking its place. They would escape because they had to. But, oh, god, it would be difficult.

After a brief discussion about using their shoulders to ram the door open, Aiden took a step back and then hit the door as hard as he could. The door bounced and shook in the frame but otherwise, nothing happened.

In fact, the impact hurt Aiden much worse than it did the door. He immediately cried out, bent forward, grabbed his head and chest while moaning in pain. Wren gently rubbed his back. Aiden's cries of pain only lasted a few seconds before he jerked his body around and away from Wren. Throwing up bile and dry heaving interrupted his continued whimpers of pain.

"Oh, god, that hurt," Aiden moaned after he had stopped heaving. "Okay, that isn't going to work. It hurts too much and the door is still closed."

Wren rubbed Aiden's back while he thought about alternative solutions. Were there other ways to knock down a door? Then he remembered something that had happened to a friend of his when he was a kid. "What about kicking a hole in the door? These doors are super flimsy. I mean, I used to have one of these at home and when I was a kid, a friend of mine in elementary school kicked a hole in the door while we were playing around."

"Okay, but I need another moment," Aiden said, still hunched over.

Wren nodded, then turned to the door and kicked it. After the first kick, he moaned. It was probably better than throwing himself at the door like Aiden had done but it still hurt an amazing amount. But they had to escape, and this was their only option. So, he did it again, then again. After trying a few different ways, he discovered if he lay on his back and kicked the door with his head still resting on the ground; then the ground helped support his head, and the pain was more bearable. It still hurt, but it was bearable, at least under these circumstances.

After a few more kicks he decided his recollection of the doors was somewhat exaggerated. That or his injury was taking all the strength out of his kicks. Wren figured it was probably a combination of the two. But he was making progress. He wasn't able to kick a hole in one kick the way he remembered, but he created a dent and after kicking for a little while a small hole emerged.

By this point, Aiden was sitting and watching, having realized he couldn't really help. When the hole was big enough to stick a hand through, he stopped Wren.

Aiden and Wren went down onto their hands and knees and pried the wood away to make the hole bigger. Eventually, it was big enough to see through. Wren looked through the hole. It was dark on the other side. He couldn't see a thing. He couldn't even see what was keeping the door from opening. It wasn't enough. They needed a bigger hole.

Wren and Aiden got back to work.

After Wren got a sliver in his hand from the cheap wood, they agreed hand protection would be helpful. Aiden and Wren looked around the empty room. Wren figured his t-shirt would be better than nothing. He pulled it off, being careful of his head, and wrapped it around his hand.

"While the view makes the task easier," Aiden said with a joking smile. "And I hate to say something that might encourage you to put your shirt back on, but there is the blanket. So, you probably don't need to use your shirt."

Wren looked at the hand he had covered in his shirt, looked over at Aiden and the blanket he had already gotten up to grab, and laughed with embarrassment. "Shut up. I have a concussion."

"So, do I," Aiden pointed out with a laugh.

"I said, shut up," Wren laughed. He tried to hold a glare but was smiling despite himself. Aiden leaned over and gave Wren a kiss before Wren put his shirt back on, they both wrapped their hands in the blanket and returned to work.

After what felt like forever, but was probably only about thirty minutes, the hole was big enough for Wren to slip through. By then they had discovered what was keeping the door shut. There was a two by four across the door, preventing it from opening. Knowing what blocked the door didn't actually help. They couldn't do anything about it until Wren was on the other side of the door.

Once the hole was big enough Wren climbed through and looked around. He was back in the open basement room with the stairs which he'd come down earlier with Tyler. He vaguely wondered how long ago that had been. He had lost all sense of time, not that it really mattered. Either way, they needed to get out as quickly as possible because no matter what time it was Tyler could return at any minute. With that in mind he focused on the room around him.

He hadn't look around much before but now he was paying attention he saw that the room was almost empty. He tried to see if there were any hidden tools, or things he could use as a tool to help pry the board free. It was hard to see. There was next to no light in the room.

"As suspected, he nailed the board to the door frame. We will either need to make the hole big enough for you or I will have to find something to pry the board free. But I can't see anything down here. It's almost pitch black," Wren explained.

"I'll keep working on the door. You see if you can find a light switch or something while I'm working."

"Ya, okay." Wren got up and slowly walked along the wall before he remembered Tyler had turned on a light at the top of the stairs when they had come down. He continued walking around the room, feeling along the wall for the stairs. Unfortunately, first he ended up finding a workbench the hard way when he walked into it and stubbed his toe.

"Fuck!"

"You okay?" Aiden called in alarm. "What happened?"

"I'm fine, just stubbed my toe on a wooden workbench or something."

"See if there are any tools on it, like a hammer or something."

"Ya, no. It's empty."

Not long after, he found the stairs by almost falling again when the wall he was leaning against suddenly disappeared.

"I found the stairs," Wren said to Aiden since he was sure Aiden couldn't see any of what he was doing. "There is a light switch at the top."

"Ya, okay. I think I almost got this hole big enough, so we might not need to worry about prying the board free, anyway. But turning on a light would be good."

Wren grunted an acknowledgment as he slowly moved up the stairs in the dark. Even though he knew they were close to escaping, Wren was gripped by fear. It was the same fear he'd had before, there was something about climbing onto the pitch-black stairs in the empty house that was almost worse than everything else he had faced.

*Well, maybe not worse,* Wren thought as he pushed through his fear and continued up the stairs. But he suspected he wouldn't be interested in going into any dark basements again any time soon. His imagination played tricks on him and he thought he could hear Tyler returning, or at least he hoped it was his mind playing tricks on him.

The world was so much less scary when the monsters weren't real.

He got to the top of the stairs and felt around for the light switch. With a huge sigh of relief as he flicked it and, just like that, the lights in the basement turned on.

# Chapter 48
## Aiden

Aiden was halfway through the hole in the door when the lights suddenly switched on. He yelled in surprise as the light blinded him. He shut his eyes quickly then slowly opened them again.

"Good job," Aiden yelled out to Wren before looking around.

With the lights on he could see the room he was entering was a small main room in the basement. There were two other doors beside the one he was leaving. He could see the empty workbench that Wren had bumped into and ahead of him was the stairs going up. Wren was just walking back down the stairs.

"You turn into Winnie the Pooh while I was upstairs?" Wren asked with a smile.

"What?" Aiden asked, completely confused.

"You stuck?" Wren clarified.

"Oh," Aiden gave a small laugh, understanding the reference. "No. Just stopped so my eyes could adjust. Wait a sec while I finish getting through."

Wren waited as Aiden wiggled through the hole. He hadn't been stuck, but it was a tight fit. He hadn't bothered making the hole any bigger than necessary. He ended up with a few new scratches for his rushed effort but he ignored them.

Once he was through, Wren put his hand down and helped Aiden stand. He didn't release Wren's hand. He needed the comfort of holding hands. They both looked around the room in silence. Another empty room.

The workbench was attached to the wall. On the side of the room lay a pile of broken chair parts.

Otherwise, there was no other furniture. Tyler had nailed the wooden board blocking the door to the door frame, but he must have brought the wood and tools and taken them when he left because there was nothing else in the room. It made Aiden wonder what Tyler's plan had been. Had he intended on abandoning them? Just leaving them to starve? There wasn't even a way for Tyler to have opened the door to pass food to them. At least not without removing the board.

Suddenly, Wren squeezed his hand and gave him a terrified look. He put his finger to his lips, silently telling Aiden to keep quiet. Aiden strained his ears, listening intently. He hadn't heard anything, but he had been pretty caught up in his own head and could have missed something. He felt his heart pound until all he could hear was the beat of his own heartbeat. They stood in silence waiting for the next crisis to start.

Aiden started feeling lightheaded and realized he was holding his breath to remain quiet and focus on listening. He still couldn't hear anything but his heart beat in his ears. He looked at Wren and gave him an inquiring look while he tried desperately to resume breathing without gasping for air. More time passes, seconds which seemed to stretch into infinity.

Finally, Wren shook his head and explained, "I thought I heard something outside, maybe a car pulling up. If Tyler returns, we will have a serious problem. We need to hurry and get out before he returns and finds us."

Aiden agreed. They needed to leave. They might not be locked in the room anymore but they were both still hurt and Tyler definitely still had the advantage. They needed to get out and get help.

Aiden hadn't said anything but the pain in his chest was getting worse. Aiden wondered if he had a cracked rib or two—as if the concussion and possible broken nose and weren't enough.

Fuck!

They had to let their hands separate as they walked up the narrow stairs. Aiden hated it. He wasn't sure if he ever wanted to let Wren go again. Bad things happened when they weren't together.

When they got to the top of the stairs, Aiden felt his heart-rate speed up in fear that this door would be locked, too. He held his breath again as he turned the handle and let the air whoosh out softly as he slowly pushed the door open.

They found themselves in a hallway. To the left was the front door and Aiden wanted to cry when he saw it. The other direction seemed to lead toward the back of the house.

Aiden rushed toward the door and Wren surprised him when he didn't immediately follow.

"The front door's locked," Wren said before he even made it to the door. Aiden tried the door, and the handle moved but he couldn't open it. He realized Tyler must have set the dead bolt. When Aiden went to unlock it, he saw what Wren was talking about. The dead bolt needed a key to unlock, even from the inside.

"Fuck!" Aiden exclaimed. He hit it with the palm of his hand and leaned against the door. *Why couldn't any of this be easy? Couldn't they catch a break, just one?*

But Wren wouldn't let him give up. "Let's go check out the back. Maybe there will be a way out back there."

Wren lead the way back down the hall past the open door to the basement. Aiden watched Wren's steps falter and a shiver passed over him as they passed the door. Then Wren turned and slammed the door shut before continuing on his way toward the back of the house.

They passed the stairs going up which they both ignored. Then the hall opened into a small kitchen.

The kitchen appeared to be empty. There were windows letting in a small amount of light but, otherwise, the counters were bare and there was no indication anyone had used this space recently. Without taking time to look around, Wren grabbed Aiden's hand and pulled him toward the outside door. The door was also locked but the deadbolt worked normally.

Wren pulled him outside into a fenced backyard. It was still dark but Aiden could see a hint of light showing on the horizon. With no clocks Aiden had no idea what time it was, but the light on the horizon suggested it must be so late it could be considered early.

The light allowed Aiden to see around the backyard. There was an untended garden against one side of the six-foot-tall fence. There was also a large birch tree whose branches were hanging over the fence from one of the neighbouring yards. There was no yard furniture although Aiden could see an area of dead grass, a reflection of what must have been a long table at one time. There was a fence around the perimeter of the yard which cast ominous shadows. Against the far fence, partially hidden in the shadows cast by over hanging trees, Aiden spotted the back gate with a large wooden arch over top. Wren must have seen it too because he was already walking in that direction using their joined hands to pull Aiden behind him.

The gate was somewhat shorter than the rest of the fence but because of the arch there was no way to climb over it, not that Aiden wanted to try with all of his injuries. Aiden couldn't help plan what they would do if the gate wouldn't open. At this point it seemed so unlikely that escape would be as easy as opening a gate. Aiden found himself waiting for the other shoe to drop when Wren easily unlatched the door.

And drop it did.

When Wren tried to push the gate open it wouldn't budge. Aiden wasn't sure if there was something on the other side preventing it from opening, but from what he could see, Aiden suspected it was just that the wood had warped so much the gate couldn't open.

Wren was clearly as frustrated by this latest development as Aiden. He pushed and pulled on the gate with no success. He kicked it, letting out a soft whimper of pain. Then he stopped, leaned against the gate, and slumped back. He couldn't even blame Tyler for this. Aiden knew it wasn't Tyler who warped the wood. He was pretty sure Tyler thought they wouldn't make it out of the room in the basement. No, this was just fate fucking with them.

Aiden moved to lean against the gate beside Wren. He didn't want to admit it out loud but even just standing around was difficult and painful. Aiden realized Wren was silently crying. That was when Aiden realized Wren—who'd kept a positive attitude and helped keep Aiden from giving up over and over—was questioning whether they would make it out of here before Tyler came back and found them.

No! Fuck that. They were escaping. He wasn't going to let them give up in the fucking backyard because of some stupid old gate. He'd scream bloody murder and wake up the whole neighbourhood if he had to.

But first, "Let's try one more time together," Aiden suggested, deliberately ignoring Wren's tears. Aiden didn't want to ignore the tears. He wanted to pull him close and not let go for a couple decades, at least, but that needed to wait until they were safe.

Wren nodded, shifting his body so he was half turned away as he wiped away his tears with a with a quick jerking motion. Aiden felt the palms of his hands and his arms tingle with the need to hug Wren and took a half step toward him before he could stop himself. They couldn't get distracted but Wren, once again, proved he was by far the strongest person Aiden knew. When he turned back toward Aiden, he had a determined smile on his face. Aiden wanted to cry with pride. Or maybe he just wanted to cry too.

"Let's do this," Wren announced and if Aiden hadn't seen the tears, he wouldn't have been sure if they had really been there.

It took a few minutes for them to figure out the best way to position themselves. The hinges indicated the gate swung in so they both needed to pull on the gate at the same time but between their injuries and the narrow space in front of the gate; it was complicated.

They ended up standing side by side as close as they could get with their hands on the top of the gate. It was awkward and Wren figured out something was wrong with Aiden's ribs when he accidentally brushed against his side and Aiden couldn't hold back a cry of pain. Luckily, other than giving Aiden a serious look, Wren ignored the discovery. It was no use dwelling on all the things that were wrong. There were too many to count and as long as they could both walk, none of their injuries mattered until they could get help.

Aiden counted to three, and they both pulled as hard as they could. The gate shifted about an inch before stopping again. They took a few seconds break then Wren counted to three, and they pulled again. They had to repeat this pattern a few times but eventually the gate suddenly sprang free, pushing them both off balance.

Wren caught himself by taking a few quick steps back, but Aiden's foot caught on something behind him and he tripped and fell, hitting his bum with the full force of his weight. He cried out and felt a wave of nausea roll through him and had only seconds to roll over onto all fours before he was throwing up again. Or rather, he was dry heaving since his stomach was long since empty. He felt tears pool in his eyes and fall down his cheeks as the pain from the concussion met with the pain of throwing up with fucking cracked ribs, or whatever was wrong with them.

Wren's cool hand rubbed up and down his back and Aiden came back to himself and realized the noise he'd been hearing was his own keening cry of pain.

"You think you can walk?" Wren asked once Aiden no longer felt as though he was trying to push his empty stomach out through his mouth. He rolled back over to lie down on the dirt and untended grass.

"Give me a moment, then I think so."

Wren just nodded and gently picked up Aiden's head and gently put it into his lap. He gently played with Aiden's hair, brushing it out of his face. It felt so good. Aiden wanted to stay like this forever, maybe go to sleep and have a nap before he did anything else. That was when he knew he needed to get up.

With Wren's help Aiden stood up. He felt unsteady on his feet for a few moments but he was pretty sure he wasn't going to fall again.

They walked through the gate and finally, finally, they were free for real!

* * *

“You think we should go wake up a neighbour?” Aiden asked as he stopped in front of the house directly beside the one they had just escaped.

Wren was quiet for a moment, torn between knowing they needed to get help and, “We don’t even know if there will be anyone home or if they would wake up if we ring the bell. I really want to get as far away as possible before Tyler gets back.”

“Look, I want to get as far away as possible, too. But I feel like shit and neither of us can walk around forever. Why don’t we go over and look around, see if it looks like someone’s there? Then if not, we can go looking elsewhere. I mean, if Tyler isn’t there now, he probably isn’t going to come back until after daybreak. He is probably sleeping somewhere.”

“But we don’t know that. He said he owns this place, but he isn’t sleeping here. So, where is he? What if the place where he is staying is next door? When I screamed for help earlier only one person came to investigate the noise. Who's to say anyone will even answer if we ring their bell.

“Plus, maybe the reason he isn’t here is that he’s not sleeping. He could drive down the block right now. We need to get away from there. We need to get away from that house,” Wren pleaded, tears streaming down his face, Aiden realized Wren was truly frightened. If he let himself think about how scared he was, Aiden would have to admit was worried about Tyler returning too.

“I can’t stay here, Aiden. I just can’t,” Wren continued to beg.

“Okay. Okay. Let’s get going.”

Wren nodded with relief and they started walking. It was slow going. They had to stop a few times to orient themselves but eventually they figured out they weren’t too far from Heritage LRT station. They had decided, for better or for worse, they would walk to the transit station and call for help there rather than trying to stop and get help from a stranger.

"They're gonna have a pay phone, or, at the very least, one of those emergency call boxes," Wren pointed out. Aiden could tell Wren really wanted to get as far away from that horrible house as they could before Tyler could return. Aiden didn't bother arguing. He wasn't sure whether he could anymore. He needed all of his energy to put one foot in front of the other and keep them from getting lost. Wren could help a little since they were in the same area of the city as his mother's house but they were walking through side streets and he didn't know the city as well as Aiden.

Their progress was slow since they weren't capable of rushing. Even with their slow progress, Aiden could see Wren visibly relaxing the further they got from the house. Aiden's everything hurt and each step was jarring his ribs and head but he also felt a bubbling relief the further they got away and the less chance they had of getting caught by Tyler again. Unfortunately, as their fear receded, so did their adrenaline which was the thing keeping them going. Aiden could tell Wren was flagging, and he wondered whether they'd make it. By his calculation they were only five or six blocks from the transit station but it might as well have been five or six kilometers based on how he felt. No, that wasn't true. Aiden was in good shape. Normally five or six kilometers would be easier than these last few blocks. His vision was tunnelling until all he could see was the sidewalk in front of his feet.

"We're at a main road," Wren announced and Aiden caught him looking at him with a worried expression.

Aiden leaned against a light post and looked around, "All right, I definitely know where we are now," He pointed to the right. "We have to walk down that way for a bit then we will get to the Century Park transit station. Remember where Heritage Mall used to be?"

"Ya, ya, I know where we are now."

"You wanna stop and rest?" Wren asked after they walked a little further. Aiden initially felt a wave of relief and gratitude at the question because he did. He wanted to stop more than anything. He was so tired and every moment on his feet was making his body hurt more. But he wasn't sure if he would be able to get up again if they stopped.

"No. Let's just get there. I won't feel safe until we are with someone that can protect us from him."

"Hey, we did pretty well at saving ourselves." Wren pointed out with a weak grin.

"Ya, sure, if you call two concussions and everything else that's wrong with us 'pretty well'."

"Well, we rescued ourselves."

"Ya, we did do that," Aiden agreed with his own tired but proud smile but he knew it was weak. He worried he might just topple over but he urged Wren to continue walking.

The sun was halfway up and traffic was increasing on the roads. This night was officially going down as the longest Aiden had ever endured and it wasn't even over yet. He gritted his teeth and kept pushing, moving one foot in front of the other. He would not let Wren down.

One foot.

Then the other.

Over and over again.

Aiden let his mind wander. All he could see was the ground in front of his feet and all he could feel was pain and the warmth of Wren's hand in his.

Eventually, they got to the transit station. At first glance Aiden couldn't see a pay phone and he didn't bother looking for it because in front of them was a white and blue box on a stand with the word EMERGENCY written along the face, a large blue button, and a speaker. This would do. If this wasn't a valid emergency than nothing was.

Wren looked at Aiden, smiled and pushed the blue button.

# Chapter 49
## Wren

After the second time the nurse found Aiden and Wren snuggled together in Aiden's bed, the day shift nurse stopped insisting on them moving into their own beds. They were sharing a room anyway, so instead she opened the curtain that usually separated their two beds and let them know that other nurses might not be as accommodating.

It didn't really matter anyway. Wren would go to battle to stay with Aiden. He was, however, relieved he didn't have to since he wasn't sure how many more battles he was up for before he had some sleep. He'd really liked to have a few hours of uninterrupted sleep but he knew that was too much to ask for because of his concussion.

At least he could finally lie down and had been given painkillers for his persistent headache. It had taken longer to get the pain killers than he would have liked. The doctors had ordered a bunch of tests including neurological testing and an MRI. He'd also had a few x-rays and a bunch of blood drawn. Unlike Aiden, who did in fact have three cracked ribs, Wren hadn't broken any bones. They were really worried about both Aiden and Wren's head injuries though. Apparently, it is a very bad thing when you lose consciousness after being hit in the head, especially if you don't wake up right away.

Aiden was being watched even more carefully than Wren because he still couldn't remember everything that had happened before he'd woken up alone with Wren. No one was sure if this was because of his concussion or because of the roofie that Tyler had put in his drink, which turned out to be Rohypnol.

The good news was they had found the drug on Tyler when he was finally caught and arrested which confirmed the results of the tests the doctors had done.

Oh yes, the best news of all was they had caught Tyler. Apparently, he'd come back to the house around ten o'clock that morning, only twenty minutes after the police had set up to arrest him. Tyler's arrest had been mostly without incident, and the police had taken him to the police station to be questioned.

It was only mostly without incident because, as McDougall had gleefully told them, Tyler had tried to overpower Johnson. She had taken him down in no uncertain terms. In the end, size only matters if your opponent doesn't know how to fight any better than you do. Tyler was a big bully, but he wasn't a trained fighter. Johnson thought that was why he used the roofie. Since Aiden was a bit taller, Tyler couldn't be certain who would win if they got into a fair fight, even if Aiden wasn't as muscular.

Aiden had hugged Wren close and cried when he heard they had arrested Tyler. Wren wasn't afraid to admit he had cried tears of relief as well. Knowing their months long ordeal was overhelped Wren accept the night of insanity.

Johnson and McDougall hadn't just come with good news. They had also told Wren and Aiden that besides the vial of Rohypnol, Tyler had had a very sharp knife, rope, and, scariest of all, bleach and two tarps.

Tarps. Fucking tarps.

And bleach.

He really had been intending to kill them. After he'd left them unconscious on the floor, Tyler had gone off—they still didn't know where—and while he was gone, he'd made a stop at Canadian Tire to buy an over-sized container of cleaning bleach and two tarps.

The silver lining—if there was one besides the fact that they'd managed to escape—the police were charging him with two counts of attempted murder in addition to a long list of other charges. The officers had started telling them exactly what Tyler was being charged with but Wren hadn't wanted to hear. He'd lived through it, then he and Aiden had had to practically relive the entire ordeal when they'd made their statement to the police. He really didn't need to hear the legal terms attached to each thing.

It didn't matter anyway. Wren only cared whether Tyler would go to jail and how long he would be stuck there before Wren had to worry about him again. Even his wishful side knew Tyler would get out eventually, Wren just hoped it wouldn't be for a long time.

For now, nothing mattered except wrapping his body around a sleeping Aiden, closing his eyes, and joining him in sweet, sweet slumber.

"You fucking assholes!" Zane's voice started Wren awake.

Groggy, he opened his eyes and saw that sometime while he was sleeping, Lucy had arrived and his mother had disappeared. She was quietly sitting in the visitor chair between his empty bed and Aiden's bed. Zane and Derek must have just arrived.

"Way to be inconsiderate!" Lucy said, rolling here eyes at Zane once she saw both Aiden and Wren were now awake. "You had to wake them. What are you on about, anyway?"

Zane came up and—gently Wren noticed—swatted both Aiden and Wren on their shins. "Not only did these assholes ruin my birthday by being kidnapped—"

"Because they did that on purpose," Lucy interjected sarcastically

"But," Zane continued, speaking louder to talk over Lucy, "But they also had the nerve to leave me at the stupid club all night completely terrified that my best friend was dead and I didn't even find out they were safe until you," Zane said pointing at Lucy. "And not either of my so-called friends, called to said they had shown up at some fucking transit station barely alive. They were on their way to the hospital so I should just go to sleep because they wouldn't be able to see any visitors for a few hours.

"As if I could possibly sleep before I saw they were both safe with my own eyes." Zane burst into tears.

Derek wrapped his arms around Zane's shoulders and although he mouthed, "Sorry," above Zane's head, Wren could see Derek looked equally tired and was misty eyed himself.

"I told her to call you so you knew we were safe," Aiden croaked through his sleepy voice. "I knew you would be worried."

Zane cried harder and through his tears Wren heard him snuffle, "I thought you were dead. You just disappeared. Some psycho was out there trying to hurt you, and then you were gone. I thought for sure he'd gotten to you and killed you both. And then I found out I was right—the psycho had gotten to both of you and was trying to kill you!"

Aiden struggled to sit up and gasped in pain as his movement overcame the pain medications pumping through his system.

"You lay back down!" Zane snapped and Aiden slumped back down. "Jesus Christ! What is wrong with you? You are hurt. Lucy says you have three broken ribs. You have a concussion. Oh, and you just escaped from a madman! Then—then, because you have to be a goddamn movie hero, you walked to safety with the broken ribs and the concussion! I can come to you."

Zane walked over and grasped Aiden's hand. Wren knew how close Aiden and Zane were. He was sure Zane had been almost as scared as him when they'd discovered Aiden was missing at the club. He wanted to give them space but he wasn't going to. He wasn't going to let Aiden go. So instead he snuggled down and let the pain medications lull him back to sleep.

But he only was allowed to sleep for twenty minutes before the nurse busted in and woke him up to do another quick neurological test. It was a new nurse. She clucked about two patients sharing a bed being against hospital policy but didn't force the issue after Lucy casually commented that she could make him move back into his bed but the moment she left the room he would be back in bed with Aiden and wouldn't it be better for both of them if he wasn't moving back and forth between beds.

Wren saw that Zane and Derek were still there. He moved to sit up to talk to them now that he was awake again. This time it was Aiden who fell asleep while they talked.

The rest of the day went the same way. Wren and Aiden napped off and on. Doctors, nurses and visitors came and went. Lucy, one of Aiden's parents, or Wren's mom seemed to always be there. Wren wondered if there was a schedule. When Aiden asked Lucy during her second shift, she shrugged and said, "Of course."

At nine o'clock, visiting hours ended, and they kicked everyone out. Wren's mother tried to stay and was visibly upset about leaving the two of them alone in the hospital but Wren give her a big hug and reminded her he wasn't alone this time.

"I'm scared if I let you out of my sight something else bad will happen," she explained.

"I know but Aiden and I make a pretty good team. We managed to save ourselves last night. Plus, Tyler is in jail."

The reminder that Tyler was in custody seemed to be the deciding factor and, with a long look back, Wren watched his mother finally leave the room.

Even if it was exhausting, it had been nice having so many people show they cared. The visitors weren't even all there to visit Aiden, although many were. It had been an eye opener for Wren, forcing him to acknowledge he really had formed friendships here in Edmonton. The ambulance had taken them to the University of Alberta Hospital, which was where Wren worked. So, a bunch of his coworkers had stopped by to say, hi. The outpouring of love and support had been an amazing change from what he'd experienced when he'd been alone for so long at the hospital in Toronto with no one except the police seeming to even care he was there, at least until his mother arrived almost three days later.

But it was exhausting. Wren was just so tired. After being socially isolated for so long, the constant company of the last eight hours made

Wren want to take a nap. Or maybe that was the painkillers and a healing body.

The night passed both much too quickly and much too slowly. Yet, despite the wake-up calls, the constant headache, and the cramped bed, Wren felt like he slept better than he had all week. When they woke up, on their own for the first time since the morning before Tyler had kidnapped them, Wren gave Aiden a kiss and thanked him.

"Even though we only did it a few times. I missed sleeping with you when I was at Barry's," Wren admitted.

"I missed you too. Maybe we can do something about that."

Wren gave Aiden a thoughtful look. "You inviting me to move in, for real this time?"

"Well, I know you wanted to get your own place and found an apartment, but ya, I am," Aiden said with a smile. "When you know, you know, and if the last forty-eight hours has taught me anything it is to take the bull by the horns because you never know when some psycho is going to suddenly try to shoot the bull."

"Or at least kidnap him," Wren laughed.

"Close enough, I'm concussed and on a bunch of painkillers." They both laughed.

"So?" Aiden pressed when Wren was silent for a moment.

Wren felt himself light up and a huge smile spread across his face. "I suppose I don't have to take the apartment. I haven't actually signed the lease yet."

"You sure you don't want to continue staying at Barry's?" Aiden joked.

"Bite your tongue. No, wait. Come here. Let me bite it."

Wren leaned over Aiden for a kiss.

When they came up for air, Wren said, "When they finally allow us to leave, I'm going home with you. I hope you never get tired of me because I'm never leaving. You invited me and now I'm going to be that house guest you can't get rid of."

“That sounds perfect. Except you’re wrong, I’ll never get tired of you and want you to leave.”

“You say that now...” Wren joked. “But first thing after getting home, you are going to fuck me.”

Aiden groaned as they kissed again. “That sounds even more perfect.” They snuggled into each other, kissing and getting a start on the rest of their life.

They broke their kiss when Wren heard someone at the curtain clear their throat. He turned over and looked over his shoulder and saw—of course—it was his father with an expression on his face which somehow showed he was both relieved and disgusted at the same time.

Some things never changed.

# Chapter 50
## Aiden

Having sex first thing after being released from the hospital ended up being off the table. Not only because Aiden really wasn't up for anything beyond lying in pain but also because it turned out Wren was discharged from the hospital a full twenty-four hours before Aiden. Wren had been reluctant to leave alone but Aiden had encouraged him to go. He argued the bed in the apartment was much more comfortable than the narrow hospital bed, it was quieter, and he wouldn't be woken up by hospital staff coming in and out of the room all the time.

None of those arguments had convinced Wren to leave.

Then Aiden pulled out the big guns. He had Wren get the bag with all of Aiden's things. He riffled inside and handed over his key to his apartment. "Go make a copy for yourself. You live there now."

Wren had smiled and finally, key in hand, had left the hospital, promising to not only make a new key, but start moving in. Aiden had smiled at the idea of coming home later to an apartment that was not just his but his and Wren's apartment.

His happiness at sending Wren to move in hadn't lasted through the night. That night without Wren in the hospital had been the worst night of Aiden's life. Possibly even worse than the time spent locked in the basement—at least then they'd been together. Maybe the night alone in the hospital had seemed so much harder because of their time locked up. Sleep was elusive and when he eventually passed out from pain medication and exhaustion, he found himself waking up almost a dozen times because of nightmares. He dreamed Wren had been captured again or that he had been taken and couldn't get to Wren. The only consistent element in his nightmares had been that Wren hadn't been with him.

At one point, Aiden had been so caught up in his fear and nightmares that he had called Wren. He'd needed to know Wren was safe. He hadn't even cared that it was after three in the morning. Based on how quickly he responded, Wren hadn't seemed bothered by the early hour—or was it late hour? Really what was three in the morning other than the middle of the night? They chatted back and forth for a while until they had gone back to sleep. Wren was quite possibly having as much difficulty sleeping as Aiden.

The next morning, he begged the doctor to let him leave. He needed to get home to Wren.

Luckily, after a few more relatively quick tests, the doctor had agreed. But hospitals always seem to run on their own time and it was well into the afternoon before he was discharged and Lucy wheeled him out of the hospital in the wheel chair he hadn't wanted to use.

As he stepped outside into the bright summer day Aiden found himself blinking back tears but it wasn't because of the sun. Aiden couldn't hold back his grin when he saw Wren climbing out of Lucy's car.

"Surprise!" Wren said softly into Aiden's shoulder as they latched onto each other, hugging as tightly as Aiden's ribs would allow.

"I stopped by your apartment to get you some clean clothes and I couldn't stand leaving his pitiful face behind. But I made him wait in the car since I knew this would happen," Lucy said rolling her eyes at how Wren and Aiden practically attached themselves at the hip. "All right, you are both going to the same place. Into the car with you."

She just rolled her eyes again but refrained from saying anything when both Wren and Aiden climbed into the backseat together.

The drive back to their apartment was quiet and uneventful. Aiden was so exhausted from his poor night's sleep, preceded by—how many nights had it been now since he'd been able to sleep without being kidnapped or interrupted? Aiden had lost count.

He rested his head on Wren's shoulder and, before he knew it, Lucy was parking in front of his apartment.

Lucy walked them into the house, joking she needed to make sure they weren't going to injure themselves getting inside. Wren had argued they had hardly injured themselves. Lucy had just shrugged and kept following them into the apartment.

"You have dinner plans tonight?" Aiden asked, glancing at Wren to see if he was okay with what he was about to propose. Wren didn't seem opposed so he continued. "I need to nap and I'm hardly up to cooking to my normal standards so I was just planning on getting something through Skip the Dishes. You are welcome to join us."

"As a thanks for everything you've done over the past few days," Wren continued. And it was true. Lucy had done so much. She had even been missing work to spend time with Aiden and Wren at the hospital. When Aiden had asked why she wasn't at work she'd waved him off saying, "You're more important and it's summer anyway."

Aiden knew it wasn't nothing though, Lucy held an important research position at a nanotechnology lab on the university campus. She seemed to always be busy. What she could do though, is flex her hours. So, while Lucy waved off spending time with them at the hospital and picking Aiden up from the hospital today, Aiden knew this meant more time she would have to work in the evenings or this weekend. He definitely owed her, whether she agreed or not.

"Hmm, free food?" Lucy asked jokingly. "Sure."

Three hours later Aiden woke from his nap. Only three hours asleep but Aiden felt refreshed and well rested for the first time in days. He could feel his pain killers wearing off. His head and ribs hurt but that was all right, everything in the world was all right as long as he was with Wren and they were both safe. Aiden looked at Wren as he continued to sleep. He noticed his legs were still wrapped around Wren's from when they'd fallen asleep. Aiden also felt Wren's hand lying against his bare stomach. Wren had somehow managed to snake his hand up under Aiden's t-shirt while they slept. Yes, everything was all right in his world.

"Hey," Wren said softly when he finally opened his eyes.

"Hey," Aiden whispered back. He leaned forward and kissed Wren gently on the lips. "I'm so happy you're here."

"Where else would I be?" Wren looked confused.

"I don't know..." Aiden moved in closer, wrapping his arm over Wren's shoulder. "If you hadn't said 'yes' when I asked you out for our first date, you'd be somewhere else—somewhere not with me."

Wren leaned in so his head was resting against Aiden's chest and listening to his heartbeat. "And my life would be so much worse."

"If we hadn't gotten together, maybe Tyler wouldn't have gone postal."

Wren glanced up. He must have seen the sincerity in Aiden's face because he kissed Aiden on the chest and answered with the same sincerity. "My life would still have been worse off. Nothing Tyler did, or could do, would make me love you less. You saved me."

"You saved yourself." Aiden hated to hear Wren put himself down. He hadn't needed to be saved by Aiden. He hadn't been broken or in need of repair because he'd always been perfect.

"Maybe, but I found the courage to be me again while I was with you."

"I love you," Aiden said simply. There really was nothing else to say.

# Epilogue
## Wren

Wren hung up his jacket with a pocket full of scarf, gloves, and tuque. He passed Aiden an empty hanger for his. He was in shock. Two years later and finally everything was over. Well, as over as it could be when Tyler could be granted parole in five years. He would finish his sentence completely eight years after that. But that was for the future. For now, Wren could look forward to five years of freedom from worry. It could have been worse.

It could have been better, too. Aiden had been hoping for life. A few of the crimes Tyler committed during that nightmarish night had him facing possible life in prison. Aiden seemed to think there was a chance he'd get that sentence. Wren had been pretty sure that was wishful thinking. But Wren wouldn't complain about Aiden's optimism. He tended to hope for the best. Wren had come to really appreciate that during their recovery.

Despite their concussions and Aiden's broken ribs, their physical recovery hadn't been too bad. Not fun but it had just taken time and patience.

Their mental recovery had been another story. They'd ended up working with a counsellor, both together and separately. Wren especially had needed help moving past his fears. If he was completely honest, the journey might never end. He would probably always struggle a little with basements and dark enclosed spaces.

He'd also started having panic attacks, certain Tyler had somehow escaped prison and was waiting around every corner. He'd been especially terrified whenever he didn't know where Aiden was and worried it meant something bad had happen. The fear became so intense that Wren had deferred the start of medical school. Luckily, the school had been understanding, given the extenuating circumstances.

With help and more support than he believed he deserved, Wren had learned how to manage his fears. He still liked to make sure Aiden was all right when they were apart, but his interest was no longer laced with panic and fear. Instead, it had just become part of how he cared. It helped that Aiden had sworn up and down he didn't mind, liked it even.

Maybe that was part of it too, learning how to really trust both himself and Aiden. Two years ago, Wren would have sworn he already trusted Aiden but Wren had discovered trust was dynamic. It was measured in degrees rather than yes or no. He had trusted Aiden since they were children. He'd learned to trust him as a lover and a partner during their initial months together, but the last two years had taught him how to trust himself and trust Aiden to be exactly what he needed, even if that was someone who forced him to make difficult choices or face his fears.

"Well, it wasn't the outcome we hoped for—"

"You hoped for, I was more realistic," Wren interrupted.

"Yes, well, it still isn't too bad. Tyler will be in jail for longer than his lawyer was asking for at least."

"Ya, I'm happy," Wren said but even he could hear his voice didn't sound happy. "It's just—it's just I wish it was done for good. I never want to even think about Tyler again and knowing he might try to track me down again when he gets out of jail is just... exhausting."

Aiden looked at him and pulled him into a hug. "It sucks, but we decided before we wouldn't let Tyler control us."

Wren nodded into Aiden's chest.

"So, we go on and live our life. You continue going to school and finish up that medical degree and become an awesome doctor. I will continue working and we will stay together. If he decides to come after us again when he's released, then we'll deal with it. Together."

"At least we have five years before he even can get out. And that's a pretty long time. You willing to commit to me for that long? You sure you won't get bored with me?" Wren repeated their ongoing joke and thought of the ring he had hidden in a sock in his drawer.

Aiden smiled affectionately. "Never. I'm with you forever and together we'll deal with whatever happens in five years, Tyler or no Tyler."

Wren let himself feel hope for the future and felt a smile spread on his face. A future with Aiden was worth any risk.

Wren pushed Aiden against the opposite wall. He went on his toes and pulled Aiden's face down toward his. "If nothing else, court is done. So, let's go celebrate," he said before kissing the ever-loving shit out of Aiden.

Aiden hummed his consent then moved along the wall. Wren hoped he was taking them to the couch where they stashed lube because he needed Aiden to get inside him—like, right now.

They fumbled toward the couch, too intent on their kiss for either of them to be watching where they were going. Luckily, neither tripped on anything until two steps from their destination. Aiden caught his foot on the coffee table, lost his balance and fell onto the couch. He pulled Wren on top of him by the unexpected move.

"Graceful," Wren laughed.

"Shut up and kiss me again. I liked that part."

Since he agreed Wren did as he was told. Except now they were finally where he wanted to be. He just needed one more thing.

"Naked. You need to be naked," Wren gasped, fumbling with his own shirt and pants, frantic in his need. "Need you."

Aiden undid the top three buttons of the nice blue shirt he wore to court before yanking the shirt off over his head. Wren wasn't sure since he was still in the middle of ripping his own pants off, but he thought he heard at least one button hit the floor.

The rest of their clothes were quickly removed. Then they were both standing naked, facing each other, panting and feeling the anticipation of what would happen next.

Wren wasn't sure how long the moment lasted. It seemed to stretch on, each breath slowing down until they lasted forever and yet no time seemed to pass at all. The tension built, snapped, and they both sprang into motion.

Aiden kissed his way up Wren's jaw and nibbled on Wren's ear. Wren could feel each one of Aiden's hot breaths against his cheek and could hear him panting. It felt as if each breath was tied directly to his cock. His own breath sped up in sync with Aiden's.

When Aiden entered him, Wren sighed in relief. This is what he'd wanted. This was what he'd needed. After a moment of enjoying the feeling of being filled Wren pushed his hips back, driving Aiden's cock further inside him. He needed more. He needed everything. He needed to give everything.

The sound of the grunt and the slapping of flesh filled the air. Their bodies moved in time with their breath, their kisses, their moans.

"Yesss," Aiden and Wren moaned together. Wren could feel his orgasm barrelling toward him.

"Need.... Gonna...." Wren tried to explain but he couldn't get the words past his ecstasy. Luckily, Aiden didn't need whole sentences to understand.

"Got you," he grunted as he wrapped his arm around Wren's body and took hold of his cock.

A few stokes and Wren couldn't hold it back, he was coming with a shout of pleasure. Aiden's own orgasm was not far behind.

Later that night, upstairs in their bed, Wren thought again about the ring he had hidden. He hadn't decided yet when or how he would propose. The one thing he was certain of was that he was going to. He thought back to something Aiden had said before they left for court today, "In the end, it didn't matter what happened because they were together and they could face anything. Hadn't they already proven that? They hadn't just survived Tyler, they had survived the aftermath—the recovery."

So, maybe it didn't matter how Wren proposed. It just mattered that they end up spending the rest of their lives together.

The End

Manufactured by Amazon.ca
Bolton, ON

16938882R00201